JONATHAN SWIFT was born in Dublin in 1667 after his father's death. He was educated at Kilkenny Grammar School and at Trinity College, Dublin, where he was censured for offences against discipline and had to obtain his degree by 'special grace'. Throughout his life, his ferocity was to alienate many people, but at the same time he counted among his close friends several distinguished men, notably Bolingbroke and Pope. Swift was ordained in Ireland in 1695 and was given a prebend at St Patrick's, Dublin, where he was later made dean. An ardent pacifist who loathed cruelty, imperialism and war, he wrote many pamphlets on religion and war and during the course of frequent visits to London did much to try and improve the political situation in Ireland. His loyalties were initially with the Whigs, but he was disgusted at their alliance with dissent in 1710 and went over to the Tories, attacking Whig ministers in the *Examiner*, which he edited. The details of his daily life in London are recounted in a series of intimate letters to Esther Johnson, published as *Journal to Stella*. He was also very close to Esther Vanhomrigh, whom he met in 1708, and his final rupture with her in about 1723 may have hastened her death. The story of their love affair is related in Swift's poem 'Cadenus and Vanessa'. Swift's masterpiece, *Gulliver's Travels*, appeared in 1726. It was an overnight success, but soon triggered heated debate, and to this day it has remained extremely controversial. *Gulliver's Travels* was the only one of his publications for which Swift received any payment (£200) and, like much of his work, it was published anonymously. Throughout his life, Swift suffered from a form of vertigo and his illness became very marked in about 1738. As a result of his increasing dementia, he was declared 'of unsound mind' in 1742 and guardians were appointed to manage his affairs. He died in 1745.

ROBERT DEMARIA, JR is Henry Noble MacCracken Professor of English at Vassar College, where he has taught since 1975. He is the author of three books about Samuel Johnson, including *Samuel Johnson and the Life of Reading* (1997), and the editor of *British Literature 1640–1789: An Anthology* (second edn, 2001). He has been a Guggenheim Foundation Fellow and a Fellow of the Center for Advanced Study in the Behavioral Sciences.

JONATHAN SWIFT

Gulliver's Travels

Edited with an Introduction and Notes by
ROBERT DEMARIA, JR

PENGUIN BOOKS

PENGUIN BOOKS

Published by the Penguin Group
Penguin Books Ltd, 80 Strand, London WC2R ORL, England
Penguin Putnam Inc., 375 Hudson Street, New York, New York 10014, USA
Penguin Books Australia Ltd, 250 Camberwell Road, Camberwell, Victoria 3124, Australia
Penguin Books Canada Ltd, 10 Alcorn Avenue, Toronto, Ontario, Canada M4V 3B2
Penguin Books India (P) Ltd, 11 Community Centre, Panchsheel Park, New Delhi – 110 017, India
Penguin Books (NZ) Ltd, Private Bag 102902, NSMC, Auckland, New Zealand
Penguin Books (South Africa) (Pty) Ltd, 24 Sturdee Avenue, Rosebank 2196, South Africa

Penguin Books Ltd, Registered Offices: 80 Strand, London WC2R ORL, England

www.penguin.com

First published by Benjamin Motte, Jr 1726

Published in Penguin Classics 2001
Reprinted with minor revisions 2003

20

Editorial material copyright © Robert DeMaria, Jr 2001, 2003
All rights reserved

The moral right of the editor has been asserted

Set in 10/12.5 pt Monotype Van Dijck
Typeset by Rowland Phototypesetting Ltd, Bury St Edmunds, Suffolk
Printed in Great Britain by Clays Ltd, St Ives plc

ISBN-13: 978-0-14-143949-5

www.greenpenguin.co.uk

Penguin Books is committed to a sustainable future
for our business, our readers and our planet.
The book in your hands is made from paper
certified by the Forest Stewardship Council.

CONTENTS

PLATES   vi

ACKNOWLEDGEMENTS   vii

INTRODUCTION   ix

FURTHER READING   xxiii

A NOTE ON THE TEXT   xxvi

TRAVELS INTO SEVERAL
REMOTE NATIONS OF THE WORLD.
IN FOUR PARTS.
BY LEMUEL GULLIVER

Advertisement   4

A Letter from Capt. Gulliver to his Cousin Sympson   5

The Publisher to the Reader   9

The Contents   11

Part I: A Voyage to Lilliput   19

Part II: A Voyage to Brobdingnag   77

Part III: A Voyage to Laputa, Balnibarbi,
*   Luggnagg, Glubbdubdrib and Japan*   141

Part IV: A Voyage to the Country of the Houyhnhnms   203

NOTES   272

TEXTUAL NOTES   298

PLATES

1. Portrait frontispiece   2
2. Title page of the first edition   3
3. Map of Lilliput and Blefuscu   20
4. Map of Brobdingnag   78
5. Map of Laputa and Neighbouring Islands   142
6. Map of Balnibarbi   157
7. Book Writing Machine in the Academy of Lagado   173
8. Map of Houyhnhnms Land   204

All plates are reproduced from a large paper copy of the first edition (1726), courtesy of the Pierpont Morgan Library, New York (PML 15810).

ACKNOWLEDGEMENTS

It is a pleasure to thank the librarians and staff members of the Christopher Wren Library, Trinity College, Cambridge, the Pierpont Morgan Library, New York and the National Art Reference Library in the Victoria and Albert Museum, London for their courtesy and for their learned assistance in the preparation of this text. I am further indebted to the Pierpont Morgan Library for permission to reproduce photographs of the plates in their large paper edition of the first edition (PML 15810).

In the notes I am indebted to many earlier editors of *Gulliver's Travels*, particularly Peter Dixon and John Chalker, editors of the last Penguin edition (1967), and Paul Turner, editor of the Oxford University Press edition (1971). As ever, I am also indebted to Vassar College for providing financial support and encouragement of my work. My colleague Eamon Grennan was kind enough to read a draft of my introduction.

INTRODUCTION

Like any work whose popularity outlives its own time, *Gulliver's Travels* can be profitably and pleasurably read in a variety of ways by a great variety of readers. In modern times, by readers habituated to the predominant fictional form of the twentieth century, it has often been read as a kind of novel. In this reading, Gulliver is the central character, and we follow his exploits on his four voyages with an interest in his experience, his achievements, his development, and his survival. Many successful adaptations of *Gulliver's Travels* for the screen, for children's books, and for pictorial representation reflect this sort of reading, and much of the continued success of the book must be attributed to that.[1] Swift certainly plays to (and with) the ancient wishes of readers for stories, and those whose wishes are strong enough may even find in the lightly sketched Mrs Gulliver a Penelope to whom this modern Ulysses returns in between and after his long and dangerous journeys. It would be folly to deny the power of the book to interest readers in this way. As important as a storybook or novelistic reading of *Gulliver* is to the book's longevity, however, there are other things going on in this text, many of which tend drastically to undercut one sort of reading that has kept it going all these years.

When the reader is no longer 'filled . . . with a mingled emotion of merriment and amazement' and 'Criticism [no longer] lost in Wonder', as Dr Johnson described the first effect of *Gulliver's Travels*, certain problems come into focus. To begin with, the main character tells us things that are startlingly out of keeping with the decorum of the sort of travel story we think we are reading. There are some breaches in expectation fairly early in Part I. Here, Gulliver is among the tiny people of Lilliput and Blefuscu, where everything in the European world is scaled down on the ratio of one to twelve. As our foreign correspondent, Gulliver gives us information about this strange place, its political life, its intrigues, and some of its customs. When Gulliver is captured by the Lilliputians and led into the city, he is chained down and billeted in a disused temple (which only well-informed readers will recognize as resembling England's Westminster Cathedral). Alarmingly, however, his account then deviates into a description of his act of defecation:

I had been for some Hours extremely pressed by the Necessities of Nature; which was no wonder, it being almost two Days since I had last disburthened myself. I was under great Difficulties between Urgency and Shame. The best Expedient I could think on, was to creep into my House, which I accordingly did; and shutting the Gate after me, I went as far as the length of my Chain would suffer, and discharged my Body of that uneasy Load. But this was the only time I was ever guilty of so uncleanly an Action; for which I cannot but hope the candid Reader will give some Allowance, after he hath maturely and impartially considered my Case, and the Distress I was in. From this time my constant Practice was, as soon as I rose, to perform that Business in open Air, at the full extent of my Chain, and due Care was taken every Morning before Company came, that the offensive Matter should be carried off in Wheelbarrows, by two Servants appointed for that purpose. I would not have dwelt so long upon a Circumstance, that perhaps at first sight may appear not very momentous, if I had not thought it necessary to justify my Character in point of Cleanliness to the World; which I am told some of my Maligners have been pleased, upon this and other Occasions, to call in question.

The tone is right, but this is not the matter one expects to find in a traveller's account. Only readers in a mood thoughtlessly to consume whatever the printed page offers can at this point avoid re-examining their assumptions about both the narrator and the book as a whole. This passage is one of many that forces readers to recognize that Swift is ridiculing the sort of travel story that he is at the same time imitating, and it arouses the uncomfortable suspicion that readers too are under attack.[2]

In Part I alone 'the reader' is invoked twenty times more, and over the course of the whole book, the numerous addresses to the 'candid', 'curious', 'courteous', or 'gentle reader' become a reminder of the way Swift is subverting both the apparent form of his story and the kind of reading which it invites, in spite of itself. By the end of Part IV, Gulliver can speak out directly against the genre he has imitated:

I could heartily wish a Law were enacted, that every Traveller before he were permitted to publish his Voyages, should be obliged to make Oath before the *Lord High Chancellor* that all he intended to print was absolutely true to the best of his Knowledge; for then the World would no longer be deceived as it usually is, while some Writers, to make their Works pass the better upon the Public, impose the grossest Falsities on the unwary Reader. I have perused several Books of Travels with great Delight in my younger Days; but having since gone over most Parts of the Globe, and been able to contradict many fabulous Accounts from my own Observation, it hath given me a great Disgust against this Part of Reading, and some Indignation to see the Credulity of Mankind so impudently abused.

So Swift has all along been chiding his readers, while encouraging them to read his book. Moreover, the satire targets more than one particular act of reading; it also takes aim at most of the assumptions that make up the mentality of a reader – assumptions about discourse, reason, and human nature. It is telling that the repeated introduction of excrement, sometimes in the form of 'medicine' recommended for the reader, is one of the clearest signals of Swift's subversive activity. Neither the polish of Swift's plain and simple prose style, nor its venerable age (nearly three hundred years) can hide the fact that this work is often as rude and as adversarial as any modern product of political activism.

Gulliver's Travels is not a novel or a story, primarily; it belongs instead to the more difficult literary genre of the satire. It is a parody of a travel book like William Dampier's *Voyages* (to which there are many specific references), but it is more importantly following the form and spirit of a long line of satirical works that begins in ancient times. Specific correspondences between *Gulliver's Travels* and certain satirical works have been carefully established; of special importance are parallels with the Greek poet Lucian, Rabelais, Sir Thomas More, and Cyrano de Bergerac.[3] However, the satirical spirit in *Gulliver's Travels* goes even deeper than the resemblances it bears to specific works. Swift was well schooled in classical writers, and he was especially well versed, as many of his contemporaries were, in the poetry of the great Roman satirists – Horace, Juvenal and Persius. A manuscript exists in the Rothschild Collection in which Swift has transcribed a translation of Juvenal's sixth and tenth satires, and his knowledge of these and other great classical satirical poems is evident throughout his writings. Occasionally Swift seems to declare his kinship to this ancient line of satirists. Towards the end of the work, for example, Gulliver speaks of the possibility of Europeans attacking the horse-like, highly rational Houyhnhnms whom he so much admires:

Imagine Twenty thousand of them breaking into the midst of an *European* Army, confounding the Ranks, overturning the Carriages, battering the Warriors' Faces into Mummy, by terrible Yerks from their hinder Hoofs. For they would well deserve the Character given to *Augustus; Recalcitrat undique tutus*. But instead of Proposals for conquering that magnanimous Nation, I rather wish they were in a Capacity or Disposition to send a sufficient Number of their Inhabitants for civilizing *Europe*, by teaching us the first Principles of Honour, Justice, Truth, Temperance, Public Spirit, Fortitude, Chastity, Friendship, Benevolence, and Fidelity. The *Names* of all which Virtues are still retained among us in Languages, and are to be met with in modern as well as ancient Authors; which I am able to assert from my own small Reading.

The Latin quotation means, 'from his secure position, he kicks out in every direction'. It comes from a poem by Horace in which he defends his calling as a satirist, while recognizing that it would be more profitable to perform in other literary kinds, like panegyric (*Satires* 2.1). In a way, Swift is speaking in the voice of Horace to defend his own identity as a satirist as he finishes his longest and most successful satirical work.

Gulliver's Travels treats all the standard topics of classical satire. Like Juvenal's tenth satire, it makes fun of the vanity of the most common of human wishes: money, power, fame, long life, learning (especially without effort), beauty, and so on. Like most great satires, it cannot be said to urge a particular virtuous course of life on its readers, though some simple, Christian triad of faith, hope, and charity may be implicitly recommended.

One important vehicle of Swift's general satire, of course, is his use of perspective. The fact that the perspective changes from Part to Part is a salient and delightful feature of the work. It can even be thought of as a conceit or a trick, resembling, as Denis Donoghue has suggested, the sort of conceit that usually propels a metaphysical poem.[4] In fact, Samuel Johnson had the same impatient response to Swift's conceit as he did to metaphysical poetry. He told Boswell, 'When once you have thought of big men and little men, it is very easy to do all the rest.'[5] 'All the rest' is not the whole book, but it does cover a great deal, especially of Parts I and II, and often it entails aspects of the general satire. For example, Gulliver's size in comparison to the Lilliputians is the device that generates all the talk about the difficulty of feeding and housing his enormous body. He is twelve times the Lilliputians in height, but it follows (in terms of the mathematical conceit) that he is twelve times their size in every dimension, so that his bulk is 12^3 or 1728 times theirs. Such enormity is gross and it is clearly meant to remind us of the grossness of the human body, a common topic in satires and sermons designed to discourage worldly pride and remind us of the importance of spirit. The same might be said about the famous episode in which Gulliver takes advantage of his size to extinguish the fire in the Lilliputian palace by directing a stream of urine on the queen's quarters. Towering in corporal superiority, he fails to consider how repulsive and humiliating this might be to the sensibilities of the queen.

On the other side of the conceit, the enormity of Gulliver tends more often to show the moral smallness, or meanness, rather than the fineness or delicacy of the Lilliputians. They distinguish differences in height that are tiny on the 'normal' European scale of things, and they are over-nice and peevish rather than precise or discerning. The contrast between the smallness of the Lilliputians and the grossness of Gulliver foreshadows the reversal of the conceit in Part II where we are shown the smallness and insignificance of Gulliver in relation to the grossness (though also, at times, the grandeur) of the Brobdingnags. Now it is Gulliver's skin that seems fine and that of his hosts that is gross. Applying his comparatively microscopic vision to their skins, he sees imperfections, cancers, and, most horribly, lice, all magnified to horrific proportions. As readers, however, we know that what he sees on the flesh of the Brobdingnags is all that human flesh is heir to; all that should serve to dampen our insupportable pride; and all that should teach us to put our faith in more durable and more inner virtues. In Part II, as in Part I, Swift can again reverse the conceit, so that we focus not on Brobdingnagian grossness but rather on Gulliver's human smallness. Perhaps the most overt and continued satirical passage in the whole book occurs after Gulliver has described European culture and European history to the Brobdingnag king. His response puts Gulliver and his brethren (us, that is) into his perspective, as he sums up: 'I cannot but conclude the Bulk of your Natives, to be the most pernicious Race of little odious Vermin that Nature ever suffered to crawl upon the Surface of the Earth.' To achieve this supremely satiric vision Swift has merely manipulated the central conceit of *Gulliver's Travels* and looked at Gulliver through the wrong end of a very big telescope.

Swift did not need Dr Johnson to tell him that there was a metaphysical predictability and mathematical dryness to his optical conceit in *Gulliver's Travels*. He clearly understood its limitations, just as he understood the limitations of metaphysical works when he parodied them in *A Tale of a Tub* and *Meditations on a Broomstick*. In *Gulliver's Travels* he is making fun of the device at the same time that he deploys it. The transformations that occur in the famous examination of the articles in Gulliver's pockets provide a detailed example of his dual approach.[6] Moreover, Swift mostly leaves this conceit behind in Parts III and IV. The change in perspective in Part IV is abstract and ontological, if there is one at all: humans change places with horses in terms of most of the qualities that define human as opposed to equine life, at least for logicians.[7] Ingenuity might imagine the reversal of common sense and academic sense as a change of perspective in Part III, but the absence of the familiar optical conceit in this part is surely a reason for its lack of popularity among most readers. Another reason is that it seems more engaged in the satire of particular, contemporary events and persons than the first two parts (though this may be an illusion). This might look like inconsistency in the book, but the genre of satire authorizes Swift to change his method in midstream (one meaning of the Latin word *satira* itself is mixture), and it vindicates his concern with relatively local issues. Classical satires could be grand and philosophical, but they also were often aimed at specific contemporary targets.

Likewise, *Gulliver's Travels*, for all its philosophic scope, is steeped in the politics of its time.

Swift may have contemplated a work like *Gulliver's Travels* as early as 1713. At that time, though born and bred in Dublin, he was in England and deeply involved in politics as a close associate of the Tory ministers who controlled Parliament from 1710 to 1714. Towards the end of that time, the Tories suffered a violent reversal of fortunes, and Whigs, led at first by Robert Walpole, gained control of the government for the rest of Swift's life and beyond. When the government he served was about to collapse, Swift returned to Ireland. As a reward for his service, though it was far below the reward he hoped for, Swift enjoyed the deanship of St Patrick's Cathedral in Dublin from 1714 on. From this somewhat disappointing post, he looked back on his days of high political intrigue in London and, to a degree, reflected on both earlier and more recent political events. He wrote a work about his years in government called *The Last Four Years of Queen Anne*, in which he defended his fallen political friends, but he was persuaded to put the work aside, and it was not published in his lifetime. He wrote *Gulliver's Travels* in Ireland from about 1721 to 1725, and published it in 1726. This work of fiction provided a safer, more artistic medium in which Swift could reflect on his period of political involvement. His eye focuses sometimes broadly and sometimes rather minutely on the politics of his era, but Swift's treatment of political history is always artistic, and it is, therefore, easy to appreciate *Gulliver's Travels*, without knowing a great deal about the history he had in mind. On the other hand, Swift's library, his life of reading, and his own political biography indicate that history was in the forefront of his interests, and readers hoping to get closer to Swift and his intentions in writing *Gulliver* must know some of the facts.

The broad context of *Gulliver's Travels* is the history of England, mainly from the execution of Charles I in 1649 (hinted at in his description of the disused temple in Part I) to the crisis of the Tory ministry which ended with the indictment and expulsion of his associates, Robert Harley, Lord Oxford and Henry Saint-John, Viscount Bolingbroke, the death of Queen Anne, and the accession of the Elector of Hanover, George I, to the English throne. A prominent event in this history, as Swift alludes to it, is the Glorious Revolution, in which the Roman Catholic James II was deposed by Parliament, and his daughter Mary and her husband William of Orange made king and queen. This event had double importance for Swift because it aroused a rebellion on the part of Irish Catholics, which was frightening both in itself and in the brutal manner in which it was crushed by William III at the Battle of Boyne. At this moment in history Swift was twenty-two years old. He left Trinity College where he had received his BA three years earlier and visited his mother in Leicester, England, where she had lived apart from him from his childhood. He then moved to Moor Park, where he served as secretary to William Temple, a veteran of the British Civil War and a highly experienced politician who had been in government most of his life.

An important aspect of the then recent history of England and Ireland was frequent and ongoing reconfiguration in the religious sphere of the political world. As the monarchy shifted, so did the laws affecting the various religious sects whom they ruled. Swift saw his position as a Church of Ireland priest (ordained in 1695) as a middle way, avoiding the extremes of Catholics or Catholic sympathizers, many of whom favoured the return of the Stuart monarchy, and the dissenters, who wanted more separation of church and state and whose relatively rationalistic form of religion Swift and many others regarded as a kind of atheism. In Anne's reign, some of the leniency afforded the dissenters by William was rolled back in legislation like the Test Act. This climate emboldened supporters of the High Church, but Jacobitism (a preference for the Stuart 'Pretender' to the throne – James Francis Edward at this time) was still treason, and it was on charges of treason that Anne's Tory ministers were driven into exile. Important events in the demise of the Tories are figured forth in *Gulliver's Travels*: the trial of Bishop Atterbury for treasonous Jacobite activities, for example, takes shape in Part III in the description of a team of crack-brained interpreters at the Academy of Lagado who 'can discover a Close Stool to signify a Privy Council, a Flock of Geese a Senate, a lame Dog an Invader . . .' Likewise, the '*Articles of Impeachment against* Quinbus Flestrin' in Part I thinly disguise the articles of impeachment actually pressed against Harley and Bolingbroke.

Although they are sometimes hard to separate from internal party politics, Swift also alludes frequently to international events of high importance in modern British history. The Treaty of Utrecht was a hotly debated and finally unpopular diplomatic achievement of the Tories, and various allusions to it surface in *Gulliver's Travels*. Utrecht put an end to the War of the Spanish Succession, a world war fought in North America as well as Europe. It involved Britain militarily and diplomatically with the Spanish, the Portuguese, the Dutch, their long-time foes the French, as well as with many smaller nations. When Spanish, Dutch, or Portuguese characters appear in *Gulliver's Travels*, their colouring reflects Swift's partisan view of these countries' politics and religion, especially as it played out in the war and the treaty that ended it. But, when it comes to this broader political context, it is especially evident that some of Swift's political concerns, though always partisan in some respects, are part and parcel of a deeper, more philosophical approach to politics. The considerable anti-war sentiment in *Gulliver's Travels* is traceable not only to Tory rhetoric about the Treaty of Utrecht but also to a traditional view held by great humanists such as Erasmus and Sir Thomas More, who, of course, had their own particular battles in mind. Likewise, the disgust expressed in *Gulliver's Travels* about the horrors of colonization falls heavily on the Spanish for a variety of specifically historical reasons, but it also comprises a general philosophical position that is comprehensible and coherent without knowledge of the Spanish activities in the 'New World'.

Of less importance but visible none the less in *Gulliver's Travels* is some of Swift's political manoeuvring in the period after his removal to Ireland and his retirement from the grand political stage in London. One of Swift's proudest political works was his effort to defeat a scheme known as Wood's Halfpence.[8] After successfully offering the Duchess of Kendall an enormous bribe, William Wood secured in London a patent to coin 360 tons of copper as Irish halfpence; his profit from this scheme would have been many millions of pounds in modern money. The Irish would have lost nearly an equivalent amount in their already small purchasing power, at least in foreign markets, because the inferior alloy would undoubtedly have been rejected in many quarters. The scheme was entirely conceived and condoned in London and represented for Swift and others another stage in Britain's long-term economic tyranny of Ireland. In February of 1724 Swift donned one of his numerous literary disguises and campaigned against the scheme in the person of William Drapier. In a series of six *Letters* over the next year Swift helped galvanize Irish opposition to Wood's scheme and ran a very serious risk of arrest for seditious libel. In August of 1725 Wood's patent was withdrawn; Swift and the Irish Parliament rejoiced.

Swift's intense involvement in the defeat of Wood's halfpenny coincided with his work on *Gulliver's Travels*. It shows up in allegorical form in five paragraphs of Part III that describe the rebellion of Lindalino (wordplay for Dublin) against Laputa, the kingdom of the flying island. These paragraphs were not printed in the first edition of 1726, the second edition of 1727 or even the heavily revised edition of 1735, presumably because the publishers feared political reprisals. They remained unprinted until 1896, and they are certainly not essential to the book. However, this episode demonstrates the way in which particular political and historical events could come to the fore in the composition of *Gulliver's Travels*. Many readers have felt that when the political particulars get this close to the surface, the art is ruined, and the book only survives as a timeless literary achievement because it rises above particular political situations or generalizes them in a way that makes the text accessible to readers increasingly removed from the context. Part III, the last to be written, has often been seen as the least successful of the four parts, and perhaps this is attributable to the way in which contemporary politics intruded on Swift in the late stages of composition. But nearly every section of *Gulliver's Travels* bears the marks of recent British political history, and nearly every section also escapes those politics to rest secure in a world of fiction and fantasy, where readers do not need an editor's notes to appreciate books, even books written in the distant past with distant historical situations in mind. Even the most specifically political passages of Part III seem to me to be achieving this transformation, as the interest of students and other new readers in all parts of the book attests.

One more aspect of the way fictional text and historical context compete for attention in *Gulliver's Travels* deserves introduction. The linguistic arena of this competition is marked out by Swift's use of the first-person singular pronoun, *I*. The *I* in *Gulliver's Travels* is, of course, Lemuel Gulliver, a character who in many ways bears little resemblance to the author who created him. As his family origins in the town of

Banbury and his education at Emanuel College, Cambridge suggest, he is probably a dissenting Protestant, whereas Swift was a conservative Church of Ireland priest. As a surgeon, and in many other ways, Gulliver is focused on the physical body and gives little thought to the spirit, which was the subject of Swift's care. As a devotee of rationalism, especially after his life among the Houyhnhnms, Gulliver has separated himself from the Christian virtues of faith, hope, and charity in a way that Swift must have condemned. Gulliver is very often an object of the satire in *Gulliver's Travels* as well as its narrator. If we do not see it earlier, Gulliver's position becomes abundantly clear when he finds himself mired in the giant cowpats of Brobdingnag, dunked in a bowl of cream, and transformed into a child's doll and a lady's toy.

Against seeing Gulliver as an object of the satire, of course, is his putative position as the author of the work. Although Swift gives us plenty of evidence to conclude that this is a sham, and hints broadly that we should know better in the first place because all human writing is a kind of falsehood, he also reverses the irony from time to time by making real connections between himself, the true author, and Gulliver. A prime example of the kind of confusion Swift delights in creating occurs in what became Gulliver's first appearance in all editions published after 1735, the 'Letter from Capt. *Gulliver*, to his Cousin *Sympson*'. Here Gulliver complains to the publisher, whom he calls his cousin Sympson, the name Swift used when he opened negotiations with Benjamin Motte for the first publication of *Gulliver's Travels*. Gulliver's complaints are very much the same complaints that Swift made in real life to Motte, through the agency of his real-life friend Charles Ford, in a letter from Dublin dated 3 January 1727. Gulliver tells Sympson, 'I do not remember I gave you Power to consent, that anything should be omitted, and much less that anything should be inserted: Therefore, as to the latter, I do here renounce everything of that Kind; particularly a Paragraph about her Majesty the late Queen *Anne*, of most pious and glorious Memory; although I did reverence and esteem her more than any of human Species.' In reality, Swift wrote to Motte: 'I have an entire Respect for the Memory of the late Queen, and am always pleased when others show the same; but that Paragraph relating to her looks so very much beside the Purpose that I cannot think it to have been written by the same Author.'[9] There are obvious differences between the two statements, and the last clause of Gulliver's remark, though possibly odd or even incomprehensible to a first reader, displays the character of Gulliver after his conversion to Houyhnhnmism in Part IV. However, the sentiments in the two statements are very much the same and Gulliver is speaking partly as Swift here.

There are other occasions on which Swift's gullible, vain spokesman is again surprisingly close to Swift in his utterances, as many critics have noticed. Robert C. Elliott discussed this relation at length, and Claude Rawson speaks of 'an intimate traffic between fictional concoction and a self-disclosure both parodied and withheld'.[10] Like others, Rawson cites the example of Swift's remark in a letter to Pope on 26 November 1725 shortly before he came to England with the manuscript of *Gulliver*: 'I tell you after all that I do not hate Mankind, it is *vous autres* who hate them because you would have them reasonable animals, and are Angry for being disappointed . . . I am no more angry with [them] than I was with the Kite that last week flew away with one of my Chickens and yet I was pleased when one of my servants shot him two days after.' This remark closely resembles the opinion of the Master Houyhnhnm, as Gulliver reports it: he 'hated the *Yahoos* of this Country, yet he no more blamed them for their odious Qualities, than he did a *Gnnayh* (a Bird of Prey) for its Cruelty'. Even when there is no verbal parallel, there are many moments where readers must feel the correspondence between Swift and Gulliver tightens, as it does any time Gulliver notices the vanity of human (or Lilliputian) wishes for fame and glory, beauty and long life. There may even be moments where Swift feels a kind of identification with his character that prevents him, on reflection, from subjecting him to further embarrassment. In the first edition, for example, Gulliver notes that the Houyhnhnms use for medicinal purposes, 'a Mixture of *their own Dung* and *Urine* forcibly put down the *Yahoo*'s Throat. This I have since often taken myself and do freely recommend it to my Countrymen for the public Good, as an admirable Specific against all Diseases produced by Repletion.' In revising and correcting the text shortly after the first printing, however, Swift substituted, 'This I have since often known to have been taken with success and do here freely recommend it to my Countrymen.' A certain tenderness for or identification with the first-person of his narrative seems to intervene here and keep Swift from subjecting 'myself' to this degradation.

The relations between the fictional Gulliver and the real Swift are complex, like the relations between Swift and the very numerous other spokespersons he creates in his works. The complexity of these relations is one of the hallmarks of Swift's writing, as is their instability. It is notable that in the recently published *Dictionary of Literary Pseudonyms in the English Language*, Swift's entry is much larger than any other writer's, comprising forty-one pseudonyms.[11] But in most of these figures there is some resemblance to Swift. In George Faulkner's edition of Swift's *Works* (1735), this Dublin publisher – with or without Swift's cooperation – elicited a recognition of similarity between Swift and Gulliver by using a portrait of the author for the frontispiece in volume I that closely resembles the portrait of Gulliver that he used as the frontispiece in volume III.[12] Similarly, most of the imaginary places in *Gulliver's Travels* are tinged with resemblances to Swift's home places of London and Dublin. Despite their variety, for example, the names for many of these places exhibit wordplay on the names *Dublin* and *London*: Lindalino and Glubbdubdrib; Mildendo, Langden, Maldonada are a few of the more obvious ways of scrambling *Dublin* and *London* that Swift lights on. The use over and over again of names that play on *London* and *Dublin* illustrates the famous Horatian tag, '*Caelum non animum mutant qui trans mare currunt*', which means, loosely translated, that no matter how far away you travel, you are (as another famous Dubliner, James Joyce, knew) always stuck with yourself.[13] This motto may be hinted at again in the names Swift creates for the principal creatures in Part IV. Both *Houyhnhnm* and *Yahoo* could be forms of the pronoun *you* or plays on parts of the word *human*. Like other great humanistic works of art, *Gulliver's Travels* is about finding oneself, and try as we might to escape into its world of fantasy, it is impossible to ignore the satirical reflections of ourselves with which Swift has peopled all his realms. That he is willing also to find himself in his satirical hall of mirrors is a mark of his wisdom as well as of his wit.

NOTES

1. For a listing of various adaptations, see the *Gulliver's Travels Website* now at http://www.jaffebros.com/lee/gulliver/index.html.

2. For a brilliant discussion of Swift's relations with his reader in *Gulliver's Travels*, see Claude Rawson, *Gulliver and the Gentle Reader*. (Publication details of most books mentioned here are in my list of Further Reading.)

3. Paul Turner points out many of these parallels in his edition of *Gulliver's Travels*.

4. See Donoghue, *Jonathan Swift*, p. 63.

5. Boswell, *The Life of Samuel Johnson*, ed. G. B. Hill, revised L. F. Powell, 6 vols. (Clarendon Press, 1934–64), 3: 319; also cited by Donoghue, *Jonathan Swift*, p. 59.

6. Perhaps this extra awareness on Swift's part is why Johnson confessed to Boswell that he found 'very great merit' in 'the inventory of articles found in the pockets of the Man Mountain . . .' (Boswell, *Life* 2: 319).

7. This was the perception of R. S. Crane in one of the best articles ever written on *Gulliver's Travels*, 'The Houyhnhnms, the Yahoos, and the History of Ideas'.

8. I rely on the account of this affair in *The Drapier's Letters*, ed. Herbert Davis, ix-lxvii.

9. Swift's *Correspondence* 3. 195.

10. Claude Rawson's 'Gulliver and Others: Reflections on Swift's I Narrators', p. 239.

11. Ed. T. J. Carty (Mansell, London, 1995).

12. See Richard Rodino (1991).

13. Horace, *Epistles* 1. 11. 27.

FURTHER READING

SWIFT'S WRITINGS

The Correspondence of Jonathan Swift, ed. Harold Williams, 5 vols. (Clarendon Press, 1963–5)

The Correspondence of Jonathan Swift, ed. David Woolley (Lang, 1999–)

The Drapier's Letters, ed. Herbert Davis (Clarendon Press, 1935)

Gulliver's Travels, ed. Paul Turner (Oxford University Press, 1971)

—— ed. Harold Williams (First Edition Club, London, 1926)

Jonathan Swift: The Complete Poems, ed. Pat Rogers (Penguin, 1983)

Journal to Stella, ed. Harold Williams, 2 vols. (Clarendon Press, 1948)

The Poems of Jonathan Swift, ed. Harold Williams, 3 vols. (1937; second edition, Clarendon Press, 1958)

The Prose Writings of Jonathan Swift, ed. Herbert Davis, 14 vols. (Blackwell, 1939–68); *Gulliver's Travels* is vol. 11, ed. Harold Williams

A Tale of a Tub, eds. A. C. Guthkelch and D. Nichol Smith, (1920; second edition, Clarendon Press, 1958)

BIOGRAPHY AND CRITICISM

Carnochan, W. B., *Lemuel Gulliver's Mirror for Man* (University of California Press, 1968)

Case, Arthur, *Four Essays on Gulliver's Travels* (Princeton University Press, 1945)

Clark, Paul Odell, 'A Gulliver Dictionary', *Studies in Philology*, 50 (1953), pp. 592–624

Crane, R. S., 'The Houyhnhnms, the Yahoos, and the History of Ideas' (1959), in *Jonathan Swift: A Critical Anthology*, ed. Denis Donoghue (Penguin, 1971) pp. 363–84

Donoghue, Denis, 'The Brainwashing of Lemuel Gulliver', *The Southern Review*, 32 (1996), pp. 128–46

—— *Jonathan Swift: A Critical Introduction* (Cambridge University Press, 1969)

Downie, J. A. ,'The Political Significance of *Gulliver's Travels*', in *Swift and His Contexts*, eds. John Irwin, Hermann J. Real and James Woolley (AMS Press, 1989), pp. 1–19

Eddy, W. A., *Gulliver's Travels, a Critical Study* (Princeton University Press, 1923)

Ehrenpreis, Irvin, *Swift: the Man, his Works, and the Age*, 3 vols. (Methuen, 1958–83)

Elliott, Robert C., *The Literary Persona* (University of Chicago Press, 1982)

Erskine-Hill, Howard, *Jonathan Swift: Gulliver's Travels* (Cambridge University Press, 1993)

Glendinning, Victoria, *Jonathan Swift: A Portrait* (Holt, 1999)

Higgins, Ian, *Swift's Politics: A Study in Disaffection* (Cambridge University Press, 1994)

LeFanu, William, *A Catalogue of Books belonging to Dr Jonathan Swift* (Cambridge Bibliographical Society, 1988)

Lock, F. P., *The Politics of Gulliver's Travels* (Clarendon Press, 1980)

—— 'The Text of *Gulliver's Travels*', *Modern Language Review*, 76 (1981) pp. 513–33

Mezciems, Jenny, 'Swift's Praise of Gulliver: Some Renaissance Background to the Travels', in *The Character of Swift's Satire*, ed. Claude Rawson (University of Delaware Press, 1983), pp. 245–81

Nokes, David, *Jonathan Swift, a Hypocrite Reversed: A Critical Biography* (Oxford University Press, 1985)

Nutall, A. D., 'Gulliver among the Horses', *Yearbook of English Studies*, 18 (1988), pp. 51–67

Orwell, George, 'Politics vs Literature: An Examination of *Gulliver's Travels* (1946), in *Jonathan Swift: A Critical Anthology*, ed. Denis Donoghue (Penguin, 1971) pp. 342–60

Rawson, Claude, *God, Gulliver and Genocide: Barbarism and the European Imagination 1492–1945* (Oxford University Press, 2001)

—— 'Gulliver and Others: Reflections on Swift's I Narrators', in *Swift, the Enigmatic Dean* (Stauffenburg Verlag, 1998), pp. 231–46

—— *Gulliver and the Gentle Reader* (Routledge and Kegan Paul, 1973)

Reilly, Edward J., ed. *Approaches to Teaching Swift's Gulliver's Travels* (Modern Language Association of America, 1988)

Rodino, Richard, ' "Splendide Mendax": Authors, Characters, and Readers in *Gulliver's Travels*', *PMLA*, 106 (1991), pp. 1054–70

Seidel, Michael, '*Gulliver's Travels* and the Contracts of Fiction', *The Cambridge Companion to the Eighteenth-Century Novel* (Cambridge University Press, 1996), pp. 72–89

Smith, Frederik N., ed. *The Genres of Gulliver's Travels* (University of Delaware Press, 1990)

Teerink, H. and Scouten, Arthur H., *A Bibliography of the Writings of Jonathan Swift*, second edition (University of Pennsylvania Press, 1963)

Treadwell, Michael, 'Benjamin Motte, Andrew Tooke and *Gulliver's Travels*', in *Proceedings of the First Münster Symposium on Jonathan Swift*, eds. Hermann J. Real and Heinz J. Vienken (Wilhelm Fink Verlag, 1985), pp. 287–304

Williams, Harold, *The Text of Gulliver's Travels* (Cambridge University Press, 1952)

Woolley, David, ' "About ten days ago . . .",' in *Swift: the Enigmatic Dean, Festschrift for Hermann Josef Real*, eds. Rudolf Freiburg, Arno Löffler and Wolfgang Zach (Stauffenburg Verlag, 1998), 291–302

—— 'Swift's Copy of *Gulliver's Travels*', in *The Art of Jonathan Swift*, ed. Clive T. Probyn (Vision Press, 1978), pp. 163–5

A NOTE ON THE TEXT

The text of this edition is based on the first edition of *Travels into Several Remote Nations of the World*, which was published by Benjamin Motte, Jr on 28 October 1726.[1] Motte probably printed this edition from a faithful transcript of Swift's manuscript. According to standard practice of the day, Motte destroyed the handwritten copy when it was no longer needed for printing and proofreading. The original manuscript is also not extant. If this were the end of the story, there would be little question about the choice of Motte's first edition as the basis for all future editions of *Gulliver's Travels*. Unfortunately, this is just the beginning of a complex publication history.

Before he printed *Gulliver's Travels*, Motte sent the manuscript to his friend and associate Andrew Tooke, requesting that he rewrite some sections in order to avoid action for libel. As soon as Swift saw the book in print, he noticed 'several passages which appear to be patched and altered', and he complained that 'his copy was basely mangled, and abused, and added to, and blotted out by the printer'.[2] Six weeks later he had his friend Charles Ford send Motte a letter complaining about the alterations and listing a number of specific corrections to be made in the next edition.[3] Motte responded to this letter by incorporating most of the specific changes in his revised 'second edition' of 1727 (he had already printed two further, unrevised editions in 1726). However, Motte did not address the major areas of complaint in Ford's letter; indeed, he may not have been able to do so because he had already destroyed the original manuscript he was asked to restore, and the letter was not specific enough about the required changes to make use of the original unneccessary.

Although Motte appears to have destroyed his manuscript in 1726,

Swift's apparently survived a little longer. Charles Ford evidently used this manuscript to correct two large paper copies of the first edition of *Gulliver's Travels*. One of these copies is now in the Forster Collection of the National Art Reference Library, in the Victoria and Albert Museum; the other is in the Pierpont Morgan Library in New York City. Ford's manuscript additions in these books do not simply restore the 'mangled' original text; in some cases they represent revisions undoubtedly desired by Swift or, conceivably, 'corrections' of Ford's own. Nevertheless, they must be granted authority, as clearly deriving from Swift's intentions. Swift also had two copies for his personal correction. The more interesting of these is in the Armagh Public Library. It is not as fully annotated as Ford's copies, and mostly repeats corrections entered more fully by Ford. However scanty, these corrections have obvious authority.

There is yet another wrinkle. Motte never printed an edition that takes Ford's (or Swift's) annotated copies into consideration; that task was taken up by the Dublin publisher George Faulkner who brought out a new edition of *Gulliver's Travels* as volume III of Swift's *Works* in 1735. Swift tried to secure one of Ford's books for Faulkner to use as a copytext, but it is not clear whether he succeeded in doing so. Whether he did or not, there are many differences between the two Ford copies and Faulkner's edition. There are, for example, a couple of passages that Faulkner, like Motte before him, balked at printing, apparently for fear of legal action and political exposure. In addition, there are very numerous small differences. Some of these are, no doubt, representative of further corrections on Swift's part, whether or not he actually read all of Faulkner's proof-sheets, as the Dublin publisher claimed; others may be a matter of differences between Faulkner's house printing style and Motte's.

In the generation of Swift scholars who flourished in the first half of the twentieth century a great battle was waged over the comparative merits of Motte's and Faulkner's editions. On the whole Sir Harold Williams had the better of Arthur Case, and as a result, Faulkner's 1735 edition has generally become the standard edition.[4] Williams is certainly successful in showing that the edition of 1735 best represents the last wishes of the author, and that standard was until recently a court of last resort for editorial decisions. We are now in a period of editorial thinking that is more pluralistic and allows for the interest and viability of various editions, being less concerned with establishing a final, standard, authoritative text. In these circumstances, and for this particular edition, it seemed possible and appropriate to present a text that preserves a sense of what the book looked like to its first readers, while including changes in that text that seem to come from the original manuscript or clearly appear to be authorial corrections.

The copytext for this edition, therefore, is the first issue of the first edition of 1726. Into this text are read the changes in the Ford copies at the Morgan Library and the Victoria and Albert Museum and a few additional changes from the Armagh copy. Even where readings of 1726 seem preferable, the Ford copies are granted the final say. Finally, added in are readings of the 1735 Faulkner edition that seem to be Swift's corrections, rather than aspects of Faulkner's house style. Obviously, it is not always easy to distinguish between the two, though looking at Swift's manuscript corrections of his *Miscellanies* of 1727 was helpful, as was looking at Swift's extant manuscripts, which are punctuated much less heavily than Faulkner's text. Changes of a word or more to the text of 1726, as well as other textual decisions that seem debatable, are recorded in the Textual Notes. For the sake of economy these notes are written in the conventional form of a textual apparatus, but they comprise only a partial version of such a scholarly instrument.

Like other Penguin Classics, the present text uses modernized spelling, but it does so in a very conservative way. I have tried to limit the modernization to those instances where spelling does not seem to run over into grammar or diction: I substitute *ed* for *'d* in the preterites and past participles of verbs; *show* for *shew*; *than* for *then*; *anybody* for *any body*; and many more. However, I have preferred antiquated forms where modernization would obscure something more than orthography: for example I leave the past tense *eat* (pronounced et), instead of changing it to modern *ate*. Among the key printed texts and the post-publication manuscripts, there is some inconsistency in Swift's use of certain forms, such as *hath* and *has*; *my* and *mine*; *a half* and *an half*; *Luggnaggians* and *Luggnuggians*, *Struldbrugs* and *Struldbruggs*. Such inconsistencies were not resolved in 1735 and have been left to stand in the present edition, as have unresolved inconsistencies in the way chapter summaries appear in the Contents and at the beginnings of the chapters themselves. Punctuation, capitals, and italics are left mostly as they are in 1726, except where they are changed in the Forster and Morgan copies of *Gulliver* or where a 1735 reading makes demonstrably better sense. In a very few instances I have taken it upon myself to modernize punctuation to make the sense easier for contemporary readers.[5] Some of the modernizations of spelling, punctuation, and capitalization result in an apparent preference for the house style of Faulkner, but that is not their intention.

EXPLANATORY NOTES

An editor must write notes, but in encountering a great literary work, especially for the first time, a reader may not wish to consult them. 'Notes are often necessary, but they are necessary evils,' as Dr Johnson said in the preface to his edition of Shakespeare. 'Particular passages are cleared by notes, but the general effect of the work is weakened. The mind is refrigerated by interruption; the thoughts are diverted from the principal subject; the reader is weary, he suspects not why; and at last throws away the book, which he has too diligently studied.'[6] If a writer can defraud a reader of literary profit and pleasure by too much dependence on a remote historical context, an editor runs at least an equal risk of aiding and abetting the crime, even as he tries to mitigate its effects. The editor of *Gulliver's Travels* runs the additional risk of becoming part of Swift's grand joke by providing glosses and interpretations of a text that is itself parodic and therefore turns sober interpretation of it into something silly, like 'metaparody'. Like other editors of Swift, I have not avoided being part of the joke, but I have tried to remember that if *Gulliver's Travels* could not be read without notes, it probably would not be read at all. Nevertheless, the curious reader, willing to suffer a little refrigeration, will find a good deal of diversion and explanation in the five hundred notes to this edition. I have tried to focus on explanatory information, and I have resisted the impulse to offer interpretive advice or to trace literary sources or parallels, except where a knowledge of them is needed to grasp the tone of a particular passage. Many of the notes are glosses on particular words that have changed meaning since Swift's time, and I have very often used definitions of these words from Johnson's *Dictionary* (1755). Johnson began work on this book a year after Swift's death; he quotes Swift a great deal throughout the book, and in his definitions he expresses a quicker sense of Swift's meanings than any reader now is likely to achieve. Many of these definitions are also a pleasure to read in themselves.

NOTES

1. The copy of the first edition, first issue (Teerink A) in the Rothschild Collection at Trinity College, Cambridge is the basis of this edition. This account of the early printing history of *Gulliver's Travels* merely summarizes the findings of David Wooley and the late Michael Treadwell, who worked carefully through the many intricacies of this problem in historical bibliography. See, especially, Treadwell, 'Benjamin Motte, Andrew Tooke and *Gulliver's Travels*', and Wooley, ' "About ten days ago . . .".'

2. Swift's *Correspondence* 3, 189–90.

3. For a complete list of these changes, see David Woolley, 'Swift's Copy of *Gulliver's Travels*'. The letter itself is in the Forster Collection in the National Art Reference Library in the Victoria and Albert Museum, London.

4. See Harold Williams, *The Text of Gulliver's Travels* and *Gulliver's Travels* (1926), introduction; Arthur Case, 'The Text of Gulliver's Travels', in *Four Essays on Gulliver's Travels*, 1–49.

5. For example, I have adjusted the use of commas in combination with parentheses and very occasionally used a semi-colon to avoid the appearance of a run-on sentence.

6. *Johnson on Shakespeare*, ed. Arthur Sherbo, *Yale Edition of the Works of Samuel Johnson*, vols. 7–8 (Yale University Press, 1968), 7: 111.

GULLIVER'S TRAVELS

Captain Lemuel Gulliver, of
Redriff Ætat. suæ 58.

PLATE I

TRAVELS

INTO SEVERAL

Remote NATIONS

OF THE

WORLD.

In ·Four PARTS.

By *LEMUEL GULLIVER*,
Firſt a SURGEON, and then a CAP-
TAIN of ſeveral SHIPS.

VOL. I.

LONDON:

Printed for BENJ. MOTTE, *at the*
Middle Temple-Gate *in* Fleet-ſtreet.
MDCCXXVI.

PLATE 2

Advertisement

Mr. Sympson's *Letter to Captain* Gulliver,[1] *prefixed to this Volume, will make a long Advertisement unnecessary. Those Interpolations complained of by the Captain, were made by a Person since deceased,[2] on whose Judgment the Publisher relied to make any Alterations that might be thought necessary. But, this Person, not rightly comprehending the Scheme of the Author, nor able to imitate his plain simple Style, thought fit among many other Alterations and Insertions, to compliment the Memory of her late Majesty, by saying,* That *she governed without a* Chief Minister.[3] *We are assured, that the Copy sent to the Bookseller in* London, *was a Transcript of the Original, which Original being in the Possession of a very worthy Gentleman in* London, *and a most intimate Friend of the Author's;[4] after he had bought the Book in Sheets,[5] and compared it with the Originals, bound it up with blank Leaves, and made those Corrections, which the Reader will find in our Edition. For, the same Gentleman did us the Favour to let us transcribe his Corrections.*

A
LETTER
FROM Capt. *GULLIVER*,
TO HIS
Cousin *SYMPSON*[1]

I hope you will be ready to own publicly, whenever you shall be called to it, that by your great and frequent Urgency you prevailed on me to publish a very loose and uncorrect Account of my Travels; with Direction to hire some young Gentlemen of either University to put them in Order, and correct the Style, as my Cousin *Dampier*[2] did by my Advice, in his Book called, *A Voyage round the World.* But I do not remember I gave you Power to consent, that anything should be omitted, and much less that anything should be inserted: Therefore, as to the latter, I do here renounce everything of that Kind; particularly a Paragraph about her Majesty the late Queen *Anne*,[3] of most pious and glorious Memory; although I did reverence and esteem her more than any of human Species. But you, or your Interpolator, ought to have considered, that as it was not my Inclination, so was it not decent to praise any Animal of our Composition before my Master *Houyhnhnm*:[4] And besides, the Fact was altogether false; for to my Knowledge, being in *England* during some Part of her Majesty's Reign, she did govern by a chief Minister; nay, even by two successively; the first whereof was the Lord of *Godolphin*, and the second the Lord of *Oxford*;[5] so that you have made me *say the thing that was not*.[6] Likewise, in the Account of the Academy of Projectors, and several Passages of my Discourse to my Master *Houyhnhnm*, you have either omitted some material Circumstances, or minced or changed them in such a Manner, that I do hardly know mine own Work. When I formerly hinted to you something of this in a Letter,[7] you were pleased to answer, that you were afraid of giving Offence; that People in Power were very watchful over the Press; and apt not only to interpret, but to punish everything which looked like an *Inuendo* (as I think you called it). But pray, how could that which I spoke so many Years ago, and at above five Thousand Leagues distance, in another Reign, be applied to any of the *Yahoos*,[8] who now are said to govern the Herd; especially, at a time when I little thought on or feared the Unhappiness of living under them. Have not I the most Reason to complain, when I see these very *Yahoos* carried by *Houyhnhnms* in a Vehicle, as if these were Brutes, and those the rational Creatures? And, indeed, to avoid so monstrous and detestable a Sight, was one principal Motive of my Retirement hither.[9]

Thus much I thought proper to tell you in Relation to yourself, and to the Trust I reposed in you.

I do in the next Place complain of my own great Want of Judgment, in being prevailed upon by the Entreaties and false Reasonings of you and some others, very much against mine own Opinion, to suffer my Travels to be published. Pray bring to your Mind how often I desired you to consider when you insisted on the Motive of *public Good*; that the Yahoos were a Species of Animals utterly incapable of Amendment by Precepts or Examples: And so it hath proved; for instead of seeing a full Stop put to all Abuses and Corruptions, at least in this little Island,[10] as I had Reason to expect: Behold, after above six Months Warning, I cannot learn that my Book hath produced one single Effect according to mine Intentions: I desired you would let me know by a Letter, when Party and Faction were extinguished; Judges learned and upright; Pleaders[11] honest and modest, with some Tincture of common Sense; and Smithfield[12] blazing with pyramids of Law Books; the young Nobility's Education entirely changed; the Physicians banished; the Female *Yahoos* abounding in Virtue, Honour, Truth and good Sense: Courts and Levees of great Ministers thoroughly weeded and swept; Wit, Merit and Learning rewarded; all Disgracers of the Press in Prose and Verse, condemned to eat nothing but their own Cotton,[13] and quench their Thirst with their own Ink. These, and a Thousand other Reformations, I firmly counted upon by your Encouragement; as indeed they were plainly deducible from the Precepts delivered in my Book. And, it must be owned, that seven Months were a sufficient Time to correct every Vice and Folly to which *Yahoos* are subject; if their Natures had been capable of the least Disposition to Virtue or Wisdom: Yet so far have you been from answering mine Expectation in any of your Letters; that on the contrary, you are loading our Carrier every week with Libels, and Keys, and Reflections,[14] and accused of reflecting upon[15] great States-Folk; of degrading human Nature (for so they have still the Confidence to style it) and of abusing the Female Sex. I find likewise, that the Writers of those Bundles are not agreed among themselves; for some of them will not allow me to be the Author of mine own Travels; and others make me Author of Books to which I am wholly a Stranger.

I find likewise, that your Printer hath been so careless as to confound the Times, and mistake the Dates of my several Voyages and Returns; neither assigning the true Year, or the true Month, or Day of the Month: And I hear the original Manuscript is all destroyed, since the Publication of my Book.[16] Neither have I any Copy left; however, I have sent you some Corrections, which you may insert, if ever there should be a second Edition: And yet I cannot stand to them, but shall leave that Matter to my judicious and candid Readers, to adjust it as they please.

I hear some of our Sea-*Yahoos* find Fault with my Sea-Language, as not proper in many Parts, nor now in Use. I cannot help it. In my first Voyages, while I was young, I was instructed by the oldest Mariners, and learned to speak as they did. But I have since found that the Sea-*Yahoos* are apt, like the Land ones, to become new fangled[17] in their Words; which the latter change every Year; insomuch, as I remember upon each Return to mine own Country, their old Dialect was so altered, that I could hardly understand the new. And I observe, when any *Yahoo* comes from *London* out of Curiosity to visit me at mine own House, we neither of us are able to deliver our Conceptions in a Manner intelligible to the other.

If the Censure of Yahoos could any Way affect me, I should have great Reason to complain, that some of them are so bold as to think my Book of Travels a mere Fiction out of mine own Brain; and have gone so far as to drop Hints, that the *Houyhnhnms*, and *Yahoos* have no more Existence than the Inhabitants of *Utopia*.[18]

Indeed I must confess, that as to the People of *Lilliput*, *Brobdingrag*, (for so the Word should have been spelt, and not erroneously *Brobdingnag*) and *Laputa*; I have never yet heard of any *Yahoo* so presumptuous as to dispute their Being, or the Facts I have related concerning them; because the Truth immediately strikes every Reader with Conviction. And, is there less Probability in my Account of the *Houyhnhnms* or *Yahoos*, when it is manifest as to the latter, there are so many Thousands even in this City, who only differ from their Brother Brutes in *Houyhnhnmland*, because they use a Sort of *Jabber*, and do not go naked. I wrote for their Amendment, and not their Approbation. The united Praise of the whole Race would be of less Consequence to me, than the neighing of those two degenerate *Houyhnhnms* I keep in my Stable; because, from these, degenerate as they are, I still improve in some Virtues, without any Mixture of Vice.

Do these miserable Animals presume to think that I am so far degenerated as to defend my Veracity; *Yahoo* as I am, it is well known through all *Houyhnhnmland*, that by the Instructions and Example of my illustrious Master, I was able in the Compass of two Years (although I confess with the utmost Difficulty) to remove that infernal Habit of Lying, Shuffling,[19] Deceiving, and Equivocating, so deeply rooted in the very Souls of all my Species; especially the *Europeans*.

I have other Complaints to make upon this vexatious Occasion; but I forbear troubling myself or you any further. I must freely confess, that since my last Return, some Corruptions of my *Yahoo* Nature have revived in me by conversing with a few of your Species, and particularly those of mine own Family, by an unavoidable Necessity; else I should never have attempted so absurd a Project as that of reforming the *Yahoo* Race in this Kingdom; but, I have now done with all such visionary[20] Schemes for ever.

THE
PUBLISHER
TO THE
READER

The Author of these Travels, Mr. *Lemuel Gulliver*, is my ancient and intimate Friend; there is likewise some Relation between us by the Mother's Side. About three Years ago, Mr. *Gulliver* growing weary of the Concourse of curious People coming to him at his House in *Redriff*,[1] made a small Purchase of Land, with a convenient House, near *Newark* in *Nottinghamshire*, his Native Country; where he now lives retired, yet in good Esteem among his Neighbours.

Although Mr. *Gulliver* was born in *Nottinghamshire*, where his Father dwelt, yet I have heard him say, his Family came from *Oxfordshire*; to confirm which, I have observed in the Churchyard at *Banbury*, in that County, several Tombs and Monuments of the *Gullivers*.[2]

Before he quitted *Redriff*, he left the Custody of the following Papers in my Hands, with the liberty to dispose of them as I should think fit. I have carefully perused them three Times: The Style is very plain and simple; and the only Fault I find is, that the Author, after the Manner of Travellers, is a little too Circumstantial.[3] There is an Air of Truth apparent through the Whole; and indeed, the Author was so distinguished for his Veracity, that it became a sort of Proverb among his Neighbours at *Redriff*, when anyone affirmed a Thing, to say, it was as true as if Mr. *Gulliver* had spoke it.

By the Advice of several worthy Persons, to whom, with the Author's Permission, I communicated these Papers, I now venture to send them into the World, hoping they may be, at least, for some time, a better Entertainment to our young Noblemen, than the common Scribbles of Politics and Party.

This Volume would have been at least twice as large, if I had not made bold to strike out innumerable Passages relating to the Winds and Tides, as well as to the Variations[4] and Bearings in the several Voyages; together with the minute Descriptions of the Management of the Ship in Storms, in the Style of Sailors: Likewise the Account of the Longitudes and Latitudes; wherein I have Reason to apprehend that Mr. *Gulliver* may be a little dissatisfied. But I was resolved to fit the Work as much as possible to the general Capacity of Readers. However, if my own Ignorance in Sea-Affairs shall have led me to commit some Mistakes, I alone am answerable for them: And if any Traveller hath a Curiosity to see the whole Work at large, as it came from the Hand of the Author, I shall be ready to gratify him.

As for any further Particulars relating to the Author, the Reader will receive Satisfaction from the first Pages of the Book.

RICHARD SYMPSON

THE CONTENTS

PART I
A VOYAGE TO LILLIPUT

CHAP. I

The Author gives some Account of himself and Family: His first Inducements to travel. He is shipwrecked, and swims for his Life: Gets safe on Shore in the Country of Lilliput: *Is made a Prisoner, and carried up the Country.*

Page 21

CHAP. II

The Emperor of Lilliput, *attended by several of the Nobility, comes to see the Author in his Confinement. The Emperor's Person and Habit described. Learned Men appointed to teach the Author their Language. He gains Favour by his mild Disposition. His Pockets are searched and his Sword and Pistols taken from him.*

Page 30

CHAP. III

The Author diverts the Emperor and his Nobility of both Sexes, in a very uncommon Manner. The Diversions of the Court of Lilliput *described. The Author hath his Liberty granted him upon certain Conditions.*

Page 38

CHAP. IV

Mildendo, *the Metropolis of* Lilliput, *described, together with the Emperor's Palace. A Conversation between the Author and a principal Secretary, concerning the Affairs of that Empire. The Author's Offers to serve the Emperor in his Wars.*

Page 45

CHAP. V

The Author by an extraordinary Stratagem prevents an Invasion. A high Title of Honour is conferred upon him. Ambasssadors arrive from the Emperor of Blefuscu, *and sue for Peace. The Empress's Apartment on fire by an Accident; the Author instrumental in saving the rest of the Palace.*

Page 49

CHAP. VI

Of the Inhabitants of Lilliput, *their Learning, Laws, and Customs, the Manner of educating their Children. The Author's way of living in that Country. His Vindication of a great Lady.*

Page 55

CHAP. VII

The Author being informed of a Design to accuse him of High Treason, makes his Escape to Blefuscu. *His Reception there.*

Page 63

CHAP. VIII

The Author, by a lucky Accident, finds Means to leave Blefuscu; *and after some Difficulties, returns safe to his Native Country.*

Page 70

PART II

A VOYAGE TO BROBDINGNAG

CHAP. I

A great Storm described, the long-boat sent to fetch Water, the Author goes with it to discover the Country. He is left on Shore, is seized by one of the Natives, and carried to a Farmer's House. His Reception there, with several Accidents that happened there. A Description of the Inhabitants.

Page 79

CHAP. II

A Description of the Farmer's Daughter. The Author carried to a Market-Town, and then to the Metropolis. The Particulars of his Journey.

Page 90

CHAP. III

The Author sent for to Court. The Queen buys him of his Master the Farmer, and presents him to the King. He disputes with his Majesty's great Scholars. An Apartment at Court provided for the Author. He is in high Favour with the Queen. He stands up for the Honour of his own Country. His Quarrels with the Queen's Dwarf.

Page 95

CHAP. IV

The Country described. A Proposal for correcting modern Maps. The King's Palace, and some Account of the Metropolis. The Author's way of travelling. The chief Temple described.

Page 103

CHAP. V

Several Adventures that happened to the Author. The Execution of a Criminal. The Author shows his Skill in Navigation.

Page 107

CHAP. VI

Several Contrivances of the Author to please the King and Queen. He shows his Skill in Music. The King inquires into the State of Europe, *which the Author relates to him. The King's Observations thereon.*

Page 116

CHAP. VII

The Author's Love of his Country. He makes a Proposal of much Advantage to the King, which is rejected. The King's great Ignorance in Politics. The Learning of that Country very imperfect and confined. Their Laws, and military Affairs, and Parties in the State.

Page 123

CHAP. VIII

The King and Queen make a Progress to the Frontiers. The Author attends them. The manner in which he leaves the Country very particularly related. He returns to England.

Page 129

PART III

A VOYAGE TO LAPUTA, BALNIBARBI, LUGGNAGG, GLUBBDUBDRIB AND JAPAN

CHAP. I

The Author sets out on his Third Voyage; is taken by Pirates. The Malice of a Dutchman. *His Arrival at an Island. He is received into* Laputa.

Page 143

CHAP. II

The Humours and Dispositions of the Laputians *described. An Account of their Learning. Of the King and his Court. The Author's Reception there. The Inhabitants*

subject to Fears and Disquietudes. An Account of the Women.
Page 148

CHAP. III

A Phenomenon solved by modern Philosophy and Astronomy. The Laputians' *great Improvements in the latter. The King's Method of suppressing Insurrections.*
Page 155

CHAP. IV

The Author leaves Laputa, *is conveyed to* Balnibarbi, *arrives at the Metropolis. A Description of the Metropolis and the Country adjoining. The Author hospitably received by a great Lord. His Conversation with that Lord.*
Page 162

CHAP. V

The Author permitted to see the grand Academy of Lagado. *The Academy largely described. The Arts wherein the Professors employ themselves.*
Page 167

CHAP. VI

A further Account of the Academy. The Author proposes some improvements, which are honourably received.
Page 174

CHAP. VII

The Author leaves Lagado, *arrives at* Maldonada. *No Ship ready. He takes a short Voyage to* Glubbdubdrib. *His Reception by the Governor.*
Page 179

CHAP. VIII

A further Account of Glubbdubdrib. *Ancient and Modern History corrected.*
Page 183

CHAP. IX

The Author's Return to Maldonada. *Sails to the Kingdom of* Luggnagg. *The*

Author confined. He is sent for to Court. The Manner of his Admittance. The King's great Lenity to his Subjects.

Page 188

CHAP. X

The Luggnaggians *commended. A particular Description of the* Struldbruggs, *with many Conversations between the Author and some eminent Persons upon that Subject.*

Page 191

CHAP. XI

The Author *leaves* Luggnagg *and sails to* Japan. *From thence he returns in a* Dutch *Ship to* Amsterdam, *and from* Amsterdam *to* England.

Page 198

PART IV

A VOYAGE TO THE COUNTRY OF THE HOUYHNHNMS

CHAP. I

The Author *sets out as Captain of a Ship. His Men conspire against him, confine him a long Time to his Cabin, set him on Shore in an unknown Land. He travels up in the Country. The* Yahoos, *a strange Sort of Animal, described. The Author meets two* Houyhnhnms.

Page 205

CHAP. II

The Author conducted by a Houyhnhnm *to his House. The House described. The Author's Reception. The Food of the* Houyhnhnms. *The Author in Distress for Want of Meat, is at last relieved. His Manner of feeding in this Country.*

Page 211

CHAP. III

The Author studious to learn the Language, the Houyhnhnm *his Master assists in teaching him. The Language described. Several* Houyhnhnms *of Quality come out of Curiosity to see the Author. He gives his Master a short Account of his Voyage.*

Page 216

CHAP. IV

The Houyhnhnms' *Notion of Truth and Falsehood. The Author's discourse disapproved by his Master. The Author gives a more particular Account of himself, and the Accidents of his Voyage.*

Page 221

CHAP. V

The Author at his Master's Command informs him of the State of England. *The Causes of War among the Princes of* Europe. *The Author begins to explain the* English *Constitution.*

Page 225

CHAP. VI

A Continuation of the State of England *under Queen* Anne. *The Character of a first Minister of State in European Courts.*

Page 231

CHAP. VII

The Author's great Love of his Native Country. His Master's Observations upon the Constitution and Administration of England, *as described by the Author, with parallel Cases and Comparisons. His Master's Observations upon Human Nature.*

Page 237

CHAP. VIII

The Author relates several Particulars of the Yahoos. *The great Virtues of the* Houyhnhnms. *The Education and Exercise of their Youth. Their general Assembly.*

Page 243

CHAP. IX

A grand Debate at the General Assembly of the Houyhnhnms, *and how it was determined. The Learning of the* Houyhnhnms. *Their Buildings. Their manner of Burials. The Defectiveness of their Language.*

Page 248

CHAP. X

The Author's Economy and happy Life among the Houyhnhnms. *His great Improvement in Virtue, by conversing with them. Their Conversations. The Author has notice given him by his Master that he must depart from the Country. He falls into a Swoon for Grief, but submits. He contrives and finishes a Canoe, by the help of a Fellow Servant, and puts to Sea at a venture.*

Page 253

CHAP. XI

The Author's dangerous Voyage. He arrives at New-Holland, *hoping to settle there. Is wounded with an Arrow by one of the Natives. Is seized and carried by Force into a* Portuguese *Ship. The great Civilities of the Captain. The Author arrives at* England.

Page 259

CHAP. XII

The Author's Veracity. His Design in publishing this Work. His Censure of those Travellers who swerve from the Truth. The Author clears himself from any sinister Ends in writing. An Objection answered. The Method of planting Colonies. His Native Country commended. The Right of the Crown to those Countries described by the Author is justified. The Difficulty of conquering them. The Author takes his last leave of the Reader: proposeth his Manner of Living for the future, gives good Advice, and concludes.

Page 266

TRAVELS

PART I
A VOYAGE TO LILLIPUT

Plate.I Part.I *Page.*I.

Hogs I

P Mintaon
I Good Fortune

I Naſſow
SUNDA
Sillabar

Straits *of* Sunda

SUMATRA

Blefuſcu
Lilliput.
Mendendo
Diſcovered, A.D. 1699.

Dimens Land.

PLATE 3

CHAP. I

*The Author gives some Account of himself and Family, his first
Inducements to travel. He is shipwrecked, and swims for his Life,
gets safe on shore in the Country of* Lilliput, *is made a Prisoner,
and carried up the Country.*

My Father had a small Estate in *Nottinghamshire*; I was the Third of
Five Sons. He sent me to *Emanuel College* in *Cambridge*,[1] at Fourteen Years
old,[2] where I resided three Years, and applied myself close to my Studies:
But the Charge of maintaining me (although I had a very scanty Allow-
ance) being too great for a narrow Fortune, I was bound Apprentice to
Mr. *James Bates*, an eminent Surgeon[3] in *London*, with whom I continued
four Years; and my Father now and then sending me small Sums of
Money, I laid them out in learning Navigation, and other Parts of the
Mathematics, useful to those who intend to travel, as I always believed
it would be some time or other my fortune to do. When I left Mr. *Bates*,
I went down to my Father; where, by the assistance of him and my
Uncle *John*, and some other Relations, I got Forty Pounds, and a Promise
of Thirty Pounds a Year to maintain me at *Leiden*:[4] There I studied
Physic two Years and seven Months, knowing it would be useful in long
Voyages.

Soon after my Return from *Leiden*, I was recommended by my good
Master Mr. *Bates*, to be Surgeon to the *Swallow*, Captain *Abraham Pannell*
Commander; with whom I continued three Years and a half, making a
Voyage or two into the *Levant*,[5] and some other Parts. When I came back,

I resolved to settle in *London*, to which Mr. *Bates*, my Master, encouraged me, and by him I was recommended to several Patients. I took Part of a small House in the *Old Jury*;[6] and being advised to alter my Condition, I married Mrs. *Mary Burton*,[7] second Daughter to Mr. *Edmond Burton*, Hosier, in *Newgate Street*, with whom I received four Hundred Pounds for a Portion.[8]

But, my good Master *Bates* dying in two Years after, and I having few Friends, my Business began to fail; for my Conscience would not suffer me to imitate the bad Practice of too many among my Brethren. Having therefore consulted with my Wife, and some of my Acquaintance, I determined to go again to Sea. I was Surgeon successively in two Ships, and made several Voyages, for six Years, to the *East* and *West Indies*, by which I got some Addition to my Fortune. My Hours of Leisure I spent in reading the best Authors, ancient and modern, being always provided with a good number of Books; and when I was ashore, in observing the Manners and Dispositions of the People, as well as learning their Language, wherein I had a great Facility by the strength of my Memory.

The last of these Voyages not proving very fortunate, I grew weary of the Sea, and intended to stay at home with my Wife and Family. I removed from the *Old Jury* to *Fetter Lane*, and from thence to *Wapping*,[9] hoping to get Business among the Sailors; but it would not turn to account. After three Years Expectation that things would mend, I accepted an advantageous Offer from Captain *William Prichard*, Master of the *Antelope*, who was making a Voyage to the *South Sea*. We set sail from *Bristol May* 4th, 1699, and our Voyage at first was very prosperous.

It would not be proper, for some Reasons, to trouble the Reader with the Particulars of our Adventures in those Seas: Let it suffice to inform him, that in our Passage from thence to the *East Indies*, we were driven by a violent Storm to the Northwest of *Van Diemen's* Land.[10] By an Observation, we found ourselves in the Latitude of 30 Degrees 2 Minutes South. Twelve of our Crew were dead by immoderate Labour, and ill Food, the rest were in a very weak Condition. On the fifth of *November*, which was the beginning of Summer in those Parts, the Weather being very hazy, the Seamen spied a Rock, within half a Cable's length[11] of the Ship; but the Wind was so strong, that we were driven directly upon it, and immediately split. Six of the Crew, of whom I was one, having let down the Boat into the Sea, made a shift to get clear of the Ship, and the Rock. We rowed by my Computation about three Leagues,[12] till we were able to work no longer, being already spent with Labour while we were in the Ship. We therefore trusted ourselves to the Mercy of the Waves, and in about half an Hour the Boat was overset by a sudden Flurry from the North. What became of my Companions in the Boat, as well as of those who escaped on the Rock, or were left in the Vessel, I cannot tell; but conclude they were all lost. For my own part, I swam as Fortune directed me, and was pushed forward by Wind and Tide. I often let my Legs drop, and could feel no bottom: But when I was almost gone, and able to struggle no longer, I found myself within my depth; and by this time the Storm was much abated. The Declivity was so small, that I walked near a Mile before I got to the shore, which I conjectured was about eight o' Clock in the Evening. I then advanced forward near half a Mile, but could not discover any sign of Houses or Inhabitants; at least I was in so weak a Condition, that I did not observe them. I was extremely tired, and with that, and the Heat of the Weather, and about half a Pint of Brandy that I drank as I left the Ship, I found myself much inclined to sleep. I lay down on the Grass, which was very short and soft, where I slept sounder than ever I remember to have done in my life, and as I reckoned, above nine Hours; for when I awaked, it was just Daylight. I attempted to rise, but was not able to stir: For as I happened to lie on my Back, I found my Arms and Legs were strongly fastened on each side to the Ground; and my Hair, which was long and thick, tied down in the same manner. I likewise felt several slender Ligatures across my Body, from my Armpits to my Thighs. I could only look upwards, the Sun began to grow hot, and the Light offended mine Eyes. I heard a confused Noise about me, but in the posture I lay, could see nothing except the Sky. In a little time I felt something alive moving on my left Leg, which advancing gently forward over my Breast, came almost up to my Chin; when bending my Eyes downwards as much as I could, I perceived it to be a human Creature not six Inches high, with a Bow and Arrow in his Hands, and a Quiver at his Back. In the mean time, I felt at least forty more of the same kind (as I conjectured) following the first. I was in the utmost Astonishment, and roared so loud, that they all ran back in a Fright; and some of them, as I was afterwards told, were hurt with the

Falls they got by leaping from my sides upon the Ground. However, they soon returned, and one of them, who ventured so far as to get a full sight of my Face, lifting up his Hands and Eyes by way of Admiration,[13] cried out in a shrill, but distinct Voice, *Hekinah Degul*:[14] The others repeated the same Words several times, but I then knew not what they meant. I lay all this while, as the Reader may believe, in great Uneasiness: at length, struggling to get loose, I had the Fortune to break the Strings, and wrench out the Pegs that fastened my left Arm to the Ground; for, by lifting it up to my Face, I discovered the Methods they had taken to bind me; and, at the same time, with a violent Pull, which gave me excessive Pain, I a little loosened the Strings that tied down my Hair on the left Side, so that I was just able to turn my Head about two Inches. But the Creatures ran off a second time, before I could seize them; whereupon there was a great Shout in a very shrill Accent, and after it ceased, I heard one of them cry aloud, *Tolgo Phonac*; when in an instant I felt above an hundred Arrows discharged on my left Hand, which pricked me like so many Needles; and besides they shot another Flight into the Air, as we do Bombs in *Europe*, whereof many, I suppose, fell on my Body (though I felt them not) and some on my Face, which I immediately covered with my left Hand. When this Shower of Arrows was over, I fell a groaning with Grief and Pain, and then striving again to get loose, they discharged another Volley larger than the first, and some of them attempted with Spears to stick me in the Sides; but, by good luck, I had on me a Buff Jerkin,[15] which they could not pierce. I thought it the most prudent Method to lie still, and my design was to continue so till Night, when my left Hand being already loose, I could easily free myself: and as for the Inhabitants, I had reason to believe I might be a Match for the greatest Armies they could bring against me, if they were all of the same size with him that I saw. But Fortune disposed otherwise of me. When the People observed I was quiet, they discharged no more Arrows: But by the Noise I heard increasing, I knew their Numbers were greater; and about four Yards from me, over against my right Ear, I heard a knocking for above an Hour, like that of People at work; when turning my Head that way, as well as the Pegs and Strings would permit me, I saw a Stage erected about a Foot and a half from the Ground, capable of holding four of the Inhabitants, with two or three Ladders to mount it: From whence one of them, who seemed to be a Person of Quality, made me a long Speech, whereof I understood not one Syllable. But I should have mentioned, that before the principal Person began his Oration, he cried out three times *Langro Dehul san* (these Words and the former were afterwards repeated and explained to me). Whereupon immediately about fifty of the Inhabitants came, and cut the Strings that fastened the left side of my Head, which gave me the Liberty of turning it to the right, and of observing the Person and Gesture of him that was to speak. He appeared to be of a middle Age, and taller than any of the other three who attended him, whereof one was a Page who held up his Train, and seemed to be somewhat longer than my middle Finger; the other two stood one on each side to support him. He acted every part of an Orator, and I could observe many Periods[16] of Threatenings, and others of Promises, Pity, and Kindness. I answered in a few Words, but in the most submissive manner, lifting up my Left Hand and both mine Eyes to the Sun, as calling him for a Witness; and being almost famished with Hunger, having not eaten a Morsel for some Hours before I left the Ship, I found the Demands of Nature so strong upon me, that I could not forbear showing my Impatience (perhaps against the strict Rules of Decency) by putting my Finger frequently on my Mouth, to signify that I wanted Food. The *Hurgo* (for so they call a great Lord, as I afterwards learnt) understood me very well. He descended from the Stage, and commanded that several Ladders should be applied to my Sides, on which above an hundred of the Inhabitants mounted, and walked towards my Mouth, laden with Baskets full of Meat, which had been provided, and sent thither by the King's Orders, upon the first Intelligence he received of me. I observed there was the Flesh of several Animals, but could not distinguish them by the Taste. There were Shoulders, Legs, and Loins, shaped like those of Mutton, and very well dressed, but smaller than the Wings of a Lark. I eat[17] them by two or three at a mouthful, and took three Loaves at a time, about the bigness of Musket Bullets. They supplied me as they could, showing a thousand Marks of wonder and astonishment at my Bulk and Appetite. I then made another Sign that I wanted Drink. They found by my eating that a small quantity would not suffice me, and being a most ingenious People, they slung up with great Dexterity one of their largest Hogsheads,[18] then rolled it towards my Hand, and beat out the

Top; I drank it off at a Draught, which I might well do, for it did not hold half a Pint, and tasted like a small Wine[19] of *Burgundy*, but much more delicious. They brought me a second Hogshead, which I drank in the same manner, and made Signs for more, but they had none to give me. When I had performed these Wonders, they shouted for Joy, and danced upon my Breast, repeating several times as they did at first, *Hekinah Degul*. They made me a Sign that I should throw down the two Hogsheads, but first warned the People below to stand out of the way, crying aloud, *Borach Mivola*, and when they saw the Vessels in the Air, there was an universal shout of *Hekinah Degul*. I confess I was often tempted, while they were passing backwards and forwards on my Body, to seize Forty or Fifty of the first that came in my reach, and dash them against the Ground. But the remembrance of what I had felt, which probably might not be the worst they could do, and the Promise of Honour I made them, for so I interpreted my submissive Behaviour, soon drove out these Imaginations.[20] Besides, I now considered myself as bound by the Laws of Hospitality to a People who had treated me with so much Expense and Magnificence. However, in my Thoughts I could not sufficiently wonder at the Intrepidity of these diminutive Mortals, who durst venture to mount and walk upon my Body, while one of my Hands was at liberty, without trembling at the very sight of so prodigious a Creature as I must appear to them. After some time, when they observed that I made no more Demands for Meat, there appeared before me a Person of high Rank from his Imperial Majesty. His Excellency having mounted on the small of my Right Leg, advanced forwards up to my Face, with about a Dozen of his Retinue. And producing his Credentials under the Signet Royal, which he applied close to my Eyes, spoke about ten Minutes, without any signs of Anger, but with a kind of determinate Resolution; often pointing forwards, which, as I afterwards found, was towards the Capital City, about half a Mile distant, whither it was agreed by his Majesty in Council that I must be conveyed. I answered in few words, but to no purpose, and made a Sign with my Hand that was loose, putting it to the other (but over his Excellency's Head, for fear of hurting him or his Train) and then to my own Head and Body, to signify that I desired my Liberty. It appeared that he understood me well enough, for he shook his Head by way of Disapprobation, and held his Hand in a

Posture to show that I must be carried as a Prisoner. However, he made other Signs to let me understand that I should have Meat and Drink enough, and very good Treatment. Whereupon I once more thought of attempting to break my Bonds, but again, when I felt the smart of their Arrows upon my Face and Hands, which were all in Blisters, and many of the Darts still sticking in them, and observing likewise that the Number of my Enemies increased, I gave Tokens to let them know that they might do with me what they pleased. Upon this the *Hurgo* and his Train withdrew with much Civility and cheerful Countenances. Soon after I heard a general Shout, with frequent repetitions of the Words, *Peplom Selan*, and I felt great Numbers of the People on my Left side relaxing the Cords to such a degree, that I was able to turn upon my Right, and to ease myself with making Water; which I very plentifully did, to the great astonishment of the People, who conjecturing by my Motions what I was going to do, immediately opened to the right and left on that side to avoid the Torrent which fell with such noise and violence from me. But before this, they had daubed my Face and both my Hands with a sort of Ointment very pleasant to the Smell, which in a few Minutes removed all the smart of their Arrows. These Circumstances, added to the Refreshment I had received by their Victuals and Drink, which were very nourishing, disposed me to sleep. I slept about eight hours, as I was afterwards assured; and it was no wonder, for the Physicians, by the Emperor's Order, had mingled a sleeping Potion in the Hogsheads of Wine.

It seems that upon the first moment I was discovered sleeping on the Ground after my Landing, the Emperor had early Notice of it by an Express,[21] and determined in Council that I should be tied in the manner I have related (which was done in the Night while I slept) that Plenty of Meat and Drink should be sent me, and a Machine prepared to carry me to the Capital City.

This Resolution perhaps may appear very bold and dangerous, and I am confident would not be imitated by any Prince in *Europe* on the like Occasion; however, in my Opinion it was extremely Prudent, as well as Generous. For supposing these People had endeavoured to kill me with their Spears and Arrows while I was asleep, I should certainly have awaked with the first sense of Smart, which might so far have roused my Rage and Strength, as to have enabled me to break the Strings wherewith

I was tied; after which, as they were not able to make Resistance, so they could expect no Mercy.

These People are most excellent Mathematicians, and arrived to a great Perfection in Mechanics[22] by the countenance and encouragement of the Emperor, who is a renowned Patron of Learning. This Prince hath several Machines fixed on Wheels for the Carriage of Trees and other great Weights. He often builds his largest Men of War, whereof some are nine foot long, in the Woods where the Timber grows, and has them carried on these Engines[23] three or four hundred Yards to the Sea. Five Hundred Carpenters and Engineers were immediately set at work to prepare the greatest Engine they had. It was a Frame of Wood raised three Inches from the Ground, about seven Foot long and four wide, moving upon twenty-two Wheels. The Shout I heard was upon the arrival of this Engine, which it seems set out in four hours after my Landing. It was brought parallel to me as I lay. But the principal Difficulty was to raise and place me in this Vehicle. Eighty Poles, each of one Foot high, were erected for this purpose, and very strong Cords of the bigness of Packthread were fastened by Hooks to many Bandages, which the Workmen had girt round my Neck, my Hands, my Body, and my Legs. Nine Hundred of the strongest Men were employed to draw up these Cords by many Pulleys fastened on the Poles, and thus in less than three Hours, I was raised and slung into the Engine, and there tied fast. All this I was told, for while the whole Operation was performing, I lay in a profound sleep, by the force of that soporiferous Medicine infused into my Liquor. Fifteen Hundred of the Emperor's largest Horses, each about four Inches and an half high, were employed to draw me towards the Metropolis, which, as I said, was half a Mile distant.

About four Hours after we began our Journey, I awaked by a very ridiculous Accident; for the Carriage being stopped a while to adjust something that was out of order, two or three of the young Natives had the Curiosity to see how I looked when I was asleep; they climbed up into the Engine, and advancing very softly to my Face, one of them, an Officer in the Guards, put the sharp end of his Half-pike a good way up into my left Nostril, which tickled my Nose like a Straw, and made me sneeze violently: whereupon they stole off unperceived, and it was three Weeks before I knew the cause of my awaking so suddenly. We made a long March the remaining part of that Day, and rested at Night with five hundred Guards on each side of me, half with Torches, and half with Bows and Arrows, ready to shoot me if I should offer to stir. The next Morning at Sunrise we continued our March, and arrived within two hundred Yards of the City Gates about Noon. The Emperor, and all his Court came out to meet us, but his great Officers would by no means suffer his Majesty to endanger his Person by mounting on my Body.

At the Place where the Carriage stopped, there stood an ancient Temple, esteemed to be the largest in the whole Kingdom, which having been polluted some Years before by an unnatural Murder,[24] was, according to the Zeal[25] of those People, looked upon as Profane, and therefore had been applied to common Uses, and all the Ornaments and Furniture carried away. In this Edifice it was determined I should lodge. The great Gate fronting to the North was about four Foot high, and almost two Foot wide, through which I could easily creep. On each side of the Gate was a small Window not above six Inches from the Ground: into that on the Left side, the King's Smiths conveyed fourscore and eleven Chains, like those that hang to a Lady's Watch in *Europe*, and almost as large, which were locked to my left Leg with six and thirty Padlocks. Over against this Temple, on t'other side of the great Highway, at twenty Foot distance, there was a Turret at least five Foot high. Here the Emperor ascended with many principal Lords of his Court, to have an opportunity of viewing me, as I was told, for I could not see them. It was reckoned that above an hundred thousand Inhabitants came out of the Town upon the same Errand; and in spite of my Guards, I believe there could not be fewer than ten thousand, at several times, who mounted upon my Body by the help of Ladders. But a Proclamation was soon issued to forbid it upon pain of Death. When the Workmen found it was impossible for me to break loose, they cut all the Strings that bound me; whereupon I rose up with as melancholy a Disposition as ever I had in my Life. But the noise and astonishment of the People at seeing me rise and walk are not to be expressed. The Chains that held my left Leg were about two Yards long, and gave me not only the Liberty of walking backwards and forwards in a Semicircle; but being fixed within four Inches of the Gate, allowed me to creep in, and lie at my full length in the Temple.

CHAP. II

The Emperor of Lilliput, *attended by several of the Nobility, comes
to see the Author in his Confinement. The Emperor's Person and
Habit described. Learned Men appointed to teach the Author their
Language. He gains Favour by his mild Disposition. His Pockets
are searched, and his Sword and Pistols taken from him.*

When I found myself on my Feet, I looked about me, and must confess
I never beheld a more entertaining Prospect. The Country round appeared
like a continued Garden, and the enclosed Fields, which were generally
forty Foot square, resembled so many Beds of Flowers. These Fields were
intermingled with Woods of half a Stang,[26] and the tallest Trees, as I
could judge, appeared to be seven foot high. I viewed the Town on my
left hand, which looked like the painted Scene of a City in a Theatre.

I had been for some Hours extremely pressed by the Necessities of
Nature; which was no wonder, it being almost two Days since I had last
disburthened myself. I was under great Difficulties between Urgency and
Shame. The best Expedient I could think on, was to creep into my House,
which I accordingly did; and shutting the Gate after me, I went as far as
the length of my Chain would suffer, and discharged my Body of that
uneasy Load. But this was the only time I was ever guilty of so uncleanly
an Action; for which I cannot but hope the candid Reader will give some
Allowance, after he hath maturely and impartially considered my Case,
and the Distress I was in. From this time my constant Practice was, as
soon as I rose, to perform that Business in open Air, at the full extent of
my Chain, and due Care was taken every Morning before Company came,
that the offensive Matter should be carried off in Wheelbarrows, by two
Servants appointed for that purpose. I would not have dwelt so long
upon a Circumstance, that perhaps at first sight may appear not very
momentous, if I had not thought it necessary to justify my Character in
point of Cleanliness to the World; which I am told some of my Maligners
have been pleased, upon this and other Occasions, to call in question.

When this Adventure was at an end, I came back out of my House,
having occasion for fresh Air. The Emperor was already descended from

the Tower, and advancing on Horseback towards me, which had like to have cost him dear; for the Beast, though very well trained, yet wholly unused to such a Sight, which appeared as if a Mountain moved before him, reared up on his hinder Feet: But that Prince, who is an excellent Horseman, kept his Seat, till his Attendants ran in, and held the Bridle, while his Majesty had time to dismount. When he alighted, he surveyed me round with great Admiration, but kept without the length of my Chain. He ordered his Cooks and Butlers, who were already prepared, to give me Victuals and Drink, which they pushed forward in a sort of Vehicles upon Wheels until I could reach them. I took those Vehicles, and soon emptied them all; twenty of them were filled with Meat, and ten with Liquor, each of the former afforded me two or three good Mouthfuls, and I emptied the Liquor of ten Vessels, which was contained in earthen Vials, into one Vehicle, drinking it off at a Draught, and so I did with the rest. The Empress, and young Princes of the Blood, of both Sexes, attended by many Ladies, sat at some distance in their Chairs; but upon the Accident that happened to the Emperor's Horse, they alighted, and came near his Person, which I am now going to describe. He is taller by almost the breadth of my Nail, than any of his Court, which alone is enough to strike an Awe into the Beholders. His Features are strong and masculine, with an *Austrian* Lip and arched Nose,[27] his Complexion olive, his Countenance erect, his Body and Limbs well proportioned, all his Motions graceful, and his Deportment majestic. He was then past his Prime, being twenty-eight Years and three Quarters old, of which he had reigned about seven, in great Felicity, and generally victorious. For the better convenience of beholding him, I lay on my side, so that my Face was parallel to his, and he stood but three Yards off: However, I have had him since many times in my Hand, and therefore cannot be deceived in the Description. His Dress was very plain and simple, and the Fashion of it between the *Asiatic* and the *European*; but he had on his Head a light Helmet of Gold, adorned with Jewels, and a Plume on the Crest. He held his Sword drawn in his Hand, to defend himself, if I should happen to break loose; it was almost three Inches long, the Hilt and Scabbard were Gold enriched with Diamonds. His Voice was shrill, but very clear and articulate, and I could distinctly hear it when I stood up. The Ladies and Courtiers were all most magnificently clad, so that the Spot they stood upon seemed to resemble a Petticoat spread on the Ground, embroidered with Figures of Gold and Silver. His Imperial Majesty spoke often to me, and I returned Answers, but neither of us could understand a Syllable. There were several of his Priests and Lawyers present (as I conjectured by their Habits) who were commanded to address themselves to me, and I spoke to them in as many Languages as I had the least smattering of, which were *High* and *Low Dutch*,[28] *Latin*, *French*, *Spanish*, *Italian*, and *Lingua Franca*;[29] but all to no purpose. After about two Hours the Court retired, and I was left with a strong Guard, to prevent the Impertinence, and probably the Malice of the Rabble, who were very impatient to crowd about me as near as they durst, and some of them had the Impudence to shoot their Arrows at me as I sat on the Ground by the Door of my House, whereof one very narrowly missed my left Eye. But the Colonel ordered six of the Ringleaders to be seized, and thought no Punishment so proper as to deliver them bound into my Hands, which some of his Soldiers accordingly did, pushing them forwards with the Butt-Ends of their Pikes into my reach; I took them all in my right Hand, put five of them into my Coat-Pocket, and as to the sixth, I made a Countenance as if I would eat him alive. The poor Man squalled terribly, and the Colonel and his Officers were in much pain, especially when they saw me take out my Penknife: But I soon put them out of fear; for, looking mildly, and immediately cutting the Strings he was bound with, I set him gently on the Ground, and away he ran; I treated the rest in the same manner, taking them one by one out of my Pocket, and I observed both the Soldiers and People were highly obliged at this Mark of my Clemency, which was represented very much to my Advantage at Court.

Towards Night I got with some difficulty into my House, where I lay on the Ground, and continued to do so about a Fortnight; during which time the Emperor gave Orders to have a Bed prepared for me. Six Hundred Beds of the common Measure were brought in Carriages, and worked up in my House; an hundred and fifty of their Beds sewn together made up the Breadth and Length, and these were four double, which however kept me but very indifferently from the Hardness of the Floor, that was of smooth Stone. By the same Computation they provided me with Sheets, Blankets, and Coverlets, tolerable enough for one who had been so long inured to Hardships as I.

As the News of my Arrival spread through the Kingdom, it brought prodigious Numbers of rich, idle, and curious People to see me; so that the Villages were almost emptied, and great Neglect of Tillage and Household Affairs must have ensued, if his Imperial Majesty had not provided by several Proclamations and Orders of State against this Inconveniency.[30] He directed that those, who had already beheld me, should return home, and not presume to come within fifty Yards of my House without Licence from Court; whereby the Secretaries of State got considerable Fees.[31]

In the mean time, the Emperor held frequent Councils to debate what Course should be taken with me; and I was afterwards assured by a particular Friend, a Person of great Quality, who was looked upon to be as much in the Secret as any, that the Court was under many Difficulties concerning me. They apprehended[32] my breaking loose, that my Diet would be very expensive, and might cause a Famine. Sometimes they determined to starve me, or at least to shoot me in the Face and Hands with poisoned Arrows, which would soon dispatch me: But again they considered, that the Stench of so large a Carcass might produce a Plague in the Metropolis, and probably spread through the whole Kingdom. In the midst of these Consultations, several Officers of the Army went to the Door of the great Council-Chamber; and two of them being admitted, gave an account of my Behaviour to the six Criminals above-mentioned, which made so favourable an Impression in the Breast of his Majesty and the whole Board in my behalf, that an Imperial Commission was issued out, obliging all the Villages nine hundred Yards round the City, to deliver in every Morning six Beeves, forty Sheep, and other Victuals for my Sustenance; together with a proportionable Quantity of Bread, and Wine, and other Liquors: for the due Payment of which, his Majesty gave Assignments[33] upon his Treasury. For this Prince lives chiefly upon his own Demesnes, seldom except upon great Occasions raising any Subsidies upon his Subjects, who are bound to attend him in his Wars at their own Expense. An Establishment was also made of six hundred Persons to be my Domestics, who had Board-Wages allowed for their Maintenance, and Tents built for them very conveniently on each side of my Door. It was likewise ordered, that three hundred Tailors should make me a Suit of Clothes after the Fashion of the Country: That six of his Majesty's greatest Scholars should be employed to instruct me in their Language: And, lastly, that the Emperor's Horses, and those of the Nobility, and Troops of Guards should be frequently exercised in my sight, to accustom themselves to me. All these Orders were duly put in execution, and in about three Weeks I made a great Progress in learning their Language; during which time, the Emperor frequently honoured me with his Visits, and was pleased to assist my Masters in teaching me. We began already to converse together in some sort; and the first Words I learnt were to express my desire that he would please to give me my Liberty, which I every day repeated on my Knees. His Answer, as I could apprehend it, was, that this must be a Work of Time, not to be thought on without the Advice of his Council, and that first I must *Lumos Kelmin pesso desmar lon Emposo*; that is, swear a Peace with him and his Kingdom. However, that I should be used with all Kindness, and he advised me to acquire by my Patience, and discreet Behaviour, the good Opinion of himself and his Subjects. He desired I would not take it ill, if he gave Orders to certain proper Officers to search me;[34] for probably I might carry about me several Weapons, which must needs be dangerous things, if they answered the Bulk of so prodigious a Person. I said, his Majesty should be satisfied, for I was ready to strip myself, and turn up my Pockets before him. This I delivered part in Words, and part in Signs. He replied, that by the Laws of the Kingdom I must be searched by two of his Officers; that he knew this could not be done without my Consent and Assistance; that he had so good an Opinion of my Generosity and Justice, as to trust their Persons in my Hands: That whatever they took from me should be returned when I left the Country, or paid for at the Rate which I would set upon them. I took up the two Officers in my Hands, put them first into my Coat-Pockets, and then into every other Pocket about me, except my two Fobs, and another secret Pocket I had no mind should be searched, wherein I had some little Necessaries that were of no consequence to any but myself. In one of my Fobs there was a Silver Watch, and in the other a small Quantity of Gold in a Purse. These Gentlemen, having Pen, Ink, and Paper about them, made an exact Inventory of everything they saw; and when they had done, desired I would set them down, that they might deliver it to the Emperor. This Inventory I afterwards translated into *English*, and is word for word as follows.

IMPRIMIS,[35] In the right Coat-Pocket of the *Great Man-Mountain* (for so I interpret the Words *Quinbus Flestrin*)[36] after the strictest search, we found only one great Piece of coarse Cloth, large enough to be a Foot-Cloth for your Majesty's chief Room of State. In the left Pocket we saw a huge Silver Chest, with a Cover of the same Metal, which we the Searchers were not able to lift. We desired it should be opened, and one of us stepping into it, found himself up to the mid Leg in a sort of Dust, some part whereof flying up to our Faces, set us both sneezing for several times together. In his right Waistcoat-Pocket, we found a prodigious Bundle of white thin Substances, folded one over another, about the bigness of three Men, tied with a strong Cable, and marked with black Figures; which we humbly conceive to be Writings, every Letter almost half as large as the Palm of our Hands. In the left, there was a sort of Engine, from the Back of which were extended twenty long Poles, resembling the Pallisado's before your Majesty's Court; wherewith we conjecture the *Man-Mountain* combs his Head, for we did not always trouble him with Questions, because we found it a great Difficulty to make him understand us. In the large Pocket on the right side of his middle Cover (so I translate the Word *Ranfu-Lo*, by which they meant my Breeches) we saw a hollow Pillar of Iron, about the length of a Man, fastened to a strong piece of Timber, larger than the Pillar; and upon one side of the Pillar were huge Pieces of Iron sticking out, cut into strange Figures, which we know not what to make of. In the left Pocket, another Engine of the same kind. In the smaller Pocket on the right side, were several round flat Pieces of white and red Metal, of different Bulk; some of the white, which seemed to be Silver, were so large and heavy, that my Comrade and I could hardly lift them. In the left Pocket were two black Pillars irregularly shaped: we could not, without difficulty, reach the top of them as we stood at the bottom of his Pocket. One of them was covered, and seemed all of a piece: But at the upper End of the other, there appeared a white round Substance, about twice the bigness of our Heads. Within each of these was enclosed a prodigious Plate of Steel; which, by our Orders, we obliged him to show us, because we apprehended they might be dangerous Engines. He took them out of their Cases, and told us, that in his own Country his Practice was to shave his Beard with one of these, and to cut his Meat with the other. There were two Pockets which we could not

35

enter: These he called his Fobs; they were two large Slits cut into the top of his middle Cover, but squeezed close by the pressure of his Belly. Out of the right Fob hung a great Silver Chain, with a wonderful kind of Engine at the bottom. We directed him to draw out whatever was fastened to that Chain; which appeared to be a Globe, half Silver, and half of some transparent Metal: For on the transparent side we saw certain strange Figures circularly drawn, and thought we could touch them, till we found our Fingers stopped by that lucid Substance. He put this Engine to our Ears, which made an incessant Noise like that of a Water-Mill. And we conjecture it is either some unknown Animal, or the God that he worships: But we are more inclined to the latter Opinion, because he assured us (if we understood him right, for he expressed himself very imperfectly) that he seldom did anything without consulting it. He called it his Oracle, and said it pointed out the Time for every Action of his Life. From the left Fob he took out a Net almost large enough for a Fisherman, but contrived to open and shut like a Purse, and served him for the same use: We found therein several massy Pieces of yellow Metal, which if they be real Gold, must be of immense Value.

Having thus, in obedience to your Majesty's Commands, diligently searched all his Pockets, we observed a Girdle about his Waist made of the Hide of some prodigious Animal; from which, on the left Side, hung a Sword of the length of five Men; and on the right, a Bag or Pouch divided into two Cells, each Cell capable of holding three of your Majesty's Subjects. In one of these Cells were several Globes or Balls of a most ponderous Metal, about the bigness of our Heads, and required a strong Hand to lift them: The other Cell contained a Heap of certain black Grains, but of no great Bulk or Weight, for we could hold above fifty of them in the Palms of our Hands.

This is an exact Inventory of what we found about the Body of the *Man-Mountain*, who used us with great Civility, and due Respect to your Majesty's Commission. Signed and Sealed on the fourth Day of the eighty-ninth Moon of your Majesty's auspicious Reign.

Clefren Frelock, Marsi Frelock.

When this Inventory was read over to the Emperor, he directed me, although in very gentle Terms, to deliver up the several Particulars. He first called for my Scimitar, which I took out, Scabbard and all. In the mean time he ordered three thousand of his choicest Troops (who then attended him) to surround me at a distance, with their Bows and Arrows just ready to discharge: but I did not observe it, for my Eyes were wholly fixed upon his Majesty. He then desired me to draw my Scimitar, which, although it had got some Rust by the Sea-Water, was in most parts exceeding bright. I did so, and immediately all the Troops gave a Shout between Terror and Surprise; for the Sun shone clear, and the Reflection dazzled their Eyes as I waved the Scimitar to and fro in my Hand. His Majesty, who is a most magnanimous Prince, was less daunted than I could expect; he ordered me to return it into the Scabbard, and cast it on the ground as gently as I could, about six foot from the end of my Chain. The next thing he demanded was one of the hollow Iron Pillars, by which he meant my Pocket-Pistols. I drew it out, and at his desire, as well as I could, expressed to him the Use of it; and charging it only with Powder, which by the closeness of my Pouch happened to escape wetting in the Sea (an Inconvenience against which all prudent Mariners take special care to provide), I first cautioned the Emperor not to be afraid, and then I let it off in the Air. The Astonishment here was much greater than at the sight of my Scimitar. Hundreds fell down as if they had been struck dead; and even the Emperor, although he stood his ground, could not recover himself in some time. I delivered up both my Pistols in the same manner, as I had done my Scimitar, and then my Pouch of Powder and Bullets; begging him that the former might be kept from the Fire, for it would kindle with the smallest Spark, and blow up his Imperial Palace into the Air. I likewise delivered up my Watch, which the Emperor was very curious to see, and commanded two of his tallest Yeomen of the Guards to bear it on a Pole upon their Shoulders, as Draymen in *England* do a Barrel of Ale. He was amazed at the continual Noise it made, and the Motion of the Minute-hand, which he could easily discern; for their Sight is much more acute than ours: and asked the Opinions of his learned Men about him, which were various and remote, as the Reader may well imagine without my repeating; although indeed I could not very perfectly understand them. I then gave up my Silver and Copper Money, my Purse with nine large Pieces of Gold, and some smaller ones; my Knife and Razor, my Comb and Silver Snuff-Box, my Handkerchief and Journal

Book. My Scimitar, Pistols, and Pouch, were conveyed in Carriages to his Majesty's Stores; but the rest of my Goods were returned me.

I had, as I before observed, one private Pocket which escaped their Search, wherein there was a pair of Spectacles (which I sometimes use for the weakness of my Eyes) a Pocket Perspective,[37] and several other little Conveniences; which being of no consequence to the Emperor, I did not think myself bound in Honour to discover, and I apprehended they might be lost or spoiled if I ventured them out of my Possession.

CHAP. III

The Author diverts the Emperor and his Nobility of both Sexes, in a very uncommon Manner. The Diversions of the Court of Lilliput described. The Author hath his Liberty granted him upon certain Conditions.

My Gentleness and good Behaviour had gained so far on the Emperor and his Court, and indeed upon the Army and People in general, that I began to conceive Hopes of getting my Liberty in a short time. I took all possible Methods to cultivate this favourable Disposition. The Natives came by degrees to be less apprehensive of any Danger from me. I would sometimes lie down, and let five or six of them dance on my Hand. And at last the Boys and Girls would venture to come and play at Hide and Seek in my Hair. I had now made a good Progress in understanding and speaking their Language. The Emperor had a mind one day to entertain me with several of the Country Shows, wherein they exceed all Nations I have known, both for Dexterity and Magnificence. I was diverted with none so much as that of the Rope-Dancers, performed upon a slender white Thread, extended about two Foot, and twelve Inches from the Ground. Upon which I shall desire liberty, with the Reader's Patience, to enlarge a little.

This Diversion is only practised by those Persons who are Candidates for great Employments, and high Favour, at Court. They are trained in this Art from their Youth, and are not always of noble Birth, or liberal

Education. When a great Office is vacant either by Death or Disgrace (which often happens) five or six of those Candidates petition the Emperor to entertain his Majesty and the Court with a Dance on the Rope, and whoever jumps the highest without falling, succeeds in the Office. Very often the Chief Ministers themselves are commanded to show their Skill, and to convince the Emperor that they have not lost their Faculty. *Flimnap*, the Treasurer,[38] is allowed to cut a Caper on the strait Rope, at least an Inch higher than any other Lord in the whole Empire. I have seen him do the Summerset[39] several times together upon a Trencher[40] fixed on the Rope, which is no thicker than a common Packthread in *England*. My Friend *Reldresal*,[41] Principal Secretary for private Affairs, is, in my opinion, if I am not partial, the second after the Treasurer; the rest of the great Officers are much upon a Par.

These Diversions are often attended with fatal Accidents, whereof great Numbers are on Record. I myself have seen two or three Candidates break a Limb. But the Danger is much greater when the Ministers themselves are commanded to show their Dexterity; for by contending to excel themselves and their Fellows, they strain so far, that there is hardly one of them who hath not received a Fall, and some of them two or three. I was assured that a Year or two before my arrival, *Flimnap* would have infallibly broke his Neck, if one of the King's Cushions,[42] that accidentally lay on the ground, had not weakened the Force of his Fall.

There is likewise another Diversion, which is only shown before the Emperor and Empress, and first Minister, upon particular Occasions. The Emperor lays on a Table three fine silken Threads of six Inches long. One is Blue, the other Red, and the third Green.[43] These Threads are proposed as Prizes for those Persons whom the Emperor hath a mind to distinguish by a peculiar Mark of his Favour. The Ceremony is performed in his Majesty's great Chamber of State, where the Candidates are to undergo a Trial of Dexterity very different from the former, and such as I have not observed the least Resemblance of in any other Country of the old or the new World. The Emperor holds a Stick in his Hands, both Ends parallel to the Horizon, while the Candidates advancing one by one, sometimes leap over the Stick, sometimes creep under it backwards and forwards several times, according as the Stick is advanced or depressed.

Sometimes the Emperor holds one end of the Stick, and his first Minister the other; sometimes the Minister has it entirely to himself. Whoever performs his part with most Agility, and holds out the longest in leaping and creeping, is rewarded with the Blue coloured Silk; the Red is given to the next, and the Green to the third, which they all wear girt twice round about the middle; and you see few great Persons about this Court, who are not adorned with one of these Girdles.

The Horses of the Army, and those of the Royal Stables, having been daily led before me, were no longer shy, but would come up to my very Feet without starting. The Riders would leap them over my Hand as I held it on the Ground, and one of the Emperor's Huntsmen, upon a large Courser, took my Foot, Shoe and all; which was indeed a prodigious Leap. I had the good fortune to divert the Emperor one day after a very extraordinary manner. I desired he would order several Sticks of two foot high, and the thickness of an ordinary Cane, to be brought me; whereupon his Majesty commanded the Master of his Woods to give Directions accordingly; and the next Morning six Woodmen arrived with as many Carriages, drawn by eight Horses to each. I took nine of these Sticks, and fixing them firmly in the Ground in a Quadrangular Figure, two foot and a half Square, I took four other Sticks, and tied them parallel at each Corner, about two foot from the Ground; then I fastened my Handkerchief to the nine Sticks that stood erect, and extended it on all sides till it was as tight as the top of a Drum; and the four parallel Sticks rising about five Inches higher than the Handkerchief, served as Ledges on each side. When I had finished my Work, I desired the Emperor to let a Troop of his best Horse, twenty-four in number, come and exercise upon this Plain. His Majesty approved of the Proposal, and I took them up one by one in my Hands, ready mounted and armed, with the proper Officers to exercise them. As soon as they got into order, they divided into two Parties, performed mock Skirmishes, discharged blunt Arrows, drew their Swords, fled and pursued, attacked and retired, and in short discovered[44] the best Military Discipline I ever beheld. The parallel Sticks secured them and their Horses from falling over the Stage; and the Emperor was so much delighted, that he ordered this Entertainment to be repeated several days, and once was pleased to be lifted up, and give the word of Command; and, with great difficulty, persuaded even the Empress herself to let me hold her in her close Chair[45] within two Yards of the Stage, from whence she was able to take a full View of the whole Performance. It was my good fortune that no ill Accident happened in these Entertainments, only once a fiery Horse that belonged to one of the Captains pawing with his Hoof struck a Hole in my Handkerchief, and his Foot slipping, he overthrew his Rider and himself; but I immediately relieved them both, and covering the Hole with one Hand, I set down the Troop with the other, in the same manner as I took them up. The Horse that fell was strained in the left Shoulder, but the Rider got no Hurt, and I repaired my Handkerchief as well as I could; however I would not trust to the Strength of it any more in such dangerous Enterprises.

About two or three days before I was set at liberty, as I was entertaining the Court with these kind of Feats, there arrived an Express to inform his Majesty that some of his Subjects riding near the Place where I was first taken up, had seen a great black Substance lying on the Ground, very oddly shaped, extending its Edges round as wide as his Majesty's Bedchamber, and rising up in the middle as high as a Man; that it was no living Creature, as they at first apprehended, for it lay on the Grass without Motion, and some of them had walked round it several times: That by mounting upon each others Shoulders, they had got to the top, which was flat and even, and stamping upon it they found it was hollow within; that they humbly conceived it might be something belonging to the *Man-Mountain*, and if his Majesty pleased, they would undertake to bring it with only five Horses. I presently[46] knew what they meant, and was glad at heart to receive this Intelligence.[47] It seems upon my first reaching the Shore after our Shipwreck, I was in such confusion, that before I came to the Place where I went to sleep, my Hat which I had fastened with a String to my Head while I was rowing, and had stuck on all the time I was swimming, fell off after I came to Land; the String, as I conjecture, breaking by some Accident which I never observed, but thought my Hat had been lost at Sea. I entreated his Imperial Majesty to give Orders it might be brought to me as soon as possible, describing to him the Use and the Nature of it: And the next day the Waggoners arrived with it, but not in a very good condition; they had bored two Holes in the Brim, within an Inch and a half of the Edge, and fastened two Hooks in the Holes; these Hooks were tied by a long Cord to the

Harness, and thus my Hat was dragged along for above half an *English* Mile: but the Ground in that Country being extremely smooth and level, it received less Damage than I expected.

Two Days after this Adventure, the Emperor having ordered that Part of his Army which quarters in and about his Metropolis to be in a readiness, took a fancy of diverting himself in a very singular manner. He desired I would stand like a *Colossus*,[48] with my Legs as far asunder as I conveniently could. He then commanded his General (who was an old experienced Leader, and a great Patron of mine) to draw up the Troops in close Order, and march them under me, the Foot by Twenty-four in a breast, and the Horse by Sixteen, with Drums beating, Colours flying, and Pikes advanced. This Body consisted of three thousand Foot, and a thousand Horse. His Majesty gave Orders, upon pain of Death, that every Soldier in his March should observe the strictest Decency, with regard to my Person; which, however, could not prevent some of the younger Officers from turning up their Eyes as they passed under me. And, to confess the Truth, my Breeches were at that time in so ill a Condition, that they afforded some Opportunities for Laughter and Admiration.

I had sent so many Memorials and Petitions for my Liberty, that his Majesty at length mentioned the Matter first in the Cabinet, and then in a full Council; where it was opposed by none, except *Skyresh Bolgolam*,[49] who was pleased, without any provocation, to be my mortal Enemy. But it was carried against him by the whole Board, and confirmed by the Emperor. That Minister was *Galbet*, or Admiral of the Realm, very much in his Master's Confidence, and a Person well versed in Affairs, but of a morose and sour Complexion.[50] However, he was at length persuaded to comply; but prevailed that the Articles and Conditions upon which I should be set free, and to which I must swear, should be drawn up by himself. These Articles were brought to me by *Skyresh Bolgolam* in Person, attended by two Under-Secretaries, and several Persons of Distinction. After they were read, I was demanded to swear to the Performance of them; first in the manner of my own Country, and afterwards in the method prescribed by their Laws; which was to hold my right Foot in my left Hand, to place the middle Finger of my right Hand on the Crown of my Head, and my Thumb on the Tip of my right Ear. But because the

Reader may perhaps be curious to have some Idea of the Style and Manner of Expression peculiar to that People, as well as to know the Articles upon which I recovered my Liberty, I have made a Translation of the whole Instrument[51] word for word, as near as I was able, which I here offer to the Public.

GOLBASTO   MOMAREN   EVLAME   GURDILO   SHEFIN MULLY ULLY GUE, most Mighty Emperor of *Lilliput*, Delight and Terror of the Universe, whose Dominions extend five thousand Blustrugs (about twelve Miles in Circumference) to the Extremities of the Globe; Monarch of all Monarchs, taller than the Sons of Men; whose Feet press down to the Centre, and whose Head strikes against the Sun: At whose Nod the Princes of the Earth shake their Knees; pleasant as the Spring, comfortable as the Summer, fruitful as Autumn, dreadful as Winter. His most sublime Majesty proposeth to the *Man-Mountain*, lately arrived to our Celestial Dominions, the following Articles, which by a solemn Oath he shall be obliged to perform.

FIRST, The *Man-Mountain* shall not depart from our Dominions, without our Licence under our Great Seal.

2ᵈ, He shall not presume to come into our Metropolis, without our express Order; at which time the Inhabitants shall have two Hours warning to keep within their Doors.

3ᵈ, THE said *Man-Mountain* shall confine his Walks to our principal High Roads, and not offer to walk or lie down in a Meadow or Field of Corn.[52]

4ᵗʰ, As he walks the said Roads, he shall take the utmost care not to trample upon the Bodies of any of our loving Subjects, their Horses, or Carriages, nor take any of our said Subjects into his Hands, without their own Consent.

5ᵗʰ, IF an Express requires extraordinary Dispatch, the *Man-Mountain* shall be obliged to carry in his Pocket the Messenger and Horse a Six Days Journey once in every Moon, and return the said Messenger back (if so required) safe to our Imperial Presence.

6ᵗʰ, HE shall be our Ally against our Enemies in the Island of *Blefuscu*,[53] and do his utmost to destroy their Fleet, which is now preparing to invade Us.

7th, THAT the said *Man-Mountain* shall, at his times of leisure, be aiding and assisting to our Workmen, in helping to raise certain great Stones, towards covering the Wall of the principal Park, and other our Royal Buildings.

8th, THAT the said *Man-Mountain* shall, in two Moons time, deliver in an exact Survey of the Circumference of our Dominions by a Computation of his own Paces round the Coast.

LASTLY, That upon his solemn Oath to observe all the above Articles, the said *Man-Mountain* shall have a daily Allowance of Meat and Drink sufficient for the Support of 1728 of our Subjects, with free Access to our Royal Person, and other Marks of our Favour. Given at our Palace at *Belfaborac* the twelfth Day of the Ninety-first Moon of our Reign.

I swore and subscribed to these Articles with great Cheerfulness and Content, although some of them were not so honourable as I could have wished; which proceeded wholly from the Malice of *Skyresh Bolgolam* the High Admiral: whereupon my Chains were immediately unlocked, and I was at full liberty; the Emperor himself in Person did me the Honour to be by at the whole Ceremony. I made my Acknowledgements by prostrating myself at his Majesty's Feet: But he commanded me to rise; and after many gracious Expressions, which, to avoid the Censure of Vanity, I shall not repeat, he added, that he hoped I should prove a useful Servant, and well deserve all the Favours he had already conferred upon me, or might do for the future.

The Reader may please to observe, that in the last Article for the Recovery of my Liberty, the Emperor stipulates to allow me a Quantity of Meat and Drink sufficient for the Support of 1728 *Lilliputians*. Some time after, asking a Friend at Court how they came to fix on that determinate Number; he told me, that his Majesty's Mathematicians, having taken the Height of my Body by the help of a Quadrant, and finding it to exceed theirs in the Proportion of Twelve to One, they concluded from the Similarity of their Bodies, that mine must contain at least 1728 of theirs, and consequently would require as much Food as was necessary to support that number of *Lilliputians*. By which, the Reader may conceive an Idea of the Ingenuity of that People, as well as the prudent and exact Economy of so great a Prince.

CHAP. IV

Mildendo,[54] *the Metropolis of* Lilliput, *described, together with the Emperor's Palace. A Conversation between the Author and a principal Secretary, concerning the Affairs of that Empire: The Author's Offers to serve the Emperor in his Wars.*

The first Request I made after I had <u>obtained my Liberty</u>, was, that I might have Licence to see *Mildendo*, the Metropolis; which the Emperor easily granted me, but with a special Charge to do no hurt, either to the Inhabitants, or their Houses. The People had notice by Proclamation of my design to visit the Town. The Wall which encompassed it, is two foot and an half high, and at least eleven Inches broad, so that a Coach and Horses may be driven very safely round it; and it is flanked with strong Towers at ten foot distance. I stepped over the great Western Gate, and passed very gently, and sideling through the two principal Streets, only in my short Waistcoat, for fear of damaging the Roofs and Eves of the Houses with the Skirts of my Coat. I walked with the utmost Circumspection, to avoid treading on any Stragglers, that might remain in the Streets, although the Orders were very strict, that all People should keep in their Houses, at their own Peril. The Garret Windows and Tops of Houses were so crowded with Spectators, that I thought in all my Travels I had not seen a more populous Place. The City is an exact Square, each side of the Wall being five hundred foot long. The two great Streets which run cross and divide it into four Quarters, are five foot wide. The Lanes and Alleys which I could not enter, but only viewed them as I passed, are from twelve to eighteen Inches. The Town is capable of holding five hundred thousand Souls.[55] The Houses are from three to five Storeys. The Shops and Markets well provided.

The Emperor's Palace is in the Centre of the City, where the two great Streets meet. It is enclosed by a Wall of two foot high, and twenty foot distant from the Buildings. I had his Majesty's Permission to step over this Wall; and the Space being so wide between that and the Palace, I could easily view it on every side. The outward Court is a Square of forty foot, and includes two other Courts: In the inmost are the Royal

Apartments, which I was very desirous to see, but found it extremely difficult; for the great Gates, from one Square into another, were but eighteen Inches high, and seven Inches wide. Now the Buildings of the outer Court were at least five foot high, and it was impossible for me to stride over them, without infinite Damage to the Pile,[56] although the Walls were strongly built of hewn Stone, and four Inches thick. At the same time the Emperor had a great desire that I should see the Magnificence of his Palace; but this I was not able to do till three Days after, which I spent in cutting down with my Knife some of the largest Trees in the Royal Park, about an hundred Yards distant from the City. Of these Trees I made two Stools, each about three foot high, and strong enough to bear my Weight. The People having received notice a second time, I went again through the City to the Palace, with my two Stools in my Hands. When I came to the side of the outer Court, I stood upon one Stool, and took the other in my hand: This I lifted over the Roof, and gently set it down on the Space between the first and second Court, which was eight foot wide. I then stepped over the Buildings very conveniently from one Stool to the other, and drew up the first after me with a hooked Stick. By this Contrivance I got into the inmost Court; and lying down upon my side, I applied my Face to the Windows of the middle Storeys, which were left open on purpose, and discovered the most splendid Apartments that can be imagined. There I saw the Empress, and the young Princes in their several Lodgings, with their chief Attendants about them. Her Imperial Majesty was pleased to smile very graciously upon me, and gave me out of the Window her Hand to kiss.

But I shall not anticipate the Reader with further Descriptions of this kind, because I reserve them for a greater Work, which is now almost ready for the Press, containing a general Description of this Empire, from its first Erection, through a long Series of Princes, with a particular Account of their Wars and Politics, Laws, Learning, and Religion; their Plants and Animals, their peculiar Manners and Customs, with other Matters very curious and useful; my chief design at present being only to relate such Events and Transactions as happened to the Public, or to myself, during a Residence of about nine Months in that Empire.

One Morning, about a Fortnight after I had obtained my Liberty, *Reldresal* Principal Secretary (as they style him) of private Affairs, came to my House, attended only by one Servant. He ordered his Coach to wait at a distance, and desired I would give him an Hour's Audience; which I readily consented to, on account of his Quality, and Personal Merits, as well as the many good Offices he had done me during my Solicitations at Court. I offered to lie down, that he might the more conveniently reach my Ear; but he chose rather to let me hold him in my hand during our Conversation. He began with Compliments on my Liberty, said he might pretend to some Merit in it; but, however, added, that if it had not been for the present Situation of things at Court, perhaps I might not have obtained it so soon. For, *said he*, as flourishing a Condition as we may appear to be in to Foreigners, we labour under two mighty Evils; a violent Faction at home, and the Danger of an Invasion by a most potent Enemy from abroad. As to the first, you are to understand, that for above seventy Moons past, there have been two struggling Parties in this Empire, under the Names of *Tramecksan*, and *Slamecksan*,[57] from the high and low Heels on their Shoes, by which they distinguish themselves. It is alledged indeed, that the high Heels are most agreeable to our ancient Constitution: But however this be, his Majesty hath determined to make use of only low Heels in the Adminis-tration of the Government, and all Offices in the Gift of the Crown, as you cannot but observe; and particularly, that his Majesty's Imperial Heels are lower at least by a *Drurr* than any of his Court (*Drurr* is a Measure about the fourteenth Part of an Inch). The Animosities between these two Parties run so high, that they will neither eat nor drink, nor talk with each other. We compute the *Tramecksan*, or High-Heels, to exceed us in number; but the Power is wholly on our side. We apprehend his Imperial Highness, the Heir to the Crown, to have some Tendency towards the High-Heels;[58] at least, we can plainly discover one of his Heels higher than the other, which gives him a Hobble in his Gait. Now, in the midst of these intestine Disquiets, we are threatened with an Invasion from the Island of *Blefuscu*, which is the other great Empire of the Universe, almost as large and powerful as this of his Majesty. For as to what we have heard you affirm, that there are other Kingdoms and States in the World,[59] inhabited by human Creatures as large as yourself, our Philosophers are in much doubt, and would rather conjecture that you dropped from the Moon, or one of the Stars; because it is certain, that an hundred Mortals of your Bulk would, in a short time, destroy all the Fruits and Cattle of his Majesty's Dominions. Besides, our Histories of six thousand Moons make no mention of any other Regions, than the two great Empires of *Lilliput* and *Blefuscu*. Which two mighty Powers have, as I was going to tell you, been engaged in a most obstinate War for six and thirty Moons past. It began upon the following Occasion. It is allowed on all hands, that the primitive way of breaking Eggs before we eat them, was upon the larger End: But his present Majesty's Grand-father,[60] while he was a Boy, going to eat an Egg, and breaking it according to the ancient Practice, happened to cut one of his Fingers. Whereupon the Emperor his Father published an Edict, commanding all his Subjects, upon great Penalties, to break the smaller End of their Eggs. The People so highly resented this Law, that our Histories tell us there have been six Rebellions raised on that account; wherein one Emperor lost his Life, and another his Crown.[61] These civil Commotions were constantly fomented by the Monarchs of *Blefuscu*; and when they were quelled, the Exiles always fled for Refuge to that Empire. It is computed, that eleven thousand Persons have, at several times, suffered Death, rather than submit to break their Eggs at the smaller End. Many hundred large Volumes have been published upon this Controversy: But the Books of the *Big-Endians* have been long forbidden, and the whole Party rendered incapable by Law of holding Employments.[62] During the Course of these Troubles, the Emperors of *Blefuscu* did frequently expostulate by their Ambassadors, accusing us of making a Schism in Religion,[63] by offending against a fundamental Doctrine of our great Prophet *Lustrog*, in the fifty-fourth Chapter of the *Blundecral* (which is their *Alcoran*). This, however, is thought to be a mere Strain upon the Text: For the Words are these; *That all true Believers shall break their Eggs at the convenient End*: and which is the convenient End, seems, in my humble Opinion, to be left to every Man's Conscience, or at least in the power of the Chief Magistrate to determine. Now the *Big-Endian* Exiles have found so much Credit in the Emperor of *Blefuscu's* Court, and so much private Assistance and Encouragement from their Party here at home, that a bloody War hath been carried on between the two Empires for six and thirty Moons with various Success; during which time we have lost forty Capital Ships, and a much greater number of smaller Vessels, together with thirty thousand of our best Seamen and Soldiers; and the Damage received by the Enemy is reckoned to be somewhat greater than Ours. However, they have now equipped a numerous Fleet, and are just preparing to make a Descent upon us; and his Imperial Majesty placing great Confidence in your Valour and Strength, hath commanded Me to lay this Account of his Affairs before You.

I desired the Secretary to present my humble Duty to the Emperor, and to let him know, that I thought it would not become Me, who was a Foreigner, to interfere with Parties; but I was ready, with the hazard of my Life, to defend his Person and State against all Invaders.

CHAP. V

*The Author by an extraordinary Stratagem prevents an Invasion.
A high Title of Honour is conferred upon him. Ambassadors arrive
from the Emperor of Blefuscu, and sue for Peace. The Empress's
Apartment on fire by an Accident; the Author instrumental in
saving the rest of the Palace.*

The Empire of *Blefuscu* is an Island situated to the North North-East side of *Lilliput*, from whence it is parted only by a Channel of eight hundred Yards wide. I had not yet seen it, and upon this Notice of an intended Invasion, I avoided appearing on that side of the Coast, for fear of being discovered by some of the Enemy's Ships, who had received no Intelligence of me, all Intercourse between the two Empires having been strictly forbidden during the War, upon pain of Death, and an Embargo laid by our Emperor upon all Vessels whatsoever. I communicated to his Majesty a Project I had formed of seizing the Enemy's whole Fleet; which, as our Scouts assured us, lay at Anchor in the Harbour ready to sail with the first fair Wind. I consulted the most experienced Seamen, upon the depth of the Channel, which they had often plumbed, who told me, that in the middle at high Water it was seventy *Glumgluffs* deep, which is about six foot of *European* Measure; and the rest of it fifty *Glumgluffs* at most. I walked towards the North-East Coast over against *Blefuscu*, and lying down behind a Hillock, took out my small Pocket Perspective-Glass, and viewed the Enemy's Fleet at Anchor, consisting of about fifty Men of War, and a great Number of Transports: I then came back to my House, and gave Order (for which I had a Warrant) for a great Quantity of the strongest Cable and Bars of Iron. The Cable was about as thick as Packthread, and the Bars of the length and size of a Knitting-Needle. I trebled the Cable to make it stronger, and for the same reason I twisted three of the Iron Bars together, bending the Extremities into a Hook. Having thus fixed fifty Hooks to as many Cables, I went back to the North-East Coast, and putting off my Coat, Shoes, and Stockings, walked into the Sea in my Leathern Jerkin, about half an hour before high Water. I waded with what Haste I could, and swam in the middle about thirty Yards till I felt ground; I arrived at the Fleet in less than half an hour. The Enemy was so frighted when they saw me, that they leaped out of their Ships, and swam to shore, where there could not be fewer than thirty thousand Souls. I then took my Tackling, and fastening a Hook to a hole at the Prow of each, I tied all the Cords together at the End. While I was thus employed, the Enemy discharged several thousand Arrows, many of which stuck in my Hands and Face; and besides the excessive smart, gave me much disturbance in my Work. My greatest Apprehension was for my Eyes, which I should have infallibly lost, if I had not suddenly thought of an Expedient. I kept among other little Necessaries a pair of Spectacles in a private Pocket, which, as I observed before, had escaped the Emperor's Searchers. These I took out and fastened as strongly as I could upon my Nose, and thus armed went on boldly with my Work in spite of the Enemy's Arrows, many of which struck against the Glasses of my Spectacles, but without any other Effect, further than a little to discompose them. I had now fastened all the Hooks, and taking the Knot in my Hand, began to pull; but not a Ship would stir, for they were all too fast held by their Anchors, so that the boldest part of my Enterprise remained. I therefore let go the Cord, and leaving the Hooks fixed to the Ships, I resolutely cut with my Knife the Cables that fastened the Anchors, receiving above two hundred Shots in my Face and Hands; then I took up the knotted End of the Cables to which my Hooks were tied, and with great ease drew fifty of the Enemy's largest Men of War after me.

The *Blefuscudians*, who had not the least Imagination of what I intended, were at first confounded with Astonishment. They had seen me cut the Cables, and thought my Design was only to let the Ships run adrift, or fall foul on each other: but when they perceived the whole Fleet moving in Order, and saw me pulling at the End, they set up such a scream of Grief and Despair, that it is almost impossible to describe or conceive. When I had got out of danger, I stopped a while to pick out the Arrows that stuck in my Hands and Face, and rubbed on some of the same Ointment that was given me at my first arrival, as I have formerly mentioned. I then took off my Spectacles, and waiting about an Hour till the Tide was a little fallen, I waded through the middle with my Cargo, and arrived safe at the Royal Port of *Lilliput*.

The Emperor and his whole Court stood on the Shore expecting the Issue of this great Adventure. They saw the Ships move forward in a large Half-Moon, but could not discern me, who was up to my Breast in Water. When I advanced to the middle of the Channel, they were yet more in pain because I was under Water to my Neck. The Emperor concluded me to be drowned, and that the Enemy's Fleet was approaching in a hostile manner: But he was soon eased of his Fears, for the Channel growing shallower every step I made, I came in a short time within hearing, and holding up the end of the Cable by which the Fleet was fastened, I cried in a loud Voice, *Long live the most puissant Emperor of Lilliput!* This great Prince received me at my Landing with all possible Encomiums, and created me a *Nardac* upon the spot, which is the highest Title of Honour among them.

His Majesty desired I would take some other Opportunity of bringing all the rest of his Enemy's Ships into his Ports. And so unmeasurable is the Ambition of Princes, that he seemed to think of nothing less than reducing the whole Empire of *Blefuscu* into a Province, and governing it by a Viceroy; of destroying the *Big-Endian* Exiles, and compelling that People to break the smaller end of their Eggs, by which he would remain the sole Monarch of the whole World. But I endeavoured to divert him from this Design, by many Arguments drawn from the Topics[64] of Policy as well as Justice: And I plainly protested, that I would never be an Instrument of bringing a Free and Brave People into Slavery. And when the Matter was debated in Council, the wisest part of the Ministry were of my Opinion.

This open bold Declaration of mine was so opposite to the Schemes and Politics of his Imperial Majesty, that he could never forgive it; he mentioned it in a very artful manner at Council, where I was told that some of the wisest appeared, at least by their Silence, to be of my opinion; but others, who were my secret Enemies, could not forbear some Expressions, which by a side-wind reflected on me. And from this time began an Intrigue between his Majesty, and a Junto[65] of Ministers maliciously bent against me, which broke out in less than two Months, and had like to have ended in my utter Destruction. Of so little weight are the greatest Services to Princes, when put into the Balance with a Refusal to gratify their Passions.

About three Weeks after this Exploit, there arrived a solemn Embassy from *Blefuscu*, with humble Offers of a Peace;[66] which was soon concluded upon Conditions very advantageous to our Emperor, wherewith I shall not trouble the Reader. There were six Ambassadors, with a Train of about five hundred Persons, and their Entry was very magnificent, suitable to the Grandeur of their Master, and the Importance of their Business. When their Treaty was finished, wherein I did them several good Offices by the Credit I now had, or at least appeared to have at Court, their Excellencies, who were privately told how much I had been their Friend, made me a Visit in Form.[67] They began with many Compliments upon my Valour and Generosity, invited me to that Kingdom in the Emperor their Master's Name, and desired me to show them some Proofs of my prodigious Strength, of which they had heard so many Wonders; wherein I readily obliged them, but shall not trouble the Reader with the Particulars.

When I had for some time entertained their Excellencies to their infinite Satisfaction and Surprise, I desired they would do me the Honour to present my most humble Respects to the Emperor their Master, the Renown of whose Virtues had so justly filled the whole World with Admiration, and whose Royal Person I resolved to attend before I returned to my own Country: accordingly, the next time I had the honour to see our Emperor, I desired his general Licence to wait on the *Blefuscudian* Monarch, which he was pleased to grant me, as I could plainly perceive, in a very cold manner; but could not guess the Reason, till I had a Whisper from a certain Person, that *Flimnap* and *Bolgolam* had represented my Intercourse with those Ambassadors as a mark of Disaffection, from which I am sure my Heart was wholly free. And this was the first time I began to conceive some imperfect Idea of Courts and Ministers.

It is to be observed, that these Ambassadors spoke to me by an Interpreter, the Languages of both Empires differing as much from each other as any two in *Europe*, and each Nation priding itself upon the Antiquity, Beauty, and Energy of their own Tongues, with an avowed Contempt for that of their Neighbour; yet our Emperor standing upon the advantage he had got by the seizure of their Fleet, obliged them to deliver their Credentials, and make their Speech in the *Lilliputian* Tongue. And it must be confessed, that from the great Intercourse of Trade and Commerce between both Realms, from the continual Reception of Exiles, which is mutual among them, and from the Custom in each Empire to send their young Nobility and richer Gentry to the other, in order to polish themselves, by seeing the World, and understanding Men and Manners; there are few Persons of Distinction, or Merchants, or Seamen, who dwell in the Maritime Parts, but what can hold Conversation in both Tongues; as I found some Weeks after, when I went to pay my respects to the Emperor of *Blefuscu*, which in the midst of great Misfortunes, through the Malice of my Enemies, proved a very happy Adventure to me, as I shall relate in its proper place.

The Reader may remember, that when I signed those Articles upon which I recovered my Liberty, there were some which I disliked upon account of their being too servile, neither could anything but an extreme Necessity have forced me to submit. But being now a *Nardac*, of the highest Rank in that Empire, such Offices were looked upon as below my Dignity, and the Emperor (to do him Justice) never once mentioned them to me. However, it was not long before I had an Opportunity of doing his Majesty, at least as I then thought, a most signal Service. I was alarmed at Midnight with the Cries of many hundred People at my Door; by which being suddenly awaked, I was in some kind of Terror. I heard the word *Burglum* repeated incessantly: several of the Emperor's Court making their Way through the Crowd, entreated me to come immediately to the Palace, where her Imperial Majesty's Apartment was on fire, by the carelessness of a Maid of Honour, who fell asleep while she was reading a Romance.[68] I got up in an instant; and Orders being given to clear the way before me, and it being likewise a Moonshine Night, I made a shift to get to the Palace without trampling on any of the People. I found they had already applied Ladders to the Walls of the Apartment, and were well provided with Buckets, but the Water was at some distance. These Buckets were about the size of a large Thimble, and the poor People supplied me with them as fast as they could; but the Flame was so violent, that they did little good. I might easily have stifled it with my Coat, which I unfortunately left behind me for haste, and came away only in my Leathern Jerkin. The Case seemed wholly desperate and deplorable, and this magnificent Palace would have infallibly been burnt down to the ground, if, by a Presence of Mind, unusual to me, I had not suddenly thought of an Expedient. I had the Evening before drank plentifully of a most delicious Wine, called *Glimigrim* (the *Blefuscudians* call it *Flunec*,[69] but ours is esteemed the better sort), which is very diuretic. By the luckiest Chance in the World, I had not discharged myself of any part of it. The Heat I had contracted by coming very near the Flames, and by my labouring to quench them, made the Wine begin to operate by Urine; which I voided in such a Quantity, and applied so well to the proper Places, that in three Minutes the Fire was wholly extinguished, and the rest of that noble Pile, which had cost so many Ages in erecting, preserved from Destruction.

It was now Daylight, and I returned to my House, without waiting to congratulate with the Emperor; because, although I had done a very eminent piece of Service, yet I could not tell how his Majesty might resent the manner by which I had performed it: For, by the fundamental Laws of the Realm, it is Capital[70] in any Person, of what Quality soever, to make water within the Precincts of the Palace. But I was a little comforted by a Message from his Majesty, that he would give Orders to the Grand Justiciary for passing my Pardon in form; which, however, I could not obtain. And I was privately assured, that the Empress conceiving the greatest Abhorrence of what I had done,[71] removed to the most distant side of the Court, firmly resolved that those Buildings should never be repaired for her Use; and, in the presence of her chief Confidants, could not forbear vowing Revenge.

CHAP. VI

Of the Inhabitants of Lilliput; *their Learning, Laws, and
Customs, the Manner of Educating their Children. The Author's
Way of living in that Country. His Vindication of a great Lady.*

Although I intend to leave the Description of this Empire to a
particular Treatise, yet in the mean time I am content to gratify the
curious Reader with some general Ideas. As the common Size of the
Natives is somewhat under six Inches high, so there is an exact Proportion
in all other Animals, as well as Plants and Trees: For instance, the tallest
Horses and Oxen are between four and five Inches in height, the Sheep
an Inch and a half, more or less; their Geese about the bigness of a
Sparrow, and so the several Gradations downwards, till you come to the
smallest, which, to my sight, were almost invisible; but Nature hath
adapted the Eyes of the *Lilliputians* to all Objects proper for their view:
They see with great exactness, but at no great distance. And to show the
sharpness of their Sight towards Objects that are near, I have been much
pleased with observing a Cook pulling a Lark,[72] which was not so large
as a common Fly; and a young Girl threading an invisible Needle with
invisible Silk. Their tallest Trees are about seven foot high; I mean some
of those in the great Royal Park, the Tops whereof I could but just reach
with my Fist clenched. The other Vegetables are in the same Proportion;
but this I leave to the Reader's Imagination.

I shall say but little at present of their Learning, which for many Ages
hath flourished in all its Branches among them: But their manner of
writing is very peculiar, being neither from the left to the right, like the
Europeans'; nor from the right to the left, like the *Arabians'*; nor from up
to down, like the *Chinese*; nor from down to up, like the *Cascagians'*;[73] but
aslant from one Corner of the Paper to the other, like our Ladies in
England.

They bury their Dead with their Heads directly downwards, because
they hold an Opinion that in eleven thousand Moons they are all to rise
again, in which Period the Earth (which they conceive to be flat) will
turn upside down, and by this means they shall, at their Resurrection,

be found ready standing on their Feet. The Learned among them confess the Absurdity of this Doctrine, but the Practice still continues, in compliance to the Vulgar.

There are some Laws and Customs in this Empire very peculiar, and if they were not so directly contrary to those of my own dear Country, I should be tempted to say a little in their justification. It is only to be wished that they were as well executed. The first I shall mention relates to Informers. All Crimes against the State are punished here with the utmost severity; but if the Person accused maketh his Innocence plainly to appear upon his Trial, the Accuser is immediately put to an ignominious Death; and out of his Goods or Lands, the innocent Person is quadruply recompensed for the Loss of his Time, for the Danger he underwent, for the Hardship of his Imprisonment, and for all the Charges he hath been at[74] in making his Defence. Or, if that Fund be deficient, it is largely[75] supplied by the Crown. The Emperor does also confer on him some public Mark of his Favour, and Proclamation is made of his Innocence through the whole City.

They look upon Fraud as a greater Crime than Theft, and therefore seldom fail to punish it with Death; for they allege, that Care and Vigilance, with a very common Understanding, may preserve a Man's Goods from Thieves, but Honesty has no fence[76] against superior Cunning: and since it is necessary that there should be a perpetual Intercourse of Buying and Selling, and dealing upon Credit, where Fraud is permitted and connived at,[77] or hath no Law to punish it, the honest Dealer is always undone, and the Knave gets the advantage. I remember when I was once interceding with the King for a Criminal who had wronged his Master of a great Sum of Money, which he had received by Order, and ran away with; and happening to tell his Majesty, by way of Extenuation, that it was only a breach of Trust; the Emperor thought it monstrous in me to offer, as a Defence, the greatest Aggravation of the Crime: and truly I had little to say in return, farther than the common Answer, that different Nations had different Customs; for, I confess, I was heartily ashamed.

Although we usually call Reward and Punishment the two Hinges upon which all Government turns, yet I could never observe this Maxim to be put in practice by any Nation except that of *Lilliput*. Whoever can there bring sufficient Proof that he hath strictly observed the Laws of his Country for seventy-three Moons, hath a claim to certain Privileges, according to his Quality and Condition of Life, with a proportionable Sum of Money out of a Fund appropriated for that Use: He likewise acquires the Title of *Snilpall*, or *Legal*, which is added to his Name, but does not descend to his Posterity. And these People thought it a prodigious Defect of Policy among us, when I told them that our Laws were enforced only by Penalties, without any mention of Reward. It is upon this account that the Image of Justice, in their Courts of Judicature, is formed with six Eyes, two before, as many behind, and on each side one, to signify Circumspection; with a Bag of Gold open in her Right Hand, and a Sword sheathed in her Left, to show she is more disposed to Reward than to Punish.

In choosing Persons for all Employments, they have more regard to good Morals than to great Abilities; for, since Government is necessary to Mankind, they believe that the common Size of Human Understandings, is fitted to some Station or other, and that Providence never intended to make the Management of public Affairs a Mystery, to be comprehended only by a few Persons of sublime Genius, of which there seldom are three born in an Age: but they suppose Truth, Justice, Temperance, and the like, to be in every Man's power; the Practice of which Virtues, assisted by Experience and a good Intention, would qualify any Man for the Service of his Country, except where a Course of Study is required. But they thought the want of Moral Virtues was so far from being supplied by superior Endowments of the Mind, that Employments could never be put into such dangerous Hands as those of Persons so qualified; and at least, that the Mistakes committed by Ignorance in a virtuous Disposition, would never be of such fatal Consequence to the Public Weal, as the Practices of a Man whose Inclinations led him to be corrupt, and had great Abilities to manage, and multiply, and defend his Corruptions.

In like manner, the Disbelief of a Divine Providence renders a Man uncapable of holding any Public Station;[78] for since Kings avow themselves to be the Deputies of Providence, the *Lilliputians* think nothing can be more absurd than for a Prince to employ such Men as disown the Authority under which he acts.

In relating these and the following Laws, I would only be understood to mean the original Institutions, and not the most scandalous Corruptions into which these People are fallen by the degenerate Nature of Man. For as to that infamous Practice of acquiring great Employments by dancing on the Ropes, or Badges of Favour and Distinction by leaping over Sticks, and creeping under them, the Reader is to observe, that they were first introduced by the Grandfather of the Emperor now reigning, and grew to the present height, by the gradual increase of Party and Faction.

Ingratitude is among them a capital Crime, as we read it to have been in some other Countries; for they reason thus, that whoever makes ill Returns to his Benefactor, must needs be a common Enemy to the rest of Mankind, from whom he hath received no Obligation, and therefore such a Man is not fit to live.

Their Notions relating to the Duties of Parents and Children differ extremely from ours. For, since the Conjunction of Male and Female is founded upon the great Law of Nature, in order to propagate and continue the Species, the *Lilliputians* will needs have it, that Men and Women are joined together like other Animals, by the Motives of Concupiscence; and that their Tenderness towards their Young proceeds from the like natural Principle: for which reason they will never allow, that a Child is under any Obligation to his Father for begetting him, or to his Mother for bringing him into the World; which, considering the Miseries of human Life, was neither a Benefit in itself, or intended so by his Parents, whose Thoughts in their Love-Encounters were otherwise employed. Upon these, and the like Reasonings, their Opinion is, that Parents are the last of all others to be trusted with the Education of their own Children: and therefore they have in every Town public Nurseries, where all Parents, except Cottagers[79] and Labourers, are obliged to send their Infants of both Sexes to be reared and educated when they come to the Age of twenty Moons, at which time, they are supposed to have some Rudiments of Docility.[80] These Schools are of several kinds, suited to different Qualities, and to both Sexes. They have certain Professors well skilled in preparing Children for such a condition of Life as befits the Rank of their Parents, and their own Capacities as well as Inclinations. I shall first say something of the Male Nurseries, and then of the Female.

The Nurseries for Males of Noble or Eminent Birth, are provided with Grave and Learned Professors, and their several Deputies. The Clothes and Food of the Children are plain and simple. They are bred up in the Principles of Honour, Justice, Courage, Modesty, Clemency, Religion, and Love of their Country; they are always employed in some Business, except in the times of Eating and Sleeping, which are very short, and two Hours for Diversions, consisting of bodily Exercises. They are dressed by Men till four Years of Age, and then are obliged to dress themselves, although their Quality[81] be ever so great; and the Women Attendants, who are aged proportionably to ours at fifty, perform only the most menial Offices. They are never suffered to converse with Servants, but go together in small or greater numbers to take their Diversions, and always in the presence of a Professor, or one of his Deputies; whereby they avoid those early bad Impressions of Folly and Vice to which our Children are subject. Their Parents are suffered to see them only twice a Year; the Visit is to last but an hour. They are allowed to kiss the Child at Meeting and Parting; but a Professor, who always stands by on those occasions, will not suffer them to whisper, or use any fondling Expressions, or bring any Presents of Toys, Sweetmeats, and the like.

The Pension from each Family for the Education and Entertainment of a Child, upon failure of due payment, is levied by the Emperor's Officers.

The Nurseries for Children of ordinary Gentlemen, Merchants, Traders, and Handicrafts, are managed proportionably after the same manner; only those designed for Trades, are put out Apprentices at Eleven years old, whereas those of Persons of Quality continue in their Nurseries till Fifteen, which answers to One and Twenty with us: but the Confinement is gradually lessened for the last three Years.

In the Female Nurseries, the young Girls of Quality are educated much like the Males, only they are dressed by orderly Servants of their own Sex, but always in the presence of a Professor or Deputy, till they come to dress themselves, which is at five Years old. And if it be found that these Nurses ever presume to entertain the Girls with frightful or foolish Stories, or the common Follies practised by Chamber-Maids among us, they are publicly whipped thrice about the City, imprisoned for a Year, and banished for Life to the most desolate Part of the Country. Thus the young Ladies there are as much ashamed of being Cowards and Fools, as the Men, and despise all personal Ornaments beyond Decency and Cleanliness: neither did I perceive any Difference in their Education, made by their Difference of Sex, only that the Exercises of the Females were not altogether so robust, and that some Rules were given them relating to domestic Life, and a smaller Compass of Learning was enjoined them: For their Maxim is, that among People of Quality, a Wife should be always a reasonable and agreeable Companion, because she cannot always be young. When the Girls are twelve Years old, which among them is the marriageable Age, their Parents or Guardians take them home, with great Expressions of Gratitude to the Professors, and seldom without Tears of the young Lady and her Companions.

In the Nurseries of Females of the meaner sort, the Children are instructed in all kinds of Works proper for their Sex, and their several degrees: Those intended for Apprentices are dismissed at nine Years old, the rest are kept to thirteen.

The meaner Families who have Children at these Nurseries, are obliged, besides their annual Pension, which is as low as possible, to return to the Steward of the Nursery a small monthly Share of their Gettings, to be a Portion for the Child; and therefore all Parents are limited in their Expenses by the Law. For the *Lilliputians* think nothing can be more unjust, than for People, in subservience to their own Appetites, to bring Children into the World, and leave the Burthen of supporting them on the Public. As to Persons of Quality, they give Security to appropriate a certain Sum for each Child, suitable to their Condition; and these Funds are always managed with good Husbandry, and the most exact Justice.

The Cottagers and Labourers keep their Children at home, their Business being only to till and cultivate the Earth, and therefore their Education is of little consequence to the Public; but the Old and Diseased among them are supported by Hospitals:[82] for Begging is a Trade unknown in this Kingdom.

And here it may perhaps divert the curious Reader, to give some account of my Domestic,[83] and my manner of living in this Country, during a Residence of nine Months and thirteen Days. Having a Head mechanically turned, and being likewise forced by necessity, I had made for myself a Table and Chair convenient enough, out of the largest Trees in the Royal Park. Two hundred Sempstresses were employed to make me Shirts, and Linnen for my Bed and Table, all of the strongest and coarsest kind they could get; which, however, they were forced to quilt together in several Folds, for the thickest was some degrees finer than Lawn.[84] Their Linnen is usually three Inches wide, and three foot make a Piece. The Sempstresses took my Measure as I lay on the ground, one standing at my Neck, and another at my Mid-Leg, with a strong Cord extended, that each held by the end, while the third measured the length of the Cord with a Rule of an Inch long. Then they measured my right Thumb, and desired no more; for by a mathematical Computation, that twice round the Thumb is once round the Wrist, and so on to the Neck and the Waist, and by the help of my old Shirt, which I displayed on the Ground before them for a Pattern, they fitted me exactly. Three hundred Tailors were employed in the same manner to make me Clothes; but they had another Contrivance for taking my Measure. I kneeled down, and they raised a Ladder from the Ground to my Neck; upon this Ladder one of them mounted, and let fall a Plumb-line from my Collar to the Floor, which just answered the length of my Coat; but my Waist and Arms I measured myself. When my Clothes were finished, which was done in my House (for the largest of theirs would not be able to hold them), they looked like the Patch-Work made by the Ladies in *England*, only that mine were all of a Colour.

I had three hundred Cooks to dress my Victuals, in little convenient Huts built about my House, where they and their Families lived, and prepared me two Dishes apiece. I took up twenty Waiters in my Hand, and placed them on the Table, an hundred more attended below on the Ground, some with Dishes of Meat, and some with Barrels of Wine, and other Liquors, slung on their Shoulders; all which the Waiters above drew up as I wanted, in a very ingenious manner, by certain Cords, as we draw the Bucket up a Well in *Europe*. A Dish of their Meat was a good Mouthful, and a Barrel of their Liquor a reasonable Draught. Their Mutton yields to ours, but their Beef is excellent. I have had a Sirloin so large, that I have been forced to make three Bits[85] of it; but this is rare. My Servants were astonished to see me eat it Bones and all, as in our Country we do the Leg of a Lark. Their Geese and Turkeys I usually eat

at a Mouthful, and I must confess they far exceed ours. Of their smaller
Fowl I could take up twenty or thirty at the end of my Knife.

One day his Imperial Majesty being informed of my way of living,
desired that himself, and his Royal Consort, with the young Princes of
the Blood of both Sexes, might have the Happiness (as he was pleased to
call it) of dining with me. They came accordingly, and I placed them upon
Chairs of State on my Table, just over-against me, with their Guards about
them. *Flimnap* the Lord High Treasurer attended there likewise, with
his white Staff; and I observed he often looked on me with a sour Countenance, which I would not seem to regard, but eat more than usual, in honour
to my dear Country, as well as to fill the Court with Admiration. I
have some private Reasons to believe, that this Visit from his Majesty
gave *Flimnap* an opportunity of doing me ill Offices to his Master. That
Minister had always been my secret Enemy, though he outwardly caressed
me more than was usual to the Moroseness of his Nature. He represented to the Emperor the low Condition of his Treasury; that he was
forced to take up Money at great Discount; that Exchequer Bills would
not circulate under nine *per Cent.* below Par;[86] that in short I had cost
his Majesty above a Million and a half of *Sprugs* (their greatest Gold
Coin, about the bigness of a Spangle); and upon the whole, that it would
be advisable in the Emperor to take the first fair Occasion of dismissing
me.

I am here obliged to vindicate the Reputation of an excellent Lady,
who was an innocent Sufferer upon my account. The Treasurer took a
fancy to be jealous of his Wife, from the Malice of some Evil Tongues,
who informed him that her Grace had taken a violent Affection for my
Person, and the Court-Scandal ran for some time, that she once came
privately to my Lodging. This I solemnly declare to be a most infamous
Falsehood, without any Grounds, farther than that her Grace was pleased
to treat me with all innocent Marks of Freedom and Friendship. I own
she came often to my House, but always publicly, nor ever without three
more in the Coach, who were usually her Sister and young Daughter,
and some particular Acquaintance; but this was common to many other
Ladies of the Court. And I still appeal to my Servants round, whether
they at any time saw a Coach at my Door without knowing what Persons
were in it. On those Occasions, when a Servant had given me notice, my

Custom was to go immediately to the Door; and after paying my Respects, to take up the Coach and two Horses very carefully in my Hands (for if there were six Horses, the Postillion[87] always unharnessed four) and place them on a Table, where I had fixed a moveable Rim quite round, of five Inches high, to prevent Accidents. And I have often had four Coaches and Horses at once on my Table full of Company, while I sat in my Chair leaning my Face towards them; and when I was engaged with one Set, the Coachmen would gently drive the others round my Table. I have passed many an Afternoon very agreeably in these Conversations. But I defy the Treasurer, or his two Informers (I will name them, and let them make their best of it), *Clustril* and *Drunlo*, to prove that any Person ever came to me *incognito*, except the Secretary *Reldresal*, who was sent by express Command of his Imperial Majesty, as I have before related. I should not have dwelt so long upon this Particular, if it had not been a Point wherein the Reputation of a great Lady is so nearly concerned, to say nothing of my own; though I had then the Honour to be a *Nardac*, which the Treasurer himself is not, for all the World knows he is only a *Clumglum*, a Title inferior by one degree, as that of a Marquis is to a Duke in *England*, although I allow he preceded me in right of his Post. These false Informations, which I afterwards came to the knowledge of, by an Accident not proper to mention, made *Flimnap* the Treasurer show his Lady for some time an ill Countenance, and me a worse; and although he were at last undeceived and reconciled to her, yet I lost all Credit with him, and found my Interest decline very fast with the Emperor himself, who was indeed too much governed by that Favourite.

CHAP. VII

The Author being informed of a Design to accuse him of High Treason, makes his Escape to Blefuscu. *His Reception there.*

Before I proceed to give an account of my leaving this Kingdom, it may be proper to inform the Reader of a private Intrigue which had been for two Months forming against me.

I had been hitherto all my Life a Stranger to Courts, for which I was unqualified by the Meanness of my Condition. I had indeed heard and read enough of the Dispositions of great Princes and Ministers; but never expected to have found such terrible Effects of them in so remote a Country, governed, as I thought, by very different Maxims from those in *Europe*.

When I was just preparing to pay my Attendance on the Emperor of *Blefuscu*, a considerable Person at Court (to whom I had been very serviceable at a time when he lay under the highest Displeasure of his Imperial Majesty) came to my House very privately at night in a close Chair, and without sending his Name, desired admittance: The Chair-Men were dismissed; I put the Chair, with his Lordship in it, into my Coat-Pocket; and giving Orders to a trusty Servant to say I was indisposed and gone to sleep, I fastened the Door of my House, placed the Chair on the Table, according to my usual custom, and sat down by it. After the common Salutations were over, observing his Lordship's Countenance full of Concern; and inquiring into the reason, he desired I would hear him with patience in a Matter that highly concerned my Honour and my Life. His Speech was to the following effect, for I took Notes of it as soon as he left me.

You are to know, said he, that several Committees of Council have been lately called in the most private manner on your account: And it is but two days since his Majesty came to a full Resolution.

You are very sensible that *Skyris Bolgolam* (*Galbet*, or High Admiral) hath been your mortal Enemy almost ever since your Arrival. His original Reasons I know not, but his hatred is much increased since your great Success against *Blefuscu*, by which his Glory, as Admiral, is obscured. This Lord, in conjunction with *Flimnap* the High Treasurer, whose Enmity against you is notorious on account of his Lady, *Limtoc* the General, *Lalcon* the Chamberlain, and *Balmuff* the grand Justiciary, have prepared Articles of Impeachment against you, for Treason, and other capital Crimes.

This Preface made me so impatient, being conscious of my own Merits and Innocence, that I was going to interrupt; when he entreated me to be silent, and thus proceeded.

Out of Gratitude for the Favours you have done me, I procured

Information of the whole Proceedings, and a Copy of the Articles, wherein I venture my Head for your Service.

Articles of Impeachment against Quinbus Flestrin (*the* Man-Mountain).[88]

ARTICLE I

WHEREAS, by a Statute made in the Reign of his Imperial Majesty *Calin Deffar Plune*, it is enacted, That whoever shall make water within the Precincts of the Royal Palace, shall be liable to the Pains and Penalties of High-Treason: Notwithstanding, the said *Quinbus Flestrin*, in open breach of the said Law, under colour[89] of extinguishing the Fire kindled in the Apartment of his Majesty's dear Imperial Consort, did maliciously, traitorously, and devilishly, by discharge of his Urine, put out the said Fire kindled in the said Apartment, lying and being within the Precincts of the said Royal Palace, against the Statute in that Case provided, &c. against the Duty, &c.

ARTICLE II

THAT the said *Quinbus Flestrin* having brought the Imperial Fleet of *Blefuscu* into the Royal Port, and being afterwards commanded by his Imperial Majesty to seize all the other Ships of the said Empire of *Blefuscu*, and reduce that Empire to a Province, to be governed by a Viceroy from hence, and to destroy and put to death not only all the *Big-Endian Exiles*, but likewise all the People of that Empire, who would not immediately forsake the *Big-Endian* Heresy: He the said *Flestrin*, like a false Traitor against his most Auspicious, Serene, Imperial Majesty, did petition to be excused from the said Service, upon pretence of unwillingness to force the Consciences, or destroy the Liberties and Lives of an innocent People.

ARTICLE III

THAT, whereas certain Ambassadors arrived from the Court of *Blefuscu* to sue for Peace in his Majesty's Court: He the said *Flestrin* did, like a false Traitor, aid, abet, comfort, and divert the said Ambassadors, although he knew them to be Servants to a Prince who was lately an open Enemy to his Imperial Majesty, and in open War against his said Majesty.

ARTICLE IV

THAT the said *Quinbus Flestrin*, contrary to the Duty of a faithful Subject, is now preparing to make a Voyage to the Court and Empire of *Blefuscu*, for which he hath received only verbal Licence from his Imperial Majesty; and under Colour of the said Licence, doth falsely and traitorously intend to take the said Voyage, and thereby to aid, comfort, and abet the Emperor of *Blefuscu*, so late an Enemy, and in open War with his Imperial Majesty aforesaid.

There are some other Articles, but these are the most important, of which I have read you an Abstract.

In the several Debates upon this Impeachment, it must be confessed that his Majesty gave many marks of his great Lenity, often urging the Services you had done him, and endeavouring to extenuate your Crimes. The Treasurer and Admiral insisted that you should be put to the most painful and ignominious Death, by setting fire on your House at Night, and the General was to attend with twenty thousand Men armed with poisoned Arrows to shoot you on the Face and Hands. Some of your Servants were to have private Orders to strew a poisonous Juice on your Shirts, which would soon make you tear your own Flesh, and die in the utmost Torture.[90] The General came into the same Opinion, so that for a long time there was a Majority against you. But his Majesty resolving, if possible, to spare your Life, at last brought off the Chamberlain.

Upon this Incident, *Reldresal* Principal Secretary for private Affairs, who always approved himself your true Friend, was commanded by the Emperor to deliver his Opinion, which he accordingly did; and therein justified the good Thoughts you have of him. He allowed your Crimes to be great, but that still there was room for Mercy, the most commendable Virtue in a Prince, and for which his Majesty was so justly celebrated. He said the Friendship between you and him was so well known to the World, that perhaps the most honourable Board might think him partial: However, in obedience to the Command he had received, he would freely offer his Sentiments. That if his Majesty, in consideration of your Services, and pursuant to his own merciful Disposition, would please to spare your Life, and only give order to put out both your Eyes, he humbly conceived, that by this Expedient,[91] Justice might in some measure be satisfied, and all the World would applaud the Lenity of the Emperor, as well as the fair and generous Proceedings of those who have the Honour to be his Counsellors. That the loss of your Eyes would be no impediment to your bodily strength, by which you might still be useful to his Majesty. That Blindness is an addition to Courage, by concealing Dangers from us; that the Fear you had for your Eyes, was the greatest Difficulty in bringing over the Enemy's Fleet, and it would be sufficient for you to see by the Eyes of the Ministers, since the greatest Princes do no more.

This Proposal was received with the utmost Disapprobation by the whole Board. *Bolgolam*, the Admiral, could not preserve his Temper; but rising up in Fury, said, he wondered how the Secretary durst presume to give his Opinion for preserving the Life of a Traitor: That the Services you had performed, were, by all true Reasons of State, the great Aggravation of your Crimes; that you, who were able to extinguish the Fire, by discharge of Urine in her Majesty's Apartment (which he mentioned with horror) might, at another time, raise an Inundation by the same Means, to drown the whole Palace; and the same Strength which enabled you to bring over the Enemy's Fleet, might serve, upon the first Discontent to carry it back: That he had good Reasons to think you were a *Big-Endian* in your Heart;[92] and as Treason begins in the Heart before it appears in Overt Acts, so he accused you as a Traitor on that account, and therefore insisted you should be put to death.

The Treasurer was of the same Opinion; he showed to what straits his Majesty's Revenue was reduced by the charge of maintaining you, which would soon grow insupportable: That the Secretary's Expedient of putting out your Eyes was so far from being a Remedy against this Evil, that it would probably increase it, as it is manifest from the common practice of blinding some kind of Fowl, after which they fed the faster, and grew sooner fat: That his sacred Majesty and the Council, who are your Judges, were in their own Consciences fully convinced of your Guilt, which was a sufficient Argument to condemn you to Death, without the formal Proofs required by the strict Letter of the Law.

But his Imperial Majesty fully determined against capital Punishment, was graciously pleased to say, that since the Council thought the loss of your Eyes too easy a Censure, some other may be inflicted hereafter. And your Friend the Secretary humbly desiring to be heard again, in answer to what the Treasurer had objected concerning the great Charge his Majesty was at in maintaining you, said, that his Excellency, who had the sole disposal of the Emperor's Revenue, might easily provide against that Evil, by gradually lessening your Establishment;[93] by which, for want of sufficient Food, you would grow weak and faint, and lose your Appetite, and consequently decay and consume in a few Months; neither would the Stench of your Carcass be then so dangerous, when it should become more than half diminished; and immediately upon your Death, five or six Thousand of his Majesty's Subjects might, in two or three days, cut your Flesh from your Bones, take it away by Cart-loads, and bury it in distant parts to prevent Infection, leaving the Skeleton as a Monument of Admiration to Posterity.

Thus by the great Friendship of the Secretary, the whole Affair was compromised. It was strictly enjoined, that the Project of starving you by degrees should be kept a Secret, but the Sentence of putting out your Eyes was entered on the Books; none dissenting except *Bolgolam* the Admiral, who being a Creature of the Empress, was perpetually instigated by her Majesty to insist upon your Death, she having borne perpetual Malice against you, on account of that infamous and illegal Method you took to extinguish the Fire in her Apartment.

In three days your Friend the Secretary will be directed to come to your House, and read before you the Articles of Impeachment; and then to signify the great Lenity[94] and Favour of his Majesty and Council, whereby you are only condemned to the loss of your Eyes, which his Majesty doth not question you will gratefully and humbly submit to; and twenty of his Majesty's Surgeons will attend, in order to see the Operation well performed, by discharging very sharp-pointed Arrows into the Balls of your Eyes, as you lie on the Ground.

I leave to your Prudence what Measures you will take; and to avoid Suspicion, I must immediately return in as private a manner as I came.

His Lordship did so, and I remained alone, under many Doubts and Perplexities of Mind.

It was a Custom introduced by this Prince and his Ministry (very different, as I have been assured, from the Practices of former Times), that after the Court had decreed any cruel Execution, either to gratify the Monarch's Resentment, or the Malice of a Favourite, the Emperor made a Speech to his whole Council, expressing his great Lenity and Tenderness, as Qualities known and confessed by all the World. This Speech was immediately published through the Kingdom; nor did any-thing terrify the People so much as those Encomiums on his Majesty's Mercy; because it was observed, that the more these Praises were enlarged and insisted on, the more inhuman was the Punishment, and the Sufferer more innocent. And as to myself, I must confess, having never been designed for a Courtier either by my Birth or Education, I was so ill a Judge of Things, that I could not discover the Lenity and Favour of this Sentence, but conceived it (perhaps erroneously) rather to be rigorous than gentle. I sometimes thought of standing my Trial, for although I could not deny the Facts alleged in the several Articles, yet I hoped they would admit of some Extenuations. But having in my Life perused many State Trials, which I ever observed to terminate as the Judges thought fit to direct, I durst not rely on so dangerous a Decision, in so critical a Juncture, and against such powerful Enemies. Once I was strongly bent upon Resistance, for while I had Liberty, the whole Strength of that Empire could hardly subdue me, and I might easily with Stones pelt the Metropolis to pieces; but I soon rejected that Project with Horror, by remembering the Oath I had made to the Emperor, the Favours I received from him, and the high Title of *Nardac* he conferred upon me. Neither had I so soon learned the Gratitude of Courtiers, to persuade myself that his Majesty's present Severities acquitted me of all past Obligations.

At last I fixed upon a Resolution, for which it is probable I may incur some Censure, and not unjustly; for I confess I owe the preserving my Eyes, and consequently my Liberty, to my own great Rashness and want of Experience: because if I had then known the Nature of Princes and Ministers, which I have since observed in many other Courts, and their Methods of treating Criminals less obnoxious than myself, I should with great alacrity and readiness have submitted to so easy a Punishment. But hurried on by the Precipitancy of Youth, and having his Imperial Maj-esty's Licence to pay my Attendance upon the Emperor of *Blefuscu*, I took this Opportunity, before the three Days were elapsed, to send a Letter to my Friend the Secretary, signifying my Resolution of setting out that Morning for *Blefuscu* pursuant to the leave I had got; and without waiting for an Answer, I went to that side of the Island where our Fleet lay. I seized a large Man of War, tied a Cable to the Prow, and lifting up the Anchors, I stripped myself, put my Clothes (together with my Coverlet, which I brought under my Arm) into the Vessel, and drawing it after me between wading and swimming, arrived at the Royal Port of *Blefuscu*, where the People had long expected me; they lent me two Guides to direct me to the Capital City, which is of the same Name. I held them in my Hands until I came within two hundred Yards of the Gate, and desired them to signify my Arrival to one of the Secretaries, and let him know, I there waited his Majesty's Commands. I had an Answer in about an Hour, that his Majesty, attended by the Royal Family, and great Officers of the Court, was coming out to receive me. I advanced a Hundred Yards. The Emperor, and his Train, alighted from their Horses, the Empress and Ladies from their Coaches, and I did not perceive they were in any Fright or Concern. I lay on the Ground to kiss his Majesty's and the Empress's Hand. I told his Majesty that I was come according to my Promise, and with the Licence of the Emperor my Master, to have the Honour of seeing so Mighty a Monarch, and to offer him any Service in my power, consistent with my Duty to my own Prince; not mentioning a Word of my Disgrace, because I had hitherto no regular Information of it, and might suppose myself wholly ignorant of any such Design; neither could I reasonably conceive that the Emperor would discover the Secret while I was out of his power: wherein, however, it soon appeared I was deceived.

I shall not trouble the Reader with the particular Account of my Reception at this Court, which was suitable to the Generosity of so great a Prince; nor of the Difficulties I was in for want of a House and Bed, being forced to lie on the Ground, wrapped up in my Coverlet.

CHAP. VIII

The Author, by a lucky Accident, finds Means to leave Blefuscu; *and after some Difficulties, returns safe to his Native Country.*

Three Days after my Arrival, walking out of Curiosity to the North-East Coast of the Island, I observed, about half a League off, in the Sea, somewhat that looked like a Boat overturned. I pulled off my Shoes and Stockings, and wading two or three Hundred Yards, I found the Object to approach nearer by force of the Tide, and then plainly saw it to be a real Boat, which I supposed might, by some Tempest, have been driven from a Ship; whereupon I returned immediately towards the City, and desired his Imperial Majesty to lend me twenty of the tallest Vessels he had left after the Loss of his Fleet, and three thousand Seamen under the Command of his Vice-Admiral. This Fleet sailed round, while I went back the shortest way to the Coast where I first discovered the Boat; I found the Tide had driven it still nearer. The Seamen were all provided with Cordage, which I had beforehand twisted to a sufficient strength. When the Ships came up, I stripped myself, and waded till I came within an hundred Yards of the Boat, after which I was forced to swim till I got up to it. The Seamen threw me the end of the Cord, which I fastened to a Hole in the fore-part of the Boat, and the other end to a Man of War: But I found all my Labour to little purpose; for being out of my depth, I was not able to work. In this Necessity, I was forced to swim behind, and push the Boat forwards as often as I could, with one of my Hands; and the Tide favouring me, I advanced so far, that I could just hold up my Chin and feel the Ground. I rested two or three Minutes, and then gave the Boat another Shove, and so on till the Sea was no higher than my Armpits; and now the most laborious part being over, I took out my other Cables which were stowed in one of the Ships, and fastening them first to the Boat, and then to nine of the Vessels which attended me; the Wind being favourable the Seamen towed, and I shoved till we arrived within forty Yards of the Shore, and waiting till the Tide was out, I got dry to the Boat, and by the assistance of two thousand Men, with Ropes and Engines, I made a shift to turn it on its Bottom, and found it was but little damaged.

I shall not trouble the Reader with the Difficulties I was under by the help of certain Paddles, which cost me ten days making, to get my Boat to the Royal Port of *Blefuscu*, where a mighty concourse of People appeared upon my arrival, full of Wonder at the sight of so prodigious a Vessel. I told the Emperor that my good Fortune had thrown this Boat in my way, to carry me to some place from whence I might return into my native Country, and begged his Majesty's Orders for getting Materials to fit it up, together with his Licence to depart; which, after some kind Expostulations, he was pleased to grant.

I did very much wonder, in all this time, not to have heard of any Express relating to me from our Emperor to the Court of *Blefuscu*. But I was afterwards given privately to understand, that his Imperial Majesty, never imagining I had the least notice of his Designs, believed I was only gone to *Blefuscu* in performance of my Promise, according to the Licence he had given me, which was well known at our Court, and would return in a few days when that Ceremony was ended. But he was at last in pain at my long absence; and, after consulting with the Treasurer, and the rest of that Cabal, a Person of Quality was dispatched with the Copy of the Articles against me. This Envoy had Instructions to represent to the Monarch of *Blefuscu*, the great Lenity of his Master, who was content to punish me no further than with the loss of my Eyes; that I had fled from Justice,[95] and if I did not return in two Hours, I should be deprived of my Title of *Nardac*, and declared a Traitor. The Envoy further added, that in order to maintain the Peace and Amity between both Empires, his Master expected, that his Brother of *Blefuscu* would give Orders to have me sent back to *Lilliput*, bound Hand and Foot, to be punished as a Traitor.

The Emperor of *Blefuscu* having taken three Days to consult, returned an Answer consisting of many Civilities and Excuses. He said, that as for sending me bound, his Brother knew it was impossible; that although I had deprived him of his Fleet, yet he owed great Obligations to me for many good Offices I had done him in making the Peace. That however both their Majesties would soon be made easy; for I had found a prodigious Vessel on the Shore, able to carry me on the Sea, which he had given order to fit up with my own Assistance and Direction, and he hoped in a few Weeks both Empires would be freed from so insupportable an Encumbrance.

With this Answer the Envoy returned to *Lilliput*, and the Monarch of *Blefuscu* related to me all that had passed, offering me at the same time (but under the strictest Confidence) his gracious Protection, if I would continue in his Service; wherein although I believed him sincere, yet I resolved never more to put any confidence in Princes or Ministers, where I could possibly avoid it; and therefore, with all due Acknowledgements for his favourable Intentions, I humbly begged to be excused. I told him, that since Fortune, whether good or evil, had thrown a Vessel in my way, I was resolved to venture myself in the Ocean, rather than be an occasion of Difference between two such mighty Monarchs. Neither did I find the Emperor at all displeased; and I discovered by a certain Accident, that he was very glad of my Resolution, and so were most of his Ministers.

These Considerations moved me to hasten my Departure somewhat sooner than I intended; to which the Court, impatient to have me gone, very readily contributed. Five hundred Workmen were employed to make two Sails to my Boat, according to my Directions, by quilting thirteen fold of their strongest Linnen together. I was at the pains of making Ropes and Cables, by twisting ten, twenty or thirty of the thickest and strongest of theirs. A great Stone that I happened to find, after a long Search by the Sea-shore, served me for an Anchor. I had the Tallow of three hundred Cows for greasing my Boat, and other Uses. I was at incredible pains in cutting down some of the largest Timber Trees for Oars and Masts, wherein I was, however, much assisted by his Majesty's Ship-Carpenters, who helped me in smoothing them, after I had done the rough Work.

In about a Month, when all was prepared, I sent to receive his Majesty's Commands, and to take my leave. The Emperor and Royal Family came out of the Palace; I lay down on my Face to kiss his Hand, which he very graciously gave me; so did the Empress, and young Princes of the Blood. His Majesty presented me with fifty Purses of two hundred *Sprugs* apiece, together with his Picture at full length, which I put immediately into one of my Gloves, to keep it from being hurt. The Ceremonies at my Departure were too many to trouble the Reader with at this time.

I stored the Boat with the Carcasses of an hundred Oxen, and three hundred Sheep, with Bread and Drink proportionable, and as much Meat ready dressed as four hundred Cooks could provide. I took with me six Cows and two Bulls alive, with as many Ewes and Rams, intending to carry them into my own Country, and propagate the Breed. And to feed them on board, I had a good Bundle of Hay, and a Bag of Corn. I would gladly have taken a Dozen of the Natives, but this was a thing the

Emperor would by no means permit; and besides a diligent Search into my Pockets, his Majesty engaged my Honour not to carry away any of his Subjects, although with their own Consent and Desire.

Having thus prepared all things as well as I was able, I set sail on the twenty-fourth Day of *September*, 1701, at six in the Morning; and when I had gone about four Leagues to the Northward, the Wind being at South-East, at six in the Evening, I descried a small Island about half a League to the North-West. I advanced forward, and cast Anchor on the Lee-side of the Island, which seemed to be uninhabited. I then took some Refreshment, and went to my rest. I slept well, and I conjecture at least six Hours, for I found the Day broke in two Hours after I awaked. It was a clear Night. I eat my Breakfast before the Sun was up; and heaving Anchor, the Wind being favourable, I steered the same Course that I had done the Day before, wherein I was directed by my Pocket-Compass. My Intention was to reach, if possible, one of those Islands, which I had reason to believe lay to the North-East of *Van Diemen's* Land. I discovered nothing all that Day; but upon the next, about three in the Afternoon, when I had by my Computation made twenty-four Leagues from *Blefuscu*, I descried a Sail steering to the South-East; my Course was due East. I hailed her, but could get no Answer; yet I found I gained upon her, for the Wind slackened. I made all the sail I could, and in half an hour she spied me, then hung out her Ancient,[96] and discharged a Gun. It is not easy to express the Joy I was in upon the unexpected hope of once more seeing my beloved Country, and the dear Pledges I had left in it. The Ship slackened her Sails, and I came up with her between five and six in the Evening, *September* 26; but my Heart leapt within me to see her *English* Colours. I put my Cows and Sheep into my Coat-Pockets, and got on board with all my little Cargo of Provisions. The Vessel was an *English* Merchant-Man, returning from *Japan* by the *North* and *South-Seas*;[97] the Captain, Mr. *John Biddel* of *Deptford*, a very civil Man, and an excellent Sailor. We were now in the Latitude of 30 Degrees South; there were about fifty Men in the Ship; and here I met an old Comrade of mine, one *Peter Williams*, who gave me a good Character to the Captain. This Gentleman treated me with Kindness, and desired I would let him know what place I came from last, and whither I was bound; which I did in a few Words, but he thought I was raving, and that the Dangers I underwent

had disturbed my Head; whereupon I took my black Cattle and Sheep
out of my Pocket, which, after great Astonishment, clearly convinced
him of my Veracity. I then showed him the Gold given me by the Emperor
of *Blefuscu*, together with his Majesty's Picture at full length, and some
other Rarities of that Country. I gave him two Purses of two hundred
Sprugs each, and promised, when we arrived in *England*, to make him a
Present of a Cow and a Sheep big with Young.

I shall not trouble the Reader with a particular Account of this
Voyage, which was very prosperous for the most part. We arrived in the
*Downs*⁹⁸ on the 13th of *April* 1702. I had only one Misfortune, that the
Rats on board carried away one of my Sheep; I found her Bones in a Hole,
picked clean from the Flesh. The rest of my Cattle I got safe on shore,
and set them a grazing in a Bowling-Green at *Greenwich*, where the
Fineness of the Grass made them feed very heartily, although I had
always feared the contrary: neither could I possibly have preserved them
in so long a Voyage, if the Captain had not allowed me some of his best
Biscuit, which rubbed to Powder, and mingled with Water, was their
constant Food. The short time I continued in *England*, I made a considerable Profit by showing my Cattle to many Persons of Quality, and others:
and before I began my second Voyage, I sold them for six hundred Pounds.
Since my last return, I find the Breed is considerably increased, especially
the Sheep; which I hope will prove much to the Advantage of the Woollen
Manufacture,⁹⁹ by the Fineness of the Fleeces.

I stayed but two Months with my Wife and Family; for my insatiable
Desire of seeing foreign Countries would suffer me to continue no longer.
I left fifteen hundred Pounds with my Wife, and fixed her in a good House
at *Redriff*. My remaining Stock I carried with me, part in Money, and
part in Goods, in hopes to improve my Fortunes. My eldest Uncle *John*
had left me an Estate in Land, near *Epping*,¹⁰⁰ of about Thirty Pounds a
Year; and I had a long Lease of the *Black-Bull* in *Fetter-Lane*,¹⁰¹ which
yielded me as much more: so that I was not in any danger of leaving my
Family upon the Parish. My Son *Johnny*, named so after his Uncle, was
at the Grammar School,¹⁰² and a towardly¹⁰³ Child. My Daughter *Betty*
(who is now well married, and has Children) was then at her Needle-
Work. I took leave of my Wife, and Boy and Girl, with Tears on both
sides, and went on board the *Adventure*, a Merchant-Ship of three hundred

Tons, bound for *Surat*,[104] Captain *John Nicholas* of *Liverpool* Commander. But my Account of this Voyage must be referred to the Second Part of my Travels.

The End of the First Part

TRAVELS

PART II
A VOYAGE TO BROBDINGNAG

Plate, II Part, II *Page.* 1.

BROBDINGNAG

Flanflasnic

Lorbrulgrud

Difcovered, A D 1703

NORTH AMERICA

Streights of Annan

C Blanco

St Sebaftian

C Mendocino

NEW ALBION

Mount St Martin

Pto Sr Francis Drake

P Monterey

PLATE 4[1]

CHAP. I

A great Storm described, the long-boat sent to fetch Water,
the Author goes with it to discover the Country. He is left on Shore,
is seized by one of the Natives, and carried to a Farmer's House.
His Reception there, with several Accidents that happened there.
A Description of the Inhabitants.

Having been condemned by Nature and Fortune to an active and
restless Life, in ten Months after my Return, I again left my native
Country, and took Shipping in the *Downs* on the 20*th* Day of *June* 1702
in the *Adventure*, Capt. *John Nicholas* a *Cornish* Man Commander, bound
for *Surat*. We had a very prosperous Gale[2] till we arrived at the *Cape of
Good Hope*, where we landed for fresh Water, but discovering a Leak we
unshipped our Goods, and wintered there; for the Captain falling sick of
an Ague, we could not leave the *Cape* till the end of *March*. We then set
sail, and had a good Voyage till we passed the *Straits* of *Madagascar*; but
having got Northward of that Island, and to about five Degrees South
Latitude, the Winds, which in those Seas are observed to blow a constant
equal Gale between the North and West from the beginning of *December*
to the beginning of *May*, on the 19th of *April* began to blow with much
greater Violence, and more Westerly than usual, continuing so for twenty
Days together, during which time we were driven a little to the East of
the *Molucca* Islands,[3] and about three Degrees Northward of the Line,[4]
as our Captain found by an Observation he took the 2*d* of *May*, at which
time the Wind ceased, and it was a perfect Calm, whereat I was not a

little rejoiced. But he being a Man well experienced in the Navigation of those Seas bid us all prepare against a Storm, which accordingly happened the Day following: For a Southern Wind, called the Southern *Monsoon*, began to set in.

Finding it was like to overblow,⁵ we took in our Sprit-sail, and stood by to hand the Fore-sail; but making foul Weather, we looked the Guns were all fast, and handed the Missen. The Ship lay very broad off, so we thought it better spooning before the Sea, than trying or hulling. We reefed the Foresail and set him, we hauled aft the Foresheet; the Helm was hard a Weather. The Ship wore bravely. We belayed the Fore-down-hall; but the Sail was split, and we hauled down the Yard, and got the Sail into the Ship, and unbound all the things clear of it. It was a very fierce Storm; the Sea broke strange and dangerous. We hauled off upon the Lanyard of the Whipstaff, and helped the Man at Helm. We would not get down our Top-Mast, but let all stand, because she scudded before the Sea very well, and we knew that the Top-Mast being aloft, the Ship was the wholesomer, and made better way through the Sea, seeing we had Searoom. When the Storm was over, we set Foresail and Mainsail, and brought the Ship to. Then we set the Missen, Maintop-Sail and the Foretop-Sail. Our Course was East North-east, the Wind was at South-west. We got the Starboard Tacks aboard, we cast off our Weather-braces and Lifts; we set in the Lee-braces, and hauled forward by the Weather-bowlings, and hauled them tight, and belayed them, and hauled over the Missen Tack to Windward, and kept her full and by as near as she would lie.

During this Storm, which was followed by a strong Wind West South-west, we were carried by my Computation about five hundred Leagues to the East, so that the oldest Sailor on Board could not tell in what part of the World we were. Our Provisions held out well, our Ship was staunch, and our Crew all in good Health; but we lay in the utmost Distress for Water. We thought it best to hold on the same Course rather than turn more Northerly, which might have brought us to the North-west parts of great *Tartary*,⁶ and into the frozen Sea.

On the 16*th* Day of *June* 1703 a Boy on the Top-mast discovered Land. On the 17*th* we came in full View of a great Island or Continent (for we knew not whether), on the South side whereof was a small Neck of Land jutting out into the Sea, and a Creek too shallow to hold a Ship of above one hundred Tuns. We cast Anchor within a League of this Creek, and our Captain sent a dozen of his Men well armed in the Long-boat, with Vessels for Water if any could be found. I desired his leave to go with them, that I might see the Country, and make what Discoveries I could. When we came to Land we saw no River or Spring, nor any sign of Inhabitants. Our Men therefore wandered on the Shore to find out some fresh Water near the Sea, and I walked alone about a Mile on the other Side, where I observed the Country all barren and rocky. I now began to be weary, and seeing nothing to entertain my Curiosity, I returned gently down towards the Creek; and the Sea being full in my View, I saw our Men already got into the Boat, and rowing for Life to the Ship. I was going to hollow[7] after them, although it had been to little purpose, when I observed a huge Creature walking after them in the Sea, as fast as he could: He waded not much deeper than his Knees, and took prodigious strides: But our Men had the start of him half a League, and the Sea thereabouts being full of sharp pointed Rocks, the Monster was not able to overtake the Boat. This I was afterwards told, for I durst not stay to see the Issue of that Adventure; but ran as fast as I could the way I first went; and then climbed up a steep Hill which gave me some Prospect of the Country. I found it fully cultivated; but that which first surprised me was the Length of the Grass, which in those Grounds that seemed to be kept for Hay, was above twenty foot high.

I fell into a high Road, for so I took it to be, though it served to the Inhabitants only as a foot Path through a Field of Barley. Here I walked on for some time, but could see little on either Side, it being now near Harvest, and the Corn rising at least forty Foot. I was an Hour walking to the end of this Field, which was fenced in with a Hedge of at least one hundred and twenty Foot high, and the Trees so lofty that I could make no Computation of their Altitude. There was a Stile to pass from this Field into the next. It had four Steps, and a Stone to cross over when you came to the uppermost. It was impossible for me to climb this Stile, because every Step was six Foot high, and the upper Stone above twenty. I was endeavouring to find some Gap in the Hedge, when I discovered one of the Inhabitants in the next Field advancing towards the Stile, of the same size with him whom I saw in the Sea pursuing our Boat. He appeared as tall as an ordinary Spire-steeple, and took about ten Yards at every Stride, as near as I could guess. I was struck with the utmost Fear and Astonishment, and ran to hide myself in the Corn, from whence I saw him at the top of the Stile, looking back into the next Field on the right hand, and heard him call in a Voice many degrees louder than a speaking Trumpet; but the Noise was so high in the Air, that at first I certainly thought it was Thunder. Whereupon seven Monsters like himself came towards him with Reaping-Hooks in their Hands, each Hook about the largeness of six Scythes. These People were not so well clad as the first, whose Servants or Labourers they seemed to be. For, upon some Words he spoke, they went to reap the Corn in the Field where I lay. I kept from them at as great a distance as I could, but was forced to move with extreme Difficulty, for the Stalks of the Corn were sometimes not above a Foot distant, so that I could hardly squeeze my Body betwixt them. However, I made a shift to go forward till I came to a part of the Field where the Corn had been laid by the Rain and Wind. Here it was impossible for me to advance a step: for the Stalks were so interwoven that I could not creep through, and the Beards of the fallen Ears so strong and pointed that they pierced through my Clothes into my Flesh. At the same time I heard the Reapers not above an hundred Yards behind me. Being quite dispirited with Toil, and wholly overcome by Grief and Despair, I lay down between two Ridges, and heartily wished I might there end my Days. I bemoaned my desolate Widow, and Fatherless Children. I lamented my own Folly and Wilfulness in attempting a second Voyage against the Advice of all my Friends and Relations. In this terrible Agitation of Mind I could not forbear thinking of *Lilliput*, whose Inhabitants looked upon me as the greatest Prodigy that ever appeared in the World: where I was able to draw an Imperial Fleet in my Hand, and perform those other Actions which will be recorded for ever in the Chronicles of that Empire, while Posterity shall hardly believe them, although attested by Millions. I reflected what a Mortification it must prove to me to appear as inconsiderable in this Nation as one single *Lilliputian* would be among us. But, this I conceived was to be the least of my Misfortunes: For, as human Creatures are observed to be more savage and cruel in Proportion to their Bulk,[8] what could I expect but to be a Morsel in the Mouth of the first among these enormous Barbarians that should happen to seize me? Undoubtedly Philosophers are in the right when they tell us, that nothing is great or little otherwise than by Comparison. It might have pleased Fortune to let the *Lilliputians* find some Nation, where the People were as diminutive with respect to them, as they were to me. And who knows but that even this prodigious Race of Mortals might be equally over-matched in some distant part of the World, whereof we have yet no Discovery?

Scared and confounded as I was, I could not forbear going on with these Reflections, when one of the Reapers approaching within ten Yards of the Ridge where I lay, made me apprehend that with the next Step I should be squashed to Death under his Foot, or cut in two with his Reaping Hook. And therefore when he was again about to move, I screamed as loud as Fear could make me. Whereupon the huge Creature trod short, and looking round about under him for some time, at last espied me as I lay on the Ground. He considered a while with the Caution of one who endeavours to lay hold on a small dangerous Animal in such a manner that it shall not be able either to scratch or to bite him, as I myself have sometimes done with a *Weasel* in *England*. At length he ventured to take me up behind by the middle between his Forefinger and Thumb, and brought me within three Yards of his Eyes, that he might behold my Shape more perfectly. I guessed his Meaning, and my good Fortune gave me so much Presence of Mind, that I resolved not to struggle in the least as he held me in the Air above sixty Foot from the Ground, although he grievously pinched my Sides, for fear I should slip through his Fingers. All I ventured was to raise my Eyes towards the Sun, and place my Hands together in a supplicating Posture, and to speak some Words in an humble melancholy Tone, suitable to the Condition I then was in. For I apprehended every Moment that he would dash me against the Ground, as we usually do any little hateful Animal which we have a mind to destroy. But my good Star would have it, that he appeared pleased with my Voice and Gestures, and began to look upon me as a Curiosity, much wondering to hear me pronounce articulate Words, although he could not understand them. In the mean time I was not able to forbear groaning and shedding Tears, and turning my Head towards my Sides; letting him know, as well as I could, how cruelly I was hurt by the Pressure of his Thumb and Finger. He seemed to apprehend my Meaning; for, lifting up the Lappet[9] of his Coat, he put me gently into it, and immediately ran along with me to his Master, who was a substantial Farmer, and the same Person I had first seen in the Field.

The Farmer having (as I supposed by their Talk) received such an Account of me as his Servant could give him, took a piece of a small Straw, about the size of a walking Staff, and therewith lifted up the Lappets of my Coat; which it seems he thought to be some kind of Covering that Nature had given me. He blew my Hairs aside to take a better view of my Face. He called his Hinds[10] about him, and asked them (as I afterwards learned) whether they had ever seen in the Fields any little Creature that resembled me. He then placed me softly on the Ground upon all four, but I got immediately up, and walked slowly backwards and forwards, to let those People see I had no Intent to run away. They all sat down in a Circle about me, the better to observe my Motions. I pulled off my Hat, and made a low Bow towards the Farmer. I fell on my Knees, and lifted up my Hands and Eyes, and spoke several Words as loud as I could: I took a Purse of Gold out of my Pocket, and humbly presented it to him. He received it on the Palm of his Hand, then applied it close to his Eye, to see what it was, and afterwards turned it several times with the Point of a Pin (which he took out of his Sleeve), but could make nothing of it. Whereupon I made a Sign that he should place his Hand on the Ground. I took the Purse, and opening it, poured all the Gold into his Palm. There were six *Spanish*-Pieces of four Pistoles[11] each, besides twenty or thirty smaller Coins. I saw him wet the Tip of his little Finger upon his Tongue, and take up one of my largest Pieces, and then another, but he seemed to be wholly ignorant what they were. He made me a Sign to put them again into my Purse, and the Purse again into my Pocket, which after offering to him several times, I thought it best to do.

The Farmer by this time was convinced I must be a rational Creature. He spoke often to me, but the Sound of his Voice pierced my Ears like that of a Water-Mill,[12] yet his Words were articulate enough. I answered as loud as I could, in several Languages, and he often laid his Ear within two Yards of me, but all in vain, for we were wholly unintelligible to each other. He then sent his Servants to their Work, and taking his

Handkerchief out of his Pocket, he doubled and spread it on his left Hand, which he placed flat on the Ground with the Palm upwards, making me a Sign to step into it, as I could easily do, for it was not above a Foot in thickness. I thought it my part to obey, and for fear of falling, laid myself at Length upon the Handkerchief, with the Remainder of which he lapped me up to the Head for further Security, and in this manner carried me home to his House. There he called his Wife, and showed me to her; but she screamed and ran back as Women in *England* do at the Sight of a Toad or a Spider. However, when she had a while seen my Behaviour, and how well I observed the signs her Husband made, she was soon reconciled, and by degrees grew extremely tender of me.

It was about twelve at Noon, and a Servant brought in Dinner. It was only one substantial Dish of Meat (fit for the plain Condition of an Husband-Man) in a Dish of about four and twenty Foot Diameter. The Company were the Farmer and his Wife, three Children, and an old Grandmother: When they were sat down, the Farmer placed me at some distance from him on the Table, which was thirty Foot high from the Floor. I was in a terrible Fright, and kept as far as I could from the Edge for fear of falling. The Wife minced a bit of Meat, then crumbled some Bread on a Trencher, and placed it before me. I made her a low Bow, took out my Knife and Fork, and fell to eat, which gave them exceeding Delight. The Mistress sent her Maid for a small Dram-cup, which held about three Gallons, and filled it with Drink: I took up the Vessel with much difficulty in both Hands, and in a most respectful manner drank to her Ladyship's Health, expressing the Words as loud as I could in *English*, which made the Company laugh so heartily, that I was almost deafened with the Noise. This Liquor tasted like a small Cider, and was not unpleasant. Then the Master made me a sign to come to his Trencher side; but as I walked on the Table, being in great surprise all the time, as the indulgent Reader will easily conceive and excuse, I happened to stumble against a Crust, and fell flat on my Face, but received no hurt. I got up immediately, and observing the good People to be in much concern, I took my Hat (which I held under my Arm out of good Manners) and waving it over my Head, made three Huzza's to show I had got no Mischief by my Fall. But advancing forwards toward my Master (as I

shall henceforth call him) his youngest Son who sat next him, an arch[13]
Boy of about ten Years old, took me up by the Legs, and held me so high
in the Air, that I trembled every Limb; but his Father snatched me from
him, and at the same time gave him such a Box on the left Ear, as would
have felled an *European* Troop of Horse to the Earth, ordering him to be
taken from the Table. But, being afraid the Boy might owe me a spite,
and well remembering how mischievous all Children among us naturally
are to Sparrows, Rabbits, young Kittens, and Puppy Dogs, I fell on my
Knees, and pointing to the Boy, made my Master to understand, as well
as I could, that I desired his Son might be pardoned. The Father complied,
and the Lad took his Seat again; whereupon I went to him and kissed his
Hand, which my Master took, and made him stroke me gently with it.

In the midst of Dinner my Mistress's favourite Cat leapt into her Lap.
I heard a noise behind me like that of a dozen Stocking-Weavers at work;
and turning my Head I found it proceeded from the purring of this
Animal, who seemed to be three times larger than an Ox, as I computed
by the View of her Head, and one of her Paws, while her Mistress was
feeding and stroking her. The Fierceness of this Creature's Countenance
altogether discomposed me; though I stood at the further End of the
Table, above fifty Foot off, and although my Mistress held her fast for
fear she might give a spring, and seize me in her Talons. But it happened
there was no Danger; for the Cat took not the least Notice of me when
my Master placed me within three Yards of her. And as I have been
always told, and found true by Experience in my Travels, that flying, or
discovering Fear before a fierce Animal, is a certain way to make it pursue
or attack you, so I resolved in this dangerous Juncture to show no manner
of Concern. I walked with Intrepidity five or six times before the very
Head of the Cat, and came within half a Yard of her; whereupon she drew
herself back, as if she were more afraid of me: I had less Apprehension
concerning the Dogs, whereof three or four came into the Room, as it is
usual in Farmers' Houses; one of which was a Mastiff equal in bulk to
four Elephants, and a Greyhound somewhat taller than the Mastiff, but
not so large.

When Dinner was almost done, the Nurse came in with a Child of a
Year old in her Arms, who immediately spied me, and began a Squall
that you might have heard from *London-Bridge* to *Chelsea*,[14] after the usual

Oratory of Infants, to get me for a Plaything. The Mother out of pure Indulgence took me up, and put me towards the Child, who presently seized me by the Middle, and got my Head in his Mouth, where I roared so loud that the Urchin was frighted, and let me drop, and I should infallibly have broke my Neck if the Mother had not held her Apron under me. The Nurse to quiet her Babe made use of a Rattle, which was a kind of hollow Vessel filled with great Stones, and fastened by a Cable to the Child's Waist: But all in vain, so that she was forced to apply the last Remedy by giving it suck. I must confess no Object ever disgusted me so much as the sight of her monstrous Breast, which I cannot tell what to compare with, so as to give the curious Reader an Idea of its Bulk, Shape and Colour. It stood prominent six Foot, and could not be less than sixteen in Circumference. The Nipple was about half the Bigness of my Head, and the Hue both of that and the Dug so varified with Spots, Pimples and Freckles, that nothing could appear more nauseous: For I had a near sight of her, she sitting down the more conveniently to give Suck, and I standing on the Table. This made me reflect upon the fair Skins of our *English* Ladies, who appear so beautiful to us, only because they are of our own size, and their Defects not to be seen but through a Magnifying Glass, where we find by Experiment that the smoothest and whitest Skins look rough and coarse, and ill coloured.

I remember when I was at *Lilliput*, the Complexions of those diminutive People appeared to me the fairest in the World, and talking upon this subject with a Person of Learning there, who was an intimate Friend of mine, he said that my Face appeared much fairer and smoother when he looked on me from the Ground, than it did upon a nearer View when I took him up in my Hand, and brought him close, which he confessed was at first a very shocking sight. He said he could discover great Holes in my Skin, that the Stumps of my Beard were ten times stronger than the Bristles of a Boar, and my Complexion made up of several Colours altogether disagreeable: Although I must beg leave to say for myself, that I am as fair as most of my Sex and Country, and very little Sunburnt by all my Travels. On the other side, discoursing of the Ladies in that Emperor's Court, he used to tell me, one had Freckles, another too wide a Mouth, a third too large a Nose, nothing of which I was able to distinguish. I confess this Reflection was obvious enough; which however

I could not forbear, lest the Reader might think those vast Creatures
were actually deformed: For I must do them Justice to say they are a
comely Race of People; and particularly the Features of my Master's
Countenance, although he were but a Farmer, when I beheld him from
the Height of sixty Foot, appeared very well proportioned.

When Dinner was done, my Master went out to his Labourers, and as
I could discover by his Voice and Gesture, gave his Wife a strict Charge
to take care of me. I was very much tired and disposed to sleep, which
my Mistress perceiving, she put me on her own Bed, and covered me
with a clean white Handkerchief, but larger and coarser than the Main
Sail of a Man of War.

I slept about two Hours, and dreamed I was at home with my Wife
and Children, which aggravated my Sorrows when I awaked and found
myself alone in a vast Room, between two and three hundred Foot wide,
and above two hundred high, lying in a Bed twenty Yards wide. My
Mistress was gone about her household Affairs, and had locked me in.
The Bed was eight Yards from the Floor. Some natural Necessities
required me to get down: I durst not presume to call, and if I had, it
would have been in vain with such a Voice as mine at so great a distance
from the Room where I lay to the Kitchen where the Family kept. While
I was under these Circumstances two Rats crept up the Curtains, and
ran smelling backwards and forwards on the Bed. One of them came up
almost to my Face, whereupon I rose in a Fright, and drew out my
Hanger[15] to defend myself. These horrible Animals had the Boldness to
attack me on both sides, and one of them held his Fore-feet at my Collar;
but I had the good Fortune to rip up his Belly before he could do me any
Mischief. He fell down at my Feet, and the other seeing the Fate of his
Comrade, made his Escape, but not without one good Wound on the
Back, which I gave him as he fled, and made the Blood run trickling from
him. After this Exploit I walked gently to and fro on the Bed, to recover
my Breath and Loss of Spirits. These Creatures were of the size of a large
Mastiff, but infinitely more nimble and fierce, so that if I had taken off
my Belt[16] before I went to sleep, I must have infallibly been torn to
pieces and devoured. I measured the Tail of the dead Rat, and found it
to be two Yards long wanting an Inch; but it went against my Stomach
to drag the Carcass off the Bed, where it lay still bleeding; I observed it

had yet some Life, but with a strong Slash cross the Neck I thoroughly dispatched it.

Soon after my Mistress came into the Room, who seeing me all bloody, ran and took me up in her Hand. I pointed to the dead *Rat*, smiling and making other Signs to show I was not hurt, whereat she was extremely rejoiced, calling the Maid to take up the dead *Rat* with a pair of Tongs, and throw it out of the Window. Then she set me on a Table where I showed her my Hanger all bloody, and wiping it on the Lappet of my Coat, returned it to the Scabbard. I was pressed to do more than one Thing, which another could not do for me, and therefore endeavoured to make my Mistress understand that I desired to be set down on the Floor; which after she had done, my Bashfulness would not suffer me to express myself further than by pointing to the Door, and bowing several times. The good Woman with much Difficulty at last perceived what I would be at, and taking me up again in her Hand, walked into the Garden where she set me down. I went on one side about two hundred Yards, and beckoning to her not to look or to follow me, I hid myself between two Leaves of Sorrel, and there discharged the Necessities of Nature.

I hope the gentle Reader will excuse me for dwelling on these and the like Particulars, which however insignificant they may appear to grovelling vulgar Minds, yet will certainly help a Philosopher to enlarge his Thoughts and Imagination, and apply them to the Benefit of public as well as private Life, which was my sole Design in presenting this and other Accounts of my Travels to the World; wherein I have been chiefly studious of Truth, without affecting any Ornaments of Learning or of Style. But the whole Scene of this Voyage made so strong an Impression on my Mind, and is so deeply fixed in my Memory, that in committing it to Paper I did not omit one material Circumstance: However, upon a strict Review, I blotted out several Passages of less Moment which were in my first Copy, for fear of being censured as tedious and trifling, whereof Travellers are often, perhaps not without Justice, accused.

CHAP. II

*A Description of the Farmer's Daughter. The Author carried
to a Market-Town, and then to the Metropolis. The Particulars
of his Journey.*

My Mistress had a Daughter of nine Years old, a Child of towardly
Parts for her Age, very dextrous at her Needle, and skilful in dressing
her Baby.[17] Her Mother and she contrived to fit up the Baby's Cradle
for me against Night: the Cradle was put into a small Drawer of a Cabinet,
and the Drawer placed upon a hanging Shelf for fear of the *Rats*. This was
my Bed all the time I stayed with those People, though made more
convenient by degrees, as I began to learn their Language, and make my
Wants known. This young Girl was so handy, that after I had once or
twice pulled off my Clothes before her, she was able to dress and undress
me, although I never gave her that Trouble when she would let me do
either myself. She made me seven Shirts, and some other Linen of as fine
Cloth as could be got, which indeed was coarser than Sackcloth; and
these she constantly washed for me with her own Hands. She was likewise
my School-Mistress to teach me the Language: When I pointed to
anything, she told me the name of it in her own Tongue, so that in a few
Days I was able to call for whatever I had a mind to. She was very good
natured, and not above forty Foot high, being little for her Age. She gave
me the Name of *Grildrig*,[18] which the Family took up, and afterwards the
whole Kingdom. The Word imports what the *Latins* call *Nanunculus*,[19]
the *Italians Homunceletino*, and the *English Mannikin*. To her I chiefly owe
my Preservation in that Country: We never parted while I was there; I
called her my *Glumdalclitch*,[20] or little Nurse: And I should be guilty of
great Ingratitude if I omitted this honourable Mention of her Care and
Affection towards me, which I heartily wish it lay in my Power to requite
as she deserves, instead of being the innocent but unhappy Instrument
of her Disgrace, as I have too much reason to fear.

It now began to be known and talked of in the Neighbourhood, that
my Master had found a strange Animal in the Field about the bigness of
a *Splacknuck*, but exactly shaped in every part like a human Creature;

which it likewise imitated in all its Actions; seemed to speak in a little Language[21] of its own, had already learned several Words of theirs, went erect upon two Legs, was tame and gentle, would come when it was called, do whatever it was bid, had the finest Limbs in the World, and a Complexion fairer than a Nobleman's Daughter of three Years old. Another Farmer who lived hard by, and was a particular Friend of my Master, came on a Visit on purpose to inquire into the Truth of this Story. I was immediately produced, and placed upon a Table, where I walked as I was commanded, drew my Hanger, put it up again, made my Reverence to my Master's Guest, asked him in his own Language how he did, and told him he was welcome, just as my little Nurse had instructed me. This Man, who was old and dim sighted, put on his Spectacles to behold me better, at which I could not forbear laughing very heartily, for his Eyes appeared like the Full Moon shining into a Chamber at two Windows. Our People, who discovered the cause of my Mirth, bore me company in Laughing, at which the old Fellow was Fool enough to be Angry and out of Countenance. He had the Character of a great Miser, and to my Misfortune he well deserved it by the cursed Advice he gave my Master to show me as a Sight upon a Market-Day in the next Town, which was half an hour's riding, about two and twenty Miles from our House. I guessed there was some Mischief contriving, when I observed my Master and his Friend whispering long together, sometimes pointing at me; and my Fears made me fancy that I overheard and understood some of their Words. But, the next Morning *Glumdalclitch* my little Nurse told me the whole Matter, which she had cunningly picked out from her Mother. The poor Girl laid me on her Bosom, and fell a weeping with Shame and Grief. She apprehended some Mischief would happen to me from rude vulgar Folks, who might squeeze me to Death or break one of my Limbs by taking me in their Hands. She had also observed how modest I was in my Nature, how nicely I regarded my Honour, and what an Indignity I should conceive it to be exposed for Money as a public Spectacle to the meanest of the People. She said, her *Papa* and *Mamma* had promised that *Grildrig* should be hers, but now she found they meant to serve her as they did last Year, when they pretended to give her a Lamb, and yet, as soon as it was fat, sold it to a Butcher. For my own part, I may truly affirm that I was less concerned than my

Nurse. I had a strong Hope which never left me, that I should one Day recover my Liberty; and as to the Ignominy of being carried about for a Monster, I considered myself to be a perfect Stranger in the Country, and that such a Misfortune could never be charged upon me as a Reproach if ever I should return to *England*; since the King of *Great Britain* himself, in my Condition, must have undergone the same Distress.

My Master, pursuant to the Advice of his Friend, carried me in a Box the next Market day to the neighbouring Town, and took along with him his little Daughter my Nurse upon a Pillion²² behind him. The Box was close on every side, with a little Door for me to go in and out, and a few Gimlet-holes²³ to let in Air. The Girl had been so careful to put the Quilt of her Baby's Bed into it, for me to lie down on. However, I was terribly shaken and discomposed in this Journey, though it were but of half an Hour. For the Horse went about forty Foot at every Step, and trotted so high, that the Agitation was equal to the rising and falling of a Ship in a great Storm, but much more frequent: Our Journey was somewhat further than from *London* to St. *Albans*. My Master alighted at an Inn which he used to frequent; and after consulting a while with the Inn-keeper, and making some necessary Preparations, he hired the *Grultrud*, or Cryer, to give notice through the Town of a strange Creature to be seen at the Sign of the Horn and Crown not so big as a *Splacnuck* (an Animal in that Country very finely shaped, about six Foot long) and in every part of the Body resembling an human Creature, could speak several Words, and perform an hundred diverting Tricks.

I was placed upon a Table in the largest Room of the Inn, which might be near three hundred Foot Square. My little Nurse stood on a low Stool close to the Table, to take care of me, and direct what I should do. My Master, to avoid a Crowd, would suffer only thirty People at a time to see me. I walked about on the Table as the Girl commanded; she asked me Questions as far as she knew my Understanding of the Language reached, and I answered them as loud as I could. I turned about several times to the Company, paid my humble Respects, said they were wel-come, and used some other Speeches I had been taught. I took up a Thimble filled with Liquor, which *Glumdalclitch* had given me for a Cup, and drank their Health. I drew out my Hanger, and flourished with it after the manner of Fencers in *England*. My Nurse gave me part of a

Straw, which I exercised as a Pike, having learned the Art in my Youth. I was that day shown to twelve Sets of Company, and as often forced to go over again with the same Fopperies, till I was half dead with Weariness and Vexation. For, those who had seen me made such wonderful Reports, that the People were ready to break down the Doors to come in. My Master for his own Interest would not suffer anyone to touch me except my Nurse; and, to prevent danger, Benches were set round the Table at such a distance as put me out of everybody's reach. However, an unlucky School-Boy aimed a hazel Nut directly at my Head, which very narrowly missed me; otherwise, it came with so much violence that it would have infallibly knocked out my Brains, for it was almost as large as a small Pumpion:24 But I had the Satisfaction to see the young Rogue well beaten, and turned out of the Room.

My Master gave public notice, that he would show me again the next Market-Day, and in the mean time he prepared a more convenient Vehicle for me, which he had reason enough to do; for I was so tired with my first Journey, and with entertaining Company for eight Hours together, that I could hardly stand upon my Legs, or speak a Word. It was at least three Days before I recovered my Strength; and that I might have no rest at home, all the neighbouring Gentlemen from an hundred Miles round, hearing of my Fame, came to see me at my Master's own House. There could not be fewer than thirty Persons with their Wives and Children (for the Country was very populous); and my Master demanded the rate of a full Room whenever he showed me at Home, although it were only to a single Family. So that for some time I had but little ease every Day of the Week (except *Wednesday*, which is their Sabbath) although I were not carried to the Town.

My Master finding how profitable I was like to be, resolved to carry me to the most considerable Cities of the Kingdom. Having therefore provided himself with all things necessary for a long Journey, and settled his affairs at Home, he took leave of his Wife, and upon the 17*th* of *August* 1703 about two Months after my Arrival, we set out for the Metropolis, situated near the middle of that Empire, and about three thousand Miles distance from our House: My Master made his Daughter *Glumdalclitch* ride behind him. She carried me on her Lap in a Box tied about her waist. The Girl had lined it on all sides with the softest Cloth she could get, well quilted underneath, furnished it with her Baby's Bed, provided me with Linen and other Necessaries, and made everything as convenient as she could. We had no other Company but a Boy of the House, who rode after us with the Luggage.

My Master's Design was to show me in all the Towns by the way, and to step out of the Road for fifty or an hundred Miles, to any Village or Person of Quality's House where he might expect Custom. We made easy Journeys of not above seven or eightscore Miles a Day: For *Glumdal-clitch*, on purpose to spare me, complained she was tired with the trotting of the Horse. She often took me out of my Box at my own Desire, to give me Air, and show me the Country, but always held me fast by a Leading-string. We passed over five or six Rivers many degrees broader and deeper than the *Nile* or the *Ganges*; and there was hardly a Rivulet so small as the *Thames* at *London-Bridge*. We were ten Weeks in our Journey, and I was shown in eighteen large Towns besides many Villages and private Families.

On the 26*th* Day of *October*, we arrived at the Metropolis, called in their Language *Lorbrulgrud*,[25] or *Pride of the Universe*. My Master took a Lodging in the principal Street of the City, not far from the Royal Palace, and put out Bills[26] in the usual Form, containing an exact Description of my Person and Parts. He hired a large Room between three and four hundred Foot wide. He provided a Table sixty Foot in diameter, upon which I was to act my Part, and palisadoed it round three Foot from the edge, and as many high, to prevent my falling over. I was shown ten times a Day to the Wonder and Satisfaction of all People. I could now speak the Language tolerably well, and perfectly understood every Word that was spoken to me. Besides, I had learned their Alphabet, and could make a shift to explain a Sentence here and there; for *Glumdalclitch* had been my Instructor while we were at home, and at leisure Hours during our Journey. She carried a little Book in her Pocket, not much larger than a *Sanson's Atlas*;[27] it was a common Treatise for the use of young Girls, giving a short Account of their Religion; out of this she taught me my Letters, and interpreted the Words.

CHAP. III

*The Author sent for to Court. The Queen buys him of his Master
the Farmer, and presents him to the King. He disputes with his
Majesty's great Scholars. An Apartment at Court provided for the
Author. He is in high Favour with the Queen. He stands up for the
Honour of his own Country. His Quarrels with the Queen's Dwarf.*

The frequent Labours I underwent every Day made in a few Weeks a
very considerable change in my Health: The more my Master got by me,
the more unsatiable he grew. I had quite lost my Stomach, and was
almost reduced to a Skeleton. The Farmer observed it, and concluding I
soon must die, resolved to make as good a Hand of me as he could. While
he was thus reasoning and resolving with himself, a *Slardral*, or Gentleman
Usher, came from Court, commanding my Master to carry me immediately thither for the Diversion of the Queen and her Ladies. Some of the
latter had already been to see me, and reported strange Things of my
Beauty, Behaviour, and good Sense. Her Majesty and those who attended
her were beyond Measure delighted with my Demeanour. I fell on my
Knees, and begged the Honour of kissing her Imperial Foot; but this
Gracious Princess held out her little Finger towards me (after I was set
on a Table) which I embraced in both my Arms, and put the tip of it,
with the utmost respect, to my Lip. She made me some general Questions
about my Country and my Travels, which I answered as distinctly and
in as few Words as I could. She asked whether I would be content to live
at Court. I bowed down to the board of the Table, and humbly answered
that I was my Master's Slave, but if I were at my own Disposal, I should
be proud to devote my Life to her Majesty's Service. She then asked my
Master whether he were willing to sell me at a good Price. He, who
apprehended I could not live a Month, was ready enough to part with
me, and demanded a thousand pieces of Gold, which were ordered
him on the spot, each piece being about the bigness of eight hundred
Moydores;[28] but, allowing for the proportion of all Things between that
Country and *Europe*, and the high price of Gold among them, was hardly
so great a sum as a thousand Guineas would be in *England*. I then said to

the Queen, since I was now her Majesty's most humble Creature and Vassal, I must beg the favour, that *Glumdalclitch*, who had always tended me with so much care and kindness, and understood to do it so well, might be admitted into her Service, and continue to be my Nurse and Instructor. Her Majesty agreed to my Petition, and easily got the Farmer's consent, who was glad enough to have his Daughter preferred at Court: and the poor Girl herself was not able to hide her Joy: My late Master withdrew, bidding me farewell, and saying he had left me in a good Service; to which I replied not a Word, only making him a slight bow.

The Queen observed my coldness, and when the Farmer was gone out of the Apartment, asked me the reason. I made bold to tell her Majesty that I owed no other Obligation to my late Master, than his not dashing out the Brains of a poor harmless Creature found by chance in his Field; which Obligation was amply recompensed by the gain he had made in showing me through half the Kingdom, and the price he had now sold me for. That the Life I had since led, was laborious enough to kill an Animal of ten times my Strength. That my Health was much impaired by the continual drudgery of entertaining the Rabble every hour of the Day, and that if my Master had not thought my Life in danger, her Majesty perhaps would not have got so cheap a bargain. But as I was out of all fear of being ill treated under the protection of so great and good an Empress, the Ornament of Nature, the Darling of the World, the Delight of her Subjects, the Phoenix of the Creation; so, I hoped my late Master's apprehensions would appear to be groundless, for I already found my Spirits to revive by the Influence of her most August Presence.

This was the sum of my Speech, delivered with great Improprieties and Hesitation; the latter part was altogether framed in the Style peculiar to that People, whereof I learned some Phrases from *Glumdalclitch*, while she was carrying me to Court.

The Queen giving great Allowance for my Defectiveness in speaking, was however surprised at so much Wit and good Sense in so diminutive an Animal. She took me in her own Hands, and carried me to the King, who was then retired to his Cabinet. His Majesty, a Prince of much Gravity, and austere Countenance, not well observing my Shape at first View, asked the Queen after a cold Manner, how long it was since she grew fond of a *Splacnuck*; for such it seems he took me to be, as I lay upon my Breast in her Majesty's right Hand. But this Princess, who hath an infinite deal of Wit and Humour, set me gently on my Feet upon the Scrutore,[29] and commanded me to give His Majesty an Account of myself, which I did in a very few Words; and *Glumdalclitch*, who attended at the Cabinet door, and could not endure I should be out of her sight, being admitted, confirmed all that had passed from my Arrival at her Father's House.

The King, although he be as learned a Person as any in his Dominions, and had been educated in the Study of Philosophy,[30] and particularly Mathematics; yet when he observed my Shape exactly, and saw me walk erect, before I began to speak, conceived I might be a piece of Clockwork (which is in that Country arrived to a very great Perfection), contrived by some ingenious Artist.[31] But, when he heard my Voice, and found what I delivered to be regular and rational, he could not conceal his Astonishment. He was by no means satisfied with the Relation I gave him of the Manner I came into his Kingdom, but thought it a Story concerted between *Glumdalclitch* and her Father, who had taught me a Set of Words to make me sell at a higher Price. Upon this Imagination he put several other Questions to me, and still received rational Answers, no otherwise defective than by a Foreign Accent, and an imperfect Knowledge in the Language, with some rustic Phrases which I had learned at the Farmer's House, and did not suit the polite Style of a Court.

His Majesty sent for three great Scholars who were then in their weekly waiting (according to the Custom in that Country). These Gentlemen, after they had a while examined my Shape with much Nicety, were of different Opinions concerning me. They all agreed that I could not be produced according to the regular Laws of Nature,[32] because I was not framed with a Capacity of preserving my Life, either by Swiftness, or climbing of Trees, or digging Holes in the Earth. They observed by my Teeth, which they viewed with great Exactness, that I was a carnivorous Animal; yet most Quadrupeds being an Overmatch for me, and Field-Mice, with some others, too nimble, they could not imagine how I should be able to support myself, unless I fed upon Snails and other Insects, which they offered by many learned Arguments to evince that I could not possibly do. One of these Virtuosi[33] seemed to think that I might be an Embryo, or abortive Birth. But this Opinion was rejected by the other two, who observed my Limbs to be perfect and finished, and that I had lived several Years, as it was manifested from my Beard, the Stumps whereof they plainly discovered through a Magnifying Glass. They would not allow me to be a Dwarf, because my Littleness was beyond all degrees of Comparison; for, the Queen's favourite Dwarf, the smallest ever known in that Kingdom, was near thirty Foot high. After much Debate, they concluded unanimously that I was only *Relplum Scalcath*, which is interpreted literally, *Lusus Naturae*;[34] a Determination exactly agreeable to the Modern Philosophy of *Europe*, whose Professors, disdaining the old Evasion of *occult Causes*,[35] whereby the Followers of *Aristotle* endeavour in vain to disguise their Ignorance, have invented this wonderful Solution of all Difficulties to the unspeakable Advancement of human Knowledge.

After this decisive Conclusion, I entreated to be heard a Word or two. I applied myself to the King, and assured His Majesty that I came from a Country which abounded with several Millions of both Sexes, and of my own Stature; where the Animals, Trees, and Houses were all in Proportion, and where by consequence I might be as able to defend myself, and to find Sustenance, as any of his Majesty's Subjects could do here; which I took for a full Answer to those Gentlemen's Arguments. To this they only replied with a Smile of Contempt, saying, That the Farmer had instructed me very well in my Lesson. The King, who had a much better Understanding, dismissing his learned Men, sent for the Farmer, who by good Fortune was not yet gone out of Town: Having therefore first examined him privately, and then confronted him with me and the young Girl, his Majesty began to think that what we told him might possibly be true. He desired the Queen to order that a particular Care should be taken of me, and was of opinion, that *Glumdalclitch* should still continue in her Office of tending me, because he observed we had a great Affection for each other. A convenient Apartment was provided for her at Court; she had a sort of Governess appointed to take care of her Education, a Maid to dress her, and two other Servants for menial Offices; but, the Care of me was wholly appropriated to herself. The Queen commanded her own Cabinet-maker to contrive a Box that might serve me for a Bed-chamber, after the Model that *Glumdalclitch* and I should agree upon. This Man was a most ingenious Artist, and according to my Directions, in three Weeks finished for me a wooden Chamber of sixteen Foot square, and twelve high, with Sash Windows, a Door, and two

Closets, like a *London* Bed-chamber. The Board that made the Ceiling was to be lifted up and down by two Hinges, to put in a Bed ready furnished by her Majesty's Upholsterer, which *Glumdalclitch* took out every Day to air, made it with her own Hands, and letting it down at Night, locked up the Roof over me. A Nice Workman, who was famous for little Curiosities, undertook to make me two Chairs, with Backs and Frames, of a Substance not unlike Ivory, and two Tables, with a Cabinet to put my Things in. The Room was quilted on all sides, as well as the Floor and the Ceiling, to prevent any Accident from the Carelessness of those who carried me, and to break the Force of a Jolt when I went in a Coach. I desired a Lock for my Door to prevent Rats and Mice from coming in: The Smith after several Attempts made the smallest that was ever seen among them, for I have known a larger at the Gate of a Gentleman's House in *England.* I made a shift to keep the Key in a Pocket of my own, fearing *Glumdalclitch* might lose it. The Queen likewise ordered the thinnest Silks that could be gotten, to make me clothes, not much thicker than an *English* Blanket, very cumbersome till I was accustomed to them. They were after the Fashion of the Kingdom, partly resembling the *Persian*, and partly the *Chinese*, and are a very grave decent Habit.

The Queen became so fond of my Company, that she could not dine without me. I had a Table placed upon the same at which her Majesty eat, just at her left Elbow, and a Chair to sit on. *Glumdalclitch* stood upon a Stool on the Floor, near my Table, to assist and take care of me. I had an entire Set of Silver Dishes and Plates, and other Necessaries, which in Proportion to those of the Queen, were not much bigger than what I have seen of the same kind in a *London* Toy-shop, for the Furniture of a Baby-house: These my little Nurse kept in her Pocket, in a Silver Box, and gave me at Meals as I wanted them, always cleaning them herself. No Person dined with the Queen but the two Princesses Royal, the elder sixteen Years old, and the younger at that time thirteen and a Month. Her Majesty used to put a Bit of Meat upon one of my Dishes, out of which I carved for myself; and her Diversion was to see me eat in Miniature. For the Queen (who had indeed but a weak Stomach) took up at one Mouthful, as much as a dozen *English* Farmers could eat at a Meal, which to me was for some time a very nauseous sight. She would craunch[36] the Wing of a Lark, Bones and all, between her Teeth, although it were nine times as large as that of a full-grown Turkey; and put a Bit of Bread in her Mouth, as big as two twelvepenny Loaves. She drank out of a golden Cup, above a Hogshead at a Draught. Her Knives were twice as long as a Scythe set straight upon the Handle. The Spoons, Forks, and other Instruments were all in the same Proportion. I remember when *Glumdalclitch* carried me out of Curiosity to see some of the Tables at Court, where ten or a dozen of these enormous Knives and Forks were lifted up together, I thought I had never till then beheld so terrible a Sight.

It is the Custom that every *Wednesday* (which as I have before observed, was their Sabbath) the King and Queen, with the Royal Issue of both Sexes, dine together in the Apartment of his Majesty, to whom I was now become a great Favourite; and at these Times my little Chair and Table were placed at his left Hand before one of the Salt-cellars. This Prince took a Pleasure in conversing with me, inquiring into the Manners, Religion, Laws, Government, and Learning of *Europe*, wherein I gave him the best Account I was able. His Apprehension[37] was so clear, and his Judgment so exact, that he made very wise Reflections and Observations upon all I said. But, I confess, that after I had been a little too copious in talking of my own beloved Country, of our Trade, and Wars by Sea and Land, of our Schisms in Religion, and Parties in the State; the Prejudices of his Education prevailed so far, that he could not forbear taking me up in his right Hand, and stroking me gently with the other, after an hearty Fit of laughing, asked me whether I were a *Whig* or a *Tory*. Then turning to his first Minister, who waited behind him with a white Staff, near as tall as the Mainmast of the Royal *Sovereign*; he observed how contemptible a Thing was human Grandeur, which could be mimicked by such diminutive Insects as I: And yet, said he, I dare engage, these Creatures have their Titles and Distinctions of Honour; they contrive little Nests and Burrows, that they call Houses and Cities; they make a Figure in Dress and Equipage; they love, they fight, they dispute, they cheat, they betray. And thus he continued on, while my Colour came and went several times, with Indignation to hear our noble Country, the Mistress of Arts and Arms, the Scourge of *France*, the Arbitress of *Europe*, the Seat of Virtue, Piety, Honour and Truth, the Pride and Envy of the World, so contemptuously treated.

But, as I was not in a condition to resent Injuries, so, upon mature Thoughts, I began to doubt whether I were injured or no. For, after having been accustomed several Months to the Sight and Converse of this People, and observed every Object upon which I cast my Eyes to be of proportionable Magnitude, the Horror I had first conceived from their Bulk and Aspect was so far worn off, that if I had then beheld a Company of *English* Lords and Ladies in their Finery and Birthday Clothes,[38] acting their several Parts in the most courtly manner of Strutting, and Bowing and Prating; to say the Truth, I should have been strongly tempted to laugh as much at them as this King and his Grandees did at me. Neither indeed could I forbear smiling at myself, when the Queen used to place me upon her Hand towards a Looking-Glass, by which both our Persons appeared before me in full View together; and there could nothing be more ridiculous than the Comparison: So that I really began to imagine myself dwindled many Degrees below my usual Size.

Nothing angered and mortified me so much as the Queen's Dwarf, who being of the lowest Stature that was ever in that Country (for I verily think he was not full thirty Foot high) became insolent at seeing a Creature so much beneath him, that he would always affect to swagger and look big as he passed by me in the Queen's Antechamber, while I was standing on some Table talking with the Lords or Ladies of the Court, and he seldom failed of a small Word or two upon my Littleness; against which I could only revenge myself by calling him *Brother*, challenging him to wrestle, and such Repartees as are usual in the Mouths of *Court Pages*. One Day at Dinner this malicious little Cub was so nettled with something I had said to him, that raising himself upon the Frame of her Majesty's Chair, he took me up by the middle, as I was sitting down, not thinking any harm, and let me drop into a large Silver Bowl of Cream, and then ran away as fast as he could. I fell over Head and Ears, and if I had not been a good Swimmer, it might have gone very hard with me; for *Glumdalclitch* in that instant happened to be at the other End of the Room, and the Queen was in such a Fright that she wanted Presence of Mind to assist me. But my little Nurse ran to my Relief, and took me out, after I had swallowed above a Quart of Cream. I was put to bed; however I received no other Damage than the Loss of a suit of Clothes, which was utterly spoiled. The Dwarf was soundly whipped, and as a further Punishment, forced to drink up the Bowl of Cream, into which he had thrown me; neither was he ever restored to Favour: For, soon after the Queen bestowed him on a Lady of high Quality, so that I saw him no more, to my very great Satisfaction; for I could not tell to what Extremity such a malicious Urchin might have carried his Resentment.

He had before served me a scurvy Trick, which set the Queen a Laughing, although at the same time she were heartily vexed, and would have immediately cashiered him, if I had not been so generous as to intercede. Her Majesty had taken a Marrow-bone upon her Plate, and after knocking out the Marrow, placed the Bone again in the Dish erect as it stood before; the Dwarf watching his Opportunity, while *Glumdalclitch* was gone to the Sideboard, mounted upon the Stool she stood on to take care of me at Meals, took me up in both Hands, and squeezing my Legs together, wedged them into the Marrow-bone above my Waist, where I stuck for some time, and made a very ridiculous Figure. I believe it was near a Minute before anyone knew what was become of me, for I thought it below me to cry out. But, as Princes seldom get their Meat hot, my Legs were not scalded, only my Stockings and Breeches in a sad condition. The Dwarf at my Entreaty had no other Punishment than a sound whipping.

I was frequently rallied[39] by the Queen upon Account of my Fearfulness, and she used to ask me whether the People of my Country were as great Cowards as myself. The Occasion was this. The Kingdom is much pestered with Flies in Summer, and these odious Insects, each of them as big as a *Dunstable* Lark,[40] hardly gave me any rest while I sat at Dinner, with their continual humming and buzzing about my Ears. They would sometimes alight upon my Victuals, and leave their loathsome Excrement or Spawn behind, which to me was very visible, though not to the Natives of that Country, whose large Optics were not so acute as mine in viewing smaller Objects. Sometimes they would fix upon my Nose or Forehead, where they stung me to the quick, smelling very offensively, and I could easily trace that viscous Matter, which our Naturalists tell us enables those Creatures to walk with their Feet upwards upon a Ceiling. I had much ado to defend myself against these detestable Animals, and could not forbear starting when they came on my Face. It was the common Practice of the Dwarf to catch a number of these Insects in his Hand as Schoolboys do among us, and let them out suddenly under my Nose on purpose to frighten me, and divert the Queen. My Remedy was to cut them in Pieces with my Knife as they flew in the Air, wherein my Dexterity was much admired.

I remember one Morning when *Glumdalclitch* had set me in my Box upon a Window, as she usually did in fair Days to give me Air (for I durst not venture to let the Box be hung on a Nail out of the Window, as we do with Cages in *England*) after I had lifted up one of my Sashes, and sat down at my Table to eat a piece of Sweet Cake for my Breakfast, above twenty Wasps, allured by the smell, came flying into the Room, humming louder than the Drones of as many Bagpipes. Some of them seized my Cake, and carried it piecemeal away, others flew about my Head and Face, confounding me with the Noise, and putting me in the utmost terror of their Stings. However I had the Courage to rise and draw my Hanger, and attack them in the Air. I dispatched four of them, but the rest got away, and I presently shut my Window. These Insects were as large as Partridges, I took out their Stings, found them an Inch and a half long, and as sharp as Needles. I carefully preserved them all, and having since shown them with some other Curiosities in several parts of *Europe*; upon my Return to *England* I gave three of them to *Gresham College*,[41] and kept the fourth for myself.

CHAP. IV

The Country described. A Proposal for correcting modern Maps. The King's Palace, and some Account of the Metropolis. The Author's way of travelling. The chief Temple described.

I now intend to give the Reader a short Description of this Country, as far as I travelled in it, which was not above two thousand Miles round *Lorbrulgrud* the Metropolis. For, the Queen, whom I always attended, never went further when she accompanied the King in his Progresses,[42] and there stayed till his Majesty returned from viewing his Frontiers. The whole Extent of this Prince's Dominions reacheth about six thousand Miles in Length, and from three to five in Breadth. From whence I cannot but conclude that our Geographers of *Europe* are in a great Error, by supposing nothing but Sea between *Japan* and *California*; for it was ever my Opinion, that there must be a Balance of Earth to counterpoise the great Continent of *Tartary*; and therefore they ought to correct their Maps and Charts, by joining this vast Tract of Land to the Northwest Parts of *America*, wherein I shall be ready to lend them my Assistance.

The Kingdom is a Peninsula, terminated to the Northeast by a Ridge of Mountains thirty Miles high, which are altogether impassable by reason of the Volcanoes upon the Tops. Neither do the most Learned know what sort of Mortals inhabit beyond those Mountains, or whether they be inhabited at all. On the three other Sides it is bounded by the Ocean. There is not one Seaport in the whole Kingdom, and those Parts of the Coasts into which the Rivers issue are so full of pointed Rocks, and the Sea generally so rough, that there is no venturing with the smallest of their Boats, so that these People are wholly excluded from any Commerce with the rest of the World. But the large Rivers are full of Vessels, and abound with excellent Fish, for they seldom get any from the Sea, because the Sea-fish are of the same Size with those in *Europe*, and consequently not worth catching; whereby it is manifest, that Nature, in the Production of Plants and Animals of so extraordinary a Bulk, is wholly confined to this Continent, of which I leave the Reasons to be determined by Philosophers.[43] However, now and then they take a Whale that happens to be dashed against the Rocks, which the common People feed on heartily. These Whales I have known so large that a Man could hardly carry one upon his Shoulders; and sometimes for Curiosity they are brought in Hampers to *Lorbrulgrud*: I saw one of them in a Dish at the King's Table, which passed for a Rarity, but I did not observe he was fond of it; for I think indeed the Bigness disgusted him, although I have seen one somewhat larger in *Greenland*.

The Country is well inhabited, for it contains fifty-one Cities, near an hundred walled Towns, and a great number of Villages. To satisfy my curious Reader, it may be sufficient to describe *Lorbrulgrud*. This City stands upon almost two equal Parts on each side the River that passes through. It contains above eighty thousand Houses, and about six hundred thousand Inhabitants. It is in Length three *Glonglungs*[44] (which make about fifty-four *English* Miles) and two and a half in Breadth, as I measured it myself in the Royal Map made by the King's Order, which was laid on the Ground on purpose for me, and extended an hundred Feet; I paced the Diameter and Circumference several times barefoot, and computing by the Scale, measured it pretty exactly.

The King's Palace is no regular Edifice, but an heap of Buildings about seven Miles round: The chief Rooms are generally two hundred and forty Foot high, and broad and long in Proportion. A Coach was allowed to *Glumdalclitch* and me, wherein her Governess frequently took her out to see the Town, or go among the Shops; and I was always of the Party, carried in my Box; although the Girl at my own Desire would often take me out, and hold me in her Hand, that I might more conveniently view the Houses and the People as we passed along the Streets. I reckoned our Coach to be about a Square of *Westminster Hall*, but not altogether so high; however, I cannot be very exact. One Day the Governess ordered our Coachman to stop at several Shops, where the Beggars watching their Opportunity, crowded to the sides of the Coach, and gave me the most horrible Spectacles that ever an *European* Eye beheld. There was a Woman with a Cancer in her Breast, swelled to a monstrous size, full of Holes, in two or three of which I could have easily crept, and covered my whole Body. There was a Fellow with a Wen in his Neck, larger than five Woolpacks, and another with a couple of wooden Legs, each about twenty Foot high. But, the most hateful Sight of all was the Lice crawling on their Clothes. I could see distinctly the Limbs of these Vermin with my naked Eye, much better than those of an *European* Louse through a Microscope, and their Snouts with which they rooted like Swine. They were the first I had ever beheld, and I should have been curious enough to dissect one of them, if I had proper Instruments (which I unluckily left behind me in the Ship) although indeed the Sight was so nauseous, that it perfectly turned my Stomach.

Beside the large Box in which I was usually carried, the Queen ordered a smaller one to be made for me, of about twelve Foot square, and ten high, for the Convenience of Travelling, because the other was somewhat too large for *Glumdalclitch's* Lap, and cumbersome in the Coach; it was made by the same Artist, whom I directed in the whole Contrivance. This travelling Closet was an exact Square with a Window in the middle of three of the Squares, and each Window was latticed with Iron Wire on the outside, to prevent Accidents in long Journeys. On the fourth side, which had no Window, two strong Staples were fixed, through which the

Person that carried me, when I had a mind to be on Horseback, put in a Leathern Belt, and buckled it about his Waist. This was always the Office of some grave trusty Servant in whom I could confide, whether I attended the King and Queen in their Progresses, or were disposed to see the Gardens, or pay a visit to some great Lady or Minister of State in the Court, when *Glumdalclitch* happened to be out of Order:⁴⁵ For I soon began to be known and esteemed among the greatest Officers, I suppose more upon Account of their Majesty's Favour than any Merit of my own. In Journeys, when I was weary of the Coach, a Servant on Horseback would buckle my Box, and place it on a Cushion before him; and there I had a full Prospect of the Country on three Sides from my three Windows. I had in this Closet a Field-Bed⁴⁶ and a Hammock hung from the Ceiling, two Chairs and a Table, neatly screwed to the Floor, to prevent being tossed about by the Agitation of the Horse or the Coach. And having been long used to Sea Voyages, those Motions, although sometimes very violent, did not much discompose me.

Whenever I had a mind to see the Town, it was always in my Travelling Closet, which *Glumdalclitch* held in her Lap in a kind of open Sedan, after the Fashion of the Country, borne by four Men, and attended by two others in the Queen's Livery. The People who had often heard of me, were very curious to crowd about the Sedan, and the Girl was complaisant⁴⁷ enough to make the Bearers stop, and to take me in her Hand that I might be more conveniently seen.

I was very desirous to see the chief Temple, and particularly the Tower belonging to it, which is reckoned the highest in the Kingdom. Accordingly one Day my Nurse carried me thither, but I may truly say I came back disappointed; for, the height is not above three thousand Foot, and reckoning from the Ground to the highest Pinnacle top; which allowing for the difference between the size of those People, and us in *Europe*, is no great matter for Admiration, nor at all equal in Proportion (if I rightly remember), to *Salisbury* Steeple.⁴⁸ But, not to detract from a Nation to which during my Life I shall acknowledge myself extremely obliged, it must be allowed that whatever this famous Tower wants in Height is amply made up in Beauty and Strength. For the Walls are near an hundred Foot thick, built of hewn Stone, whereof each is about forty Foot square, and adorned on all sides with Statues of Gods and Emperors cut in Marble larger than the Life, placed in their several Niches. I measured a little Finger which had fallen down from one of these Statues, and lay unperceived among some Rubbish, and found it exactly four Foot and an Inch in length. *Glumdalclitch* wrapped it up in a Handkerchief, and carried it home in her Pocket to keep among other Trinkets, of which the Girl was very fond, as Children at her Age usually are.

The King's Kitchen is indeed a noble Building, vaulted at top, and about six hundred Foot high. The great Oven is not so wide by ten Paces as the Cupola at St. *Paul*'s:⁴⁹ For I measured the latter on purpose after my Return. But if I should describe the Kitchen grate, the prodigious Pots and Kettles, the joints of Meat turning on the Spits, with many other Particulars, perhaps I should be hardly believed; at least a severe Critic would be apt to think I enlarged a little, as Travellers are often suspected to do. To avoid which censure, I fear I have run too much into the other extreme; and that if this Treatise should happen to be translated into the Language of *Brobdingnag* (which is the general name of that Kingdom), and transmitted thither, the King and his People would have reason to complain that I had done them an Injury by a false and diminutive Representation.

His Majesty seldom keeps above six hundred Horses in his Stables: They are generally from fifty-four to sixty Foot high. But, when he goes abroad on solemn Days, he is attended for State by a Militia Guard of five hundred Horse, which indeed I thought was the most splendid Sight that could be ever beheld, till I saw part of his Army in Battalia,⁵⁰ whereof I shall find another occasion to speak.

CHAP. V

Several Adventures that happened to the Author. The Execution of a Criminal. The Author shows his Skill in Navigation.

I should have lived happy enough in that Country, if my Littleness had not exposed me to several ridiculous and troublesome Accidents; some of which I shall venture to relate. *Glumdalclitch* often carried me into the Gardens of the Court in my smaller Box, and would sometimes take me out of it and hold me in her Hand, or set me down to walk. I remember, before the Dwarf left the Queen, he followed us one Day into those Gardens, and my Nurse having set me down, he and I being close together, near some Dwarf Apple trees, I must need show my Wit by a silly Allusion[51] between him and the Trees, which happens to hold in their Language as it doth in ours. Whereupon, the malicious Rogue watching his Opportunity, when I was walking under one of them, shook it directly over my Head, by which a dozen Apples, each of them near as large as a *Bristol* Barrel, came tumbling about my Ears; one of them hit me on the Back as I chanced to stoop, and knocked me down flat on my Face, but I received no other hurt, and the Dwarf was pardoned at my Desire, because I had given the Provocation.

Another day *Glumdalclitch* left me on a smooth Grass-plot to divert myself while she walked at some distance with her Governess. In the mean time there suddenly fell such a violent shower of Hail, that I was immediately by the force of it struck to the Ground: And when I was down, the Hailstones gave me such cruel Bangs all over the Body, as if I had been pelted with Tennis balls; however I made a shift to creep on all four, and shelter myself by lying flat on my Face on the Lee side of a Border of Lemon Thyme, but so bruised from Head to Foot that I could not go abroad in ten Days. Neither is this at all to be wondered at, because Nature in that Country observing the same Proportion through all her Operations, a Hailstone is near eighteen hundred times as large as one in *Europe*, which I can assert upon Experience, having been so curious to weigh and measure them.

But, a more dangerous Accident happened to me in the same Garden, when my little Nurse believing she had put me in a secure Place, which I often entreated her to do, that I might enjoy my own Thoughts, and having left my Box at home to avoid the Trouble of carrying it, went to another part of the Gardens with her Governess and some Ladies of her Acquaintance. While she was absent and out of hearing, a small white Spaniel belonging to one of the chief Gardeners, having got by accident into the Garden, happened to range near the Place where I lay. The Dog following the Scent, came directly up, and taking me in his Mouth ran straight to his Master, wagging his Tail, and set me gently on the

Ground. By good Fortune he had been so well taught, that I was carried between his Teeth without the least hurt, or even tearing my Clothes. But, the poor Gardener, who knew me well, and had a great Kindness for me, was in a terrible Fright. He gently took me up in both his Hands, and asked me how I did; but I was so amazed and out of Breath, that I could not speak a Word. In a few Minutes I came to myself, and he carried me safe to my little Nurse, who by this time had returned to the Place where she left me, and was in cruel Agonies when I did not appear, nor answer when she called; she severely reprimanded the Gardener on account of his Dog. But, the Thing was hushed up, and never known at Court; for the Girl was afraid of the Queen's Anger, and truly as to myself, I thought it would not be for my Reputation[52] that such a Story should go about.

This Accident absolutely determined *Glumdalclitch* never to trust me abroad for the future out of her Sight. I had been long afraid of this Resolution, and therefore concealed from her some little unlucky Adventures that happened in those Times when I was left by myself. Once a Kite hovering over the Garden made a stoop at me, and if I had not resolutely drawn my Hanger, and run under a thick Espalier,[53] he would have certainly carried me away in his Talons. Another time walking to the Top of a fresh Molehill, I fell to my Neck in the hole through which that Animal had cast up the Earth, and coined some Lie not worth remembering, to excuse myself for spoiling my Clothes. I likewise broke my right Shin against the Shell of a Snail, which I happened to stumble over, as I was walking alone, and thinking on poor *England*.

I cannot tell whether I were more pleased or mortified to observe in those solitary Walks, that the smaller Birds did not appear to be at all afraid of me, but would hop about within a Yard distance, looking for Worms, and other Food with as much Indifference and Security as if no Creature at all were near them. I remember, a Thrush had the Confidence to snatch out of my Hand with his Bill a piece of Cake that *Glumdalclitch* had just given me for my Breakfast. When I attempted to catch any of these Birds, they would boldly turn against me, endeavouring to pick my Fingers, which I durst not venture within their Reach; and then they would turn back unconcerned to hunt for Worms or Snails, as they did before. But, one Day I took a thick Cudgel, and threw it with all my

Strength so luckily at a Linnet, that I knocked him down, and seizing him by the Neck with both my Hands, ran with him in Triumph to my Nurse. However, the Bird who had only been stunned, recovering himself, gave me so many Boxes with his Wings on both Sides of my Head and Body, though I held him at Arm's length, and was out of the reach of his Claws, that I was twenty times thinking to let him go. But I was soon relieved by one of our Servants, who wrung off the Bird's Neck, and I had him next Day for Dinner by the Queen's Command. This Linnet, as near as I can remember, seemed to be somewhat larger than an *English* Swan.

The Maids of Honour often invited *Glumdalclitch* to their Apartments, and desired she would bring me along with her, on purpose to have the pleasure of seeing and touching me. They would often strip me naked from top to toe, and lay me at full Length in their Bosoms; wherewith I was much disgusted; because, to say the Truth, a very offensive Smell came from their Skins; which I do not mention or intend to the Disadvantage of those excellent Ladies, for whom I have all manner of Respect; but, I conceive that my Sense was more acute in proportion to my Littleness, and that those illustrious Persons were no more disagreeable to their Lovers, or to each other, than People of the same Quality are with us in *England*. And, after all, I found their natural Smell was much more supportable than when they used Perfumes, under which I immediately swooned away. I cannot forget that an intimate Friend of mine in *Lilliput* took the freedom in a warm Day, when I had used a good deal of Exercise, to complain of a strong Smell about me, although I am as little faulty that way as most of my Sex: But I suppose his faculty of Smelling was as nice[54] with regard to me, as mine was to that of this People. Upon this Point, I cannot forbear doing Justice to the Queen my Mistress, and *Glumdalclitch* my Nurse, whose Persons were as sweet as those of any Lady in *England*.

That which gave me most uneasiness among these Maids of Honour, when my Nurse carried me to visit them, was to see them use me without any manner of Ceremony, like a Creature who had no sort of Consequence. For, they would strip themselves to the Skin, and put on their Smocks[55] in my Presence, while I was placed on their Toilet[56] directly before their naked Bodies, which, I am sure, to me was very far from being a tempting

Sight, or from giving me any other emotions than those of Horror and Disgust. Their Skins appeared so coarse and uneven, so variously coloured when I saw them near, with a Mole here and there as broad as a Trencher, and Hairs hanging from it thicker than Packthreads; to say nothing further concerning the rest of their Persons. Neither did they at all scruple while I was by to discharge what they had drunk, to the quantity of at least two Hogsheads, in a Vessel that held above three Tuns.[57] The handsomest among these Maids of Honour, a pleasant frolicsome Girl of sixteen, would sometimes set me astride upon one of her Nipples, with many other Tricks, wherein the Reader will excuse me for not being over particular. But, I was so much displeased, that I entreated *Glumdalclitch* to contrive some excuse for not seeing that young Lady any more.

One Day, a young Gentleman who was Nephew to my Nurse's Governess, came and pressed them both to see an Execution. It was of a Man who had murdered one of that Gentleman's intimate Acquaintance. *Glumdalclitch* was prevailed on to be of the Company, very much against her Inclination, for she was naturally tender hearted: And, as for myself, although I abhorred such kind of Spectacles, yet my Curiosity tempted me to see something that I thought must be extraordinary. The Malefactor was fixed in a Chair upon a Scaffold erected for the purpose, and his Head cut off at a blow with a Sword of about forty Foot long. The Veins and Arteries spouted up such a prodigious quantity of Blood, and so high in the Air, that the great *Jet d'Eau* at *Versailles* was not equal for the time it lasted; and the Head when it fell on the Scaffold Floor, gave such a bounce, as made me start, although I were at least half an *English* Mile distant.

The Queen who often used to hear me talk of my Sea Voyages, and took all Occasions to divert me when I was melancholy; asked me whether I understood how to handle a Sail or an Oar, and whether a little exercise of Rowing might not be convenient for my Health. I answered, that I understood both very well. For although my proper Employment had been to be Surgeon or Doctor to the Ship, yet upon a pinch, I was forced to work like a common Mariner. But, I could not see how this could be done in their Country, where the smallest Wherry[58] was equal to a first-rate Man of War among us, and such a Boat as I could manage would never live in any of their Rivers: Her Majesty said, if I would contrive a

Boat, her own Joiner should make it, and she would provide a place for me to sail in. The Fellow was an ingenious Workman, and by my Instructions in ten Days finished a Pleasure-boat with all its Tackling, able conveniently to hold eight *Europeans*. When it was finished, the Queen was so delighted, that she ran with it in her Lap to the King, who ordered it to be put in a Cistern[59] full of Water, with me in it, by way of Trial, where I could not manage my two Sculls or little Oars for want of room. But, the Queen had before contrived another Project. She ordered the Joiner to make a wooden Trough of three hundred Foot long, fifty broad, and eight deep; which being well pitched to prevent leaking was placed on the Floor along the Wall, in an outer Room of the Palace. It had a Cock near the bottom to let out the Water when it began to grow stale, and two Servants could easily fill it in half an Hour. Here I often used to row for my own Diversion, as well as that of the Queen and her Ladies, who thought themselves well entertained with my Skill and Agility. Sometimes I would put up my Sail, and then my Business was only to steer, while the Ladies gave me a Gale with their Fans; and when they were weary, some of the Pages would blow my Sail forward with their Breath, while I showed my Art by steering Starboard or Larboard as I pleased. When I had done, *Glumdalclitch* always carried back my Boat into her Closet, and hung it on a Nail to dry.

In this Exercise I once met an Accident which had like to have cost me my Life. For, one of the Pages having put my Boat into the Trough, the Governess who attended *Glumdalclitch*, very officiously[60] lifted me up to place me in the Boat, but I happened to slip through her Fingers, and should have infallibly fallen down forty Foot upon the Floor, if by the luckiest chance in the World, I had not been stopped by a Corking-pin[61] that stuck in the good Gentlewoman's Stomacher; the Head of the Pin passed between my Shirt and the Waistband of my Breeches, and thus I was held by the middle in the Air till *Glumdalclitch* ran to my Relief.

Another time, one of the Servants, whose Office it was to fill my Trough every third Day with fresh Water, was so careless to let a huge Frog (not perceiving it) slip out of his Pail. The Frog lay concealed till I was put into my Boat, but then seeing a resting Place, climbed up, and made it lean so much on one Side, that I was forced to balance it with all my weight on the other, to prevent overturning. When the Frog was got in, it hopped at once half the length of the Boat, and then over my Head, backwards and forwards, daubing my Face and Clothes with its odious Slime. The largeness of its Features made it appear the most deformed Animal that can be conceived. However, I desired *Glumdalclitch* to let me deal with it alone. I banged it a good while with one of my Sculls, and at last forced it to leap out of the Boat.

But, the greatest Danger I ever underwent in that Kingdom, was from a Monkey, who belonged to one of the Clerks of the Kitchen. *Glumdalclitch* had locked me up in her Closet, while she went somewhere upon Business or a Visit. The Weather being very warm, the Closet Window was left open, as well as the Windows and the Door of my bigger Box, in which I usually lived, because of its Largeness and Conveniency. As I sat quietly meditating at my Table, I heard something bounce in at the Closet Window, and skip about from one side to the other; whereat although I were much alarmed, yet I ventured to look out, but not stirring from my Seat; and then I saw this frolicsome Animal, frisking and leaping up and down till at last he came to my Box, which he seemed to view with great Pleasure and Curiosity, peeping in at the Door and every Window. I retreated to the further Corner of my Room, or Box, but the Monkey looking in at every side, put me into such a fright, that I wanted presence of Mind to conceal myself under the Bed, as I might easily have done. After some time spent in peeping, grinning, and chattering, he at last espied me, and reaching one of his Paws in at the Door, as a Cat does when she plays with a Mouse, although I often shifted place to avoid him, he at length caught hold of the Lappet of my Coat (which being made of that Country Cloth, was very thick and strong) and dragged me out. He took me up in his right forefoot and held me as a Nurse does a Child she is going to suckle, just as I have seen the same sort of Creature do with a Kitten in *Europe*: And when I offered to struggle, he squeezed me so hard, that I thought it more prudent to submit. I have good reason to believe that he took me for a young one of his own Species, by his often stroking my Face very gently with his other Paw. In these Diversions he was interrupted by a Noise at the Closet Door, as if somebody were opening it; whereupon he suddenly leaped up to the Window at which he had come in, and thence upon the Leads[62] and Gutters, walking upon three Legs, and holding me in the fourth, till he clambered up to a roof that was next to ours. I heard *Glumdalclitch* give a shriek at the moment he was carrying me out. The poor Girl was almost distracted:[63] That quarter of the Palace was all in an uproar; the Servants ran for Ladders; the Monkey was seen by hundreds in the Court sitting upon the ridge of a Building, holding me like a Baby in one of his forepaws, and feeding me with the other, by cramming into my Mouth some Victuals he had squeezed out of the Bag on one side of his Chaps, and patting me when I would not eat; whereat many of the Rabble below could not forbear laughing; neither do I think they justly ought to be blamed, for without question the Sight was ridiculous enough to everybody but myself. Some of the People threw up Stones, hoping to drive the Monkey down; but this was strictly forbidden, or else very probably my Brains had been dashed out.

The Ladders were now applied, and mounted by several Men, which the Monkey observing, and finding himself almost encompassed; not being able to make speed enough with his three Legs, let me drop on a ridge Tile, and made his Escape. Here I sat for some time three hundred Yards from the Ground, expecting every moment to be blown down by the Wind, or to fall by my own Giddiness, and come tumbling over and over from the Ridge to the Eaves. But an honest Lad, one of my Nurse's Footmen, climbed up, and putting me into his Breeches Pocket, brought me down safe.

I was almost choked with the filthy stuff the Monkey had crammed down my Throat; but, my dear little Nurse picked it out of my Mouth with a small Needle, and then I fell a Vomiting, which gave me great Relief. Yet I was so weak and bruised in the Sides with the Squeezes given me by this odious Animal, that I was forced to keep my Bed a Fortnight. The King, Queen and all the Court sent every Day to inquire after my Health, and her Majesty made me several Visits during my Sickness. The Monkey was killed, and an Order made that no such Animal should be kept about the Palace.

When I attended the King after my Recovery, to return him thanks for his Favours, he was pleased to rally me a good deal upon this Adventure. He asked me what my Thoughts and Speculations were while I lay in the Monkey's Paw, how I liked the Victuals he gave me, his manner of Feeding, and whether the fresh Air on the Roof had sharpened my Stomach. He desired to know what I would have done upon such an

Occasion in my own Country. I told his Majesty, that in *Europe* we had no Monkeys, except such as were brought for Curiosities from other Places, and so small, that I could deal with a dozen of them together, if they presumed to attack me. And as for that monstrous Animal with whom I was so lately engaged (it was indeed as large as an Elephant), if my Fears had suffered me to think so far as to make use of my Hanger (looking fiercely and clapping my Hand upon the Hilt as I spoke) when he poked his Paw into my Chamber, perhaps I should have given him such a Wound, as would have made him glad to withdraw it with more haste than he put it in. This I delivered in a firm Tone, like a Person who was jealous lest his Courage should be called in question. However, my speech produced nothing else besides a loud Laughter, which all the Respect due to his Majesty from those about him could not make them contain. This made me reflect how vain an Attempt it is for a Man to endeavour doing Himself Honour among those who are out of all Degree of Equality or Comparison with him. And yet I have seen the Moral of my own Behaviour very frequent in *England* since my Return, where a little contemptible Varlet, without the least Title to Birth, Person, Wit, or common Sense, shall presume to look with Importance, and put himself upon a foot with the greatest Persons of the Kingdom.

I was every Day furnishing the Court with some ridiculous Story; and *Glumdalclitch*, although she loved me to excess, yet was arch enough to inform the Queen, whenever I committed any Folly that she thought would be diverting to her Majesty. The Girl, who had been out of order, was carried by her Governess to take the Air about an hour's distance, or thirty Miles from Town. They alighted out of the Coach near a small Footpath in a Field, and *Glumdalclitch* setting down my travelling Box, I went out of it to walk. There was a Cow-dung in the Path, and I must needs try my Activity by attempting to leap over it. I took a Run, but unfortunately jumped short, and found myself just in the middle up to my Knees. I waded through with some difficulty, and one of the Footmen wiped me as clean as he could with his Handkerchief; for I was filthily bemired, and my Nurse confined me to my Box till we returned home; where the Queen was soon informed of what had passed, and the Footmen spread it about the Court, so that all the Mirth, for some Days, was at my expense.

CHAP. VI

*Several Contrivances of the Author to please the King and Queen.
He shows his Skill in Music. The King inquires into the State of
Europe, which the Author relates to him. The King's Observations
thereon.*

I used to attend the King's Levee[64] once or twice a Week, and had
often seen him under the Barber's Hand, which indeed was at first very
terrible to behold. For, the Razor was almost twice as long as an ordinary
Scythe. His Majesty according to the Custom of the Country was only
shaved twice a Week. I once prevailed on the Barber to give me some of
the Suds or Lather, out of which I picked forty or fifty of the strongest
Stumps of Hair. I then took a piece of fine Wood, and cut it like the back
of a Comb, making several Holes in it at equal distance with as small a
Needle as I could get from *Glumdalclitch*. I fixed in the Stumps so artificially,[65] scraping and sloping them with my Knife towards the Points, that
I made a very tolerable Comb; which was a seasonable Supply, my own
being so much broken in the Teeth, that it was almost useless: Neither
did I know any Artist in that Country so nice and exact, as would
undertake to make me another.

And this puts me in mind of an Amusement wherein I spent many of
my leisure Hours. I desired the Queen's Woman to save for me the
Combings of her Majesty's Hair, whereof in time I got a good quantity,
and consulting with my Friend the Cabinet-maker, who had received
general Orders to do little Jobs for me; I directed him to make two
Chair-frames, no larger than those I had in my Box, and then to bore
little Holes with a fine Awl round those parts where I designed the Backs
and Seats; through these Holes I wove the strongest Hairs I could pick
out, just after the manner of Cane-chairs in *England*. When they were
finished, I made a Present of them to her Majesty, who kept them in her
Cabinet,[66] and used to show them for Curiosities, as indeed they were
the Wonder of everyone that beheld them. The Queen would have had
me sit upon one of these Chairs, but I absolutely refused to obey
her, protesting I would rather die a thousand Deaths than place a

dishonourable part of my Body on those precious Hairs that once adorned her Majesty's Head. Of these Hairs (as I had always a Mechanical Genius) I likewise made a neat little Purse about five Foot long, with her Majesty's Name deciphered[67] in Gold Letters, which I gave to *Glumdalclitch*, by the Queen's Consent. To say the Truth, it was more for Show than Use, being not of strength to bear the weight of the larger Coins, and therefore she kept nothing in it, but some little Toys that Girls are fond of.

The King, who delighted in Music, had frequent Consorts[68] at Court, to which I was sometimes carried, and set in my Box on a Table to hear them: But, the Noise was so great, that I could hardly distinguish the Tunes. I am confident that all the Drums and Trumpets of a Royal Army, beating and sounding together just at your Ears, could not equal it. My Practice was to have my Box removed from the Places where the Performers sat, as far as I could, then to shut the Doors and Windows of it, and draw the Window-Curtains; after which I found their Music not disagreeable.

I had learned in my Youth to play a little upon the Spinet. *Glumdalclitch* kept one in her Chamber, and a Master attended twice a Week to teach her: I call it a Spinet, because it somewhat resembled that Instrument, and was played upon in the same manner. A fancy came into my Head that I would entertain the King and Queen with an *English* Tune upon this Instrument. But this appeared extremely difficult: For, the Spinet was near sixty Foot long, each Key being almost a Foot wide, so that, with my Arms extended, I could not reach to above five Keys, and to press them down required a good smart stroke with my Fist, which would be too great a Labour, and to no purpose. The Method I contrived was this. I prepared two round Sticks about the bigness of common Cudgels; they were thicker at one end than the other, and I covered the thicker ends with a piece of a Mouse's Skin, that by rapping on them, I might neither damage the tops of the Keys, nor interrupt the Sound. Before the Spinet a Bench was placed about four Foot below the Keys, and I was put upon the Bench. I ran sideling upon it that way and this, as fast as I could, banging the proper Keys with my two Sticks, and made a shift to play a Jig, to the great Satisfaction of both their Majesties: But, it was the most violent Exercise I ever underwent, and yet I could not strike above sixteen Keys, nor, consequently, play the Bass and Treble

PART II   *A Voyage to Brobdingnag*

together, as other Artists do; which was a great Disadvantage to my Performance.

The King, who as I before observed, was a Prince of excellent Understanding, would frequently order that I should be brought in my Box, and set upon the Table in his Closet.[69] He would then command me to bring one of my Chairs out of the Box, and sit down within three Yards distance upon the top of the Cabinet, which brought me almost to a level with his Face. In this manner I had several Conversations with him. I one Day took the freedom to tell his Majesty, that the Contempt he discovered towards *Europe*, and the rest of the World, did not seem answerable to those excellent Qualities of the Mind he was Master of. That, Reason did not extend itself with the bulk of the Body: On the contrary, we observed in our Country that the tallest Persons were usually least provided with it. That among other Animals, Bees and Ants had the Reputation of more Industry, Art and Sagacity than many of the larger kinds. And that, as inconsiderable as he took me to be, I hoped I might live to do his Majesty some signal Service. The King heard me with Attention, and began to conceive a much better Opinion of me than he had ever before. He desired I would give him as exact an Account of the Government of *England* as I possibly could; because, as fond as Princes commonly are of their own Customs (for so he conjectured of other Monarchs by my former Discourses) he should be glad to hear of anything that might deserve Imitation.

Imagine with thyself, courteous Reader, how often I then wished for the Tongue of *Demosthenes* or *Cicero*,[70] that might have enabled me to celebrate the Praise of my own dear native Country in a Style equal to its Merits and Felicity.

I began my Discourse by informing his Majesty that our Dominions consisted of two Islands, which composed three mighty Kingdoms[71] under one Sovereign, besides our Plantations[72] in *America*. I dwelt long upon the Fertility of our Soil, and the Temperature[73] of our Climate. I then spoke at large upon the Constitution of an *English* Parliament, partly made up of an illustrious Body called the House of Peers, Persons of the noblest Blood, and of the most ancient and ample Patrimonies. I described that extraordinary Care always taken of their Education in Arts and Arms, to qualify them for being Counsellors born to the King and

118

Kingdom, to have a Share in the Legislature, to be Members of the highest Court of Judicature[74] from whence there could be no Appeal; and to be Champions always ready for the Defence of their Prince and Country by their Valour, Conduct and Fidelity. That these were the Ornament and Bulwark of the Kingdom, worthy Followers of their most renowned Ancestors, whose Honour had been the Reward of their Virtue, from which their Posterity were never once known to degenerate. To these were joined several holy Persons, as part of that Assembly, under the Title of Bishops,[75] whose peculiar Business it is, to take care of Religion, and of those who instruct the People therein. These were searched and sought out through the whole Nation, by the Prince and his wisest Counsellors, among such of the Priesthood, as were most deservedly distinguished by the Sanctity of their Lives, and the Depth of their Erudition; who were indeed the spiritual Fathers of the Clergy and the People.

That, the other part of the Parliament consisted of an Assembly called the House of Commons, who were all principal Gentlemen, *freely* picked and culled out by the People themselves, for their great Abilities, and Love of their Country, to represent the Wisdom of the whole Nation. And, these two Bodies make up the most august Assembly in *Europe*, to whom, in Conjunction with the Prince, the whole Legislature is committed.

I then descended to the Courts of Justice, over which the Judges, those venerable Sages and Interpreters of the Law, presided, for determining the disputed Rights and Properties of Men, as well as for the Punishment of Vice, and Protection of Innocence. I mentioned the prudent Management of our Treasury; the Valour and Achievements of our Forces by Sea and Land. I computed the Number of our People, by reckoning how many Millions there might be of each Religious Sect, or Political Party among us. I did not omit even our Sports and Pastimes, or any other Particular which I thought might redound to the Honour of my Country. And, I finished all with a brief historical Account of Affairs and Events in *England* for about an hundred Years past.

This Conversation was not ended under five Audiences, each of several Hours, and the King heard the whole with great Attention, frequently taking Notes of what I spoke, as well as Memorandums of several Questions he intended to ask me.

When I had put an end to these long Discourses, his Majesty in a sixth

Audience consulting his Notes, proposed many Doubts, Queries, and Objections, upon every Article. He asked, what Methods were used to cultivate the Minds and Bodies of our young Nobility, and in what kind of Business they commonly spent the first and teachable part of their Lives. What Course was taken to supply that Assembly when any noble Family became extinct. What Qualifications were necessary in those who were to be created new Lords: Whether the Humour[76] of the Prince, a Sum of Money to a Court-Lady, or a Prime Minister,[77] or a Design of strengthening a Party opposite to the public Interest, ever happened to be Motives in those Advancements. What Share of Knowledge these Lords had in the Laws of their Country, and how they came by it, so as to enable them to decide the Properties of their Fellow-Subjects in the last Resort. Whether they were always so free from Avarice, Partialities, or Want, that a Bribe, or some other sinister View, could have no place among them. Whether those holy Lords I spoke of were always promoted to that Rank upon account of their Knowledge in religious Matters, and the Sanctity of their Lives, had never been Compliers with the times while they were common Priests, or slavish prostitute Chaplains to some Nobleman,[78] whose Opinions they continued servilely to follow after they were admitted into that Assembly.

He then desired to know what Arts were practised in electing those whom I called Commoners. Whether, a Stranger with a strong Purse might not influence the vulgar Voters to choose him before their own Landlord, or the most considerable Gentleman in the Neighbourhood. How it came to pass, that People were so violently bent upon getting into this Assembly, which I allowed to be a great Trouble and Expense, often to the Ruin of their Families, without any Salary or Pension: Because this appeared such an exalted strain of Virtue and public Spirit, that his Majesty seemed to doubt[79] it might possibly not be always sincere: And he desired to know whether such zealous Gentlemen could have any Views of refunding themselves for the Charges and Trouble they were at, by sacrificing the Public Good to the Designs of a weak and vicious Prince in Conjunction with a corrupted Ministry. He multiplied his Questions, and sifted[80] me thoroughly upon every part of this Head,[81] proposing numberless Enquiries and Objections, which I think it not prudent or convenient to repeat.

Upon what I said in relation to our Courts of Justice, his Majesty desired to be satisfied in several Points: And, this I was the better able to do, having been formerly almost ruined by a long Suit in Chancery,[82] which was decreed for me with Costs. He asked, what Time was usually spent in determining between Right and Wrong, and what Degree of Expense. Whether Advocates and Orators had Liberty to plead in Causes manifestly known to be unjust, vexatious, or oppressive. Whether Party in Religion or Politics were observed to be of any Weight in the Scale of Justice. Whether those pleading Orators were Persons educated in the general Knowledge of Equity, or only in provincial, national, and other local Customs. Whether they or their Judges had any Part in penning those Laws which they assumed the Liberty of interpreting and glossing upon at their Pleasure. Whether they had ever at different Times pleaded for and against the same Cause, and cited Precedents to prove contrary Opinions. Whether they were a rich or a poor Corporation.[83] Whether they received any pecuniary Reward for pleading or delivering their Opinions. And particularly whether they were ever admitted as Members in the lower Senate.

He fell next upon the Management of our Treasury; and said, he thought my Memory had failed me, because I computed our Taxes at about five or six millions a Year, and when I came to mention the Issues,[84] he found they sometimes amounted to more than double;[85] for, the Notes he had taken were very particular in this Point, because he hoped, as he told me, that the Knowledge of our Conduct might be useful to him, and he could not be deceived in his Calculations. But, if what I told him were true, he was still at a loss how a Kingdom could run out of its Estate like a private Person. He asked me, who were our Creditors? and, where we should find Money to pay them? He wondered to hear me talk of such chargeable[86] and extensive Wars; that, certainly we must be a quarrelsome People, or live among very bad Neighbours, and that our Generals must needs be richer than our Kings. He asked what Business we had out of our own Islands, unless upon the Score of Trade or Treaty, or to defend the Coasts with our Fleet. Above all, he was amazed to hear me talk of a mercenary standing Army[87] in the midst of Peace, and among a Free People. He said if we were governed by our own Consent in the Persons of our Representatives, he could not imagine of whom we were afraid, or against whom we were to fight, and would hear my Opinion, whether a private Man's House might not better be defended by himself, his Children, and Family, than by half a dozen Rascals picked up at a venture in the Streets, for small Wages, who might get an hundred times more by cutting their Throats.

He laughed at my odd kind of Arithmetic (as he was pleased to call it) in reckoning the Numbers of our People by a Computation drawn from the several Sects among us in Religion and Politics. He said, he knew no Reason, why those who entertain Opinions prejudicial to the Public, should be obliged to Change, or should not be obliged to Conceal them. And as it was Tyranny in any Government to require the first, so it was Weakness not to enforce the second: For, a Man may be allowed to keep Poisons in his Closet, but not to vend them about as Cordials.

He observed, that among the Diversions of our Nobility and Gentry, I had mentioned Gaming.[88] He desired to know at what Age this Entertainment was usually taken up, and when it was laid down. How much of their Time it employed, whether it ever went so high as to affect their Fortunes. Whether mean vicious People by their Dexterity in that Art might not arrive at great Riches, and sometimes keep our very Nobles in Dependence, as well as habituate them to vile Companions, wholly take them from the Improvement of their Minds, and force them by the Losses they have received, to learn and practise that infamous Dexterity upon others.

He was perfectly astonished with the historical Account I gave him of our Affairs during the last Century, protesting it was only an heap of Conspiracies, Rebellions, Murders, Massacres, Revolutions, Banishments, the very worst Effects that Avarice, Faction, Hypocrisy, Perfidiousness, Cruelty, Rage, Madness, Hatred, Envy, Lust, Malice, or Ambition could produce.

His Majesty in another Audience was at the Pains to recapitulate the Sum of all I had spoken, compared the Questions he made with the Answers I had given; then taking me into his Hands, and stroking me gently, delivered himself in these Words, which I shall never forget, nor the manner he spoke them in. My little Friend *Grildrig*; you have made a most admirable Panegyric upon your Country. You have clearly proved that Ignorance, Idleness and Vice are the proper Ingredients for qualifying a Legislator. That Laws are best explained, interpreted, and applied by those whose Interest and Abilities lie in perverting, confounding, and eluding them. I observe among you some Lines of an Institution,[89] which in its Original might have been tolerable, but these half erased, and the rest wholly blurred and blotted by Corruptions. It doth not appear from all you have said, how any one Virtue is required towards the Procurement of any one Station among you, much less that Men are ennobled[90] on Account of their Virtue, that Priests are advanced for their Piety or Learning, Soldiers for their Conduct or Valour, Judges for their Integrity, Senators for the Love of their Country, or Counsellors for their Wisdom. As for yourself (continued the King) who have spent the greatest part of your Life in travelling, I am well disposed to hope you may hitherto have escaped many Vices of your Country. But, by what I have gathered from your own Relation, and the Answers I have with much Pains wringed and extorted from you, I cannot but conclude the Bulk of your Natives, to be the most pernicious Race of little odious Vermin that Nature ever suffered to crawl upon the Surface of the Earth.

CHAP. VII

The Author's Love of his Country. He makes a Proposal of much Advantage to the King, which is rejected. The King's great Ignorance in Politics. The Learning of that Country very imperfect and confined. Their Laws, and military Affairs, and Parties in the State.

Nothing but an extreme Love of Truth could have hindered me from concealing this part of my Story. It was in vain to discover[91] my Resentments, which were always turned into Ridicule; And I was forced to rest with Patience while my noble and most beloved Country was so injuriously treated. I am heartily sorry as any of my Readers can possibly be, that such an Occasion was given: But this Prince happened to be so curious and inquisitive upon every Particular, that it could not consist either with Gratitude or good Manners to refuse giving him what

Satisfaction I was able. Yet thus much I may be allowed to say in my own Vindication, that I artfully eluded many of his Questions, and gave to every Point a more favourable turn by many Degrees than the strictness of Truth would allow. For, I have always borne that laudable Partiality to my own Country, which *Dionysius Halicarnassensis* with so much Justice recommends to an Historian.⁹² I would hide the Frailties and Deformities of my Political Mother, and place her Virtues and Beauties in the most advantageous Light. This was my sincere Endeavour in those many Discourses I had with that mighty Monarch, although it unfortunately failed of Success.

But, great Allowances should be given to a King who lives wholly secluded from the rest of the World, and must therefore be altogether unacquainted with the Manners and Customs that most prevail in other Nations: The want of which Knowledge will ever produce many *Prejudices*, and a certain *Narrowness of Thinking*, from which we and the politer Countries of *Europe* are wholly exempted. And it would be hard indeed, if so remote a Prince's Notions of Virtue and Vice were to be offered as a Standard for all Mankind.

To confirm what I have now said, and further to show the miserable Effects of a *confined Education*, I shall here insert a Passage which will hardly obtain Belief. In hopes to ingratiate myself farther into his Majesty's Favour, I told him of an Invention discovered between three and four hundred Years ago, to make a certain Powder, into an heap of which the smallest spark of Fire falling, would kindle the whole in a Moment, although it were as big as a Mountain, and make it all fly up in the Air together, with a Noise and Agitation greater than Thunder. That, a proper quantity of this Powder rammed into an hollow Tube of Brass or Iron, according to its Bigness, would drive a Ball of Iron or Lead with such Violence and speed as nothing was able to sustain its Force. That the largest Balls thus discharged, would not only destroy whole Ranks of an Army at once, but batter the strongest Walls to the Ground, sink down Ships with a thousand Men in each, to the bottom of the Sea; and when linked together by a Chain, would cut through Masts and Rigging, divide hundreds of Bodies in the middle, and lay all waste before them. That we often put this Powder into large hollow Balls of Iron, and discharged them by an Engine into some City we were besieging, which would rip up the Pavements, tear the Houses to Pieces, burst and throw Splinters on every side, dashing out the Brains of all who came near. That I knew the Ingredients very well, which were cheap, and common; I understood the manner of compounding them, and could direct his Workmen how to make those Tubes of a Size proportionable to all other Things in his Majesty's Kingdom, and the largest need not be above an hundred Foot long; twenty or thirty of which Tubes charged with the proper quantity of Powder and Balls, would batter down the Walls of the strongest Town in his Dominions in a few Hours, or destroy the whole Metropolis, if ever it should pretend to dispute his absolute Commands. This I humbly offered to his Majesty as a small Tribute of Acknowledgement in return of so many Marks that I had received of his Royal Favour and Protection.

The King was struck with Horror at the Description I had given of those terrible Engines, and the Proposal I had made. He was amazed how so impotent and grovelling an Insect as I (these were his Expressions) could entertain such inhuman Ideas, and in so familiar a manner as to appear wholly unmoved at all the Scenes of Blood and Desolation, which I had painted as the common Effects of those destructive Machines, whereof he said, some evil Genius, Enemy to Mankind, must have been the first Contriver.[93] As for himself, he protested, that although few Things delighted him so much as new Discoveries in Art or in Nature, yet he would rather lose half his Kingdom than be privy to such a Secret, which he commanded me, as I valued my Life, never to mention any more.

A strange Effect of *narrow Principles* and *short Views!* that a Prince possessed of every Quality which procures Veneration, Love and Esteem; of strong Parts, great Wisdom and profound Learning, endued with admirable Talents for Government, and almost adored by his Subjects, should from a *nice unnecessary Scruple*, whereof in *Europe* we can have no Conception, let slip an Opportunity put into his Hands, that would have made him absolute Master of the Lives, the Liberties, and the Fortunes of his People. Neither do I say this with the least Intention to detract from the many Virtues of that excellent King, whose Character I am sensible will on this account be very much lessened in the Opinion of an *English* Reader: But, I take this Defect among them to have risen from their Ignorance, they not having hitherto reduced *Politics* into a *Science*, as the more acute Wits of *Europe* have done.[94] For, I remember very well, in a Discourse one Day with the King, when I happened to say there were several thousand Books among us written upon the *Art of Government*, it gave him (directly contrary to my Intention) a very mean Opinion of our Understandings. He professed both to abominate and despise all *Mystery*, *Refinement*, and *Intrigue*, either in a Prince or a Minister. He could not tell what I meant by *Secrets of State*, where an Enemy or some Rival Nation were not in the Case. He confined the Knowledge of governing within very *narrow Bounds*; to common Sense and Reason, to Justice and Lenity, to the speedy Determination of civil and criminal Causes; with some other obvious Topics[95] which are not worth considering. And, he gave it for his Opinion, that whoever could make two Ears of Corn, or two Blades of Grass to grow upon a spot of Ground where only one grew before, would deserve better of Mankind, and do more essential Service to his Country than the whole Race of Politicians put together.

The Learning of this People is very defective, consisting only in Morality, History, Poetry and Mathematics, wherein they must be allowed to excel. But, the last of these is wholly applied to what may be useful in Life, to the Improvement of Agriculture and all mechanical Arts; so that among us it would be little esteemed. And as to Ideas, Entities, Abstractions and Transcendentals,[96] I could never drive the least Conception into their Heads.

No Law of that Country must exceed in Words the number of Letters in their Alphabet, which consists only in two and twenty.[97] But indeed, few of them extend even to that Length. They are expressed in the most plain and simple Terms, wherein those People are not mercurial enough to discover above one Interpretation. And to write a Comment upon any Law is a capital Crime. As to the Decision of civil Causes, or Proceedings against Criminals, their Precedents are so few, that they have little Reason to boast of any extraordinary Skill in either.

They have had the Art of Printing, as well as the *Chinese*, time out of mind. But their Libraries are not very large; for that of the King's, which is reckoned the biggest, doth not amount to above a thousand Volumes, placed in a Gallery of twelve hundred Foot long, from whence I had liberty to borrow what Books I pleased. The Queen's Joiner had contrived

in one of *Glumdalclitch*'s Rooms a kind of wooden Machine five and twenty
Foot high, formed like a standing Ladder, the Steps were each fifty Foot
long: It was indeed a moveable pair of Stairs, the lowest end placed at
ten Foot distance from the Wall of the Chamber. The Book I had a mind
to read was put up leaning against the Wall. I first mounted to the upper
Step of the Ladder, and turning my Face towards the Book, began at the
top of the Page, and so walking to the right and left about eight or ten
Paces according to the length of the Lines, till I had gotten a little below
the level of my Eyes, and then descending gradually till I came to the
bottom: After which I mounted again, and began the other Page in the
same manner, and so turned over the Leaf, which I could easily do with
both my Hands, for it was as thick and stiff as a Pasteboard, and in the
largest Folios not above eighteen or twenty Foot long.

Their Style is clear, masculine, and smooth, but not florid, for they
avoid nothing more than multiplying unnecessary Words, or using various[98] Expressions. I have perused many of their Books, especially those
in History and Morality. Among the rest I was much diverted with a
little old Treatise, which always lay in *Glumdalclitch*'s Bed-chamber, and
belonged to her Governess, a grave elderly Gentlewoman, who dealt in
Writings of Morality and Devotion. The Book treats of the Weakness of
Human kind, and is in little Esteem except among the Women and the
Vulgar. However, I was curious to see what an Author of that Country
could say upon such a Subject. This Writer went through all the usual
Topics of *European* Moralists, showing how diminutive, contemptible,
and helpless an Animal was Man in his own nature; how unable to defend
himself from the Inclemencies of the Air, or the Fury of wild Beasts. How
much he was excelled by one Creature in Strength, by another in Speed,
by a third in Foresight, by a fourth in Industry. He added, that Nature
was degenerated in these latter declining Ages of the World, and could
now produce only small abortive Births in comparison of those in ancient
Times. He said it was very reasonable to think, not only that the Species
of Man were originally much larger, but also that there must have been
Giants in former Ages,[99] which, as it is asserted by History and Tradition,
so it hath been confirmed by huge Bones and Skulls casually dug up in
several Parts of the Kingdom, far exceeding the common dwindled Race
of Man in our Days. He argued, that the very Laws of Nature absolutely

required we should have been made in the beginning, of a size more large and robust, not so liable to Destruction from every little Accident of a Tile falling from an House, or a Stone cast from the Hand of a Boy, or of being drowned in a little Brook. From this way of Reasoning the Author drew several moral Applications useful in the Conduct of Life, but needless here to repeat.[100] For my own part, I could not avoid reflecting how universally this Talent was spread of drawing Lectures in Morality, or indeed rather matter of Discontent and repining from the Quarrels we raise with Nature. And, I believe upon a strict Inquiry, those Quarrels might be shown as ill-grounded among us, as they are among that People.

As to their military Affairs, they boast that the King's Army consists of an hundred and seventy-six thousand Foot, and thirty-two thousand Horse: if that may be called an Army which is made up of Tradesmen[101] in the several Cities, and Farmers in the Country, whose Commanders are only the Nobility and Gentry without Pay or Reward. They are indeed perfect enough in their Exercises, and under very good Discipline, wherein I saw no great Merit; for, how should it be otherwise, where every Farmer is under the Command of his own Landlord, and every Citizen under that of the principal Men in his own City, chosen after the manner of *Venice* by *Ballot*?

I have often seen the Militia of *Lorbrulgrud* drawn out to Exercise in a great Field near the City, of twenty Miles square. They were in all not above twenty-five thousand Foot, and six thousand Horse; but it was impossible for me to compute their Number, considering the space of Ground they took up. A *Cavalier* mounted on a large Steed might be about an hundred Foot high. I have seen this whole Body of Horse upon a Word of Command draw their Swords at once, and brandish them in the Air. Imagination can figure nothing so grand, so surprising and so astonishing. It looked as if ten thousand Flashes of Lightning were darting at the same time from every Quarter of the Sky.

I was curious to know how this Prince, to whose Dominions there is no Access from any other Country, came to think of Armies, or to teach his People the Practice of military Discipline. But I was soon informed, both by Conversation, and Reading their Histories. For, in the course of many Ages they have been troubled with the same Disease to which the Whole Race of Mankind is subject; the Nobility often contending for

Power, the People for Liberty, and the King for absolute Dominion. All which, however happily tempered by the Laws of the Kingdom, have been sometimes violated by each of the three Parties, and have once or more occasioned Civil Wars, the last whereof was happily put an end to by this Prince's Grandfather by a general Composition;[102] and the Militia then settled with common Consent hath been ever since kept in the strictest Duty.

CHAP. VIII

The King and Queen make a Progress to the Frontiers. The Author attends them. The manner in which he leaves the Country very particularly related. He returns to England.

I had always a strong Impulse that I should sometime recover my Liberty, though it was impossible to conjecture by what Means, or to form any Project with the least hope of succeeding. The Ship in which I sailed was the first ever known to be driven within Sight of that Coast, and the King had given strict Orders, that if at any time another appeared, it should be taken ashore, and with all its Crew and Passengers brought in a Tumbril[103] to *Lorbrulgrud*. He was strongly bent to get me a Woman of my own size, by whom I might propagate the Breed: But I think I should rather have died than undergone the Disgrace of leaving a Posterity to be kept in Cages like tame Canary Birds, and perhaps in time sold about the Kingdom to Persons of Quality for Curiosities. I was indeed treated with much Kindness; I was the Favourite of a great King and Queen, and the Delight of the whole Court, but it was upon such a foot as ill became the Dignity of Human Kind. I could never forget those domestic Pledges I had left behind me. I wanted to be among People with whom I could converse upon even Terms, and walk about the Streets and Fields without fear of being trod to Death like a Frog or a young Puppy. But, my Deliverance came sooner than I expected, and in a manner not very common: The whole Story and Circumstances of which I shall faithfully relate.

I had now been two Years in this Country; and, about the beginning of the third, *Glumdalclitch* and I attended the King and Queen in a Progress to the South Coast of the Kingdom. I was carried as usual in my Travelling-Box, which, as I have already described, was a very convenient Closet of twelve Foot wide. And, I had ordered a Hammock to be fixed by silken Ropes from the four Corners at the Top, to break the Jolts, when a Servant carried me before him on Horseback, as I sometimes desired, and would often sleep in my Hammock while we were upon the Road. On the Roof of my Closet, just over the middle of the Hammock, I ordered the Joiner to cut out a Hole of a Foot square to give me Air in hot Weather as I slept, which Hole I shut at pleasure with a Board that drew backwards and forwards through a Groove.

When we came to our Journey's end, the King thought proper to pass a few Days at a Palace he hath near *Flanflasnic*, a City within eighteen *English* Miles of the Sea-side. *Glumdalclitch* and I were much fatigued; I had gotten a small Cold, but the poor Girl was so ill as to be confined to her Chamber. I longed to see the Ocean, which must be the only Scene of my Escape, if ever it should happen. I pretended to be worse than I really was, and desired leave to take the fresh Air of the Sea, with a Page whom I was very fond of, and who had sometimes been trusted with me. I shall never forget with what Unwillingness *Glumdalclitch* consented, nor the strict charge she gave the Page to be careful of me, bursting at the same time into a Flood of Tears, as if she had some foreboding of what was to happen. The Boy took me out of my Box about half an hour's walk from the Palace, towards the Rocks on the Sea-shore. I ordered him to set me down, and lifting up one of my Sashes, cast many a wistful melancholy Look towards the Sea. I found myself not very well, and told the Page that I had a mind to take a Nap in my Hammock, which I hoped would do me good. I got in, and the Boy shut the Window close down to keep out the Cold. I soon fell asleep, and all I can conjecture is, that while I slept, the Page, thinking no Danger could happen, went among the Rocks to look for Bird's eggs, having before observed him from my Window searching about, and picking up one or two in the Clefts. Be that as it will, I found myself suddenly awaked with a violent Pull upon the Ring which was fastened at the top of my Box for the Conveniency of Carriage.[104] I felt my Box raised very high in the Air, and then borne forward with prodigious Speed. The first Jolt had like to have shaken me out of my Hammock, but afterwards the Motion was easy enough. I called out several times as loud as I could raise my Voice, but all to no purpose. I looked towards my Windows, and could see nothing but the Clouds and Sky. I heard a Noise just over my Head like the clapping of Wings, and then began to perceive the woeful Condition I was in; that some Eagle had got the Ring of my Box in his Beak, with an intent to let it fall on a Rock like a Tortoise in a Shell, and then pick out my Body, and devour it. For the Sagacity[105] and Smell of this Bird enable him to discover his Quarry at a great distance, though better concealed than I could be within a two-Inch Board.

In a little time I observed the noise and flutter of Wings to increase very fast, and my Box was tossed up and down like a Signpost in a windy Day. I heard several Bangs or Buffets, as I thought, given to the Eagle (for such I am certain it must have been that held the Ring of my Box in his Beak) and then all on a sudden felt myself falling perpendicularly down for above a Minute, but with such incredible Swiftness that I almost lost my Breath. My Fall was stopped by a terrible Squash, that sounded louder to my Ears than the Cataract of *Niagara*;[106] after which I was quite in the dark for another Minute, and then my Box began to rise so high that I could see Light from the tops of my Windows. I now perceived that I was fallen into the Sea. My Box, by the Weight of my Body, the Goods that were in, and the broad Plates of Iron fixed for strength at the four Corners of the top and bottom, floated about five Foot deep in Water. I did then, and do now suppose that the Eagle which flew away with my Box was pursued by two or three others, and forced to let me drop while he was defending himself against the rest, who hoped to share in the Prey. The Plates of Iron fastened at the bottom of the Box (for those were the strongest), preserved the Balance while it fell, and hindered it from being broken on the surface of the Water. Every joint of it was well grooved, and the Door did not move on Hinges, but up and down like a Sash, which kept my Closet so tight that very little Water came in. I got with much Difficulty out of my Hammock, having first ventured to draw back the Slip-board on the Roof already mentioned, contrived on purpose to let in Air, for want of which I found myself almost stifled.

How often did I then wish myself with my dear *Glumdalclitch*, from whom one single Hour had so far divided me! And I may say with Truth, that in the midst of my own Misfortunes I could not forbear lamenting my poor Nurse, the Grief she would suffer for my Loss, the Displeasure of the Queen, and the Ruin of her Fortune. Perhaps many Travellers have not been under greater Difficulties and Distress than I was at this Juncture, expecting every Moment to see my Box dashed in Pieces, or at least overset by the first violent Blast, or a rising Wave. A Breach in one single Pane of Glass would have been immediate Death: Nor could anything have preserved the Windows, but the strong Lattice Wires placed on the outside against Accidents in Travelling. I saw the Water ooze in at several Crannies, although the Leaks were not considerable, and I endeavoured to stop them as well as I could. I was not able to lift up the Roof of my Closet, which otherwise I certainly should have done, and sat on the top of it, where I might at least preserve myself some Hours longer than by being shut up, as I may call it, in the Hold. Or, if I escaped these Dangers for a Day or two, what could I expect but a miserable Death of Cold and Hunger! I was four Hours under these Circumstances, expecting and indeed wishing every Moment to be my last.

I have already told the Reader that there were two strong Staples fixed upon that side of my Box which had no Window, and into which the Servant who used to carry me on horseback would put a leathern Belt, and buckle it about his Waist. Being in this disconsolate state, I heard or at least thought I heard some kind of grating Noise on that side of my Box where the Staples were fixed, and soon after I began to fancy that the Box was pulled or towed along in the Sea; for I now and then felt a sort of tugging which made the Waves rise near the tops of my Windows, leaving me almost in the dark. This gave me some faint hopes of Relief, although I was not able to imagine how it could be brought about. I ventured to unscrew one of my Chairs, which were always fastened to the Floor; and having made a hard shift to screw it down again directly under the Slipping-board that I had lately opened, I mounted on the Chair, and putting my Mouth as near as I could to the Hole, I called for help in a loud Voice, and in all the Languages I understood. I then fastened my Handkerchief to a Stick I usually carried, and thrusting it up the Hole, waved it several times in the Air, that if any Boat or Ship were near, the Seamen might conjecture some unhappy Mortal to be shut up in this Box.

I found no effect from all I could do, but plainly perceived my Closet to be moved along; and in the space of an Hour, or better, that side of the Box where the Staples were, and had no Window, struck against something that was hard. I apprehended it to be a Rock, and found myself tossed more than ever. I plainly heard a Noise upon the Cover of my Closet, like that of a Cable, and the grating of it as it passed through the Ring. I then found myself hoisted up by degrees at least three Foot higher than I was before. Whereupon, I again thrust up my Stick and Handkerchief, calling for Help till I was almost hoarse. In return to which, I heard a great Shout repeated three times, giving me such Transports of Joy as are not to be conceived but by those who feel them. I now heard a trampling over my Head, and somebody calling through the Hole with a loud Voice in the *English* Tongue: If there be anybody below let them speak. I answered, I was an *Englishman*, drawn by ill Fortune into the greatest Calamity that ever any Creature underwent, and begged, by all that was moving, to be delivered out of the Dungeon I was in. The Voice replied, I was safe, for my Box was fastened to their Ship; and the Carpenter should immediately come, and saw an Hole in the Cover, large enough to pull me out. I answered, that was needless, and would take up too much time, for there was no more to be done, but let one of the Crew put his Finger into the Ring, and take the Box out of the Sea into the Ship, and so into the Captain's Cabin. Some of them upon hearing me talk so wildly thought I was mad; others laughed; for indeed it never came into my head that I was now got among People of my own Stature and Strength. The Carpenter came, and in a few Minutes sawed a Passage about four Foot square, then let down a small Ladder, upon which I mounted, and from thence was taken into the Ship in a very weak Condition.

The Sailors were all in Amazement, and asked me a thousand Questions, which I had no Inclination to answer. I was equally confounded at the Sight of so many Pygmies, for such I took them to be, after having so long accustomed mine Eyes to the monstrous Objects I had left. But the Captain, Mr. *Thomas Wilcocks*, an honest worthy *Shropshire* Man, observing I was ready to faint, took me into his Cabin, gave me a Cordial to comfort me, and made me *turn in* upon his own Bed, advising me to take a little Rest, of which I had great need. Before I went to sleep I gave him to understand that I had some valuable Furniture in my Box too good to be lost; a fine Hammock, an handsome Field-Bed, two Chairs, a Table, and a Cabinet: That my Closet was hung on all sides, or rather quilted with Silk and Cotton: That if he would let one of the Crew bring my Closet into his Cabin, I would open it there before him, and show him my Goods. The Captain hearing me utter these Absurdities, concluded I was raving: However (I suppose to pacify me), he promised to give Order as I desired, and going upon Deck sent some of his Men down into my Closet, from whence (as I afterwards found) they drew up all my Goods, and stripped off the Quilting; but the Chairs, Cabinet and Bedstead being screwed to the Floor, were much damaged by the Ignorance of the Seamen, who tore them up by Force. Then they knocked off some of the Boards for the use of the Ship, and when they had got all they had a mind for, let the Hulk drop into the Sea, which by reason of many Breaches made in the bottom and sides, sunk to rights.[107] And indeed I was glad not to have been a Spectator of the Havoc they made; because I am confident it would have sensibly[108] touched me, by bringing former Passages into my Mind, which I had rather forget.

I slept some Hours, but perpetually disturbed with Dreams of the Place I had left, and the Dangers I had escaped. However, upon waking I found myself much recovered. It was now about eight o' Clock at Night, and the Captain ordered Supper immediately, thinking I had already fasted too long. He entertained me with great Kindness, observing me not to look wildly, or talk inconsistently; and when we were left alone, desired I would give him a Relation of my Travels, and by what Accident I came to be set adrift in that monstrous wooden Chest. He said, that about twelve o' Clock at Noon, as he was looking through his Glass, he spied it at a distance, and thought it was a Sail, which he had a mind to make,[109] being not much out of his course, in hopes of buying some Biscuit, his own beginning to fall short. That upon coming nearer, and finding his Error, he sent out his Long-boat to discover what I was; that his Men came back in a Fright, swearing they had seen a swimming House. That he laughed at their Folly, and went himself in the Boat,

ordering his Men to take a strong Cable along with them. That the
Weather being calm, he rowed round me several times, observed my
Windows, and the wire Lattices that defended them. That he discovered
two Staples upon one Side, which was all of Boards, without any Passage
for Light. He then commanded his Men to row up to that Side, and
fastening a Cable to one of the Staples, ordered them to tow my Chest
(as he called it) towards the Ship. When it was there, he gave Directions
to fasten another Cable to the Ring fixed in the Cover, and to raise up
my Chest with Pullies, which all the Sailors were not able to do above
two or three Foot. He said, they saw my Stick and Handkerchief thrust
out of the Hole, and concluded, that some unhappy Men must be shut
up in the Cavity. I asked whether he or the Crew had seen any prodigious
Birds in the Air about the time he first discovered me. To which he
answered, that discoursing this matter with the Sailors while I was asleep,
one of them said he had *observed* three Eagles flying towards the North,
but remarked nothing of their being larger than the usual Size, which I
suppose must be imputed to the great Height they were at: and he could
not guess the reason of my Question. I then asked the Captain how far
he reckoned we might be from Land; he said, by the best Computation
he could make, we were at least an hundred Leagues. I assured him, that
he must be mistaken by almost half, for I had not left the Country from
whence I came above two Hours before I dropped into the Sea. Whereupon
he began again to think that my Brain was disturbed, of which he gave
me a Hint, and advised me to go to Bed in a Cabin he had provided. I
assured him I was well refreshed with his good Entertainment and
Company, and as much in my Senses as ever I was in my Life. He then
grew serious, and desired to ask me freely whether I were not troubled
in Mind by the Consciousness of some enormous Crime, for which I was
punished at the Command of some Prince, by exposing me in that Chest,
as great Criminals in other Countries have been forced to Sea in a leaky
vessel without Provisions: For, although he should be sorry to have taken
so ill a Man into his Ship, yet he would engage his Word to set me safe
on Shore in the first Port where we arrived. He added, that his Suspicions
were much increased by some very absurd Speeches I had delivered at
first to the Sailors, and afterwards to himself, in relation to my Closet or
Chest, as well as by my odd Looks and Behaviour while I was at Supper.

I begged his Patience to hear me tell my Story, which I faithfully did from the last time I left *England* to the Moment he first discovered me. And, as Truth always forceth its way into rational Minds; so, this honest worthy Gentleman, who had some Tincture of Learning, and very good Sense, was immediately convinced of my Candour and Veracity. But further to confirm all I had said, I entreated him to give Order that my Cabinet should be brought, of which I had the Key in my Pocket (for he had already informed me how the Seamen disposed of my Closet), I opened it in his Presence, and showed him the small Collection of Rarities I made in the Country from whence I had been so strangely delivered. There was the Comb I had contrived out of the Stumps of the King's Beard, and another of the same Materials, but fixed into a paring of her Majesty's Thumb-nail, which served for the Back. There was a Collection of Needles and Pins from a Foot to half a Yard long. Four Wasp Stings, like Joiners' Tacks: Some Combings of the Queen's Hair: A gold Ring which one Day she made me a Present of in a most obliging manner, taking it from her little Finger, and throwing it over my Head like a Collar. I desired the Captain would please to accept this Ring in return of his Civilities, which he absolutely refused. I showed him a Corn that I had cut off with my own Hand from a Maid of Honour's Toe; it was about the Bigness of a *Kentish* Pippin,[110] and grown so hard, that when I returned to *England*, I got it hollowed into a Cup and set in Silver. Lastly, I desired him to see the Breeches I had then on, which were made of a Mouse's Skin.

I could force nothing on him but a Footman's Tooth, which I observed him to examine with great Curiosity, and found he had a Fancy for it. He received it with abundance of Thanks, more than such a Trifle could deserve. It was drawn by an unskilful Surgeon in a Mistake from one of *Glumdalclitch*'s Men, who was afflicted with the Toothache, but it was as sound as any in his Head. I got it cleaned, and put it into my Cabinet. It was about a Foot long, and four Inches in Diameter.

The Captain was very well satisfied with this plain Relation I had given him; and said, he hoped when we returned to *England*, I would oblige the World by putting it in Paper, and making it public. My Answer was, that I thought we were already overstocked with Books of Travels: That nothing could now pass which was not extraordinary, wherein I doubted some Authors less consulted Truth than their own Vanity or Interest, or the Diversion of ignorant Readers. That my Story could contain little besides common Events, without those ornamental Descriptions of strange Plants, Trees, Birds, and other Animals, or of the barbarous Customs and Idolatry of savage People, with which most Writers abound. However, I thanked him for his good Opinion, and promised to take the matter into my Thoughts.

He said he wondered at one thing very much, which was to hear me speak so loud, asking me whether the King or Queen of that Country were thick of Hearing. I told him it was what I had been used to for above two Years past, and that I admired as much at the Voices of him and his Men, who seemed to me only to whisper, and yet I could hear them well enough. But, when I spoke in that Country, it was like a Man talking in the Street to another looking out from the Top of a Steeple, unless when I was placed on a Table, or held in any Person's Hand. I told him I had likewise observed another thing, that when I first got into the Ship, and the Sailors stood all about me, I thought they were the most little contemptible Creatures I had ever beheld. For, indeed, while I was in that Prince's Country, I could never endure to look in a Glass after my Eyes had been accustomed to such prodigious Objects, because the Comparison gave me so despicable a Conceit of myself. The Captain said, that while we were at Supper, he observed me to look at everything with a sort of Wonder, and that I often seemed hardly able to contain my Laughter, which he knew not well how to take, but imputed it to some Disorder in my Brain. I answered, it was very true, and I wondered how I could forbear, when I saw his Dishes of the size of a silver Three-pence, a Leg of Pork hardly a Mouthful, a Cup not so big as a Nutshell: and so I went on, describing the rest of his Household-stuff and Provisions after the same manner. For although the Queen had ordered a little Equipage of all things necessary while I was in her Service, yet my Ideas were wholly taken up with what I saw on every side of me, and I winked at[111] my own Littleness as People do at their own Faults. The Captain understood my Raillery very well, and merrily replied with the old *English* Proverb, that he doubted my Eyes were bigger than my Belly, for he did not observe my Stomach so good, although I had fasted all Day; and continuing in his Mirth, protested he would have gladly given an hundred Pounds to have seen my Closet in the Eagle's Bill, and afterwards in its fall from so great an height into the Sea; which would certainly have been a most astonishing Object, worthy to have the Description of it transmitted to future Ages: And the Comparison of *Phaeton*[112] was so obvious, that he could not forbear applying it, although I did not much admire the Conceit.

The Captain having been at *Tonquin*[113] was in his return to *England* driven North eastward to the Latitude of 44 Degrees, and of Longitude 143.[114] But meeting a Trade Wind two Days after I came on board him, we sailed Southward a long time, and coasting *New-Holland*[115] kept our Course West-south-west, and then South-south-west till we doubled the *Cape of Good Hope*. Our Voyage was very prosperous, but I shall not trouble the Reader with a Journal of it. The Captain called in at one or two Ports and sent in his Long-boat for Provisions and fresh Water, but I never went out of the Ship till we came into the Downs, which was on the 3d. Day of *June* 1706, about nine Months after my Escape. I offered to leave my Goods in Security for Payment of my Freight; but the Captain protested he would not receive one Farthing. We took kind leave of each other, and I made him promise he would come to see me at my house in *Redriff*. I hired a Horse and Guide for five Shillings, which I borrowed of the Captain.

As I was on the Road, observing the Littleness of the Houses, the Trees, the Cattle and the People, I began to think myself in *Lilliput*. I was afraid of trampling on every Traveller I met, and often called aloud to have them stand out of the way, so that I had like to have gotten one or two broken Heads for my Impertinence.

When I came to my own House, for which I was forced to inquire, one of the Servants opening the Door, I bent down to go in (like a Goose under a Gate) for fear of striking my Head. My Wife ran out to embrace me, but I stooped lower than her Knees, thinking she could otherwise never be able to reach my Mouth. My Daughter kneeled to ask me Blessing, but I could not see her till she arose, having been so long used to stand with my Head and Eyes erect to above sixty Foot; and then I went to take her up with one Hand, by the Waist. I looked down upon the Servants and one or two Friends who were in the House, as if they had been Pygmies, and I a Giant. I told my Wife she had been too thrifty, for I found she had starved herself and her Daughter to nothing. In short, I behaved myself so unaccountably, that they were all of the Captain's Opinion when he first saw me, and concluded I had lost my Wits. This I mention as an Instance of the great Power of Habit and Prejudice.

In a little time I and my Family and Friends came to a right Understanding: But my Wife protested I should never go to Sea any more; although my evil Destiny so ordered that she had not Power to hinder me, as the Reader may know hereafter. In the mean time I here conclude the Second Part of my unfortunate Voyages.

The End of the Second Part

TRAVELS

PART III
A VOYAGE TO LAPUTA, BALNIBARBI, LUGGNAGG, GLUBBDUBDRIB AND JAPAN

Plate III. Part. III. Page. 1.

Parts Unknown

Land of
St James Bay
Robbin I.
Companys
IESSO
Salmon B.
Land
Stats I.
C. Canal
Sea of Corea
Sando I.
Tarpui
Niuala
Toy
Red Pt.
Inaba
Meaco
Iedo
Bosho Pt.
JAPON
Surungo
Barnevelts
Ongeluckig. I.
Tonsa. I.
Bungo. I.
South. I.
Dimeris Straits.
I. Tanaxuma.
Sialo
LUGN AGG
Glangurn
Traldragdub
Clamrgnig
Maldonada
I Deserta
Glubbdubdrib
Urac
Tonal

Laputa
BALNIBARBI
Lagado
Dicovered. A.D. 1701

PLATE 5

CHAP. I

The Author sets out on his Third Voyage, is taken by Pirates.
The Malice of a Dutchman. His Arrival at an Island. He is
received into Laputa.

I had not been at home above ten Days, when Captain *William Robinson*, a *Cornish* Man, Commander of the *Hope-well*, a stout Ship of Three Hundred Tons, came to my House. I had formerly been Surgeon of another Ship where he was Master, and a fourth part Owner, in a Voyage to the *Levant*; He had always treated me more like a Brother than an inferior Officer, and hearing of my Arrival made me a Visit, as I apprehended only out of Friendship, for nothing passed more than what is usual after long Absences. But repeating his Visits often, expressing his Joy to find me in good Health, asking whether I were now settled for Life, adding that he intended a Voyage to the *East Indies*, in two Months; at last he plainly invited me, though with some Apologies, to be Surgeon of the Ship; that I should have another Surgeon under me besides our two Mates; that my Salary should be double to the usual Pay; and that having experienced my Knowledge in Sea-Affairs to be at least equal to his, he would enter into any Engagement to follow my Advice, as much as if I had share in the Command.

He said so many other obliging things, and I knew him to be so honest a Man, that I could not reject his Proposal; the Thirst I had of seeing the World, notwithstanding my past Misfortunes, continuing as violent as ever. The only Difficulty that remained, was to persuade my Wife, whose consent however I at last obtained by the prospect of Advantage she proposed[1] to her Children.

We set out the 5th Day of *August*, 1706 and arrived at Fort St. *George*,[2] the 11th of *April* 1707. We stayed there three Weeks to refresh our Crew, many of whom were sick. From thence we went to *Tonquin*, where the Captain resolved to continue some time, because many of the Goods he intended to buy were not ready, nor could he expect them to be dispatched in some Months. Therefore in hopes to defray some of the Charges he must be at, he bought a Sloop, loaded it with several sorts of Goods, wherewith the *Tonquinese* usually trade to the Neighbouring Islands, and putting Fourteen Men on Board, whereof three were of the Country, he appointed me Master of the Sloop, and gave me power to Traffic for two Months, while he transacted his Affairs at *Tonquin*.

We had not Sailed above three Days, when a great Storm arising, we were driven five Days to the North-North-East, and then to the East, after which we had fair Weather, but still with a pretty strong Gale from the West. Upon the tenth Day we were chased by two Pirates, who soon overtook us; for my Sloop was so deep loaden, that she sailed very slow; neither were we in a Condition to defend ourselves.

We were boarded about the same time by both the Pirates, who entered furiously at the Head of their Men, but finding us all prostrate upon our Faces (for so I gave order), they pinioned us with strong Ropes, and setting a Guard upon us, went to search the Sloop.

I observed among them a *Dutchman*, who seemed to be of some Authority, though he was not Commander of either Ship. He knew us by our Countenances to be *Englishmen*, and jabbering to us in his own Language, swore we should be tied Back to Back, and thrown into the Sea. I spoke *Dutch* tolerably well; I told him who we were, and begged him in consideration of our being Christians and Protestants, of neighbouring Countries, in strict Alliance,[3] that he would move the Captains to take some pity on us. This inflamed his Rage, he repeated his Threatenings, and turning to his Companions, spoke with great Vehemence, in the *Japanese* Language, as I suppose, often using the word *Christianos*.

The largest of the two Pirate Ships was Commanded by a *Japanese* Captain, who spoke a little *Dutch*, but very imperfectly. He came up to me, and after several Questions, which I answered in great Humility, he said we should not die. I made the Captain a very low Bow, and then turning to the *Dutchman*, said, I was sorry to find more Mercy in a Heathen, than in a Brother Christian. But I had soon reason to repent those foolish Words; For that malicious Reprobate, having often endeavoured in vain to persuade both the Captains that I might be thrown into the Sea (which they would not yield to after the Promise made me, that I should not die), however prevailed so far as to have a Punishment inflicted on me, worse in all human Appearance than Death itself. My Men were sent by an equal Division into both the Pirate-Ships, and my Sloop new manned. As to myself, it was determined that I should be set adrift, in a small Canoe, with Paddles and a Sail, and four Days' Provisions, which last the *Japanese* Captain was so kind to double out of his own Stores, and would permit no Man to search me. I got down into the Canoe, while the *Dutchman* standing upon the Deck, loaded me with all the Curses and injurious Terms his Language could afford.

About an Hour before we saw the Pirates, I had taken an Observation, and found we were in the Latitude of 46 N. and of Longitude 183.[4] When I was at some distance from the Pirates, I discovered by my Pocket Glass several Islands to the South-East. I set up my Sail, the Wind being fair, with a design to reach the nearest of those Islands, which I made a shift to do in about three Hours. It was all Rocky, however I got many Birds' Eggs, and striking Fire I kindled some Heath and dry Seaweed, by which I roasted my Eggs. I eat no other Supper, being resolved to spare my Provisions as much as I could. I passed the Night under the shelter of a Rock, strowing some Heath under me, and slept pretty well.

The next Day I sailed to another Island, and thence to a third and fourth, sometimes using my Sail, and sometimes my Paddles. But not to trouble the Reader with a particular Account of my Distresses, let it suffice that on the 5th Day, I arrived at the last Island in my sight, which lay South-South-East to the former.

This Island was at a greater distance than I expected, and I did not reach it in less than five Hours. I encompassed it almost round before I could find a convenient Place to land in, which was a small Creek, about three times the wideness of my Canoe. I found the Island to be all rocky, only a little intermingled with Tufts of Grass, and sweet-smelling Herbs. I took out my small Provisions, and after having refreshed myself, I secured the remainder in a Cave, whereof there were great Numbers. I gathered plenty of Eggs upon the Rocks, and got a Quantity of dry Seaweed, and parched Grass, which I designed to kindle the next Day, and roast my Eggs as well as I could. (For I had about me my Flint, Steel, Match, and Burning-glass.)[5] I lay all Night in the Cave where I had lodged my Provisions. My Bed was the same dry Grass and Seaweed which I intended for Fuel. I slept very little, for the Disquiets of my Mind prevailed over my Weariness, and kept me awake. I considered how impossible it was to preserve my Life, in so desolate a Place, and how miserable my End must be. Yet I found myself so listless and desponding, that I had not the Heart to rise, and before I could get Spirits enough to creep out of my Cave, the Day was far advanced. I walked a while among the Rocks, the Sky was perfectly clear, and the Sun so hot, that I was forced to turn my Face from it: When all on a sudden it became obscured, as I thought, in a manner very different from what happens by the Interposition of a Cloud. I turned back, and perceived a vast Opaque Body between me and the Sun, moving forwards towards the Island: It seemed to be about two Miles high, and hid the Sun six or seven Minutes, but I did not observe the Air to be much colder, or the Sky more darkened, than if I had stood under the shade of a Mountain. As it approached nearer over the Place where I was, it appeared to be a firm Substance, the Bottom flat, smooth, and shining very bright from the Reflection of the Sea below. I stood upon a Height about two Hundred Yards from the Shore, and saw this vast Body descending almost to a Parallel with me, at less than an *English* Mile distance. I took out my Pocket-Perspective, and could plainly discover Numbers of People moving up and down the Sides of it, which appeared to be Sloping, but what those People were doing, I was not able to distinguish.

The natural Love of Life gave me some inward Motions of Joy, and I was ready to entertain a Hope, that this Adventure might some way or other help to deliver me from the desolate Place and Condition I was in. But at the same time the Reader can hardly conceive my Astonishment, to behold an Island in the Air, inhabited by Men, who were able (as it should seem) to raise, or sink, or put it into a Progressive Motion, as they pleased. But not being at that time in a disposition to philosophize upon this Phenomenon, I rather chose to observe what Course the Island would take, because it seemed for a while to stand still. Yet soon after it advanced nearer, and I could see the Sides of it, encompassed with several Gradations of Galleries, and Stairs, at certain Intervals, to descend from one to the other. In the lowest Gallery, I beheld some People Fishing with long Angling Rods, and others looking on. I waved my Cap (for my Hat was long since worn out) and my Handkerchief towards the Island; and upon its nearer approach, I called and shouted with the utmost strength of my Voice; and then looking circumspectly, I beheld a Crowd gathered to that side which was most in my View. I found by their pointing towards me and to each other, that they plainly discovered me, although they made no return to my shouting. But I could see four or five Men running in great Haste up the Stairs to the Top of the Island, who then disappeared. I happened rightly to conjecture, that these were sent for Orders to some Person in Authority upon this Occasion.

The number of People increased, and in less than half an Hour, the Island was moved and raised in such a manner, that the lowest Gallery appeared in a Parallel of less than an Hundred Yards distance from the Height where I stood. I then put myself into the <u>most supplicat</u>ing Postures, and <u>spoke in the humblest Acce</u>nt, but received no Answer. Those who stood nearest over-against me, seemed to be Persons of Distinction, as I supposed by their Habit. They conferred earnestly with each other, looking often upon me. At length one of them called out in a clear, polite, smooth Dialect, not unlike in sound to the *Italian*; and therefore I returned an Answer in that Language, hoping at least that the Cadence might be more agreeable to his Ears. Although neither of us understood the other, yet my meaning was easily known, for the People saw the Distress I was in.

They made Signs for me to come down from the Rock, and go towards the Shore, which I accordingly did; and the flying Island being raised to a convenient Height, the Verge directly over me, a Chain was let down from the lowest Gallery, with a Seat fastened to the Bottom, to which I fixed myself, and was drawn up by Pullies.

CHAP. II

The Humours[6] *and Dispositions of the* Laputians *described.
An Account of their Learning. Of the King and his Court. The
Author's Reception there. The Inhabitants subject to Fears and
Disquietudes. An Account of the Women.*

At my alighting I was surrounded by a Crowd of People, but those
who stood nearest seemed to be of better Quality. They beheld me with
all the Marks and Circumstances of Wonder, neither indeed was I much
in their Debt; having never till then seen a Race of Mortals so singular
in their Shapes, Habits, and Countenances. Their Heads were all reclined
either to the Right, or the Left; one of their Eyes turned inward, and the
other directly up to the Zenith. Their outward Garments were adorned
with the Figures of Suns, Moons, and Stars, interwoven with those of
Fiddles, Flutes, Harps, Trumpets, Guitars, Harpsicords, and many more
Instruments of Music, unknown to us in *Europe*. I observed here and there
many in the Habit of Servants, with a blown Bladder fastened like a Flail
to the end of a short Stick, which they carried in their Hands. In each
Bladder was a small Quantity of dried Peas or little Pebbles (as I was
afterwards informed). With these Bladders they now and then flapped
the Mouths and Ears of those who stood near them, of which Practice I
could not then conceive the meaning; It seems, the Minds of these People
are so taken up with intense Speculations, that they neither can speak,
nor attend to the Discourses of others, without being roused by some
external Taction[7] upon the Organs of Speech and Hearing; for which
reason, those Persons who are able to afford it always keep a *Flapper* (the
Original is *Climenole*) in their Family, as one of their Domestics, nor ever
walk abroad or make Visits without him. And the Business of this Officer
is, when two or three more Persons are in Company, gently to strike
with his Bladder the Mouth of him who is to speak, and the Right Ear of
him or them to whom the Speaker addresseth himself. This *Flapper* is
likewise employed diligently to attend his Master in his Walks, and upon
occasion to give him a soft Flap on his Eyes, because he is always so
wrapped up in Cogitation, that he is in manifest danger of falling down

every Precipice, and bouncing his Head against every Post, and in the Streets, of Justling others, or being Justled himself into the Kennel.[8]

It was necessary to give the Reader this Information, without which he would be at the same Loss with me, to understand the Proceedings of these People, as they conducted me up the Stairs, to the Top of the Island, and from thence to the Royal Palace. While we were Ascending, they forgot several times what they were about, and left me to myself, till their Memories were again roused by their *Flappers*; For they appeared altogether unmoved by the Sight of my Foreign Habit and Countenance, and by the Shouts of the Vulgar,[9] whose Thoughts and Minds were more disengaged.

At last we entered the Palace, and proceeded into the Chamber of Presence, where I saw the King seated on his Throne, attended on each side by Persons of Prime Quality. Before the Throne, was a large Table filled with Globes and Spheres, and Mathematical Instruments of all kinds. His Majesty took not the least Notice of us, although our Entrance was not without sufficient Noise, by the Concourse of all Persons belonging to the Court. But, he was then deep in a Problem, and we attended at least an Hour, before he could solve it. There stood by him on each side, a young Page, with Flaps in their Hands, and when they saw he was at Leisure, one of them gently struck his Mouth, and the other his Right Ear, at which he started like one awaked on the sudden, and looking towards me, and the Company I was in, recollected the Occasion of our coming, whereof he had been informed before. He spoke some words, whereupon immediately a young Man with a Flap came up to my side, and flapped me gently on the Right Ear, but I made Signs, as well as I could, that I had no occasion for such an Instrument; which as I afterwards found gave His Majesty and the whole Court a very mean Opinion of my Understanding. The King, as far as I could conjecture, asked me several Questions, and I addressed myself to him in all the Languages I had. When it was found, that I could neither understand nor be understood, I was conducted by the King's order to an Apartment in his Palace (this Prince being distinguished above all his Predecessors for his Hospitality to Strangers), where two Servants were appointed to attend me. My Dinner was brought, and four Persons of Quality, whom I remembered to have seen very near the King's Person, did me the Honour to dine with me. We had two Courses, of three Dishes each. In the first Course, there was a Shoulder of Mutton, cut into an Equilateral Triangle, a piece of Beef into a Rhomboid, and a Pudding into a Cycloid.[10] The second Course was two Ducks, trussed up into the Form of Fiddles; Sausages and Puddings resembling Flutes and Hautboys,[11] and a Breast of Veal in the shape of a Harp. The Servants cut our Bread into Cones, Cylinders, Parallelograms, and several other Mathematical Figures.

While we were at Dinner, I made bold to ask the Names of several things in their Language; and those Noble Persons, by the Assistance of their *Flappers*, delighted to give me Answers, hoping to raise my Admiration of their great Abilities, if I could be brought to Converse with them. I was soon able to call for Bread, and Drink, or whatever else I wanted.

After Dinner my company withdrew, and a Person was sent to me by the King's Order, attended by a *Flapper*. He brought with him Pen, Ink, and Paper, and three or four Books, giving me to understand by Signs, that he was sent to teach me the Language. We sat together four Hours, in which time I wrote down a great Number of Words in Columns, with the Translations over against them. I likewise made a Shift to learn several short Sentences. For my Tutor would order one of my Servants to fetch something, to turn about, to make a Bow, to sit, or stand, or walk, and the like. Then I took down the Sentence in writing. He showed me also in one of his Books, the Figures of the Sun, Moon, and Stars, the Zodiac, the Tropics, and Polar Circles, together with the Denominations of many Figures of Planes and Solids. He gave me the Names and Descriptions of all the Musical Instruments, and the general Terms of Art[12] in playing on each of them. After he had left me, I placed all my Words with their Interpretations in Alphabetical Order. And thus in a few Days, by the help of a very faithful Memory, I got some insight into their Language.

The Word, which I interpret the *Flying* or *Floating Island*, is in the Original, *Laputa*, whereof I could never learn the true Etymology.[13] *Lap* in the old obsolete Language signifieth <u>High</u>, and *Untuh* a *Governor*, from which they say by Corruption was derived *Laputa* from *Lapuntuh*. But I do not approve of this Derivation, which seems to be a little strained. I ventured to offer to the Learned among them a Conjecture of my own, that *Laputa* was *quasi Lap outed*; *Lap* signifying properly the dancing of the Sun Beams in the Sea, and *outed*, a Wing, which however I shall not obtrude, but submit to the Judicious Reader.

Those to whom the King had entrusted me, observing how ill I was clad, ordered a Tailor to come next Morning, and take my Measure for a Suit of Clothes. This Operator did his Office after a different manner from those of his Trade in *Europe*. He first took my Altitude by a Quadrant, and then with Rule and Compasses, described the Dimensions and Outlines of my whole Body, all which he entered upon Paper, and in Six Days brought my Clothes very ill made, and quite out of shape, by happening to mistake a Figure in the Calculation. But my Comfort was, that I observed such Accidents very frequent and little regarded.

During my Confinement for want of Clothes, and by an Indisposition that held me some Days longer, I much enlarged my Dictionary; and when I went next to Court, was able to understand many things the King spoke, and to return him some kind of Answers. His Majesty had given Orders that the Island should move North-East and by East, to the Vertical Point over *Lagado*,[14] the Metropolis of the whole Kingdom below upon the firm Earth. It was about Ninety Leagues distant, and our Voyage lasted four Days and an Half. I was not in the least sensible of the progressive Motion made in the Air by the Island. On the second Morning about Eleven o' Clock, the King himself in Person, attended by his Nobility, Courtiers, and Officers, having prepared all their Musical Instruments, played on them for three Hours without Intermission, so that I was quite stunned with the noise; Neither could I possibly guess the meaning till my Tutor informed me. He said that the People of their Island had their Ears adapted to hear the Music of the Spheres,[15] which always played at certain Periods, and the Court was now prepared to bear their Part in whatever Instrument they most excelled.

In our Journey towards *Lagado* the Capital City, his Majesty ordered that the Island should stop over certain Towns, and Villages, from whence he might receive the Petitions of his Subjects. And to this purpose several Packthreads were let down with small Weights at the bottom. On these Packthreads the People strung their Petitions, which mounted up directly like the scraps of Paper fastened by Schoolboys at the end of the String that holds their Kite. Sometimes we received Wine and Victuals from below, which were drawn up by Pullies.

The Knowledge I had in Mathematics gave me great Assistance in acquiring their Phraseology, which depended much upon that Science and Music; and in the latter I was not unskilled. Their Ideas are perpetually conversant in Lines and Figures. If they would, for Example, praise the Beauty of a Woman or any other Animal, they describe it by Rhombs, Circles, Parallelograms, Ellipses, and other Geometrical Terms, or by words of Art drawn from Music, needless here to repeat. I observed in the King's Kitchen all sorts of Mathematical and Musical Instruments, after the Figures of which they cut up the Joints[16] that were served to his Majesty's Table.

Their Houses are very ill built, the Walls Bevil,[17] without one Right Angle in any Apartment, and this defect ariseth from the Contempt they bear to practical Geometry; which they despise as Vulgar and Mechanic,[18] those Instructions they give being too refined for the Intellectuals[19] of their Workmen, which occasions perpetual mistakes. And although they are dextrous enough upon a Piece of Paper in the management of the Rule, the Pencil and the Divider,[20] yet in the common Actions and behaviour of Life, I have not seen a more clumsy, awkward, and unhandy People, nor so slow and perplexed in their Conceptions upon all other Subjects, except those of Mathematics and Music. They are very bad Reasoners, and vehemently given to Opposition, unless when they happen to be of the right Opinion, which is seldom their case. Imagination, Fancy, and Invention, they are wholly strangers to, nor have any Words in their Language by which those Ideas can be expressed; the whole compass of their Thoughts and Mind being shut up within the two forementioned Sciences.

Most of them, and especially those who deal in the Astronomical Part, have great Faith in Judicial Astrology,[21] although they are ashamed to own it publicly. But, what I chiefly admired, and thought altogether unaccountable, was the strong Disposition I observed in them towards News and Politics, perpetually inquiring into Public Affairs, giving their Judgments in matters of State; and passionately disputing every Inch of a Party Opinion. I have indeed observed the same Disposition among most of the Mathematicians I have known in *Europe*,[22] although I could never discover the least Analogy between the two Sciences; unless those People suppose, that because the smallest Circle hath as many Degrees as the largest, therefore the Regulation and Management of the World require no more Abilities than the handling and turning of a Globe. But, I rather take this Quality to spring from a very common Infirmity of Human Nature, inclining us to be more curious and conceited in Matters where we have least Concern, and for which we are least adapted either by Study or Nature.

These People are under continual Disquietudes, never enjoying a Minute's Peace of Mind; and their Disturbances proceed from Causes which very little affect the rest of Mortals. Their Apprehensions arise from several Changes they dread in the Celestial Bodies.[23] For Instance; that the Earth by the continual approaches of the Sun towards it, must in course of Time be absorbed or swallowed up. That the Face of the Sun will by Degrees be encrusted with its own Effluvia, and give no more Light to the World. That, the Earth very narrowly escaped a brush from the Tail of the last Comet, which would have infallibly reduced it to Ashes; and that the next, which they have calculated for one and Thirty Years hence, will probably destroy us. For, if in its Perihelion it should approach within a certain Degree of the Sun (as by their Calculations they have reason to dread), it will conceive a Degree of Heat ten Thousand times more intense than that of Red-hot glowing Iron; and in its Absence from the Sun, carry a Blazing Tail ten hundred Thousand and fourteen Miles long; through which if the Earth should pass at the distance of one Hundred Thousand Miles from the *Nucleus* or main Body of the Comet, it must in its Passage be set on Fire, and reduced to Ashes. That the Sun daily spending its Rays without any Nutriment to supply them, will at last be wholly consumed and annihilated; which must be attended with the Destruction of this Earth, and of all the Planets that receive their Light from it.

They are so perpetually alarmed with the Apprehensions of these and the like impending Dangers, that they can neither sleep quietly in their Beds, nor have any relish for the common Pleasures or Amusements of Life. When they meet an Acquaintance in the Morning, the first Question is about the Sun's Health, how he looked at his Setting and Rising, and what hopes they have to avoid the stroke of the approaching Comet. This Conversation they are apt to run into with the same Temper that Boys discover, in delighting to hear terrible stories of Spirits and

Hobgoblins, which they greedily listen to, and dare not go to Bed for fear.

The Women of the Island have abundance of Vivacity; they contemn their Husbands, and are exceedingly fond of Strangers, whereof there is always a considerable Number from the Continent below, attending at Court, either upon Affairs of the several Towns and Corporations, or their own particular Occasions, but are much despised, because they want the same Endowments. Among these the Ladies choose their Gallants: But the Vexation is, that they act with too much Ease and Security, for the Husband is always so rapt in Speculation, that the Mistress and Lover may proceed to the greatest Familiarities before his Face, if he be but provided with Paper and Implements, and without his *Flapper* at his side.

The Wives and Daughters lament their Confinement to the Island, although I think it the most delicious spot of Ground in the World; and although they live here in the greatest Plenty and Magnificence, and are allowed to do whatever they please, they long to see the World, and take the Diversions of the Metropolis, which they are not allowed to do without a particular Licence from the King; and this is not easy to be obtained, because the People of Quality have found by frequent Experience, how hard it is to persuade their Women to return from below. I was told that a great Court Lady, who had several Children, is married to the Prime Minister, the richest Subject in the Kingdom, a very graceful Person, extremely fond of her, and lives in the finest Palace of the Island, went down to *Lagado*, on the Pretense of Health, there hid herself for several Months, till the King sent a Warrant to search for her, and she was found in an obscure Eating House all in Rags, having pawned her Clothes to maintain an old deformed Footman, who beat her every Day, and in whose Company she was taken much against her Will. And although her Husband received her with all possible Kindness, and without the least Reproach, she soon after contrived to steal down again with all her Jewels, to the same Gallant, and hath not been heard of since.

This may perhaps pass with the Reader rather for an *European* or *English* Story, than for one of a Country so remote. But he may please to consider, that the Caprices of Womankind are not limited by any Climate or Nation, and that they are much more uniform than can be easily imagined.

In about a Month's time I had made a tolerable proficiency in their Language, and was able to answer most of the King's Questions, when I had the Honour to attend him. His Majesty discovered not the least Curiosity to inquire into the Laws, Government, History, Religion, or Manners of the Countries where I had been, but confined his Questions to the state of Mathematics, and received the Account I gave him, with great Contempt and Indifference, though often roused by his *Flapper* on each side.

CHAP. III

*A Phenomenon solved by modern Philosophy and Astronomy.
The* Laputians' *great Improvements in the Latter. The King's
Method of suppressing Insurrections.*

I desired leave of this Prince to see the Curiosities of the Island, which he was graciously pleased to grant, and ordered my Tutor to attend me. I chiefly wanted to know to what Cause in Art or in Nature, it owed its several Motions, whereof I will now give a Philosophical Account[24] to the Reader.

The Flying or Floating Island is exactly circular, its Diameter 7837 Yards, or about four Miles and an Half, and consequently contains ten Thousand Acres. It is three Hundred Yards thick. The bottom or under Surface, which appears to those who view it from below, is one even regular Plate of Adamant, shooting up to the Height of about two Hundred Yards. Above it lie the several Minerals in their usual order, and over all is a Coat of rich Mould ten or twelve Foot deep. The Declivity of the upper Surface, from the Circumference to the Centre, is the natural Cause why all the Dews and Rains which fall upon the Island, are conveyed in small Rivulets towards the middle, where they are emptied into four large Basins, each of about half a Mile in Circuit, and two Hundred Yards distant from the Centre. From these Basins the Water is continually exhaled by the Sun in the Daytime, which effectually prevents their overflowing. Besides, as it is in the Power of the Monarch to raise the Island above the Region of Clouds and Vapours, he can prevent the falling of Dews and Rains whenever he pleases. For the highest Clouds cannot rise above two Miles, as Naturalists agree, at least they were never known to do in that Country.

At the Centre of the Island there is a Chasm about fifty Yards in Diameter, from whence the Astronomers descend into a large Dome, which is therefore called *Flandona Gagnole*,[25] or the *Astronomer's Cave*, situated at the Depth of a Hundred Yards beneath the upper Surface of the Adamant. In this Cave are twenty Lamps continually burning, which from the Reflection of the Adamant cast a strong Light into every Part. The place is stored with great variety of Sextants, Quadrants, Telescopes, Astrolabs, and other Astronomical Instruments. But the greatest Curiosity, upon which the Fate of the Island depends, is a Loadstone of a prodigious size, in shape resembling a Weaver's Shuttle. It is in length six Yards, and in the thickest part at least three Yards over. This Magnet is sustained by a very strong Axle of Adamant passing through its middle, upon which it plays, and is poised so exactly that the weakest Hand can turn it. It is hooped round with an hollow Cylinder of Adamant, four Foot deep, as many thick, and twelve Yards in Diameter, placed Horizontally, and supported by eight Adamantine Feet, each six Yards high. In the middle of the Concave side there is a Groove twelve Inches deep, in which the Extremities of the Axle are lodged, and turned round as there is occasion.

The stone cannot be moved from its Place by any Force, because the Hoop and its Feet are one continued Piece with that Body of Adamant which constitutes the bottom of the Island.

By means of this Loadstone, the Island is made to rise and fall, and move from one place to another. For, with respect to that part of the Earth over which the Monarch presides, the Stone is endued at one of its sides with an attractive Power, and at the other with a repulsive. Upon placing the Magnet erect with its attracting End towards the Earth, the Island descends; but when the repelling Extremity points downwards, the Island mounts directly upwards. When the Position of the Stone is oblique, the Motion of the Island is so too. For in this Magnet the Forces always act in Lines parallel to its Direction.

By this oblique Motion the Island is conveyed to different Parts of the Monarch's Dominions. To explain the manner of its Progress, let *A B*

Plate IIII. Part.III.   Page.39.

PLATE 6

represent a Line drawn cross the Dominions of *Balnibarbi*, let the Line
c d represent the Loadstone, of which let *d* be the repelling end, and *c* the
attracting end, the Island being over *C*; let the Stone be placed in the
Position *c d* with its repelling end downwards; then the Island will be
driven upwards obliquely towards *D*. When it is arrived at *D*, let the
Stone be turned upon its Axle till its attracting end points towards *E*,
and then the Island will be carried obliquely towards *E*; where if the
Stone be again turned upon its Axle till it stands in the Position *E F*,
with its repelling Point downwards, the Island will rise obliquely towards
F, where by directing the attracting end towards *G*, the Island may be
carried to *G*, and from *G* to *H*, by turning the Stone, so as to make its
repelling Extremity point directly downwards. And thus by changing
the Situation of the Stone as often as there is occasion, the Island is made
to rise and fall by turns in an oblique Direction, and by those alternate
Risings and Fallings (the Obliquity being not considerable) is conveyed
from one part of the Dominions to the other.

But it must be observed, that this Island cannot move beyond the
extent of the Dominions below, nor can it rise above the height of four
Miles. For which the Astronomers (who have written large Systems
concerning the Stone) assign the following Reason: That the Magnetic
Virtue does not extend beyond the distance of four Miles, and that the
Mineral which acts upon the Stone in the Bowels of the Earth, and in
the Sea about six Leagues distant from the Shore, is not diffused through
the whole Globe, but terminated with the Limits of the King's Dominions;
and it was easy from the great Advantage of such a superior Situation,
for a Prince to bring under his Obedience whatever Country lay within
the Attraction of that Magnet.

When the Stone is put parallel to the Plane of the Horizon, the Island
standeth still; for in that Case, the Extremities of it being at equal
distance from the Earth, act with equal Force, the one in drawing
downwards, the other in pushing upwards, and consequently no Motion
can ensue.

This Loadstone is under the Care of certain Astronomers, who from
time to time give it such Positions as the Monarch directs. They spend
the greatest part of their Lives in observing the celestial Bodies, which
they do by the Assistance of Glasses[26] far excelling ours in Goodness.

For, although their largest Telescopes do not exceed three Feet, they magnify much more than those of an hundred Yards among us, and at the same time show the Stars with greater Clearness. This Advantage hath enabled them to extend their Discoveries much farther than our Astronomers in *Europe*; for they have made a Catalogue of ten thousand fixed Stars, whereas the largest of ours do not contain above one third Part of that Number. They have likewise discovered two lesser Stars, or *Satellites*, which revolve about *Mars*,[27] whereof the innermost is distant from the Centre of the primary Planet exactly three of his Diameters, and the outermost five; the former revolves in the space of ten Hours, and the latter in twenty-one and an half; so that the Squares of their Periodical Times are very near in the same Proportion with the Cubes of their distance from the Centre of *Mars*, which evidently shows them to be governed by the same Law of Gravitation,[28] that influences the other Heavenly Bodies.

They have observed ninety-three different Comets, and settled their Periods with great Exactness. If this be true (and they affirm it with great Confidence), it is much to be wished that their Observations were made public, whereby the Theory of Comets, which at present is very lame and defective, might be brought to the same Perfection with other parts of Astronomy.

The King would be the most absolute Prince in the Universe, if he could but prevail on a Ministry to join with him; but these having their Estates below on the Continent, and considering that the Office of a Favourite hath a very uncertain Tenure, would never consent to the enslaving their Country.

If any Town should engage in Rebellion or Mutiny, fall into violent Factions, or refuse to pay the usual Tribute, the King hath two Methods of reducing them to Obedience. The first and the mildest Course is by keeping the Island hovering over such a Town,[29] and the Lands about it, whereby he can deprive them of the Benefit of the Sun and the Rain, and consequently afflict the Inhabitants with Death and Diseases. And if the Crime deserve it, they are at the same time pelted from above with great Stones, against which they have no Defence but by creeping into Cellars or Caves, while the Roofs of their Houses are beaten to pieces. But if they still continue obstinate, or offer to raise Insurrections, he proceeds to the last Remedy, by letting the Island drop directly upon their Heads, which makes a universal Destruction both of Houses and Men. However, this is an Extremity to which the Prince is seldom driven, neither indeed is he willing to put it in Execution, nor dare his Ministers advise him to an Action, which as it would render them odious to the People, so it would be a great Damage to their own Estates, which lie all below, for the Island is the King's Demesne.

But there is still indeed a more weighty Reason, why the Kings of this Country have been always averse from executing so terrible an Action, unless upon the utmost Necessity. For if the Town intended to be destroyed should have in it any tall Rocks, as it generally falls out in the larger Cities, a Situation probably chosen at first with a View to prevent such a Catastrophe; or if it abound in high Spires or Pillars of Stone, a sudden Fall might endanger the Bottom or under Surface of the Island, which although it consist as I have said of one entire Adamant two hundred Yards thick, might happen to crack by too great a Shock, or burst by approaching too near the Fires from the Houses below, as the Backs both of Iron and Stone will often do in our Chimneys. Of all this the People are well apprised, and understand how far to carry their Obstinacy, where their Liberty or Property is concerned. And the King, when he is highest provoked, and most determined to press a City to Rubbish, orders the Island to descend with great gentleness, out of a Pretence of Tenderness to his People, but indeed for fear of breaking the Adamantine Bottom; in which Case it is the Opinion of all their Philosophers, that the Loadstone could no longer hold it up, and the whole Mass would fall to the Ground.

About three years before my Arrival[30] among them, while the King was in his Progress over his Dominions, there happened an extraordinary Accident which had like to have put a Period to the Fate of that Monarchy, at least as it is now instituted. Lindalino[31] the second City in the Kingdom was the first his Majesty visited in his Progress. Three Days after his Departure, the Inhabitants who had often complained of great Oppressions, shut the Town Gates, seized on the Governor, and with incredible Speed and Labour erected four large Towers one at every Corner of the City (which is an exact Square) equal in Height to a strong pointed Rock that stands directly in the Centre of the City. Upon the

Top of each Tower, as well as upon the Rock, they fixed a great Loadstone, and in case their Design should fail, they had provided a vast Quantity of the most combustible Fuel, hoping to burst therewith the adamantine Bottom of the Island, if the Loadstone Project should miscarry.

It was eight Months before the King had perfect Notice that the Lindalinians were in Rebellion. He then commanded that the Island should be wafted over the City. The People were unanimous, and had laid in Store of Provisions, and a great River runs through the middle of the Town. The King hovered over them several Days to deprive them of the Sun and the Rain. He ordered many Packthreads to be let down, yet not a Person offered to send up a Petition, but instead thereof, very bold Demands, the Redress of all their Grievances, great Immunities,[32] the Choice of their own Governor, and other the like Exorbitances. Upon which his Majesty commanded all the Inhabitants of the Island to cast great Stones from the lower Gallery into the Town; but the Citizens had provided against this Mischief by conveying their Persons and Effects into the four Towers, and other strong Buildings, and Vaults under Ground.

The King being now determined to reduce this proud People, ordered that the Island should descend gently within forty Yards of the Top of the Towers and Rock. This was accordingly done; but the Officers employed in that Work found the Descent much speedier than usual, and by turning the Loadstone could not without great Difficulty keep it in a firm Position, but found the Island inclining to fall. They sent the King immediate Intelligence of this astonishing Event, and begged his Majesty's Permission to raise the Island higher; the King consented, a general Council was called, and the Officers of the Loadstone ordered to attend. One of the oldest and expertest among them obtained Leave to try an Experiment. He took a strong Line of an hundred Yards, and the Island being raised over the Town above the attracting Power they had felt, he fastened a Piece of Adamant to the End of his Line which had in it a Mixture of Iron mineral, of the same Nature with that whereof the Bottom or lower Surface of the Island is composed, and from the lower Gallery let it down slowly towards the Top of the Towers. The Adamant was not descended four Yards, before the Officer felt it drawn so strongly downwards, that he could hardly pull it back. He then threw down several small Pieces of Adamant, and observed that they were all violently attracted by the Top of the Tower. The same Experiment was made on the other three Towers, and on the Rock with the same Effect.

This Incident broke entirely the King's Measures and (to dwell no longer on other Circumstances) he was forced to give the Town their own Conditions.

I was assured by a great Minister, that if the Island had descended so near the Town, as not to be able to raise itself, the Citizens were determined to fix it for ever, to kill the King and all his Servants, and entirely change the Government.

By a fundamental Law of this Realm, neither the King nor either of his two elder Sons are permitted to leave the Island, nor the Queen till she is past Child-bearing.[33]

CHAP. IV

The Author leaves Laputa, *is conveyed to* Balnibarbi, *arrives at the Metropolis. A Description of the Metropolis and the Country adjoining. The Author hospitably received by a great Lord. His Conversation with that Lord.*

Although I cannot say that I was ill treated in this Island, yet I must confess I thought myself too much neglected, not without some degree of Contempt. For neither Prince nor People appeared to be curious in any part of Knowledge, except Mathematics and Music, wherein I was far their inferior, and upon that account very little regarded.

On the other side, after having seen all the Curiosities of the Island, I was very desirous to leave it, being heartily weary of those People. They were indeed excellent in two Sciences for which I have great Esteem, and wherein I am not unversed, but at the same time so abstracted and involved in Speculation that I never met with such disagreeable Companions. I conversed only with Women, Tradesmen, *Flappers*, and Court-Pages during two Months of my Abode here, by which at last I rendered myself extremely contemptible, yet these were the only People from whom I could ever receive a reasonable Answer.

I had obtained by hard Study a good degree of Knowledge in their Language; I was weary of being confined to an Island where I received so little Countenance,[34] and resolved to leave it with the first Opportunity.

There was a great Lord at Court, nearly related to the King, and for that reason alone used with Respect. He was universally reckoned the most Ignorant and stupid Person among them. He had performed many eminent Services for the Crown, had great natural and acquired Parts, adorned with Integrity and Honour, but so ill an Ear for Music, that his Detractors reported he had been often known to beat Time in the wrong Place; neither could his Tutors without extreme difficulty teach him to demonstrate the most easy Proposition in the Mathematics. He was pleased to show me many Marks of Favour, often did me the Honour of a Visit, desired to be informed in the Affairs of *Europe*, the Laws and Customs, the Manners and Learning of the several Countries where I had travelled. He listened to me with great Attention, and made very wise Observations on all I spoke. He had two *Flappers* attending him for State, but never made use of them except at Court, and in Visits of Ceremony, and would always command them to withdraw when we were alone together.

I entreated this Illustrious Person to intercede in my behalf with his Majesty for leave to depart, which he accordingly did, as he was pleased to tell me, with Regret: For, indeed he had made me several Offers very Advantageous, which however I refused with Expressions of the highest Acknowledgement.

On the 16th Day of *February*, I took leave of His Majesty and the Court. The King made me a Present to the value of about two Hundred Pounds *English*, and my Protector his Kinsman as much more, together with a Letter of Recommendation to a Friend of his in *Lagado*, the Metropolis; The Island being then hovering over a Mountain about two Miles from it, I was let down from the lowest Gallery, in the same manner as I had been taken up.

The Continent, as far as it is subject to the Monarch of the *Flying Island*, passes under the general Name of *Balnibarbi*, and the Metropolis, as I said before, is called *Lagado*. I felt some little Satisfaction in finding myself on firm Ground. I walked to the City without any concern, being clad like one of the Natives, and sufficiently instructed to converse with them. I soon found out the Person's House to whom I was recommended, presented my Letter from his Friend the Grandee in the Island, and was received with much Kindness. This great Lord, whose name was *Munodi*, ordered me an Apartment in his own House, where I continued during my stay, and was entertained in a most hospitable Manner.

The next Morning after my Arrival he took me in his Chariot to see the Town, which is about half the bigness of *London*, but the Houses very strangely Built, and most of them out of Repair. The People in the Streets walked fast, looked wild, their Eyes fixed, and were generally in Rags. We passed through one of the Town-Gates, and went about three Miles into the Country, where I saw many Labourers working with several sorts of Tools in the Ground, but was not able to conjecture what they were about, neither did I observe any expectation either of Corn or Grass, although the Soil appeared to be excellent. I could not forbear admiring at these odd Appearances both in Town and Country, and I made bold to desire my Conductor, that he would be pleased to explain to me what could be meant by so many busy Heads, Hands and Faces, both in the Streets and the Fields, because I did not discover any good Effects they produced; but on the contrary, I never knew a Soil so unhappily cultivated, Houses so ill contrived and so ruinous, or a People whose Countenances and Habit expressed so much Misery and Want.

This Lord *Munodi* was a Person of the first Rank, and had been some Years Governor of *Lagado*, but by a Cabal of Ministers was discharged for Insufficiency.[35] However the King treated him with Tenderness, as a well-meaning Man, but of a low contemptible Understanding.

When I gave that free Censure of the Country and its Inhabitants, he made no further Answer than by telling me, that I had not been long enough among them to form a Judgment; and that the different Nations of the World had different Customs, with other common Topics to the same Purpose. But when we returned to his Palace, he asked me how I liked the Building, what Absurdities I observed, and what Quarrel I had with the Dress and Looks of his Domestics. This he might safely do, because everything about him was Magnificent, Regular and Polite. I answered, that his Excellency's Prudence, Quality, and Fortune, had exempted him from those defects which Folly and Beggary had produced in others. He said if I would go with him to his Country House about twenty Miles distant, where his Estate lay, there would be more leisure for this kind of Conversation. I told his Excellency that I was entirely at his Disposal, and accordingly we set out next Morning.

During our Journey, he made me observe the several Methods used by Farmers in managing their Lands, which to me were wholly unaccountable, for except in some very few Places, I could not discover one Ear of Corn or Blade of Grass. But, in three Hours travelling, the Scene was wholly altered; we came into a most beautiful Country; Farmers' Houses at small distances, neatly built, the Fields enclosed, containing Vineyards, Corn-grounds and Meadows. Neither do I remember to have seen a more delightful Prospect. His Excellency observed my Countenance to clear up; he told me with a Sigh, that there his Estate began, and would continue the same till we should come to his House. That his Countrymen ridiculed and despised Him for managing his Affairs no better, and for setting so ill an Example to the Kingdom, which however was followed by very few, such as were old and wilful, and weak like himself.

We came at length to the House, which was indeed a noble Structure, built according to the best Rules of Ancient Architecture. The Fountains, Gardens, Walks, Avenues, and Groves were all disposed with exact Judgment and Taste. I gave due Praises to everything I saw, whereof his Excellency took not the least Notice till after Supper, when, there being no third Companion, he told me with a very melancholy Air, that he doubted he must throw down his Houses in Town and Country, to rebuild them after the present Mode, destroy all his Plantations,[36] and cast others in such a Form as modern Usage required, and give the same Directions to all his Tenants, unless he would submit to incur the Censure of Pride, Singularity, Affectation, Ignorance, Caprice, and perhaps increase His Majesty's Displeasure.

That the Admiration I appeared to be under, would cease or diminish when he had informed me of some Particulars, which probably I never heard of at Court, the People there being too much taken up in their own Speculations, to have regard to what passed here below.

The Sum of his Discourse was to this Effect. That about Forty Years ago, certain Persons went up to *Laputa* either upon Business or Diversion, and after five Months continuance came back with a very little smattering in Mathematics, but full of Volatile Spirits acquired in that Airy Region.

That these Persons upon their Return began to dislike the Management of everything below, and fell into Schemes of putting all Arts, Sciences, Languages, and Mechanics upon a new Foot. To this End they procured a Royal Patent for erecting an Academy of PROJECTORS[37] in *Lagado*; And the Humour prevailed so strongly among the People, that there is not a Town of any Consequence in the Kingdom without such an Academy. In these Colleges, the Professors contrive new Rules and Methods of Agriculture and Building, and new Instruments and Tools for all Trades and Manufactures, whereby, as they undertake, one Man shall do the Work of ten; a Palace may be built in a Week, of Materials so durable as to last for ever without repairing. All the Fruits of the Earth shall come to Maturity at whatever Season we think fit to choose, and increase an Hundred Fold more than they do at present, with innumerable other happy Proposals. The only Inconvenience is, that none of these Projects are yet brought to Perfection, and in the mean time the whole Country lies miserably waste, the Houses in Ruins, and the People without Food or Clothes. By all which, instead of being discouraged, they are fifty times more violently bent upon prosecuting their Schemes, driven equally on by Hope and Despair; That as for himself, being not of an Enterprising Spirit, he was content to go on in the old Forms, to live in the Houses his Ancestors had built, and Act as they did in every part of Life without Innovation. That, some few other Persons of Quality and Gentry had done the same, but were looked on with an Eye of Contempt and Ill Will, as Enemies to Art, ignorant, and ill Commonwealths-men,[38] preferring their own Ease and Sloth before the general Improvement of their Country.

His Lordship added, that he would not by any further Particulars prevent[39] the Pleasure I should certainly take in viewing the Grand Academy, whither he was resolved I should go. He only desired me to observe a ruined Building upon the side of a Mountain about three Miles distant, of which he gave me this Account. That he had a very convenient Mill within half a Mile of his House, turned by a Current from a large River, and sufficient for his own Family as well as a great number of his Tenants. That, about seven Years ago, a Club of those Projectors came to him with Proposals to destroy this Mill, and build another on the side of that Mountain, on the long Ridge whereof a long Canal must be cut for a Repository of Water, to be conveyed up by Pipes and Engines to supply the Mill: Because the Wind and Air upon a Height agitated the Water, and thereby made it fitter for Motion: And because the Water descending down a Declivity would turn the Mill with half the Current of a River whose Course is more upon a Level. He said, that being then not very well with the Court, and pressed by many of his Friends, he complied with the Proposal; and after employing an Hundred Men for two Years, the Work miscarried, the Projectors went off, laying the blame entirely upon him, railing at him ever since, and putting others upon the same Experiment, with equal Assurance of Success, as well as equal Disappointment.

In a few Days we came back to Town, and His Excellency, considering the bad Character he had in the Academy, would not go with me himself, but recommended me to a Friend of his to bear me Company thither. My Lord was pleased to represent me as a great Admirer of Projects, and a Person of much Curiosity and easy Belief, which indeed was not without Truth, for I had myself been a sort of Projector in my younger Days.

CHAP. V

The Author permitted to see the grand Academy of Lagado. *The Academy largely*[40] *described. The Arts wherein the Professors employ themselves.*

This Academy is not an entire single Building, but a Continuation of several Houses on both sides of a Street, which growing waste[41] was purchased and applied to that Use.

I was received very kindly by the Warden, and went for many Days to the Academy. Every Room hath in it one or more Projectors, and I believe I could not be in fewer than five Hundred Rooms.

The first Man I saw was of a meagre Aspect, with sooty Hands and Face, his Hair and Beard long, ragged and singed in several places. His Clothes, Shirt, and Skin were all of the same Colour. He had been eight Years upon a Project for extracting Sunbeams out of Cucumbers, which were to be put into Vials hermetically Sealed, and let out to warm the Air in raw inclement Summers. He told me, he did not doubt in eight Years more, he should be able to supply the Governor's Gardens with Sunshine at a reasonable Rate; but he complained that his Stock was low, and entreated me to give him something as an Encouragement to Ingenuity,[42] especially since this had been a very dear Season for Cucumbers. I made him a small Present, for my Lord had furnished me with Money on purpose, because he knew their Practice of begging from all who go to see them.

I went into another Chamber, but was ready to hasten back, being almost overcome with a horrible stink. My Conductor pressed me forward, conjuring me in a Whisper to give no offence, which would be highly resented, and therefore I durst not so much as stop my Nose. The Projector of this Cell was the most Ancient Student of the Academy. His Face and Beard were of a pale Yellow; His Hands and Clothes daubed over with Filth. When I was presented to him, he gave me a very close Embrace (a Compliment I could well have excused). His Employment from his first coming into the Academy was an Operation to reduce human Excrement to its original Food, by separating the several Parts, removing the Tincture which it receives from the Gall, making the Odour exhale, and scumming off the Saliva. He had a weekly Allowance from the Society of a Vessel filled with Human Ordure, about the bigness of a *Bristol* Barrel.

I saw another at work to calcine[43] Ice into Gun Powder, who likewise showed me a Treatise he had written concerning the Malleability of Fire, which he intended to publish.

There was a most ingenious Architect who had contrived a new Method for building Houses, by beginning at the Roof and working downwards to the Foundation, which he justified to me by the like Practice of those two prudent Insects the Bee and the Spider.

There was a Man born blind, who had several Apprentices in his own Condition: Their Employment was to mix Colours for Painters, which their Master taught them to distinguish by feeling and smelling. It was indeed my Misfortune to find them at that time not very perfect in their Lessons, and the Professor himself happened to be generally mistaken: This Artist is much encouraged and esteemed by the whole Fraternity.

In another Apartment I was highly pleased with a Projector, who had found a Device of Plowing the Ground with Hogs, to save the Charges of Plows, Cattle, and Labour. The Method is this: In an Acre of Ground you bury at six Inches distance, and eight deep, a quantity of Acorns, Dates, Chesnuts, and other Mast or Vegetables whereof these Animals are fondest: then you drive six hundred or more of them into the Field, where in a few Days they will root up the whole Ground in search of their Food, and make it fit for Sowing, at the same time manuring it with their Dung; it is true upon Experiment they found the Charge and Trouble very great, and they had little or no Crop. However, it is not doubted that this Invention may be capable of great Improvement.

I went into another Room, where the Walls and Ceiling were all hung round with Cobwebs, except a narrow Passage for the Artist to go in and out. At my Entrance he called aloud to me not to disturb his Webs. He lamented the fatal Mistake the World had been so long in of using Silkworms, while we had such plenty of Domestic Insects, who infinitely excelled the former, because they understood how to weave as well as spin. And he proposed farther, that by employing Spiders, the Charge of dying Silks should be wholly saved, whereof I was fully convinced when he showed me a vast number of Flies most beautifully coloured, wherewith he fed his Spiders, assuring us, that the Webs would take a Tincture from them; and as he had them of all Hues, he hoped to fit everybody's Fancy, as soon as he could find proper Food for the Flies of certain Gums, Oils, and other glutinous Matter to give a Strength and Consistence to the Threads.

There was an Astronomer who had undertaken to place a Sun Dial upon the great Weathercock on the Townhouse,[44] by adjusting the annual and diurnal Motions of the Earth and Sun, so as to answer and coincide with all accidental Turnings by the Wind.

I was complaining of a small Fit of the Colic, upon which my Conductor led me into a Room, where a great Physician resided, who was famous for curing that Disease by contrary Operations from the same Instrument. He had a large pair of Bellows with a long slender Muzzle of Ivory. This he conveyed eight Inches up the Anus, and drawing in the Wind, he affirmed he could make the Guts as lank as a dried Bladder. But when the Disease was more stubborn and violent, he let in the Muzzle while

the Bellows were full of Wind, which he discharged into the Body of the
Patient, then withdrew the Instrument to replenish it, clapping his
Thumb strongly against the Orifice of the Fundament; and this being
repeated three or four times, the adventitious Wind would rush out,
bringing the noxious along with it (like Water put into a Pump) and the
Patient recover. I saw him try both Experiments upon a Dog, but could
not discern any Effect from the former. After the latter, the Animal was
ready to burst, and made so violent a Discharge, as was very offensive to
me and my Companions. The Dog died on the Spot, and we left the
Doctor endeavouring to recover him by the same Operation.

I visited many other Apartments, but shall not trouble my Reader
with all the Curiosities I observed, being studious of Brevity.

I had hitherto seen only one side of the Academy, the other being
appropriated to the Advancers of speculative Learning, of whom I shall
say something when I have mentioned one illustrious Person more, who
is called among them *the universal Artist*. He told us he had been thirty
Years employing his Thoughts for the Improvement of human Life. He
had two large Rooms full of wonderful Curiosities, and fifty Men at work.
Some were condensing Air into a dry tangible Substance, by extracting
the Nitre, and letting the Aqueous or fluid Particles percolate; others
softening Marble for Pillows and Pincushions; others petrifying the Hoofs
of a living Horse to preserve them from foundering.[45] The Artist himself
was at that time busy upon two great Designs; the first to sow Land with
Chaff, wherein he affirmed the true seminal Virtue[46] to be contained, as
he demonstrated by several Experiments which I was not skilful enough
to comprehend. The other was, by a certain Composition of Gums,
Minerals, and Vegetables outwardly applied, to prevent the Growth of
Wool upon two young Lambs; and he hoped in a reasonable time to
propagate the Breed of naked Sheep all over the Kingdom.

We crossed a Walk to the other part of the Academy, where, as I have
already said, the Projector in speculative Learning resided.

The first Professor I saw was in a very large Room, with forty Pupils
about him. After Salutation, observing me to look earnestly upon a
Frame, which took up the greatest part of both the Length and Breadth
of the Room, he said perhaps I might wonder to see him employed in a
Project for improving speculative Knowledge by practical and mechanical

Operations. But the World would soon be sensible of its Usefulness, and he flattered himself that a more noble exalted Thought never sprung in any other Man's Head. Everyone knew how laborious the usual Method is of attaining to Arts and Sciences; whereas by his Contrivance, the most ignorant Person at a reasonable Charge, and with a little bodily Labour, may write Books in Philosophy, Poetry, Politics, Law, Mathematics and Theology, without the least Assistance from Genius or Study. He then led me to the Frame, about the sides whereof all his Pupils stood in Ranks. It was twenty Foot Square, placed in the middle of the Room. The Superficies was composed of several bits of Wood, about the bigness of a Die, but some larger than others. They were all linked together by slender Wires. These bits of Wood were covered on every Square with Paper pasted on them, and on these Papers were written all the Words of their Language in their several Moods, Tenses, and Declensions, but without any Order. The Professor then desired me to observe, for he was going to set his Engine at Work. The Pupils at his Command took each of them hold of an Iron Handle, whereof there were forty fixed round the Edges of the Frame, and giving them a sudden turn, the whole Disposition of the Words was entirely changed. He then commanded six and thirty of the Lads to read the several Lines softly as they appeared upon the Frame; and where they found three or four Words together that might make part of a Sentence, they dictated to the four remaining Boys who were Scribes. This Work was repeated three or four times, and at every turn the Engine was so contrived, that the Words shifted into new places, as the square bits of Wood moved upside down.

Six Hours a day the young Students were employed in this Labour, and the Professor showed me several Volumes in large Folio already collected, of broken Sentences, which he intended to piece together, and out of those rich Materials to give the World a complete Body of all Arts and Sciences; which however might be still improved, and much expedited, if the Public would raise a Fund for making and employing five hundred such Frames in *Lagado*, and oblige the Managers to contribute in common their several Collections.

He assured me, that this Invention had employed all his Thoughts from his Youth, that he had emptied the whole Vocabulary into his Frame, and made the strictest Computation of the general Proportion there is in the Book between the Numbers of Particles, Nouns, and Verbs, and other Parts of Speech.

I made my humblest Acknowledgement to this illustrious Person for his great Communicativeness, and promised if ever I had the good Fortune to return to my Native Country, that I would do him Justice, as the sole Inventer of this wonderful Machine; the Form and Contrivance of which I desired leave to delineate upon Paper as in the Figure here annexed. I told him, although it were the Custom of our Learned in *Europe* to steal Inventions from each other, who had thereby at least this advantage, that it became a Controversy which was the right Owner, yet I would take such Caution, that he should have the Honour entire without a Rival.[47]

We next went to the School of Language, where three Professors sat in Consultation upon improving that of their own Country.[48]

The first Project was to shorten Discourse by cutting Polysyllables into one, and leaving out Verbs and Participles, because in reality all things imaginable are but Nouns.

The other Project was a Scheme for entirely abolishing all Words whatsoever; and this was urged as a great Advantage in point of Health as well as Brevity. For, it is plain, that every Word we speak is in some Degree a Diminution of our Lungs by Corrosion, and consequently contributes to the shortening of our Lives. An Expedient was therefore offered, that since Words are only Names for *Things*,[49] it would be more convenient for all Men to carry about them, such *Things* as were necessary to express the particular Business they are to discourse on. And this Invention would certainly have taken Place, to the great Ease as well as Health of the Subject, if the Women in conjunction with the Vulgar and Illiterate had not threatened to raise a Rebellion, unless they might be allowed the Liberty to speak with their Tongues, after the manner of their Ancestors; Such constant irreconcileable Enemies to Science are the Common People. However, many of the most Learned and Wise adhere to the New Scheme of expressing themselves by *Things*, which hath only this Inconvenience attending it, that if a Man's Business be very great, and of various kinds, he must be obliged in Proportion to carry a greater Bundle of *Things* upon his Back, unless he can afford one or two strong Servants to attend him. I have often beheld two of those Sages almost sinking under the Weight of their Packs, like Peddlers among us; who when

Plate.V.Part.III.

PLATE 7

they met in the Streets would lay down their Loads, open their Sacks and hold Conversation for an Hour together; then put up their Implements, help each other to resume their Burthens, and take their Leave.

But for short Conversations a Man may carry Implements in his Pockets and under his Arms, enough to supply him, and in his House he cannot be at a loss; Therefore the Room where Company meet who practise this Art, is full of all *Things* ready at Hand, requisite to furnish Matter for this kind of Artificial[50] Converse.

Another great Advantage proposed by this Invention, was that it would serve as an Universal Language[51] to be understood in all civilized Nations, whose Goods and Utensils are generally of the same kind, or nearly resembling, so that their Uses might easily be comprehended. And thus Ambassadors would be qualified to treat with foreign Princes or Ministers of State to whose Tongues they were utter Strangers.

I was at the Mathematical School, where the Master taught his Pupils after a Method scarce imaginable to us in *Europe*. The Proposition and Demonstration were fairly written on a thin Wafer, with Ink composed of a Cephalic Tincture.[52] This the Student was to swallow upon a fasting Stomach, and for three Days following eat nothing but Bread and Water. As the Wafer digested, the Tincture mounted to his Brain, bearing the Proposition along with it. But the Success hath not hitherto been answerable, partly by some Error in the *Quantum*[53] or Composition, and partly by the Perverseness of Lads, to whom this Bolus is so nauseous that they generally steal aside, and discharge it upwards before it can operate, neither have they been yet persuaded to use so long an Abstinence as the Prescription requires.

CHAP. VI

A further Account of the Academy. The Author proposes some
improvements, which are honourably received.

In the School of Political Projectors I was but ill entertained, the Professors appearing in my Judgment wholly out of their Senses, which is a Scene that never fails to make me melancholy. These unhappy People were proposing Schemes for persuading Monarchs to choose Favourites[54] upon the Score of their Wisdom, Capacity and Virtue; of teaching Ministers to consult the Public Good; of rewarding Merit, great Abilities and eminent Services; of instructing Princes to know their true Interest by placing it on the same Foundation with that of their People: Of choosing for Employments Persons qualified to exercise them; with many other wild impossible Chimeras,[55] that never entered before into the heart of Man to conceive, and confirmed in me the old Observation, that there is nothing so extravagant and irrational which some Philosophers have not maintained for Truth.

But, however I shall so far do Justice to this Part of the Academy, as to acknowledge that all of them were not so visionary. There was a most Ingenious Doctor who seemed to be perfectly versed in the whole Nature and System of Government. This illustrious Person had very usefully employed his Studies in finding out effectual Remedies for all Diseases and Corruptions, to which the several kinds of public Administration are subject by the Vices or Infirmities of those who govern, as well as by the Licentiousness of those who are to obey. For instance; Whereas all Writers and Reasoners have agreed, that there is a strict universal Resemblance between the Natural and the Political Body; can there be anything more evident, than that the health of both must be preserved, and the Diseases cured by the same Prescriptions? It is allowed, that Senates and great Councils are often troubled with redundant, ebullient, and other peccant Humours,[56] with many Diseases of the Head, and more of the Heart; with strong Convulsions, with grievous Contractions of the Nerves and Sinews in both Hands, but especially the Right: With Spleen, Flatus,[57] Vertigoes and Deliriums; with Scrofulous[58] Tumours full of fetid purulent Matter; with sour frothy Ructations,[59] with Canine Appetites[60] and crudeness of Digestion, besides many others needless to mention. This Doctor therefore proposed, that upon the meeting of a Senate, certain Physicians should attend at the three first Days of their sitting, and at the Close of each day's Debate, feel the Pulses of every Senator; after which having maturely considered, and consulted upon the Nature of the several Maladies, and the methods of Cure, they should on the fourth Day return to the Senate House, attended by their

Apothecaries stored with proper Medicines, and before the Members sat, administer to each of them Lenitives, Aperitives, Abstersives, Corrosives, Restringents, Palliatives, Laxatives, Cephalalgicks, Ictericks, Apophleg-maticks, Acousticks,[61] as their several cases required, and according as these Medicines should operate, repeat, alter, or omit them at the next Meeting.

This Project could not be of any great Expense to the Public, and would in my poor opinion, be of much Use for the dispatch of Business in those Countries where Senates have any share in the Legislative Power, beget Unanimity, shorten Debates, open a few Mouths which are now closed, and close many more which are now open; curb the Petulancy of the Young, and correct the Positiveness of the Old; rouse the Stupid, and damp the Pert.

Again, Because it is a general Complaint that the Favourites of Princes are troubled with short and weak Memories; the same Doctor proposed, that whoever attended a First Minister, after having told his business with the utmost Brevity, and in the plainest Words; should at his Departure give the said Minister a Tweak by the Nose, or a kick in the Belly, or tread on his Corns, or lug him thrice by both Ears, or run a Pin into his Breech, or pinch his Arm black and blue, to prevent Forgetfulness: and at every Levee Day repeat the same Operation, till the Business were done or absolutely refused.

He likewise directed, that every Senator in the great Council of a Nation, after he had delivered his Opinion, and argued in the Defence of it, should be obliged to give his Vote directly contrary; because if that were done, the Result would infallibly terminate in the Good of the Public.

When Parties in a State are violent, he offered a wonderful Contrivance to reconcile them. The Method is this. You take an Hundred Leaders of each Party, you dispose them into Couples of such whose Heads are nearest of a size; then let two nice Operators saw off the *Occiput*[62] of each Couple at the same time, in such a manner that the Brain may be equally divided. Let the *Occiputs* thus cut off be interchanged, applying each to the head of his opposite Party-man. It seems indeed to be a Work that requireth some exactness, but the Professor assured us, that if it were dextrously performed, the Cure would be infallible. For he argued thus;

that the two half Brains being left to debate the Matter between themselves within the space of one Skull, would soon come to a good Understanding, and produce that Moderation as well as Regularity of thinking, so much to be wished for in the Heads of those, who imagine they come into the World only to watch and govern its Motion; And as to the difference of Brains in Quantity or Quality, among those who are Directors in Faction; the Doctor assured us from his own knowledge, that it was a perfect Trifle.

I heard a very warm Debate between two Professors, about the most commodious and effectual ways and means of raising Money without grieving the Subject. The first affirmed the justest Method would be to lay a certain Tax upon Vices and Folly, and the Sum fixed upon every Man, to be rated after the fairest manner by a Jury of his Neighbours. The second was of an Opinion directly contrary, to tax those Qualities of Body and Mind for which Men chiefly value themselves, the Rate to be more or less according to the Degrees of excelling, the Decision whereof should be left entirely to their own Breast. The highest Tax was upon Men, who are the greatest Favourites of the other Sex, and the Assessments according to the Number and Natures of the Favours they have received; for which they are allowed to be their own Vouchers. Wit, Valour, and Politeness were likewise proposed to be largely Taxed, and collected in the same manner, by every Person giving his own Word for the Quantum of what he possessed. But as to Honour, Justice, Wisdom, and Learning, they should not be taxed at all, because they are Qualifications of so singular a kind, that no Man will either allow them in his Neighbour, or value them in himself.

The Women were proposed to be taxed according to their Beauty and skill in Dressing, wherein they had the same Privilege with the Men, to be determined by their own Judgment. But Constancy, Chastity, good Sense, and good Nature were not rated, because they would not bear the Charge of Collecting.

To keep Senators in the Interest of the Crown, it was proposed that the Members should raffle for Employments, every Man first taking an Oath, and giving Security that he would Vote for the Court, whether he won or no, after which the Losers had in their Turn the liberty of Raffling upon the next Vacancy. Thus Hope and Expectation would be kept alive;

none would complain of broken Promises, but impute their Disappointments wholly to Fortune, whose Shoulders are broader and stronger than those of a Ministry.

Another Professor showed me a large Paper of Instructions for discovering Plots and Conspiracies against the Government. He advised great Statesmen to examine into the Diet of all suspected Persons; their times of eating; upon which side they lay in Bed; with which Hand they wiped their Posteriors; To take a strict View of their Excrements,[63] and from the Colour, the Odour, the Taste, the Consistence, the Crudeness, or Maturity of Digestion, form a Judgment of their Thoughts and Designs. Because Men are never so Serious, Thoughtful, and Intent, as when they are at Stool, which he found by frequent Experiment: For in such Conjunctures, when he used merely as a Trial, to consider which was the best way of murdering the King, his Ordure would have a Tincture of Green, but quite different when he thought only of raising an Insurrection or burning the Metropolis.

The whole Discourse was written with great Acuteness, containing many Observations both curious and useful for Politicians, but as I conceived not altogether complete. This I ventured to tell the Author, and offered if he pleased to supply him with some Additions. He received my Proposition with more Compliance than is usual among Writers, especially those of the projecting Species, professing he would be glad to receive farther Information.

I told him[64] that in the Kingdom of *Tribnia*,[65] by the Natives called *Langden*, where I had sojourned some time in my Travels, the Bulk of the People consist wholly of Discoverers, Witnesses, Informers, Accusers, Prosecutors, Evidences, Swearers, together with their several Subservient and Subaltern Instruments, all under Colours and Conduct of Ministers of State and their Deputies. The Plots in that Kingdom are usually the Workmanship of those Persons who desire to raise their own Characters of profound Politicians, to restore new Vigour to a crazy Administration, to stifle or divert general Discontents, to fill their Pockets with Forfeitures and raise or sink the Opinion of public Credit,[66] as either shall best answer their private Advantage. It is first agreed and settled among them what suspected Persons shall be accused of a Plot: then effectual Care is taken to secure all their Letters and Papers and put the Criminals in

Chains. These Papers are delivered to a set of Artists very dextrous in finding out the mysterious Meanings of Words, Syllables, and Letters. For Instance, they can discover a Close Stool to signify a Privy Council, a Flock of Geese a Senate, a lame Dog an Invader,[67] a Codshead a ———[king], the Plague a standing Army, a Buzzard a Prime Minister, the Gout a High Priest, a Gibbet a Secretary of State, a Chamber-pot a Committee of Grandees, a Sieve a Court Lady, a Broom a Revolution, a Mouse-Trap an Employment,[68] a Bottomless pit the Treasury, a sink the Court,[69] a Cap & Bells a Favourite, a broken Reed a Court of Justice, an empty Tun a General, a running Sore the Administration.

Where this Method fails, they have two others more effectual, which the Learned among them call Acrostics and Anagrams. First they can decipher all initial Letters into political Meanings. Thus *N* shall signify a Plot, *B* a Regiment of Horse, *L* a Fleet at Sea. Or secondly, by transposing the Letters of the Alphabet in any suspected Paper, they can discover the deepest Designs of a discontented Party. So for example, if I should say in a Letter to a Friend, *Our Brother* Tom *has just got the Piles*, a skilful Decipherer would discover that the same Letters which compose that Sentence, may be analysed into the following Words; *Resist, a Plot is brought Home, The Tour*.[70] And this is the Anagrammatic Method.

The Professor made me great Acknowledgements for communicating these Observations, and promised to make honourable mention of me in his Treatise.

I saw nothing in this Country that could invite me to a longer Continuance, and began to think of returning home to *England*.

CHAP. VII

The Author leaves Lagado, *arrives at* Maldonada.[71] *No Ship
ready. He takes a short Voyage to* Glubbdubdrib.[72] *His
Reception by the Governor.*

The Continent of which this Kingdom is a part, extends itself, as I have reason to believe, Eastward to that unknown Tract of *America*,

Westward of *California*, and North to the Pacific Ocean, which is not above a hundred and fifty Miles from *Lagado*, where there is a good Port and much Commerce with the great Island of *Luggnagg*,[73] situated to the North-West about 29 Degrees North Latitude, and 140 Longitude.[74] This Island of *Luggnagg* stands South-Eastwards of *Japan*, about an hundred Leagues distant. There is a strict Alliance between the *Japanese* Emperor and the King of *Luggnagg*, which affords frequent Opportunities of sailing from one Island to the other. I determined therefore to direct my Course this Way in order to my return to *Europe*. I hired two Mules with a Guide to show me the way, and carry my small Baggage. I took leave of my noble Protector, who had shown me so much Favour, and made me a generous Present at my Departure.

My Journey was without any Accident or Adventure worth relating. When I arrived at the Port of *Maldonada* (for so it is called), there was no Ship in the Harbour bound for *Luggnagg*, nor like to be in some time. The Town is about as large as *Portsmouth*. I soon fell into some Acquaintance, and was very hospitably received. A Gentleman of Distinction said to me, that since the Ships bound for *Luggnagg* could not be ready in less than a *Month*, it might be no disagreeable Amusement for me to take a Trip to the little Island of *Glubbdubdrib*, about five Leagues off to the South-West. He offered himself and a Friend to accompany me, and that I should be provided with a small convenient Bark[75] for the Voyage.

Glubbdubdrib, as nearly as I can interpret the Word, signifies the Island of *Sorcerers* or *Magicians*. It is about one third as large as the Isle of *Wight*,[76] and extremely Fruitful: It is governed by the Head of a certain Tribe, who are all Magicians. This Tribe marries only among each other, and the eldest in Succession is Prince or Governor. He hath a noble Palace and a Park of about three thousand Acres, surrounded by a Wall of hewn Stone twenty Foot high. In this Park are several smaller Enclosures for Cattle, Corn, and Gardening.

The Governor and his Family are served and attended by Domestics of a kind somewhat unusual. By his skill in Necromancy, he hath a Power of calling whom he pleaseth from the Dead, and commanding their Service for twenty-four Hours, but no longer; nor can he call the same Persons up again in less than three Months, except upon very extraordinary Occasions.

When we arrived at the Island, which was about Eleven in the Morning, one of the Gentlemen who accompanied me, went to the Governor, and desired admittance for a Stranger, who came on purpose to have the Honour of attending on his Highness. This was immediately granted, and we all three entered the Gate of the Palace between two Rows of Guards, armed and dressed after a very antic[77] manner, and something in their Countenances that made my Flesh creep with a Horror I cannot express. We passed through several Apartments between Servants of the same sort, ranked on each side as before, till we came to the Chamber of Presence, where after three profound Obeisances, and a few general Questions, we were permitted to sit on three Stools near the lowest Step of his Highness's Throne. He understood the Language of *Balnibarbi*, although it were different from that of his Island. He desired me to give him some account of my Travels; and to let me see that I should be treated without Ceremony, he dismissed all his Attendants with a turn of his Finger, at which to my great Astonishment they vanished in an Instant, like Visions in a Dream, when we awake on a sudden. I could not recover myself in some time, till the Governor assured me that I should receive no hurt; and observing my two Companions to be under no Concern, who had been often entertained in the same manner, I began to take Courage, and related to his Highness a short History of my several Adventures, yet not without some Hesitation, and frequently looking behind me to the Place where I had seen those Domestic Spectres. I had the Honour to dine with the Governor, where a new Set of Ghosts served up the Meat, and waited at Table. I now observed myself to be less terrified than I had been in the Morning. I stayed till Sunset, but humbly desired his Highness to excuse me for not accepting his Invitation of lodging in the Palace. My two Friends and I lay at a private House in the Town adjoining, which is the Capital of this little Island; and the next Morning we returned to pay our Duty to the Governor, as he was pleased to command us.

After this manner we continued in the Island for ten Days, most part of every Day with the Governor, and at Night in our Lodging. I soon grew so familiarized to the sight of Spirits, that after the third or fourth time they gave me no Emotion at all; or if I had any Apprehensions left, my Curiosity prevailed over them. For his Highness the Governor ordered me to call up whatever Persons I would choose to name, and in whatever Numbers among all the Dead from the beginning of the World to the present time, and command them to answer any Questions I should think fit to ask; with this condition, that my Questions must be confined within the compass of the times they lived in. And one thing I might depend upon, that they would certainly tell me truth, for Lying was a Talent of no use in the lower World.

I made my humble Acknowledgements to his Highness for so great a Favour. We were in a Chamber, from whence there was a fair Prospect into the Park. And because my first Inclination was to be entertained with Scenes of Pomp and Magnificence, I desired to see *Alexander the Great*, at the Head of his Army just after the Battle of *Arbela*,[78] which upon a Motion of the Governor's Finger immediately appeared in a large Field under the Window, where we stood. *Alexander* was called up into the Room: it was with great difficulty that I understood his *Greek*, and had but little of my own. He assured me upon his Honour that he was not Poisoned, but died of a Fever by excessive Drinking.[79]

Next I saw *Hannibal* passing the *Alps*, who told me he had not a drop of Vinegar in his Camp.[80]

I saw *Caesar* and *Pompey*[81] at the Head of their Troops just ready to engage. I saw the former in his last great Triumph. I desired that the Senate of *Rome* might appear before me in one large Chamber, and a modern Representative, in Counterview in another. The first seemed to be an Assembly of Heroes and Demigods; the other a Knot of Pedlars, Pickpockets, Highwaymen and Bullies.

The Governor at my Request gave the Sign for *Caesar* and *Brutus*[82] to advance towards us. I was struck with a profound Veneration at the sight of *Brutus*, and could easily discover the most consummate Virtue, the greatest Intrepidity, and firmness of Mind, the truest Love of his Country, and general Benevolence for Mankind in every Lineament of his Countenance. I observed with much pleasure, that these two Persons were in good Intelligence with each other, and *Caesar* freely confessed to me, that the greatest Actions of his own Life were not equal by many Degrees to the Glory of taking it away. I had the Honour to have much Conversation with *Brutus*, and was told that his Ancestors *Junius*,[83] *Socrates*,[84] *Epaminondas*,[85] *Cato* the Younger,[86] Sir *Thomas More*[87] and himself, were perpetually together: a *Sextumvirate* to which all the Ages of the World cannot add a Seventh.

It would be tedious to trouble the Reader with relating what vast numbers of Illustrious Persons were called up, to gratify that insatiable Desire I had to see the World in every Period of Antiquity placed before me. I chiefly fed my Eyes with beholding the Destroyers of Tyrants and Usurpers, and the Restorers of Liberty to oppressed and injured Nations. But it is impossible to express the Satisfaction I received in my own Mind, after such a manner as to make it a suitable Entertainment to the Reader.

Dantes inferno

CHAP. VIII

A further Account of Glubbdubdrib. *Ancient and Modern History corrected.*

Having a desire to see those Ancients, who were most renowned for Wit and Learning, I set apart one day on purpose. I proposed that *Homer* and *Aristotle* might appear at the Head of all their Commentators; but these were so numerous that some hundreds were forced to attend in the Court and outward Rooms of the Palace. I knew and could distinguish those two Heroes at first sight, not only from the Crowd, but from each other. *Homer* was the taller and comelier Person of the two, walked very erect for one of his Age, and his Eyes were the most quick and piercing I ever beheld.[88] *Aristotle* stooped much, and made use of a staff. His Visage was meagre, his Hair lank and thin, and his Voice hollow. I soon discovered that both of them were perfect Strangers to the rest of the Company, and had never seen or heard of them before. And I had a Whisper from a Ghost, who shall be nameless, that these Commentators always kept in the most distant Quarters from their Principals in the lower World, through a Consciousness of Shame and Guilt, because they had so horribly misrepresented the meaning of those Authors to Posterity. I introduced *Didymus* and *Eustathius*[89] to *Homer*, and prevailed on him to treat them better than perhaps they deserved, for he soon found they wanted a Genius to enter into the Spirit of a Poet. But *Aristotle* was out of all Patience with the account I gave him of *Scotus* and *Ramus*,[90] as I presented them to him, and he asked them whether the rest of the Tribe were as great Dunces as themselves.

I then desired the Governor to call up *Descartes* and *Gassendi*,[91] with whom I prevailed to explain their Systems to *Aristotle*. This great Philosopher freely acknowledged his own Mistakes in Natural Philosophy, because he proceeded in many things upon Conjecture, as all Men must do; and he found, that *Gassendi*, who had made the Doctrine of *Epicurus*[92] as palatable as he could, and the *Vortices* of *Descartes* were equally exploded. He predicted the same Fate to *Attraction*,[93] whereof the present Learned are such zealous Asserters. He said, that new Systems of Nature were but new Fashions, which would vary in every Age; and even those who pretend to demonstrate them from Mathematical Principles, would flourish but a short Period of time, and be out of Vogue when that was determined.

I spent five Days in conversing with many others of the ancient Learned. I saw most of the first Roman Emperors. I prevailed on the Governor to call up *Eliogabulus*'s Cooks[94] to dress us a Dinner, but they could not show us much of their Skill, for want of Materials. A *Helot* of *Agesilaus*[95] made us a Dish of *Spartan* Broth, but I was not able to get down a second Spoonful.

The two Gentlemen who conducted me to the Island were pressed by their private Affairs to return in three Days, which I employed in seeing some of the modern Dead, who had made the greatest Figure for two or three hundred Years past in our own and other Countries of *Europe*; and having been always a great Admirer of old illustrious Families, I desired the Governor would call up a dozen or two of Kings with their Ancestors in order for eight or nine Generations. But my Disappointment was grievous and unexpected. For instead of a long train with Royal Diadems, I saw in one Family two Fiddlers, three spruce Courtiers, and an *Italian* Prelate. In another a Barber, an Abbot, and two Cardinals. I have too great a Veneration for Crowned Heads to dwell any longer on so nice a Subject. But as to Counts, Marquesses, Dukes, Earls, and the like I was not so scrupulous. And I confess it was not without some Pleasure that I found myself able to trace the particular Features, by which certain

Families are distinguished up to their Originals. I could plainly discover
from whence one Family derives a long Chin, why a second hath abounded
with Knaves for two Generations, and Fools for two more; why a third
happened to be crack-brained, and a fourth to be Sharpers. Whence it
came what *Polydore Virgil* says of a certain great House, *Nec Vir fortis, nec
Faemina Casta.*[96] How Cruelty, Falsehood, and Cowardice grew to be
Characteristics by which certain Families are distinguished as much as
by their Coat of Arms. Who first brought the Pox[97] into a noble House,
which hath lineally descended in scrofulous Tumours to their Posterity.
Neither could I wonder at all this, when I saw such an Interruption of
Lineages by Pages, Lackies, Valets, Coachmen, Gamesters, Captains, and
Pick-pockets.

I was chiefly disgusted with modern History. For having strictly
examined all the Persons of greatest Name in the Courts of Princes for an
hundred Years past, I found how the World had been misled by prostitute
Writers, to ascribe the greatest Exploits in War to Cowards, the Wisest
Counsel to Fools, Sincerity to Flatterers, *Roman* Virtue to Betrayers of
their Country, Piety to Atheists, Chastity to Sodomites, Truth to
Informers. How many innocent and excellent Persons had been condemned to Death or Banishment, by the practising[98] of great Ministers
upon the Corruption of Judges, and the Malice of Faction. How many
Villains had been exalted to the highest places of Trust, Power, Dignity,
and Profit: How great a share in the Motions and Events of Courts,
Councils, and Senates might be challenged by Bawds, Whores, Pimps,
Parasites, and Buffoons: How low an Opinion I had of human Wisdom
and Integrity, when I was truly informed of the Springs and Motives of
great Enterprises and Revolutions in the World, and of the contemptible
Accidents to which they owed their Success.

Here I discovered the Roguery and Ignorance of those who pretend
to write *Anecdotes*, or secret History,[99] who send so many Kings to their
Graves with a Cup of Poison; will repeat the Discourse between a Prince
and Chief Minister, where no Witness was by; unlock the Thoughts and
Cabinets of Ambassadors and Secretaries of State, and have the perpetual
Misfortune to be mistaken. Here I discovered the secret Causes of many
great Events that have surprised the World, how a Whore can govern
the Back-stairs, the Back-stairs a Council, and the Council a Senate. A

General confessed in my Presence, that he got a Victory purely by the force of Cowardice and ill Conduct: and an Admiral that for want of proper Intelligence, he beat the Enemy to whom he intended to betray the Fleet. Three Kings protested to me, that in their whole Reigns they did never once prefer any Person of Merit, unless by Mistake or Treachery of some Minister in whom they confided: Neither would they do it if they were to live again; and they showed with great strength of Reason, that the Royal Throne could not be supported without Corruption, because that positive, confident restive Temper, which Virtue infused into Man, was a perpetual Clog to public Business.

I had the Curiosity to Inquire in a particular manner, by what Method great Numbers had procured to themselves high Titles of Honour, and prodigious Estates; and I confined my Inquiry to a very modern Period: however without grating upon present times, because I would be sure to give no Offence even to Foreigners (for I hope the Reader need not be told that I do not in the least intend my own Country in what I say upon this occasion) a great number of Persons concerned were called up, and upon a very slight Examination, discovered such a Scene of Infamy, that I cannot reflect upon it without some Seriousness. Perjury, Oppression, Subornation, Fraud, Pandarism, and the like *Infirmities* were amongst the most excusable Arts they had to mention, and for these I gave, as it was reasonable, great Allowance. But when some confessed they owed their Greatness and Wealth to Sodomy or Incest, others to the prostituting of their own Wives and Daughters; others to the betraying their Country or their Prince; some to Poisoning, more to the perverting of Justice in order to destroy the innocent: I hope I may be pardoned if these Discoveries inclined me a little to abate of that profound Veneration which I am naturally apt to pay to Persons of high Rank, who ought to be treated with the utmost Respect due to their sublime Dignity, by us their Inferiors.

I had often read of some great Services done to Princes and States, and desired to see the Persons by whom those Services were performed. Upon Inquiry I was told that their Names were to be found on no Record, except a few of them whom History hath represented as the vilest Rogues and Traitors. As to the rest, I had never once heard of them. They all appeared with dejected Looks, and in the meanest Habit, most of them

telling me they died in Poverty and Disgrace, and the rest on a Scaffold
or a Gibbet.

Among the rest there was one Person whose Case appeared a little
singular.[100] He had a Youth about eighteen Years old standing by his
side. He told me he had for many Years been Commander of a Ship, and
in the Sea Fight at *Actium*,[101] had the good Fortune to break through the
Enemy's great Line of Battle, sink three of their Capital Ships, and take
a fourth, which was the sole Cause of *Antony*'s Flight, and of the Victory
that ensued; that the Youth standing by him, his only Son, was killed in
the Action. He added, that upon the Confidence of some Merit, this War
being at an end, he went to *Rome*, and solicited at the Court of *Augustus*
to be preferred to a greater Ship, whose Commander had been killed; but
without any regard to his Pretensions, it was given to a Youth who had
never seen the Sea, the Son of a *Libertina*,[102] who waited on one of the
Emperor's Mistresses. Returning back to his own Vessels, he was charged
with neglect of Duty, and the Ship given to a Favourite Page of *Publicola*
the Vice-Admiral; whereupon he retired to a poor Farm, at a great
distance from *Rome*, and there ended his Life. I was so curious to know
the truth of this Story, that I desired *Agrippa*[103] might be called, who
was Admiral in that Fight. He appeared and confirmed the whole Account,
but with much more Advantage to the Captain, whose Modesty had
extenuated or concealed a great part of his Merit.

I was surprised to find Corruption grown so high and so quick in that
Empire, by the force of Luxury so lately introduced, which made me less
wonder at many parallel Cases in other Countries, where Vices of all
kinds have reigned so much longer, and where the whole Praise as well
as Pillage hath been engrossed by the chief Commander,[104] who perhaps
had the least Title to either.

As every Person called up made exactly the same appearance he had
done in the World, it gave me melancholy Reflections to observe how
much the Race of human kind was degenerate among us, within these
hundred Years past. How the Pox under all its Consequences and Denominations had altered every Lineament of an *English* Countenance, shortened
the size of Bodies, unbraced the Nerves, relaxed the Sinews and Muscles,
introduced a sallow Complexion, and rendered the Flesh loose and *Rancid*.

I descended so low as to desire that some *English* Yeomen of the old stamp, might be summoned to appear, once so famous for the Simplicity of their Manners, Diet and Dress, for Justice in their Dealings, for their true Spirit of Liberty, for their Valour and Love of their Country. Neither could I be wholly unmoved after comparing the Living with the Dead, when I considered how all these pure native Virtues were prostituted for a piece of Money by their Grandchildren, who in selling their Votes, and managing at Elections have acquired every Vice and Corruption that can possibly be learned in a Court.

CHAP. IX

The Author's Return to Maldonada. *Sails to the Kingdom of* Luggnagg. *The Author confined. He is sent for to Court. The Manner of his Admittance. The King's great Lenity to his Subjects.*

The Day of our Departure being come, I took leave of his Highness the Governor of *Glubbdubdrib*, and returned with my two Companions to *Maldonada*, where after a Fortnight's waiting, a Ship was ready to sail for *Luggnagg*. The two Gentlemen and some others were so generous and kind as to furnish me with Provisions, and see me on board. I was a Month in this Voyage. We had one violent Storm, and were under a necessity of steering Westward to get into the Trade Wind which holds for above sixty Leagues. On the 21st of *April*, 1709 we sailed in the River *Clumegnig*,[105] which is a Seaport Town, at the South-East Point of *Luggnagg*. We cast Anchor within a League of the Town, and made a Signal for a Pilot. Two of them came on board in less than half an Hour, by whom we were guided between certain Shoals and Rocks which are very dangerous in the Passage to a large Basin, where a Fleet may ride in safety within a Cable's Length of the Town Wall.

Some of our Sailors, whether out of Treachery or Inadvertence, had informed the Pilots that I was a Stranger and a great Traveller, whereof these gave notice to a Custom-House Officer, by whom I was examined very strictly upon my landing. This Officer spoke to me in the Language of *Balnibarbi*, which by the force of much Commerce is generally understood in that Town, especially by Seamen, and those employed in the Customs. I gave him a short Account of some Particulars, and made my Story as plausible and consistent as I could; but I thought it necessary to disguise my Country, and call myself an *Hollander*, because my Intentions were for *Japan*, and I knew the *Dutch* were the only *Europeans* permitted to enter into that Kingdom.[106] I therefore told the Officer, that having been Shipwrecked on the Coast of *Balnibarbi*, and cast on a Rock, I was received up into *Laputa*, or the flying Island (of which he had often heard) and was now endeavouring to get to *Japan*, from whence I might find a Convenience of returning to my own Country. The Officer said I must be confined till he could receive Orders from Court, for which he would write immediately, and hoped to receive an Answer in a fortnight. I was carried to a convenient Lodging, with a Sentry placed at the Door; however I had the Liberty of a large Garden, and was treated with Humanity enough, being maintained all the time at the King's Charge. I was invited by several Persons, chiefly out of Curiosity, because it was reported that I came from Countries very remote of which they had never heard.

I hired a young Man who came in the same Ship to be an Interpreter; he was a Native of *Luggnagg*, but had lived some Years at *Maldonada*, and was a perfect Master of both Languages. By his Assistance I was able to hold a Conversation with those who came to visit me; but this consisted only of their Questions, and my Answers.

The Dispatch came from Court about the time we expected. It contained a Warrant for conducting me and my Retinue to *Traldragdubh* or *Trildrogdrib* (for it is pronounced both ways as near as I can remember) by a party of Ten Horse. All my Retinue was that poor Lad for an Interpreter, whom I persuaded into my Service, and at my humble Request, we had each of us a Mule to ride on. A Messenger was dispatched half a day's Journey before us, to give the King notice of my Approach, and to desire that his Majesty would please to appoint a Day and Hour, when it would be his gracious Pleasure that I might have the Honour to *lick the Dust before his Footstool*.[107] This is the Court Style, and I found it to be more than matter of form. For upon my Admittance two Days after my arrival, I was commanded to crawl on my Belly, and lick the Floor as I advanced; but on account of my being a Stranger, care was taken to have it swept so clean that the Dust was not offensive. However, this was a peculiar Grace, not allowed to any but Persons of the highest Rank, when they desire an Admittance. Nay, sometimes the Floor is strewed with Dust on purpose, when the Person to be admitted happens to have powerful Enemies at Court. And I have seen a great Lord with his Mouth so crammed, that when he had crept to the proper Distance from the Throne, he was not able to speak a Word. Neither is there any Remedy, because it is Capital for those who receive an Audience to spit or wipe their Mouths in his Majesty's Presence. There is indeed another Custom, which I cannot altogether approve of. When the King hath a mind to put any of his Nobles to Death in a gentle indulgent manner, he commands to have the Floor strewed with a certain brown Powder, of a deadly Composition, which being licked up infallibly kills him in twenty-four Hours. But in Justice to this Prince's great Clemency, and the care he hath of his Subjects' Lives (wherein it were much to be wished that the Monarchs of *Europe* would imitate him), it must be mentioned for his Honour, that strict orders are given to have the infected parts of the Floor well washed after every such Execution, which if his Domestics neglect, they are in danger of incurring his Royal Displeasure. I myself heard him give Directions, that one of his Pages should be whipped, whose turn it was to give notice about washing the Floor after an Execution, but maliciously had omitted it, by which Neglect a young Lord of great Hopes coming to an Audience, was unfortunately poisoned, although the King at that time had no design against his Life. But this good Prince was so gracious, as to forgive the poor Page his Whipping, upon promise that he would do so no more, without special Orders.

To return from this Digression; when I had crept within four Yards of the Throne, I raised myself gently upon my Knees, and then striking my Forehead seven times on the Ground, I pronounced the following Words, as they had been taught me the Night before, *Ickpling Gloffthrobb Squutserumm blhiop Mlashnalt Zwin tnodbalkguffh Slhiophad Gurdlubh Asht.* This is the Compliment established by the Laws of the Land for all Persons admitted to the King's Presence. It may be rendered into *English* thus: *May your celestial Majesty outlive the Sun, eleven Moons and an half.* To this the King returned some Answer, which although I could not understand, yet I replied as I had been directed; *Fluft drin Yalerick Dwuldom prastrad mirpush*, which properly signifies, *My Tongue is in the Mouth of my Friend*, and by this Expression was meant that I desired leave to bring my Interpreter; whereupon the young Man already mentioned was accordingly introduced, by whose Intervention I answered as many Questions as his Majesty could put in above an Hour. I spoke in the *Balnibarbian* Tongue, and my Interpreter delivered my Meaning in that of *Luggnagg*.

The King was much delighted with my Company, and ordered his *Bliffmarklub* or high Chamberlain to appoint a Lodging in the Court for me and my Interpreter, with a daily Allowance for my Table, and a large Purse of Gold for my common Expenses.

I stayed three Months in this Country out of perfect Obedience to his Majesty, who was pleased highly to Favour me, and made me very honourable Offers. But, I thought it more consistent with Prudence and Justice to pass the remainder of my Days with my Wife and Family.

CHAP. X

The Luggnuggians *commended. A particular Description of the* Struldbrugs, *with many Conversations between the Author and some eminent Persons upon that Subject.*

The *Luggnuggians* are a polite and generous People, and although they are not without some share of that Pride which is peculiar to all *Eastern* Countries, yet they show themselves courteous to Strangers, especially such who are countenanced by the Court. I had many Acquaintance among Persons of the best Fashion, and being always attended by my Interpreter, the Conversation we had was not disagreeable.

One Day in much good Company I was asked by a Person of Quality, whether I had seen any of their *Struldbrugs* or *Immortals*. I said I had not, and desired he would explain to me what he meant by such an Appellation applied to a mortal Creature. He told me, that sometimes, though very rarely, a Child happened to be born in a Family with a red circular Spot in the Forehead, directly over the left Eyebrow, which was an infallible Mark that it should never die. The Spot, as he described it, was about the Compass of a Silver Threepence, but in the course of Time grew larger, and changed its Colour; for at twelve Years old it became Green, so continued till Five and Twenty, then turned to a deep Blue; at Five and Forty it grew coal Black, and as large as an *English* Shilling,[108] but never admitted any farther Alteration. He said these Births were so rare, that he did not believe there could be above Eleven Hundred *Struldbrugs* of both Sexes in the whole Kingdom, of which he computed about fifty in the Metropolis, and among the rest a young Girl born about three Years ago. That these Productions were not peculiar to any Family but a mere effect of Chance, and the Children of the *Struldbruggs* themselves, were equally mortal with the rest of the People.

I freely own myself to have been struck with inexpressible Delight upon hearing this Account: And the Person who gave it me happening to understand the *Balnibarbian* Language, which I spoke very well, I could not forbear breaking out into expressions perhaps a little too Extravagant. I cried out as in a Rapture; Happy Nation where every Child hath at least a chance for being immortal! Happy People who enjoy so many living Examples of Ancient Virtue, and have Masters ready to instruct them in the Wisdom of all former Ages! But, happiest beyond all comparison are those excellent *Struldbruggs*, who being born exempt from that universal Calamity of human Nature, have their Minds free and disengaged, without the weight and depression of Spirits caused by the continual Apprehension of Death. I discovered my Admiration that I had not observed any of these illustrious Persons at Court: the black Spot on the Forehead, being so remarkable a Distinction, that I could not have easily overlooked it: And it was impossible that his Majesty, a most Judicious Prince, should not provide himself with a good number of such wise and able Counsellors. Yet perhaps the Virtue of those Reverend Sages was too strict for the Corrupt and Libertine Manners of a Court. And we often find by Experience that young Men are too opinionative and volatile to be guided by the sober Dictates of their Seniors. However, since the King was pleased to allow me Access to his Royal Person, I was resolved upon the very first occasion to deliver my Opinion to him on this Matter freely, and at large by the help of my Interpreter; and whether he would please to take my Advice or no, yet in one thing I was determined, that his Majesty having frequently offered me an Establishment[109] in this Country, I would with great thankfulness accept the Favour, and pass my Life here in the Conversation of those superior Beings the *Struldbruggs*, if they would please to admit me.

The Gentleman to whom I addressed my Discourse, because (as I have already observed) he spoke the Language of *Balnibarbi*, said to me with a sort of a Smile, which usually ariseth from Pity to the Ignorant, that he was glad of any occasion to keep me among them, and desired my Permission to explain to the Company what I had spoke. He did so, and they talked together for some time in their own Language, whereof I understood not a Syllable, neither could I observe by their Countenances what impression my Discourse had made on them. After a short Silence the same Person told me, that his Friends and mine (so he thought fit to express himself) were very much pleased with the judicious Remarks I had made on the great Happiness and Advantages of immortal Life, and they were desirous to know in a particular manner, what Scheme of Living I should have formed to myself, if it had fallen to my Lot to have been born a *Struldbrugg*.

I answered, it was easy to be Eloquent on so copious and delightful a Subject, especially to me who have been often apt to amuse myself with Visions of what I should do if I were a King, a General, or a great Lord: And upon this very Case I had frequently run over the whole System how I should employ myself, and pass the time if I were sure to live for ever.

That, if it had been my good Fortune to come into the World a *Struldbrugg*, as soon as I could discover my own Happiness by understanding the difference between Life and Death, I would first resolve by all Arts and Methods whatsoever to procure myself Riches. In the pursuit of which by Thrift and Management, I might reasonably expect in about two Hundred Years, to be the Wealthiest Man in the Kingdom. In the second place, I would from my earliest Youth apply myself to the study of Arts and Sciences, by which I should arrive in time to excel all others in Learning. Lastly I would carefully record every Action and Event of Consequence that happened in the Public, impartially draw the Characters of the several Successions of Princes, and great Ministers of State, with my own Observations on every Point. I would exactly set down the several changes in Customs, Languages, Fashions, Dress, Diet and

Diversions. By all which Acquirements, I should be a living Treasury of Knowledge and Wisdom, and certainly become the Oracle of the Nation.

I would never marry after threescore, but live in an hospitable manner, yet still on the saving side. I would entertain myself in forming and directing the Minds of hopeful young Men, by convincing them from my own Remembrance, Experience and Observation, fortified by numerous Examples, of the usefulness of Virtue in public and private Life. But, my Choice and constant Companions should be a set of my own immortal Brotherhood, among whom I would elect a dozen from the most Ancient down to my own Contemporaries. Where any of these wanted Fortunes, I would provide them with convenient Lodges round my own Estate, and have some of them always at my Table, only mingling a few of the most valuable among you Mortals, whom length of Time would harden me to lose with little or no Reluctance, and treat your Posterity after the same manner, just as a Man diverts himself with the Annual Succession of Pinks and Tulips in his Garden, without regretting the loss of those which withered the preceding Year.

These *Struldbruggs* and I would mutually communicate our Observations and Memorials through the Course of Time, remark the several Gradations by which Corruption steals into the World, and oppose it in every step, by giving perpetual Warning and Instruction to Mankind; which, added to the strong Influence of our own Example, would probably prevent that continual Degeneracy of Human Nature so justly complained of in all Ages.

Add to all this the pleasure of seeing the various Revolutions of States and Empires, the Changes in the lower and upper World, ancient Cities in Ruins, and obscure Villages become the Seats of Kings; Famous Rivers lessening into shallow Brooks, the Ocean leaving one Coast dry, and overwhelming another: The Discovery of many Countries yet unknown. Barbarity overrunning the politest Nations, and the most barbarous become civilized. I should then see the Discovery of the *Longitude*, the *perpetual Motion*, the *Universal Medicine*, and many other great Inventions brought to the utmost Perfection.[110]

What wonderful Discoveries should we make in Astronomy, by outliving and confirming our own Predictions, by observing the Progress and Returns of Comets, with the changes of Motion in the Sun, Moon and Stars.

I enlarged upon many other Topics which the natural desire of endless Life and sublunary Happiness could easily furnish me with. When I had ended, and the Sum of my Discourse had been interpreted as before, to the rest of the Company, there was a good deal of Talk among them in the Language of the Country, not without some Laughter at my Expense. At last the same Gentleman who had been my Interpreter said, he was desired by the rest to set me right in a few Mistakes, which I had fallen into through the common Imbecility[111] of human Nature, and upon that allowance was less answerable for them. That, this Breed of *Struldbruggs* was peculiar to their Country, for there were no such People either in *Balnibarbi* or *Japan*, where he had the Honour to be Ambassador from his Majesty, and found the Natives in both those Kingdoms very hard to believe[112] that the Fact was possible, and it appeared from my Astonishment when he first mentioned the matter to me, that I received it as a thing wholly new, and scarcely to be credited. That in the two Kingdoms above mentioned, where during his Residence he had conversed very much, he observed long Life to be the universal Desire and Wish of Mankind. That whoever had one Foot in the Grave, was sure to hold back the other as strongly as he could. That the oldest had still hopes of living one Day longer, and looked on Death as the greatest Evil, from which Nature always prompted him to retreat; only in this Island of *Luggnagg*, the Appetite for living was not so eager, from the continual Example of the *Struldbruggs* before their Eyes.

That the System of Living contrived by me was unreasonable and unjust,[113] because it supposed a Perpetuity of Youth, Health, and Vigour, which no Man could be so foolish to hope, however extravagant he may be in his Wishes. That the Question therefore was not whether a Man would choose to be always in the Prime of Youth, attended with Prosperity and Health, but how he would pass a perpetual Life under all the usual Disadvantages which old Age brings along with it. For although few Men will avow their Desires of being immortal upon such hard Conditions, yet in the two Kingdoms before mentioned of *Balnibarbi* and *Japan*, he observed that every Man desired to put off Death for some time longer, let it approach ever so late, and he rarely heard of any Man who died willingly, except he were incited by the Extremity of Grief or Torture. And he appealed to me whether in those Countries I had travelled as well as my own, I had not observed the same general Disposition.

After this Preface he gave me a particular Account of the *Struldbruggs* among them. He said they commonly acted like Mortals, till about thirty Years old, after which by degrees they grew melancholy and dejected, increasing in both till they came to four-score. This he learned from their own Confession; for otherwise there not being above two or three of that Species born in an Age, they were too few to form a general Observation by. When they came to four-score Years, which is reckoned the Extremity of living in this Country, they had not only all the Follies and Infirmities of other old Men, but many more which arose from the dreadful Prospect of never dying. They were not only Opinionative, Peevish, Covetous, Morose, Vain, Talkative, but uncapable of Friendship, and dead to all natural Affection, which never descended below their Grandchildren. Envy and impotent Desires are their prevailing Passions. But those Objects against which their Envy seems principally directed, are the Vices of the younger sort, and the Deaths of the old. By reflecting on the former, they find themselves cut off from all possibility of Pleasure; and whenever they see a Funeral, they lament and repine that others are gone to an Harbour of Rest, to which they themselves never can hope to arrive. They have no Remembrance of anything but what they learned and observed in their Youth and middle Age, and even that is very imperfect. And for the Truth or Particulars of any Fact, it is safer to depend on common Traditions than upon their best Recollections. The least miserable among them appear to be those who turn to Dotage, and entirely lose their Understandings; these meet with more Pity and Assistance, because they want[114] many bad Qualities which abound in others.

If a *Struldbrugg* happen to marry one of his own kind, the Marriage is dissolved of course[115] by the Courtesy of the Kingdom, as soon as the younger of the two comes to be four-score. For the Law thinks it a reasonable Indulgence, that those who are condemned without any Fault of their own to a perpetual Continuance in the World, should not have their Misery doubled by the Load of a Wife.

As soon as they have completed the term of eighty Years, they are looked on as dead in Law; their Heirs immediately succeed to their Estates, only a small Pittance is reserved for their Support, and the poor ones are maintained at the public Charge. After that Period they are held incapable of any Employment of Trust or Profit, they cannot purchase Lands or take Leases, neither are they allowed to be Witnesses in any Cause, either Civil or Criminal, not even for the Decision of Meers and Bounds.[116]

At Ninety they lose their Teeth and Hair, they have at that age no Distinction of Taste, but eat and drink whatever they can get, without Relish or Appetite. The Diseases they were subject to still continue without increasing or diminishing. In talking they forget the common Appellations of things, and the Names of Persons, even of those who are their nearest Friends and Relations. For the same reason they never can amuse themselves with reading, because their Memory will not serve to carry them from the beginning of a Sentence to the end; and by this Defect they are deprived of the only Entertainment whereof they might otherwise be capable.

The Language of this Country being always upon the Flux, the *Struldbruggs* of one Age do not understand those of another, neither are they able after two hundred Years to hold any Conversation (farther than by a few general Words) with their Neighbours the Mortals, and thus they lie under the Disadvantage of living like Foreigners in their own Country.

This was the Account given me of the *Struldbruggs*, as near as I can remember. I afterwards saw five or six of different Ages, the youngest not above two hundred Years old, who were brought to me at several times by some of my Friends; but although they were told that I was a great Traveller, and had seen all the World, they had not the least Curiosity to ask me a Question; only desired I would give them *Slumskudask*, or a Token of Remembrance, which is a modest way of begging, to avoid the Law that strictly forbids it, because they are provided for by the Public, although indeed with a very scanty Allowance.

They are despised and hated by all sorts of People; when one of them is born, it is reckoned ominous, and their Birth is recorded very particularly; so that you may know their Age by consulting the Registry, which however hath not been kept above a thousand Years past, or at least hath been destroyed by time or public Disturbances. But the usual way of computing how old they are, is by asking them what Kings or great Persons they can remember, and then consulting History, for

infallibly the last Prince in their Mind did not begin his Reign after they
were four-score Years old.

They were the most mortifying Sight I ever beheld, and the Women
more horrible than the Men. Besides the usual Deformities in extreme
Old Age, they acquired an additional Ghastliness in proportion to their
number of Years, which is not to be described, and among half a Dozen I
soon distinguished which was the eldest, although there was not above
a Century or two between them.

The Reader will easily believe, that from what I had heard and seen,
my keen Appetite for perpetuity of Life was much abated. I grew heartily
ashamed of the pleasing Visions I had formed, and thought no Tyrant
could invent a Death into which I would not run with Pleasure from such
a Life. The King heard of all that had passed between me and my Friends
upon this Occasion, and rallied me very pleasantly, wishing I would send
a Couple of *Struldbruggs* to my own Country, to arm our People against
the Fear of Death; but this it seems is forbidden by the fundamental
Laws of the Kingdom, or else I should have been well content with the
trouble and expense of transporting them.

I could not but agree that the Laws of this Kingdom, relating to the
Struldbruggs, were founded upon the strongest Reasons, and such as any
other Country would be under the Necessity of enacting in the like
Circumstances. Otherwise, as Avarice is the necessary Consequent of old
Age, those Immortals would in time become Proprietors of the whole
Nation, and engross[117] the Civil Power, which, for want of Abilities to
manage, must end in the Ruin of the Public.

CHAP. XI

The Author leaves Luggnagg *and sails to* Japan. *From thence he
returns in a* Dutch *Ship to* Amsterdam, *and from* Amsterdam
to England.

I thought this Account of the *Struldbruggs* might be some Entertainment to the Reader, because it seems to be a little out of the common

Way;[118] at least I do not remember to have met the like in any Book of Travels that hath come to my Hands: And if I am deceived, my Excuse must be, that it is necessary for Travellers, who describe the same Country, very often to agree in dwelling on the same Particulars, without deserving the Censure of having borrowed or transcribed from those who wrote before them.

There is indeed a perpetual Commerce between this Kingdom and the great Empire of *Japan*, and it is very probable that the *Japanese* Authors may have given some Account of the *Struldbruggs*; but my Stay in *Japan* was so short, and I was so entirely a Stranger to that Language, that I was not qualified to make any Inquiries. But I hope the *Dutch* upon this notice will be curious and able enough to supply my Defects.

His Majesty having often pressed me to accept some Employment in his Court, and finding me absolutely determined to return to my Native Country, was pleased to give me his Licence to depart, and honoured me with a Letter of Recommendation under his own Hand to the Emperor of *Japan*. He likewise presented me with Four Hundred forty-four large Pieces of Gold (this Nation delighting in even Numbers) and a red Diamond which I sold in *England* for Eleven Hundred Pounds.

On the Sixth Day of *May*, 1709, I took a solemn Leave of his Majesty, and all my Friends. This Prince was so gracious as to order a Guard to conduct me to *Glanguenstald*, which is a Royal Port to the *South-West* Part of the Island. In Six Days I found a Vessel ready to carry me to *Japan*, and spent Fifteen Days in the Voyage. We landed at a small Port-Town called *Xamoschi*,[119] situated on the South-East part of *Japan*; the Town lies on the *Western* Point where there is a narrow Strait, leading *Northward* into a long Arm of the Sea, upon the *North-West* Part of which, *Yedo*[120] the Metropolis stands. At Landing I showed the Custom-House Officers my Letter from the King of *Luggnagg* to his Imperial Majesty. They knew the Seal perfectly well, it was as broad as the Palm of my Hand. The Impression was, *A King lifting up a lame Beggar from the Earth.* The Magistrates of the Town hearing of my Letter, received me as a Public Minister; they provided me with Carriages and Servants, and bore my Charges to *Yedo*, where I was admitted to an Audience, and delivered my Letter, which was opened with great Ceremony, and explained to the Emperor by an Interpreter, who then gave me notice by his Majesty's

Order, that I should signify my Request, and whatever it were, it should be granted for the sake of his Royal Brother of *Luggnagg*. This Interpreter was a Person employed to transact Affairs with the *Hollanders*, he soon conjectured by my Countenance that I was an *European*, and therefore repeated his Majesty's Commands in *Low-Dutch*,[121] which he spoke perfectly well. I answered (as I had before determined) that I was a *Dutch* Merchant, shipwrecked in a very remote Country, from whence I travelled by Sea and Land to *Luggnagg*, and then took Shipping for *Japan*, where I knew my Countrymen often traded, and with some of these I hoped to get an Opportunity of returning into *Europe*: I therefore most humbly entreated his Royal Favour to give order, that I should be conducted in safety to *Nangasac*:[122] To this I added another Petition, that for the sake of my Patron the King of *Luggnagg*, his Majesty would condescend to excuse my performing the Ceremony imposed on my Countrymen of *trampling upon the Crucifix*,[123] because I had been thrown into his Kingdom by my Misfortunes, without any intention of trading. When this latter Petition was interpreted to the Emperor, he seemed a little surprised, and said, he believed I was the first of my Countrymen who ever made any scruple in this Point, and that he began to doubt whether I was a real *Hollander* or no; but rather suspected I must be a CHRISTIAN. However, for the Reasons I had offered, but chiefly to gratify the King of *Luggnagg*, by an uncommon Mark of his Favour, he would comply with the *singularity* of my Humour, but the Affair must be managed with Dexterity, and his Officers should be commanded to let me pass as it were by Forgetfulness. For he assured me, that if the secret should be discovered by my Countrymen, the *Dutch*, they would cut my Throat in the Voyage. I returned my Thanks by the Interpreter for so unusual a Favour, and some Troops being at that time on their March to *Nangasac*, the Commanding Officer had Orders to convey me safe thither, with particular Instructions about the Business of the *Crucifix*.

On the 9th Day of *June*, 1709, I arrived at *Nangasac*, after a very long and troublesome Journey. I soon fell into Company of some *Dutch* Sailors belonging to the *Amboyna*[124] of *Amsterdam*, a stout Ship of 450 Tons. I had lived long in *Holland*, pursuing my Studies at *Leyden*, and I spoke *Dutch* well. The Seamen soon knew from whence I came last: they were curious to inquire into my Voyages and Course of Life. I made up a Story as short and probable as I could, but concealed the greatest part. I knew many Persons in *Holland*, I was able to invent Names for my Parents, whom I pretended to be obscure People in the Province of *Gelderland*. I would have given the Captain (one *Theodorus Vangrult*)[125] what he pleased to ask for my Voyage to *Holland*; but understanding I was a Surgeon, he was contented to take half the usual Rate, on Condition that I would serve him in the way of my Calling. Before we took Shipping, I was often asked by some of the Crew, Whether I had performed the Ceremony above-mentioned? I evaded the Question by general Answers, that I had satisfied the Emperor and Court in all Particulars. However, a malicious Rogue of a Skipper[126] went to an Officer, and pointing to me, told him, I had not yet *trampled on the Crucifix*: But the other, who had received Instructions to let me pass, gave the Rascal twenty Strokes on the Shoulders with a Bamboo, after which I was no more troubled with such Questions.

Nothing happened worth mentioning in this Voyage. We sailed with a fair Wind to the *Cape of Good Hope* where we stayed only to take in fresh Water. On the 16th of *April* we arrived safely at *Amsterdam*, having lost only three Men by Sickness in the Voyage, and a fourth who fell from the Foremast into the Sea, not far from the Coast of *Guinea*. From *Amsterdam* I soon after set Sail for *England* in a small Vessel belonging to that City.

On the 10th of *April* 1710, we put in at the *Downs*. I landed the next Morning, and saw once more my Native Country after an Absence of Five Years and Six Months complete. I went straight to *Redriff*, where I arrived the same Day at two in the Afternoon, and found my Wife and Family in good Health.

The End of the Third Part

TRAVELS

PART IV
A VOYAGE TO THE COUNTRY OF
THE HOUYHNHNMS

Plate.VI.Part.IIII.*Page.*I.

Edels Land

Lewins Land

Nuyts Land

I. St Francoi

I. St Pieter

Sweers I.

I. Maelsuyker

De Wits I.

HOUYHNHNMS LAND

Discovered A.D.1711

PLATE 8

CHAP. I

The Author sets out as Captain of a Ship. His Men conspire against him, confine him a long Time to his Cabin, set him on Shore in an unknown Land. He travels up in the Country. The Yahoos,[1] *a strange Sort of Animal, described. The Author meets two* Houyhnhnms.[2]

I continued at home with my Wife and Children about Five Months in a very happy Condition, if I could have learned the Lesson of knowing when I was well. I left my poor Wife big with Child, and accepted an advantageous Offer made me to be Captain of the *Adventure*, a stout Merchantman of 350 Tons: For I understood Navigation well, and being grown weary of a Surgeon's Employment at Sea, which however I could exercise upon occasion, I took a skilful young Man of that Calling, one *Robert Purefoy*,[3] into my Ship. We set sail from *Portsmouth* upon the Second Day of *August*, 1710; on the Fourteenth, we met with Captain *Pocock* of *Bristol*, at *Teneriffe*, who was going to the Bay of *Campeche* to cut Logwood.[4] On the Sixteenth, he was parted from us by a Storm; I heard since my Return, that his Ship foundered, and none escaped, but one Cabin-Boy. He was an honest Man, and a good Sailor, but a little too positive in his own Opinions, which was the Cause of his Destruction, as it hath been of several others. For, if he had followed my Advice, he might have been safe at home with his Family at this Time, as well as myself.

I had several Men die in my Ship of Calentures,[5] so that I was forced to get Recruits out of *Barbadoes*, and the *Leeward Islands*,[6] where I touched by the Direction of the Merchants who employed me, which I had soon too much cause to repent; for I found afterwards that most of them had been Buccaneers. I had Fifty Hands on board, and my Orders were, that I should trade with the *Indians*, in the *South-Sea*, and make what Discoveries I could. These Rogues whom I had picked up debauched my other Men, and they all formed a Conspiracy to seize the Ship and secure me; which they did one Morning, rushing into my Cabin, and binding me Hand and Foot, threatening to throw me overboard, if I offered to stir. I told them, I was their Prisoner, and would submit. This they made me swear to do, and then they unbound me, only fastening one of my Legs with a Chain near my Bed, and placed a Sentry at my Door with his Piece[7] charged, who was commanded to shoot me dead, if I attempted my Liberty. They sent me down Victuals and Drink, and took the Government of the Ship to themselves. Their Design was to turn Pirates, and plunder the *Spaniards*, which they could not do, till they got more Men. But first they resolved to sell the Goods in the Ship, and then go to *Madagascar* for Recruits, several among them having died since my Confinement. They sailed many Weeks, and traded with the *Indians*, but I knew not what Course they took, being kept a close Prisoner in my Cabin, and expecting nothing less than to be murdered, as they often threatened me.

Upon the Ninth Day of *May* 1711, one *James Welch* came down to my Cabin; and said he had Orders from the Captain, to set me ashore. I expostulated with him, but in vain; neither would he so much as tell me who their new Captain was. They forced me into the Long-boat, letting me put on my best Suit of Clothes, which were as good as New, and a small Bundle of Linen, but no Arms except my Hanger; and they were so civil as not to search my Pockets, into which I conveyed what Money I had, with some other little Necessaries. They rowed about a League; and then set me down on a Strand. I desired them to tell me, what Country it was. They all swore, they knew no more than myself, but said, that the Captain (as they called him) was resolved, after they had sold the Lading,[8] to get rid of me in the first Place, where they could discover Land. They pushed off immediately, advising me to make haste, for fear of being overtaken by the Tide, and so bade me Farewell.

In this desolate Condition I advanced forward, and soon got upon firm Ground, where I sat down on a Bank to rest myself, and consider what I had best to do. When I was a little refreshed, I went up into the Country, resolving to deliver myself to the first Savages I should meet, and purchase my Life from them by some Bracelets, Glass rings, and other Toys,[9] which Sailors usually provide themselves with in those Voyáges, and whereof I had some about me: The Land was divided by long Rows of Trees not regularly planted, but naturally growing; there was great plenty of Grass, and several Fields of Oats. I walked very circumspectly for fear of being surprised, or suddenly shot with an Arrow from behind or on either side. I fell into a beaten Road, where I saw many Tracks of human Feet, and some of Cows, but most of Horses. At last I beheld several Animals in a Field, and one or two of the same kind sitting in Trees. Their Shape was very singular, and deformed, which a little discomposed me, so that I lay down behind a Thicket to observe them better. Some of them coming forward near the place where I lay, gave me an Opportunity of distinctly marking their Form. Their Heads and Breasts were covered with a thick Hair, some frizzled and others lank; they had Beards like Goats, and a long ridge of Hair down their Backs, and the fore-parts of their Legs and Feet, but the rest of their Bodies were bare, so that I might see their Skins, which were of a brown buff Colour. They had no Tails, nor any Hair at all on their Buttocks, except about the *Anus*; which, I presume, Nature had placed there to defend them as they sat on the Ground; for this Posture they used, as well as lying down, and often stood on their hind Feet. They climbed high Trees, as nimbly as a Squirrel, for they had strong extended Claws before and behind, terminating in sharp points, and hooked. They would often spring, and bound, and leap with prodigious Agility. The Females were not so large as the Males, they had long lank Hair on their Heads, but none on their Faces, nor anything more than a sort of Down on the rest of their Bodies, except about the *Anus*, and *Pudenda*. Their Dugs hung between their Fore-feet, and often reached almost to the Ground as they walked. The Hair of both Sexes was of several Colours, brown, red, black, and yellow. Upon the whole, I never beheld in all my Travels so disagreeable an Animal, nor one against which I naturally conceived so strong an Antipathy. So that thinking I had seen enough, full of Contempt and Aversion, I got up and pursued the beaten Road, hoping it might direct me to the Cabin of some *Indian*. I had not gone far when I met one of these Creatures full in my way, and coming up directly to me. The ugly Monster, when he saw me, distorted several ways every Feature of his Visage, and stared as at an Object he had never seen before; then approaching nearer, lifted up his Fore-paw, whether out of Curiosity or Mischief, I could not tell. But I drew my Hanger, and gave him a good Blow with the flat Side of it, for I durst not strike him with the Edge, fearing the Inhabitants might be provoked against me, if they should come to know, that I had killed or maimed any of their Cattle. When the Beast felt the Smart, he drew back, and roared so loud, that a Herd of at least forty came flocking about me from the next Field, howling and making odious Faces; but I ran to the Body of a Tree, and leaning my Back against it, kept them off, by waving my Hanger. Several of this cursed Brood getting hold of the Branches behind leapt up in the Tree, from whence they began to discharge their Excrements on my Head: However, I escaped pretty well, by sticking close to the Stem of the Tree, but was almost stifled with the Filth, which fell about me on every side.

In the midst of this Distress, I observed them all to run away on a sudden as fast as they could, at which I ventured to leave the Tree, and pursue the Road, wondering what it was that could put them into this Fright. But looking on my Left hand, I saw a Horse walking softly in the Field: which my Persecutors having sooner discovered, was the Cause of their Flight. The Horse started a little when he came near me, but soon recovering himself, looked full in my Face with manifest Tokens of Wonder: He viewed my Hands and Feet, walking round me several times. I would have pursued my Journey, but he placed himself directly in the Way, yet looking with a very mild Aspect, never offering the least Violence. We stood gazing at each other for some time; at last I took the Boldness, to reach my Hand towards his Neck, with a Design to stroke it, using the common Style and Whistle of Jockies when they are going to handle a strange Horse. But this Animal seeming to receive my Civilities with Disdain shook his Head, and bent his Brows, softly raising up his right Forefoot to remove my Hand. Then he neighed three or four times, but in so different a Cadence, that I almost began to think he was speaking to himself in some Language of his own.

While He and I were thus employed, another Horse came up; who applying himself[10] to the first in a very formal Manner, they gently struck each other's right Hoof before, neighing several times by Turns, and varying the Sound, which seemed to be almost articulate. They went some Paces off, as if it were to confer together, walking Side by Side, backward and forward, like Persons deliberating upon some Affair of Weight, but often turning their Eyes towards me, as it were to watch that I might not escape. I was amazed to see such Actions and Behaviour in Brute Beasts, and concluded with myself, that if the Inhabitants of this Country were endued with a proportionable Degree of Reason, they must needs be the wisest People upon Earth. This Thought gave me so much Comfort, that I resolved to go forward until I could discover some House or Village, or meet with any of the Natives, leaving the two Horses to discourse together as they pleased. But the first, who was a Dapple-Grey, observing me to steal off, neighed after me in so expressive a Tone, that I fancied myself to understand what he meant; whereupon I turned back, and came near him, to expect[11] his farther Commands; but concealing my Fear as much as I could, for I began to be in some Pain, how this Adventure might terminate; and the Reader will easily believe I did not much like my present Situation.

The two Horses came up close to me, looking with great Earnestness upon my Face and Hands. The grey Steed rubbed my Hat all round with his right Fore-hoof, and discomposed it so much, that I was forced to adjust it better, by taking it off, and settling it again; whereat both he and his Companion (who was a brown Bay) appeared to be much surprised, the latter felt the Lappet of my Coat, and finding it to hang loose about me, they both looked with new Signs of Wonder. He stroked my Right hand, seeming to admire the Softness, and Colour; but he squeezed it so hard between his Hoof and his Pastern, that I was forced to roar; after which they both touched me with all possible Tenderness. They were under great Perplexity about my Shoes and Stockings, which they felt very often, neighing to each other, and using various Gestures, not unlike those of a Philosopher,[12] when he would attempt to solve some new and difficult Phenomenon.

Upon the whole, the Behaviour of these Animals was so orderly and rational, so acute and judicious, that I at last concluded, they must needs be Magicians, who had thus metamorphosed themselves upon some design, and seeing a Stranger in the way, were resolved to divert themselves with him; or perhaps were really amazed at the sight of a Man so very different in Habit, Feature and Complexion from those who might probably live in so remote a Climate. Upon the strength of this Reasoning, I ventured to address them in the following manner: Gentlemen, if you be Conjurers, as I have good Cause to believe, you can understand any Language; therefore I make bold to let your Worships know, that I am a poor distressed *Englishman*, driven by his misfortunes upon your Coast, and I entreat one of you, to let me ride upon his Back, as if he were a real Horse, to some House or Village, where I can be relieved. In return of which Favour, I will make you a Present of this Knife and Bracelet (taking them out of my Pocket). The two Creatures stood silent while I spoke, seeming to listen with great Attention; and when I had ended, they neighed frequently towards each other, as if they were engaged in serious Conversation. I plainly observed, that their Language expressed the Passions very well, and the words might with little Pains be resolved into an Alphabet more easily than the *Chinese*.[13]

I could frequently distinguish the word *Yahoo*, which was repeated by each of them several times; and although it was impossible for me to conjecture what it meant, yet while the two Horses were busy in Conversation, I endeavoured to practice this Word upon my Tongue; and as soon as they were silent, I boldly pronounced *Yahoo* in a loud Voice, imitating, at the same time, as near as I could, the Neighing of a Horse; at which they were both visibly surprised, and the Grey repeated the same Word twice, as if he meant to teach me the right Accent, wherein I spoke after him as well as I could, and found myself perceivably to improve every time, though very far from any Degree of Perfection. Then the Bay tried me with a second Word, much harder to be pronounced; but reducing it to the *English Orthography*, may be spelt thus, *Houyhnhnm*. I did not succeed in this so well as the former, but after two or three farther Trials, I had better fortune; and they both appeared amazed at my Capacity.

After some further Discourse, which I then conjectured might relate to me, the two Friends took their leaves, with the same Compliment of striking each other's Hoof; and the Grey made me signs that I should walk before him, wherein I thought it prudent to comply, till I could find a better Director. When I offered to slacken my Pace, he would cry *Hhuun, Hhuun*; I guessed his meaning, and gave him to understand, as well as I could, that I was weary, and not able to walk faster; upon which, he would stand a while to let me rest.

CHAP. II

The Author conducted by a Houyhnhnm *to his House. The House described. The Author's Reception. The Food of the* Houyhnhnms. *The Author in Distress for want of Meat, is at last relieved. His Manner of feeding in this Country.*

Having travelled about three Miles, we came to a long kind of Building, made of Timber, stuck in the Ground, and wattled across; the Roof was low, and covered with Straw. I now began to be a little comforted, and took out some Toys, which Travellers usually carry for Presents to the Savage *Indians* of *America* and other Parts, in hopes the People of the House would be thereby encouraged to receive me kindly. The Horse made me a sign to go in first; it was a large Room with a smooth Clay Floor, and a Rack and Manger extending the whole length on one side. There were three Nags, and two Mares, not eating, but some of them sitting down upon their Hams, which I very much wondered at; but wondered more to see the rest employed in domestic Business. They seemed but ordinary Cattle; however this confirmed my first Opinion, that a People who could so far civilize brute Animals, must needs excel in Wisdom all the Nations of the World. The Grey came in just after, and thereby prevented any ill Treatment, which the others might have given me. He neighed to them several times in a style of Authority, and received Answers.

Beyond this Room there were three others, reaching the length of the House, to which you passed through three Doors, opposite to each other, in the manner of a Vista;[14] we went through the second Room towards the third, here the Grey walked in first, beckoning me to attend: I waited in the second Room, and got ready my Presents, for the Master and

Mistress of the House: They were two Knives, three Bracelets of false Pearl, a small Looking-glass, and a Bead Necklace. The Horse neighed three or four times, and I waited to hear some Answers in a human Voice, but I heard no other Returns, than in the same Dialect, only one or two a little shriller, than his. I began to think that this House must belong to some Person of great Note among them, because there appeared so much Ceremony before I could gain Admittance. But, that a Man of Quality should be served all by Horses, was beyond my Comprehension. I feared my Brain was disturbed by my Sufferings and Misfortunes: I roused myself, and looked about me in the Room where I was left alone; this was furnished like the first, only after a more elegant manner. I rubbed my Eyes often, but the same Objects still occurred. I pinched my Arms and Sides, to awake myself, hoping I might be in a Dream. I then absolutely concluded, that all these Appearances could be nothing else but Necromancy and Magic. But I had no time to pursue these Reflections; for the Grey Horse came to the Door, and made me a sign to follow him into the third Room, where I saw a very comely Mare, together with a Colt and Foal, sitting on their Haunches, upon Mats of Straw, not unartfully made, and perfectly neat and clean.

The Mare soon after my Entrance, rose from her Mat, and coming up close, after having nicely observed my Hands and Face, gave me a most contemptuous Look; then turning to the Horse, I heard the word *Yahoo* often repeated betwixt them; the meaning of which word I could not then comprehend, although it were the first I had learned to pronounce; but I was soon better informed, to my everlasting Mortification: For the Horse beckoning to me with his Head, and repeating the word *Hhuun*, *Hhuun*, as he did upon the Road, which I understood was to attend him, led me out into a kind of Court, where was another Building at some Distance from the House. Here we entered, and I saw three of those detestable Creatures, which I first met after my Landing, feeding upon Roots, and the Flesh of some Animals, which I afterwards found to be that of Asses and Dogs, and now and then a Cow dead by Accident or Disease. They were all tied by the Neck with strong Withes,[15] fastened to a Beam; they held their Food between the Claws of their Forefeet, and tore it with their Teeth.

The Master Horse ordered a Sorrel Nag, one of his Servants, to untie the largest of these Animals, and take him into the Yard. The Beast and I were brought close together; and our Countenances diligently compared, both by Master and Servant, who thereupon repeated several times the word *Yahoo*. My Horror and Astonishment are not to be described, when I observed, in this abominable Animal, a perfect human Figure; the Face of it indeed was flat and broad, the Nose depressed, the Lips large, and the Mouth wide. But these Differences are common to all Savage Nations, where the Lineaments of the Countenance are distorted by the Natives suffering their Infants to lie grovelling on the Earth, or by carrying them on their Backs, nuzzling with their Face against the Mother's Shoulders. The Forefeet of the *Yahoo* differed from my Hands in nothing else, but the Length of the Nails, the Coarseness and Brownness of the Palms, and the Hairiness on the Backs. There was the same Resemblance between our Feet, with the same Differences, which I knew very well, though the Horses did not, because of my Shoes and Stockings; the same in every Part of our Bodies, except as to Hairiness and Colour, which I have already described.

The great Difficulty that seemed to stick with the two Horses, was, to see the rest of my Body so very different from that of a *Yahoo*, for which I was obliged to my Clothes, whereof they had no Conception: The Sorrel Nag offered me a Root, which he held (after their manner, as we shall describe in its proper place) between his Hoof and Pastern; I took it in my Hand, and having smelt it, returned it to him again as civilly as I could. He brought out of the *Yahoo*'s Kennel a piece of Ass's Flesh, but it smelt so offensively that I turned from it with loathing; he then threw it to the *Yahoo*, by whom it was greedily devoured. He afterwards showed me a Whisp of Hay, and a Fetlock full of Oats; but I shook my Head, to signify, that neither of these were Food for me. And indeed, I now apprehended, that I must absolutely starve, if I did not get to some of my own Species: For as to those filthy *Yahoos*, although there were few greater Lovers of Mankind, at that time, than myself; yet I confess I never saw any sensitive Being so detestable on all accounts; and the more I came near them, the more hateful they grew, while I stayed in that Country. This the Master Horse observed by my Behaviour, and therefore sent the *Yahoo* back to his Kennel. He then put his Fore-hoof to his Mouth, at which I was much surprised, although he did it with ease, and with a Motion that appeared perfectly natural, and made other signs to know what I would eat; but I could not return him such an Answer as he was able to apprehend; and if he had understood me, I did not see how it was possible to contrive any way for finding myself Nourishment. While we were thus engaged, I observed a Cow passing by, whereupon I pointed to her, and expressed a Desire to let me go and milk her. This had its effect; for he led me back into the House, and ordered a Mare-servant to open a Room, where a good store of Milk lay in Earthen and Wooden Vessels, after a very orderly and cleanly manner. She gave me a large Bowl full, of which I drank very heartily, and found myself well refreshed.

About Noon I saw coming towards the House a kind of Vehicle drawn like a Sledge by four *Yahoos*. There was in it an old Steed, who seemed to be of Quality; he alighted with his Hind feet forward, having by Accident got a Hurt in his left Forefoot. He came to dine with our Horse, who received him with great civility. They dined in the best Room, and had Oats boiled in Milk for the second Course, which the old Horse eat warm, but the rest cold. Their Mangers were placed circular in the middle of the Room, and divided into several Partitions, round which they sat on their Haunches upon Bosses of Straw. In the middle was a large Rack with Angles answering to every Partition of the Manger. So that each Horse and Mare eat their own Hay, and their own Mash of Oats and Milk, with much Decency and Regularity. The Behaviour of the young Colt and Foal appeared very modest, and that of the Master and Mistress extremely cheerful and complaisant[16] to their Guest. The Grey ordered me to stand by him, and much Discourse passed between him and his Friend concerning me, as I found by the Stranger's often looking on me, and the frequent Repetition of the word *Yahoo*.

I happened to wear my Gloves, which the Master-Grey observing, seemed perplexed, discovering signs of Wonder what I had done to my Forefeet; he put his Hoof three or four times to them, as if he would signify, that I should reduce them to their former shape, which I presently did, pulling off both my Gloves, and putting them into my Pocket. This occasioned farther Talk, and I saw the Company was pleased with my Behaviour, whereof I soon found the good Effects. I was ordered to speak the few words I understood, and while they were at Dinner, the Master taught me the Names for Oats, Milk, Fire, Water, and some others; which I could readily pronounce after him, having from my Youth a great Facility in learning Languages.

When Dinner was done, the Master Horse took me aside, and by signs and words made me understand the Concern that he was in, that I had nothing to eat. Oats in their Tongue are called *Hlunnh*. This Word I pronounced two or three times; for although I had refused them at first, yet upon second Thoughts, I considered that I could contrive to make of them a kind of Bread, which might be sufficient with Milk to keep me alive, till I could make my Escape to some other Country and to Creatures of my own Species. The Horse immediately ordered a White Mare-servant of his Family to bring me a good Quantity of Oats in a sort of wooden Tray. These I heated before the Fire as well as I could, and rubbed them till the Husks came off, which I made a shift to winnow from the Grain; I ground and beat them between two Stones, then took Water, and made them into a Paste or Cake, which I toasted at the Fire, and eat warm with Milk. It was at first a very insipid Diet, though common enough in many Parts of *Europe*,[17] but grew tolerable by Time; and having been often reduced to hard Fare in my Life, this was not the first Experiment I had made how easily Nature is satisfied. And I cannot but observe, that I never had one Hour's Sickness, while I stayed in this Island. 'Tis true, I sometimes made a shift to catch a Rabbit, or Bird, by Springes made of *Yahoos'* Hairs, and I often gathered wholesome Herbs, which I boiled, or eat as Salads with my Bread, and now and then, for a Rarity, I made a little Butter, and drank the Whey. I was at first at a great loss for Salt; but Custom soon reconciled the Want of it; and I am confident that the frequent use of Salt among us is an Effect of Luxury, and was first introduced only as a Provocative[18] to Drink; except where it is necessary for preserving of Flesh in long Voyages, or in places remote from great Markets. For we observe no Animal to be fond of it but Man: And as to myself, when I left this Country, it was a great while before I could endure the Taste of it in anything that I eat.

This is enough to say upon the Subject of my Diet, wherewith other Travellers fill their Books, as if the Readers were personally concerned, whether we fared well or ill. However, it was necessary to mention this Matter, lest the World should think it impossible that I could find

Sustenance for three Years in such a Country, and among such Inhabitants.

When it grew towards Evening, the Master Horse ordered a Place for me to lodge in; it was but Six Yards from the House, and separated from the Stable of the *Yahoos*. Here I got some Straw, and covering myself with my own Clothes, slept very sound. But I was in a short time better accommodated, as the Reader shall know hereafter, when I come to treat more particularly about my way of living.

CHAP. III

The Author studious to learn the Language, the Houyhnhnm *his Master assists in teaching him. The Language described. Several* Houyhnhnms *of Quality come out of Curiosity to see the Author. He gives his Master a short Account of his Voyage.*

My principal Endeavour was to learn the Language, which my Master (for so I shall henceforth call him) and his Children, and every Servant of his House were desirous to teach me. For they looked upon it as a Prodigy that a brute Animal should discover such Marks of a rational Creature. I pointed to every thing, and inquired the Name of it, which I wrote down in my *Journal-Book* when I was alone, and corrected my bad Accent, by desiring those of the Family to pronounce it often. In this Employment, a Sorrel Nag, one of the under Servants, was very ready to assist me.

In speaking, they pronounce through the Nose and Throat, and their Language approaches nearest to the *High Dutch* or *German*, of any I know in *Europe*; but is much more graceful and significant.[19] The Emperor Charles V made almost the same Observation, when he said, That if he were to speak to his Horse, it should be in *High Dutch*.[20]

The Curiosity and Impatience of my Master were so great, that he spent many Hours of his Leisure to instruct me. He was convinced (as he afterwards told me) that I must be a *Yahoo*, but my Teachableness, Civility and Cleanliness astonished him; which were Qualities altogether so opposite to those Animals. He was most perplexed about my Clothes, reasoning sometimes with himself, whether they were a part of my Body; for I never pulled them off till the Family were asleep, and got them on before they waked in the Morning. My Master was eager to learn from whence I came, how I acquired those Appearances of Reason, which I discovered in all my Actions, and to know my Story from my own Mouth, which he hoped he should soon do by the great Proficiency I made in learning and pronouncing their Words and Sentences. To help my Memory, I formed all I learned into the *English* Alphabet, and writ the Words down with the Translations. This last, after some time, I ventured to do in my Master's Presence. It cost me much Trouble to explain to him what I was doing; for the Inhabitants have not the least Idea of Books or Literature.

In about ten Weeks' time I was able to understand most of his Questions, and in three Months could give him some tolerable Answers. He was extremely curious to know from what Part of the Country I came, and how I was taught to imitate a rational Creature, because the *Yahoos* (whom he saw I exactly resembled in my Head, Hands and Face, that were only visible) with some appearance of Cunning, and the strongest Disposition to Mischief, were observed to be the most unteachable of all Brutes. I answered, That I came over the Sea, from a far Place, with many others of my own Kind, in a great hollow Vessel made of the Bodies of Trees. That my Companions forced me to land on this Coast, and then left me to shift for myself. It was with some Difficulty, and by the help of many Signs, that I brought him to understand me. He replied, That I must needs be mistaken, or that I *said the thing which was not.* (For they have no Word in their Language to express Lying or Falsehood.) He knew it was impossible that there could be a Country beyond the Sea, or that a parcel of Brutes could move a wooden Vessel whither they pleased upon Water. He was sure no *Houyhnhnm* alive could make such a Vessel, nor would trust *Yahoos* to manage it.

The Word *Houyhnhnm*, in their Tongue, signifies a *Horse*, and in its Etymology, *the Perfection of Nature.* I told my Master, that I was at a loss for Expression, but would improve as fast as I could; and hoped in a short time I should be able to tell him Wonders: He was pleased to direct his own Mare, his Colt and Foal, and the Servants of the Family, to take all

Opportunities of instructing me, and every Day for two or three Hours, he was at the same Pains himself: Several Horses and Mares of Quality in the Neighbourhood came often to our House upon the Report spread of a wonderful *Yahoo*, that could speak like a *Houyhnhnm*, and seemed in his Words and Actions to discover some Glimmerings of Reason. These delighted to converse with me; they put many Questions, and received such Answers, as I was able to return. By all these Advantages, I made so great a Progress, that in five Months from my Arrival, I understood whatever was spoke, and could express myself tolerably well.

The *Houyhnhnms* who came to visit my Master, out of a Design of seeing and talking with me, could hardly believe me to be a right *Yahoo*, because my Body had a different Covering from others of my Kind. They were astonished to observe me without the usual Hair or Skin, except on my Head, Face and Hands; but I discovered that Secret to my Master, upon an Accident, which happened about a Fortnight before.

I have already told the Reader, that every Night when the Family were gone to Bed, it was my Custom, to strip and cover myself with my Clothes: It happened one Morning early, that my Master sent for me, by the Sorrel Nag, who was his Valet; when he came, I was fast asleep, my Clothes fallen off on one side, and my Shirt above my Waist. I awaked at the Noise he made, and observed him to deliver his Message in some Disorder; after which he went to my Master, and in a great Fright gave him a very confused Account of what he had seen: This I presently discovered; for going as soon as I was dressed, to pay my Attendance upon his Honour, he asked me the meaning of what his Servant had reported, that I was not the same Thing when I slept as I appeared to be at other times; that his Valet assured him, some part of me was White, some Yellow, at least not so White, and some Brown.

I had hitherto concealed the Secret of my Dress, in order to distinguish myself as much as possible, from that cursed Race of *Yahoos*; but now I found it in vain to do so any longer. Besides, I considered that my Clothes and Shoes would soon wear out, which already were in a declining Condition, and must be supplied by some Contrivance from the Hides of *Yahoos* or other Brutes; whereby the whole Secret would be known. I therefore told my Master, that in the Country from whence I came, those of my kind always covered their Bodies with the Hairs of certain Animals prepared by Art, as well for Decency, as to avoid the Inclemencies of Air both hot and cold; of which, as to my own Person I would give him immediate Conviction, if he pleased to command me; only desiring his Excuse, if I did not expose those Parts, that Nature taught us to conceal. He said my Discourse was all very strange, but especially the last part; for he could not understand why Nature should teach us to conceal what Nature had given. That neither himself nor Family were ashamed of any Parts of their Bodies; but however I might do as I pleased. Whereupon, I first unbuttoned my Coat, and pulled it off. I did the same with my Waistcoat; I drew off my Shoes, Stockings and Breeches. I let my Shirt down to my Waist, and drew up the Bottom, fastening it like a Girdle about my middle to hide my Nakedness.

My Master observed the whole Performance with great Signs of Curiosity and Admiration. He took up all my Clothes in his Pastern, one Piece after another, and examined them diligently; he then stroked my Body very gently, and looked round me several times, after which he said, it was plain I must be a perfect *Yahoo*; but that I differed very much from the rest of my Species, in the Softness, Whiteness, and Smoothness of my Skin, my want of Hair in several Parts of my Body, the shape and shortness of my Claws behind and before, and my affectation of walking continually on my two Hinder-feet. He desired to see no more, and gave me leave to put on my Clothes again, for I was shuddering with Cold.

I expressed my uneasiness at his giving me so often the Appellation of *Yahoo*, an odious Animal, for which I had so utter an Hatred and Contempt. I begged he would forbear applying that Word to me, and take the same Order in his Family, and among his Friends whom he suffered to see me. I requested likewise, that the Secret of my having a false Covering to my Body might be known to none but Himself, at least as long as my present Clothing should last; for, as to what the Sorrel Nag his Valet had observed, his Honour might command him to conceal it.

All This my Master very graciously consented to, and thus the Secret was kept till my Clothes began to wear out, which I was forced to supply by several Contrivances, that shall hereafter be mentioned. In the meantime, he desired I would go on with my utmost Diligence to learn their Language, because he was more astonished at my Capacity for Speech and Reason, than at the Figure of my Body, whether it were covered or no; adding, that he waited with some Impatience to hear the Wonders which I promised to tell him.

From thenceforward he doubled the Pains he had been at to instruct me; he brought me into all Company, and made them treat me with Civility, because, as he told them privately, this would put me into good Humour, and make me more diverting.

Every Day when I waited on him, beside the Trouble he was at in teaching, he would ask me several Questions concerning myself, which I answered as well as I could; and by these means he had already received some general Ideas, though very imperfect. It would be tedious to relate the several Steps, by which I advanced to a more regular Conversation: But the first Account I gave of myself in any Order and Length, was to this purpose:

That I came from a very far Country, as I already had attempted to tell him, with about fifty more of my own Species; that we travelled upon the Seas, in a great hollow Vessel made of Wood, and larger than his Honour's House. I described the Ship to him in the best terms I could, and explained by the help of my Handkerchief displayed,[21] how it was driven forward by the Wind. That upon a Quarrel among us, I was set on shore on this Coast, where I walked forward without knowing whither, till he delivered me from the Persecution of those execrable *Yahoos*. He asked me, Who made the Ship, and how it was possible that the *Houyhnhnms* of my Country would leave it to the Management of Brutes? My Answer was, That I durst proceed no farther in my Relation, unless he would give me his Word and Honour that he would not be offended, and then I would tell him the Wonders I had so often promised. He agreed; and I went on by assuring him, that the Ship was made by Creatures like myself, who in all the Countries I had travelled, as well as in my own, were the only governing, rational Animals; and that upon my Arrival hither, I was as much astonished to see the *Houyhnhnms* act like rational Beings, as he or his Friends could be in finding some Marks of Reason in a Creature he was pleased to call a *Yahoo*, to which I owned my Resemblance in every Part, but could not account for their degenerate and brutal Nature. I said farther, That if good Fortune ever restored me to my native Country, to relate my Travels hither, as I resolved to do, everybody would believe that I *said the Thing which was not*; that I invented the Story out of my own Head; and with all possible respect to Himself, his Family, and Friends, and under his Promise of not being offended, our Countrymen would hardly think it probable, that a *Houyhnhnm* should be the presiding Creature of a Nation, and a *Yahoo* the Brute.

CHAP. IV

The Houyhnhnms' *Notion of Truth and Falsehood. The Author's Discourse disapproved by his Master. The Author gives a more particular Account of himself, and the Accidents of his Voyage.*

My Master heard me with great appearances of Uneasiness in his Countenance, because *Doubting* or *not believing*, are so little known in this Country, that the Inhabitants cannot tell how to behave themselves under such Circumstances. And I remember in frequent Discourses with my Master concerning the Nature of Manhood,[22] in other Parts of the World, having occasion to talk of *Lying*, and *false Representation*, it was with much Difficulty that he comprehended what I meant, although he had otherwise a most acute Judgment. For he argued thus; That the Use of Speech was to make us understand one another, and to receive Information of Facts; now if anyone *said the Thing which was not*, these Ends were defeated; because I cannot properly be said to understand him, and I am so far from receiving Information, that he leaves me worse than in Ignorance, for I am led to believe a Thing *Black* when it is *White*, and *Short* when it is *Long*. And these were all the Notions he had concerning that Faculty of *Lying*, so perfectly well understood among human Creatures.

To return from this Digression; when I asserted that the *Yahoos* were the only governing Animals in my Country, which my Master said was altogether past his Conception, he desired to know, whether we had *Houyhnhnms* among us, and what was their Employment: I told him, we had great Numbers, that in Summer they grazed in the Fields, and in Winter were kept in Houses, with Hay and Oats, where *Yahoo*-Servants were employed to rub their Skins smooth, comb their Manes, pick their Feet, serve them with Food, and make their Beds. I understand you well, said my Master; it is now very plain, from all you have spoken, that whatever share of Reason the *Yahoos* pretend to, the *Houyhnhnms* are your Masters; I heartily wish our *Yahoos* would be so tractable. I begged his Honour would please to excuse me from proceeding any farther, because I was very certain that the Account he expected from me would be highly displeasing. But he insisted in commanding me to let him know the best and the worst: I told him, he should be obeyed. I owned, that the *Houyhnhnms* among us, whom we called *Horses,* were the most generous and comely Animal we had; that they excelled in Strength and Swiftness; and when they belonged to Persons of Quality, employed in Travelling, Racing, or drawing Chariots, they were treated with much Kindness and Care, till they fell into Diseases, or became foundered in the Feet; and then they were sold, and used to all kind of Drudgery till they died; after which their Skins were stripped and sold for what they were worth, and their Bodies left to be devoured by Dogs and Birds of Prey.[23] But the common Race of Horses had not so good Fortune, being kept by Farmers and Carriers and other mean People, who put them to greater Labour, and fed them worse. I described as well as I could, our way of Riding, the shape and use of a Bridle, a Saddle, a Spur, and a Whip, of Harness and Wheels. I added, that we fastened Plates of a certain hard Substance called *Iron* at the Bottom of their Feet, to preserve their Hoofs from being broken by the stony Ways on which we often travelled.

My Master, after some Expressions of great Indignation, wondered how we dared to venture upon a *Houyhnhnm's* Back, for he was sure, that the weakest Servant in his House would be able to shake off the strongest *Yahoo,* or by lying down, and rolling on his Back, squeeze the Brute to Death. I answered, That our Horses were trained up from three or four Years old to the several Uses we intended them for; That if any of them proved intolerably vicious, they were employed for Carriages; that they were severely beaten while they were young, for any mischievous Tricks: That the Males, designed for common Use of Riding or Draught, were generally *castrated* about two Years after their Birth, to take down their Spirits, and make them more tame and gentle; that they were indeed sensible of Rewards and Punishments; but his Honour would please to consider, that they had not the least Tincture of Reason any more than the *Yahoos* in this Country.

It put me to the Pains of many Circumlocutions to give my Master a right Idea of what I spoke; for their Language doth not abound in Variety of Words, because their Wants and Passions are fewer than among us. But it is impossible to express his noble Resentment at our savage Treatment of the *Houyhnhnm* Race, particularly after I had explained the Manner and Use of *Castrating* Horses among us, to hinder them from propagating their Kind, and to render them more servile. He said, if it were possible there could be any Country where *Yahoos* alone were endued with Reason, they certainly must be the governing Animal, because Reason will in Time always prevail against Brutal Strength. But, considering the Frame of our Bodies, and especially of mine, he thought no Creature of equal Bulk was so ill-contrived, for employing that Reason in the common Office of Life; whereupon he desired to know whether those among whom I lived, resembled me or the *Yahoos* of his Country. I assured him, that I was as well shaped as most of my Age: but the younger and the Females were much more soft and tender, and the Skins of the latter generally as white as Milk. He said, I differed indeed from other *Yahoos*, being much more cleanly, and not altogether so deformed, but in point of real Advantage, he thought I differed for the worse. That my Nails were of no Use either to my Fore or Hinder-Feet; As to my Forefeet he could not properly call them by that Name, for he never observed me to walk upon them; that they were too soft to bear the Ground; that I generally went with them uncovered; neither was the Covering I sometimes wore on them, of the same Shape, or so strong as that on my Feet behind. That I could not walk with any Security, for if either of my Hinder-Feet slipped, I must inevitably fall. He then began to find fault with other Parts of my Body: the Flatness of my Face, the Prominence of my Nose, my Eyes placed directly in Front, so that I could not look on either Side without turning my Head: That I was not able to feed myself, without lifting one of my Forefeet to my Mouth: And therefore Nature had placed those Joints to answer that Necessity. He knew not what could be the Use of those several Clefts and Divisions in my Feet behind; that these were too soft to bear the Hardness and Sharpness of Stones without a Covering made from the Skin of some other Brute; that my whole Body wanted a Fence against Heat and Cold, which I was forced to put on and off every Day with Tediousness and Trouble. And lastly, that he observed every Animal in this Country naturally to abhor the *Yahoos*, whom the Weaker avoided, and the Stronger drove from them. So that supposing us to have the Gift of Reason, he could not see how it were possible to cure that natural Antipathy which every Creature discovered against us; nor consequently, how we could tame and render them serviceable. However, he would (as he said) debate the Matter no farther, because he was more desirous to know my own Story, the Country where I was born, and the several Actions and Events of my Life before I came hither.

I assured him, how extremely desirous I was that he should be satisfied in every Point; but I doubted much, whether it would be possible for me to explain myself on several Subjects whereof his Honour could have no Conception, because I saw nothing in his Country to which I could resemble them. That however, I would do my best, and strive to express myself by Similitudes, humbly desiring his Assistance when I wanted proper Words; which he was pleased to promise me.

I said, my Birth was of honest Parents, in an Island called *England*, which was remote from this Country, as many Days Journey as the strongest of his Honour's Servants could travel in the Annual Course of the Sun. That I was bred a Surgeon, whose Trade it is to cure Wounds and Hurts in the Body, got by Accident or Violence; that my Country was governed by a Female Man, whom we called a *Queen*. That I left it to get Riches, whereby I might maintain myself and Family when I should return. That in my last Voyage, I was Commander of the Ship, and had about fifty *Yahoos* under me, many of which died at Sea, and I was forced to supply them by others picked out from several Nations. That our Ship was twice in Danger of being sunk; the first time by a great Storm, and the second, by striking against a Rock. Here my Master interposed, by asking me, How I could persuade Strangers out of different Countries to venture with me, after the Losses I had sustained, and the Hazards I had run. I said, they were Fellows of desperate Fortunes forced to fly from the Places of their Birth, on account of their Poverty or their Crimes. Some were undone by Law suits; others spent all they had in Drinking, Whoring and Gaming; others fled for Treason; many for Murder, Theft, Poisoning, Robbery, Perjury, Forgery, Coining false Money, for committing Rapes or Sodomy, for flying from their Colours,[24] or deserting to the Enemy, and most of them had broken Prison; none of these durst return to their Native Countries for fear of being hanged, or of starving in a Jail; and therefore were under a necessity of seeking a Livelihood in other Places.

During this Discourse, my Master was pleased to interrupt me several Times; I had made use of many Circumlocutions in describing to him the Nature of the several Crimes, for which most of our Crew had been forced to fly their Country. This Labour took up several Days Conversation before he was able to comprehend me. He was wholly at a Loss to know what could be the Use or Necessity of Practising those Vices. To clear up which I endeavoured to give him some Ideas of the Desire of Power and Riches, of the terrible Effects of Lust, Intemperance, Malice and Envy. All this I was forced to define and describe by putting of Cases, and making of Suppositions. After which, like one whose Imagination was struck with something never seen or heard of before, he would lift up his Eyes with Amazement and Indignation. Power, Government, War, Law, Punishment, and a Thousand other Things had no terms, wherein that Language could express them, which made the Difficulty almost insuperable to give my Master any Conception of what I meant. But being of an excellent Understanding, much improved by Contemplation and Converse, he at last arrived at a competent Knowledge of what Human Nature in our Parts of the World is capable to perform, and desired I would give him some particular Account of that Land, which we call *Europe*, but especially of my own Country.

Jilustration

CHAP. V

The Author at his Master's Commands informs him of the State of
England. *The Causes of War among the Princes of* Europe. *The*
Author begins to explain the English *Constitution.*

The Reader may please to observe, that the following Extract of many Conversations I had with my Master, contains a Summary of the most material Points, which were discoursed at several times for above Two

Years; his Honour often desiring fuller Satisfaction as I farther improved in the *Houyhnhnm* Tongue. I laid before him, as well as I could, the whole State of *Europe*; I discoursed of Trade and Manufactures, of Arts and Sciences; and the Answers I gave to all the Questions he made, as they arose upon several Subjects, were a Fund of Conversation not to be exhausted. But I shall here only set down the Substance of what passed between us concerning my own Country, reducing it into Order as well as I can, without any Regard to Time or other Circumstances, while I strictly adhere to Truth. My only Concern is, that I shall hardly be able to do Justice to my Master's Arguments and Expressions, which must needs suffer by my want of capacity, as well as by a Translation into our barbarous[25] *English*.

In Obedience therefore to his Honour's Commands, I related to him the *Revolution* under the Prince of *Orange*,[26] the long War with *France* entered into by the said Prince, and renewed by his Successor the present Queen,[27] wherein the greatest Powers of *Christendom* were engaged, and which still continued: I computed at his Request, that about a Million of *Yahoos* might have been killed in the whole Progress of it, and perhaps a Hundred or more Cities taken, and thrice as many ships Burnt or sunk.

He asked me what were the usual Causes or Motives that made one Country go to War with another. I answered they were innumerable, but I should only mention a few of the chief. Sometimes the Ambition of Princes, who never think they have Land or People enough to govern: Sometimes the Corruption of Ministers, who engage their Master in a War in order to stifle or divert the Clamour of the Subjects against their Evil Administration. Difference in Opinions hath cost many Millions of Lives: For instance, whether *Flesh* be *Bread*, or *Bread* be *Flesh*; whether the Juice of a certain *Berry* be *Blood* or *Wine*; whether *Whistling* be a Vice or a Virtue; whether it be better to *kiss a Post*, or throw it into the Fire; what is the best Colour for a *Coat*, whether *Black*, *White*, *Red* or *Grey*; and whether it should be *long* or *short*, *narrow* or *wide*, *dirty* or *clean*, with many more.[28] Neither are any Wars so furious and bloody, or of so long Continuance, as those occasioned by Difference in Opinion, especially if it be in things indifferent.

Sometimes the Quarrel between two Princes is to decide which of them shall dispossess a Third of his Dominions, where neither of them

pretend to any Right. Sometimes one Prince quarrelleth with another,
for fear the other should quarrel with him. Sometimes a War is entered
upon, because the Enemy is too *strong*, and sometimes because he is too
weak. Sometimes our Neighbours *want* the *Things* which we *have*, or *have*
the Things which we *want*; and we both fight, till they take ours or give
us theirs. It is a very justifiable Cause of War to invade a Country after
the People have been wasted by Famine, destroyed by Pestilence, or
embroiled by Factions amongst themselves. It is justifiable to enter into
War against our nearest Ally, when one of his Towns lies convenient for
us, or a Territory of Land, that would render our Dominions round and
complete. If a Prince sends Forces into a Nation, where the People are
poor and ignorant, he may lawfully put half of them to Death, and make
Slaves of the rest, in order to civilize and reduce²⁹ them from their
barbarous Way of Living. It is a very kingly, honourable, and frequent
Practice, when one Prince desires the Assistance of another to secure him
against an Invasion, that the Assistant, when he hath driven out the
Invader, should seize on the Dominions himself, and kill, imprison or
banish the Prince he came to relieve. Alliance by Blood or Marriage, is a
frequent Cause of War between Princes, and the nearer the Kindred is,
the greater is their Disposition to quarrel: *Poor* Nations are *hungry*, and
rich Nations are *proud*, and Pride and Hunger will ever be at Variance.
For these Reasons, the Trade of a *Soldier* is held the most honourable of
all others: Because a *Soldier* is a *Yahoo* hired to kill in cold Blood as many
of his own Species, who have never offended him, as possibly he can.
There is likewise a Kind of beggarly Princes in *Europe*, not able to
make War by themselves, who hire out their Troops to richer Nations,
for so much a Day to each Man; of which they keep three fourths to
themselves, and it is the best part of their Maintenance; such are those
in Germany and other *Northern* Parts of *Europe*.

What you have told me (said my Master) upon the Subject of War,
does indeed discover most admirably the Effects of that Reason you
pretend to: However it is happy that the *Shame* is greater than the *Danger*;
and that Nature hath left you utterly uncapable of doing much Mischief.

For your Mouths lying flat with your Faces, you can hardly bite each
other to any purpose, unless by Consent. Then, as to the Claws upon
your Feet before and behind, they are so short and tender, that one of

our *Yahoos* would drive a Dozen of yours before him. And therefore in recounting the Numbers of those who have been killed in Battle, I cannot but think that you have *said the Thing which is not.*

I could not forbear shaking my Head and smiling a little at his Ignorance. And being no Stranger to the Art of War, I gave him a Description of Cannons, Culverins,[30] Muskets, Carabines,[31] Pistols, Bullets, Powder, Swords, Bayonets, Battles, Sieges, Retreats, Attacks, Undermines, Countermines,[32] Bombardments, Sea fights; Ships sunk with a Thousand Men, Twenty thousand killed on each Side; dying Groans, Limbs flying in the Air, Smoke, Noise, Confusion, Trampling to Death under Horses' Feet; Flight, Pursuit, Victory; Fields strewed with Carcasses left for Food to Dogs, and Wolves, and Birds of Prey; Plundering, Stripping, Ravishing, Burning and Destroying. And to set forth the Valour of my own dear Countrymen, I assured him, that I had seen them blow up a Hundred Enemies at once in a Siege, and as many in a Ship, and beheld the dead Bodies come down in pieces from the Clouds, to the great Diversion of the Spectators.

I was going on to more Particulars, when my Master commanded me Silence. He said, Whoever understood the Nature of *Yahoos* might easily believe it possible for so vile an Animal, to be capable of every Action I had named, if their Strength and Cunning equalled their Malice. But as my Discourse had increased his Abhorrence of the whole Species, so he found it gave him a Disturbance in his Mind, to which he was wholly a Stranger before. He thought his Ears being used to such abominable Words, might by Degrees admit them with less Detestation. That although he hated the *Yahoos* of this Country, yet he no more blamed them for their odious Qualities, than he did a *Gnnayh* (a Bird of Prey) for its Cruelty, or a sharp Stone for cutting his Hoof. But when a Creature pretending to Reason, could be capable of such Enormities, he dreaded lest the Corruption of that Faculty might be worse than Brutality itself. He seemed therefore confident, that instead of Reason, we were only possessed of some Quality fitted to increase our natural Vices; as the Reflection from a troubled Stream returns the Image of an ill-shapen Body, not only *larger*, but more *distorted.*

He added, That he had heard too much upon the Subject of War, both in this, and some former Discourses. There was another Point which a little perplexed him at present. I had informed him, that some of our Crew left their Country on account of being ruined by *Law*; that I had already explained the meaning of the Word; but he was at a Loss how it should come to pass, that the *Law* which was intended for *every* Man's Preservation, should be any Man's Ruin. Therefore he desired to be farther satisfied what I meant by *Law* and the Dispensers thereof, according to the present Practice in my own Country, because he thought Nature and Reason were sufficient Guides for a reasonable Animal,[33] as we pretended to be, in showing us what we ought to do, and what to avoid.[34]

I assured his Honour, that Law was a Science wherein I had not much conversed, further than by employing Advocates in vain, upon some Injustices that had been done me. However, I would give him all the Satisfaction I was able.

I said, there was a Society of Men among us, bred up from their Youth in the Art of proving by Words multiplied for the Purpose that White is Black, and Black is White, according as they are paid. To this Society all the rest of the People are Slaves. For Example, if my Neighbour hath a mind to my Cow, he hires a Lawyer to prove, that he ought to have my Cow from me. I must then hire another to defend my Right, it being against all Rules of Law that any Man should be allowed to speak for himself. Now, in this Case, I who am the true Owner lie under two great Disadvantages. First, my Lawyer being practised almost from his Cradle in defending Falsehood, is quite out of his Element when he would be an Advocate for Justice, which as an Office unnatural, he always attempts with great Awkwardness, if not with ill Will. The second Disadvantage is, that my Lawyer must proceed with great Caution, or else he will be reprimanded by the Judges, and abhored by his Brethren, as one that would lessen the Practice of the Law. And therefore I have but two Methods to preserve my Cow. The first is to gain over my Adversary's Lawyer with a double Fee, who will then betray his Client by insinuating that he hath Justice on his Side. The second way is for my Lawyer to make my Cause appear as unjust as he can, by allowing the Cow to belong to my Adversary; and this, if it be skilfully done, will certainly bespeak the Favour of the Bench. Now, your Honour is to know that these Judges are Persons appointed to decide all Controversies of Property, as well as for the Trial of Criminals, and picked out from the most dextrous Lawyers, who are grown old or lazy, and having been biased all their Lives against Truth and Equity lie under such a fatal Necessity of favouring Fraud, Perjury, and Oppression, that I have known several of them refuse a large Bribe from the side where Justice lay, rather than injure the *Faculty*[35] by doing anything unbecoming their Nature or their office.

It is a Maxim among these Lawyers, that whatever hath been done before, may legally be done again: And therefore they take special Care to record all the Decisions formerly made against common Justice, and the general Reason of Mankind. These, under the Name of *Precedents* they produce as Authorities to justify the most iniquitous Opinions; and the Judges never fail of decreeing accordingly.

In pleading, they studiously avoid entering into the *Merits* of the Cause; but are loud, violent and tedious in dwelling upon all *Circumstances* which are not to the Purpose. For Instance, in the Case already mentioned; They never desire to know what Claim or Title my Adversary hath to my *Cow*, but whether the said *Cow* were Red or Black, her Horns long or short; whether the Field I graze her in be round or square, whether she was milked at home or abroad, what Diseases she is subject to, and the like; after which they consult *Precedents*, adjourn the Cause, from Time to Time, and in Ten, Twenty, or Thirty Years come to an Issue.

It is likewise to be observed that this Society hath a peculiar Cant and Jargon of their own, that no other Mortal can understand, and wherein all their Laws are written, which they take special Care to multiply; whereby they have wholly confounded the very Essence of Truth and Falsehood, of Right and Wrong; so that it will take Thirty Years to decide whether the Field, left me by my Ancestors for six Generations, belongs to me or to a Stranger three hundred Miles off.

In the Trial of Persons accused for Crimes against the State the Method is much more short and commendable: The Judge first sends to sound the Disposition of those in Power, after which he can easily hang or save the Criminal, strictly preserving all due Forms of Law.

Here my Master interposing, said it was a Pity, that Creatures endowed with such prodigious abilities of Mind as these Lawyers by the Description I gave of them must certainly be, were not rather encouraged to be Instructors of others in Wisdom and Knowledge. In answer to which I assured his Honour, that in all Points out of their own Trade they were the most ignorant and stupid Generation among us, the most despicable in common Conversation, avowed Enemies to all Knowledge and Learning, and equally disposed to <u>pervert the general Reason of Mankind</u> in every other subject of Discourse, as in that of their own Profession.

CHAP. VI

A Continuation of the State of England *under Queen* Anne. *The Character of a first Minister of State in European Courts.*

My Master was yet wholly at a Loss to understand what Motives could incite this Race of Lawyers to perplex, disquiet, and weary themselves, and engage in a Confederacy of Injustice, merely for the Sake of injuring their Fellow Animals; neither could he comprehend what I meant in saying they did it for *Hire.* Whereupon I was at much Pains to describe to him the Use of *Money,* the Materials it was made of, and the Value of the Metals; that when a *Yahoo* had got a great Store of this precious Substance, he was able to purchase whatever he had a mind to, the finest Clothing, the noblest Houses, great Tracts of Land, the most costly Meats and Drinks, and have his choice of the most beautiful Females. Therefore since *Money* alone, was able to perform all these Feats, our *Yahoos* thought, they could never have enough of it to spend or to save, as they found themselves inclined from their natural Bent either to Profusion or Avarice. That the Rich Man enjoyed the Fruit of the Poor Man's Labour, and the latter were a thousand to one in proportion to the former. That the Bulk of our People were forced to live miserably, by labouring every Day for small Wages to make a few live plentifully. I enlarged myself much on these and many other Particulars to the same purpose: But his Honour was still to seek: For he went upon a supposition that all Animals had a Title to their share in the Productions of the Earth, and especially those who presided over the rest. Therefore he desired I would let him know, what these costly Meats were, and how any of us happened to want them. Whereupon I enumerated as many sorts as came into my Head, with the various Methods of dressing them, which could not be done without sending Vessels by Sea to every part of the World, as well for Liquors to Drink, as for Sauces, and innumerable other Conveniences. I assured him, that this whole Globe of Earth must be at least three times gone round, before one of our better Female *Yahoos* could get her Breakfast, or a Cup to put it in. He said, That must needs be a miserable Country which cannot furnish Food for its own Inhabitants. But what he chiefly wondered at was how such vast Tracts of Ground as I described should be wholly without *Fresh water*, and the People put to the Necessity of sending over the Sea for Drink. I replied, that *England* (the dear Place of my Nativity) was computed to produce three times the quantity of Food, more than its Inhabitants are able to consume, as well as Liquors extracted from Grain, or pressed out of the Fruit of certain Trees, which made excellent Drink, and the same Proportion in every other Convenience of Life. But in order to feed the Luxury and Intemperance of the Males, and the Vanity of the Females, we sent away the greatest Part of our necessary Things to other Countries, from whence in return we brought the Materials of Diseases, Folly, and Vice, to spend among ourselves. Hence it follows of Necessity, that vast Numbers of our People are compelled to seek their Livelihood by Begging, Robbing, Stealing, Cheating, Pimping, Forswearing,[36] Flattering, Suborning, Forging, Gaming, Lying, Fawning, Hectoring, Voting, Scribbling, Stargazing, Poisoning, Whoring, Canting, Libeling, Free-thinking,[37] and the like Occupations: every one of which Terms, I was at much Pains to make him understand.

That *Wine* was not imported among us from foreign Countries, to supply the want of Water or other Drinks, but because it was a sort of Liquid which made us merry, by putting us out of our Senses; diverted all melancholy Thoughts, begat wild extravagant Imaginations in the Brain, raised our Hopes, and banished our Fears, suspended every Office of Reason for a Time, and deprived us of the Use of our Limbs, until we fell into a profound Sleep; although it must be confessed, that we always awaked sick and dispirited, and that the Use of this Liquor filled us with Diseases, which made our Lives uncomfortable and short.

But beside all this, the Bulk of our People supported themselves by furnishing the Necessities or Conveniences of Life to the Rich, and to each other. For Instance, when I am at home and dressed as I ought to be, I carry on my Body the Workmanship of an Hundred Tradesmen; the Building and Furniture of my House employ as many more and five times the Number to adorn my Wife.

I was going on to tell him of another sort of People, who get their Livelihood by attending the Sick, having upon some Occasions informed his Honour that many of my Crew had died of Diseases. But here it was with the utmost Difficulty, that I brought him to apprehend what I meant. He could easily conceive, that a *Houyhnhnm* grew weak and heavy a few Days before his Death, or by some Accident might hurt a Limb. But that Nature, who works all Things to Perfection, should suffer any Pains to breed in our Bodies, he thought it impossible, and desired to know the Reason of so unaccountable an Evil. I told him, we fed on a thousand Things which operated contrary to each other; that we eat when we were not hungry, and drank without the Provocation of Thirst; That we sat whole Nights drinking strong Liquors without eating a Bit, which disposed us to Sloth, enflamed our Bodies, and precipitated or prevented Digestion. That prostitute Female *Yahoos* acquired a certain Malady, which bred Rottenness in the Bones of those, who fell into their Embraces; That this and many other Diseases, were propagated from Father to Son, so that great Numbers come into the World with complicated Maladies upon them; that it would be endless to give him a Catalogue of all Diseases incident to human Bodies; for they could not be fewer than five or six hundred, spread over every Limb, and Joint; in short, every Part, external and intestine, having Diseases appropriated to them. To remedy which, there was a Sort of People bred up among us, in the Profession or Pretence of curing the Sick. And because I had some Skill in the Faculty, I would in Gratitude to his Honour, let him know the whole Mystery and Method by which they proceed.

Their Fundamental is, That all Diseases arise from *Repletion*, from whence they conclude, that a great *Evacuation*[38] of the Body is necessary, either through the natural Passage, or upwards at the Mouth. Their next Business is, from Herbs, Minerals, Gums, Oils, Shells, Salts, Juices, Seaweed, Excrements, Barks of Trees, Serpents, Toads, Frogs, Spiders, Dead Men's Flesh and Bones, Birds, Beasts and Fishes, to form a

Composition for Smell and Taste the most abominable, nauseous and detestable, they can possibly contrive, which the Stomach immediately rejects with loathing; and this they call a *Vomit*; or else from the same Storehouse, with some other poisonous Additions, they command us to take in at the Orifice *above* or *below* (just as the Physician then happens to be disposed) a Medicine equally annoying and disgustful to the Bowels, which relaxing the Belly, drives down all before it, and this they call a *Purge*, or a *Clyster*. For Nature (as the Physicians allege) having intended the superior anterior Orifice only for the *intromission* of Solids and Liquids, and the inferior posterior for Ejection, these Artists ingeniously considering that in all Diseases Nature is forced out of her Seat; therefore to replace her in it, the Body must be treated in a manner directly contrary, by interchanging the Use of each Orifice, forcing Solids and Liquids in at the *Anus*, and making Evacuations at the Mouth.

But, besides real Diseases, we are subject to many that are only imaginary,[39] for which the Physicians have invented imaginary Cures; these have their several Names, and so have the Drugs that are proper for them, and with these our Female *Yahoos* are always infested.

One great Excellency in this Tribe is their Skill at *Prognostics*, wherein they seldom fail; their Predictions in real Diseases, when they rise to any Degree of Malignity, generally portending *Death*, which is always in their Power, when Recovery is not: And therefore, upon any unexpected Signs of Amendment, after they have pronounced their Sentence, rather than be accused as false Prophets, they know how to approve their Sagacity to the World by a seasonable Dose.

They are likewise of special Use to Husbands and Wives, who are grown weary of their Mates, to eldest Sons, to great Ministers of State, and often to Princes.

I had formerly upon occasion discoursed with my Master upon the Nature of *Government* in general, and particularly of our own *excellent Constitution*, deservedly the Wonder and Envy of the whole World. But having here accidentally mentioned a *Minister of State*; he commanded me some time after to inform him, what Species of *Yahoo* I particularly meant by that Appellation.

I told him,[40] that a first or *Chief Minister of State*, who was the Person I intended to describe, was a Creature wholly exempt from Joy and Grief,

Love and Hatred, Pity and Anger; at least made use of no other Passions but a violent Desire of Wealth, Power, and Titles; That he applies his Words to all Uses, except to the Indication of his Mind; That he never tells a *Truth*, but with an Intent that you should take it for a *Lie*; nor a *Lie*, but with a Design that you should take it for a *Truth*; That those he speaks worst of behind their Backs, are in the surest Way to Preferment; and whenever he begins to praise you to others or to yourself, you are from that Day forlorn. The worst Mark you can receive is a *Promise*, especially when it is confirmed with an Oath; after which every wise Man retires, and gives over all Hopes.

There are three Methods by which a Man may rise to be Chief Minister: The first is, by knowing how with Prudence to dispose of a Wife, a Daughter, or a Sister; The second, by betraying or undermining his Predecessor: And the third is, by a *furious Zeal* in public Assemblies against the Corruptions of the Court. But a Wise Prince would rather choose to employ those who practise the last of these Methods; because such Zealots prove always the most obsequious and subservient to the Will and Passions of their Master. That these *Ministers* having all Employments at their Disposal, preserve themselves in Power by bribing the Majority of a Senate or great Council; and at last by an Expedient called an *Act of Indemnity*[41] (whereof I described the Nature to him) they secured themselves from after Reckonings, and retired from the Public, laden with the Spoils of the Nation.

The Palace of a *Chief Minister* is a Seminary to breed up others in his own Trade: The Pages, Lackies, and Porters, by imitating their Master, become *Ministers of State* in their several Districts, and learn to excel in the three principal *Ingredients, of Insolency, Lying,* and *Bribery.* Accordingly, they have a *Subaltern* Court paid to them by Persons of the best Rank, and sometimes by the Force of Dexterity and Impudence, arrive through several Gradations to be Successors to their Lord.

He is usually governed by a decayed Wench or favourite Footman, who are the Tunnels through which all Graces are conveyed, and may properly be called, *in the last Resort,*[42] the Governors of the Kingdom.

One Day in Discourse my Master, having heard me mention the *Nobility* of my Country, was pleased to make me a Compliment which I could not pretend to deserve: That he was sure, I must have been born of some Noble Family, because I far exceeded in Shape, Colour, and Cleanliness, all the *Yahoos* of his Nation, although I seemed to fail in Strength, and Agility, which must be imputed to my different Way of Living from those other Brutes, and besides, I was not only endowed with the Faculty of Speech, but likewise with some Rudiments of Reason, to a Degree, that with all his Acquaintance I passed for a Prodigy.

He made me observe, that among the *Houyhnhnms*, the *White*, the *Sorrel*, and the *Iron-grey*, were not so exactly shaped as the *Bay*, the *Dapple-grey*, and the *Black*; nor born with equal Talents of the Mind, or a Capacity to improve them; and therefore continued always in the Condition of Servants, without ever aspiring to match out of their own Race, which in that Country would be reckoned monstrous and unnatural.

I made his Honour my most humble Acknowledgements for the good Opinion he was pleased to conceive of me; but assured him at the same time, that my Birth was of the lower Sort, having been born of plain honest Parents, who were just able to give me a tolerable Education: That *Nobility* among us was altogether a different Thing from the Idea he had of it; That our Young *Noblemen* are bred from their Childhood in Idleness and Luxury; that as soon as Years will permit, they consume their Vigour, and contract odious Diseases among lewd Females; and when their Fortunes are almost ruined, they marry some Woman of mean Birth, disagreeable Person, and unsound Constitution, merely for the Sake of Money, whom they hate and despise. That the Productions of such Marriages are generally scrofulous, rickety, or deformed Children, by which means the Family seldom continues above Three Generations, unless the Wife takes care to provide a healthy Father among her Neighbours, or Domestics in order to improve and continue the Breed. That a weak diseased Body, a meagre Countenance, and sallow Complexion, are the true Marks of Noble Blood; And a healthy robust Appearance is so disgraceful in a Man of Quality, that the World concludes his real Father to have been a *Groom*, or a *Coachman*. The Imperfections of his Mind run parallel with those of his Body being a Composition of Spleen, Dulness, Ignorance, Caprice, Sensuality, and Pride.

Without the Consent of *this illustrious Body* no Law can be made, repealed, or altered, and these have the Decision of all our Possessions without Appeal.

CHAP. VII

Origund Tashut ef
extremes

The Author's great Love of his Native Country. His Master's
Observations upon the Constitution and Administration of
England, *as described by the Author, with parallel Cases and*
Comparisons. His Master's Observations upon Human Nature.

The Reader may be disposed to wonder how I could prevail on myself
to give so free a Representation of my own Species, among a Race of
Mortals who were already too apt to conceive the vilest Opinion of
Human Kind from that entire Congruity betwixt me and their *Yahoos.*
But I must freely confess, that the many Virtues of those excellent
Quadrupeds placed in opposite View to human Corruptions, had so far
opened my Eyes and enlarged my Understanding, that I began to view
the Actions and Passions of Man in a very different Light, and to think
the Honour of my own Kind not worth managing;[43] which, besides, it
was impossible for me to do before a Person of so acute a Judgment as my
Master, who daily convinced me of a thousand Faults in myself, whereof
I had not the least Perception before, and which among us would never
be numbered even among human Infirmities, I had likewise learned from
his Example an utter Detestation of all Falsehood or Disguise; and *Truth*
appeared so amiable to me, that I determined upon sacrificing everything
to it.

Let me deal so candidly with the Reader, as to confess, that there was
yet a much stronger Motive for the Freedom I took in my Representation
of Things. I had not been a Year in this Country, before I contracted
such a Love and Veneration for the Inhabitants, that I entered on a firm
Resolution never to return to human Kind, but to pass the rest of my
Life among these admirable *Houyhnhnms* in the Contemplation and Practice
of every Virtue; where I could have no Example or Incitement to Vice.
But it was decreed by Fortune, my perpetual Enemy, that so great a
Felicity should not fall to my share. However, it is now some Comfort
to reflect, that in what I said of my Countrymen, I *extenuated* their Faults
as much as I durst before so strict an Examiner, and upon every Article,
gave as *favourable* a Turn as the Matter would bear. For, indeed, who is

there alive that will not be swayed by his Bias and Partiality to the Place of his Birth?

I have related the Substance of several Conversations I had with my Master, during the greatest part of the Time I had the Honour to be in his Service, but have indeed for Brevity sake omitted much more than is here set down.

When I had answered all his Questions, and his Curiosity seemed to be fully satisfied; he sent for me one Morning early, and commanding me to sit down at some distance (an Honour which he had never before conferred upon me) he said, He had been very seriously considering my whole Story, as far as it related both to myself and my Country: That he looked upon us as a sort of Animals to whose Share, by what Accident he could not conjecture, some small Pittance of *Reason* had fallen, whereof we made no other Use than by its Assistance to aggravate our *natural* Corruptions, and to acquire new ones which Nature had not given us. That we disarmed ourselves of the few Abilities she had bestowed, had been very successful in multiplying our original Wants, and seemed to spend our whole Lives in vain Endeavours to supply them by our own Inventions. That as to myself, it was manifest I had neither the Strength or Agility of a common *Yahoo*, that I walked infirmly on my hinder Feet, had found out a Contrivance to make my Claws of no Use or Defence, and to remove the Hair from my Chin, which was intended as a shelter from the Sun and the Weather. Lastly, That I could neither run with Speed, nor climb trees like my *Brethren* (as he called them) the *Yahoos* in this Country.

That our Institutions of *Government* and *Law* were plainly owing to our gross Defects in *Reason*, and by consequence, in *Virtue*; because *Reason* alone is sufficient to govern a *Rational* Creature; which was therefore a Character we had no Pretence to challenge, even from the Account I had given of my own People, although he manifestly perceived, that in order to favour them, I had concealed many Particulars, and often *said the Thing which was not*.

He was the more confirmed in this Opinion, because he observed, that as I agreed in every Feature of my Body with other *Yahoos*, except where it was to my real Disadvantage in point of Strength, Speed and Activity, the shortness of my Claws, and some other Particulars where Nature had no Part; so from the Representation I had given him of our Lives, our Manners, and our Actions, he found as near a Resemblance in the Disposition of our Minds. He said the *Yahoos* were known to hate one another more than they did any different Species of Animals; and the Reason usually assigned, was, the Odiousness of their own Shapes, which all could see in the rest, but not in themselves. He had therefore begun to think it not unwise in us to *cover* our Bodies, and by that Invention, conceal many of our own Deformities from each other, which would else be hardly supportable. But he now found he had been mistaken, and that the Dissensions of those Brutes in his Country were owing to the same Causes with ours, as I had described them. For, if (said he) you throw among Five *Yahoos* as much Food as would be sufficient for Fifty, they will, instead of eating peaceably, fall together by the Ears, each single one impatient to *have all to itself*; and therefore a Servant was usually employed to stand by while they were feeding abroad, and those kept at home were tied at a Distance from each other; that if a Cow died of Age or Accident, before a *Houyhnhnm* could secure it for his own *Yahoos*, those in the Neighbourhood, would come in Herds to seize it, and then would ensue such a Battle as I had described, with terrible Wounds made by their Claws on both Sides, although they seldom were able to kill one another, for want of such convenient Instruments of Death as we had invented. At other times the like Battles have been fought between the *Yahoos* of several Neighbourhoods without any visible Cause: Those of one District watching all Opportunities to surprise the next before they are prepared. But if they find their Project has miscarried, they return home, and, for want of Enemies, engage in what I call a *Civil War* among themselves.

That in some Fields of his Country, there are certain *shining Stones* of several Colours, whereof the *Yahoos* are violently fond, and when Part of these *Stones* is fixed in the Earth, as it sometimes happeneth, they will dig with their Claws for whole Days to get them out, then carry them away, and hide them by Heaps in their Kennels; but still looking round with great Caution, for fear their Comrades should find out their Treasure. My Master said, he could never discover the Reason of this unnatural Appetite, or how these *Stones* could be of any Use to a *Yahoo*; but now he believed it might proceed from the same Principle of *Avarice*, which I had ascribed to Mankind; that he had once, by way of Experiment, privately removed a Heap of these *Stones* from the Place where one of his *Yahoos* had buried it: Whereupon, the sordid Animal missing his Treasure, by his loud lamenting brought the whole Herd to the Place, there miserably howled, then fell to biting and tearing the rest, began to pine away, would neither eat, nor sleep, nor work, till he ordered a Servant privately to convey the *Stones* into the same Hole, and hide them as before; which when his *Yahoo* had found, he presently recovered his Spirits and good Humour, but took care to remove them to a better hiding-place, and hath ever since been a very serviceable Brute.

My Master farther assured me, which I also observed myself, That in the Fields where these *shining Stones* abound, the fiercest and most frequent Battles are fought, occasioned by perpetual Inroads of the Neighbouring *Yahoos*.

He said, it was common when two *Yahoos* discovered such a *Stone* in a Field, and were contending which of them should be the Proprietor, a third would take the Advantage, and carry it away from them both; which my Master would needs contend to have some kind of Resemblance with our *Suits at Law*; wherein I thought it for our Credit not to undeceive him; since the Decision he mentioned was much more equitable than many Decrees among us: Because the Plaintiff and Defendant there lost nothing beside the *Stone* they contended for, whereas our *Courts of Equity*,[44] would never have dismissed the Cause while either of them had anything left.

My Master continuing his Discourse, said, There was nothing that rendered the *Yahoos* more odious, than their undistinguishing Appetite to devour everything that came in their way, whether Herbs, Roots, Berries, the corrupted Flesh of Animals, or all mingled together: And it was peculiar in their Temper, that they were fonder of what they could get by Rapine or Stealth at a greater distance, than much better Food provided for them at home. If their Prey held out, they would eat till they were ready to burst, after which Nature had pointed out to them a certain *Root* that gave them a general Evacuation.

There was also another kind of *Root* very *juicy*, but somewhat rare and difficult to be found, which the *Yahoos* sought for with much Eagerness, and would suck it with great Delight; and it produced in them the same

Effects that Wine hath upon us. It would make them sometimes hug, and sometimes tear one another; they would howl and grin, and chatter, and reel and roll, and tumble, and then fall asleep in the Dirt.

I did indeed observe, that the *Yahoos* were the only Animals in this Country subject to any Diseases; which however, were much fewer than Horses have among us, and contracted not by any ill Treatment they meet with, but by the Nastiness, and Greediness of that sordid Brute. Neither has their Language any more than a general Appellation for those Maladies, which is borrowed from the Name of the Beast, and called *Hnea-Yahoo* or the *Yahoo's-Evil*, and the Cure prescribed is a Mixture of *their own Dung* and *Urine* forcibly put down the *Yahoo*'s Throat. This I have since often known to have been taken with success and do here freely recommend it to my Countrymen for the public Good, as an admirable Specific against all Diseases produced by Repletion.

As to Learning, Government, Arts, Manufactures, and the like, my Master confessed he could find little or no Resemblance between the *Yahoos* of that Country and those in ours. For, he only meant to observe what Parity there was in our Natures. He had heard indeed some curious *Houyhnhnms* observe, that in most Herds there was a sort of ruling *Yahoo* (as among us there is generally some leading or principal Stag in a Park) who was always more *deformed* in Body, and *mischievous in Disposition*, than any of the rest. That this Leader[45] had usually a Favourite as *like himself* as he could get, whose Employment was to *lick his Master's Feet and Posteriors, and drive the Female* Yahoos *to his Kennel*; for which he was now and then rewarded with a piece of Ass's Flesh. This *Favourite* is hated by the whole Herd, and therefore to protect himself, keeps always *near the Person of his Leader*. He usually continues in Office till a worse can be found; but the very Moment he is discarded, his Successor, at the Head of all the *Yahoos* in that District, Young and Old, Male and Female, come in a Body, and discharge their Excrements upon him from Head to Foot. But how far this might be applicable to our *Courts* and *Favourites*, and *Ministers of State*, my Master said I could best determine.

I *durst* make no return to this malicious Insinuation, which debased human Understanding below the Sagacity[46] of a common *Hound*, who has Judgment enough to distinguish and follow the Cry of the *ablest Dog in the Pack*, without being ever mistaken.

My Master told me, there were some Qualities remarkable in the *Yahoos*, which he had not observed me to mention, or at least very slightly, in the Accounts I had given him of human Kind; he said, Those Animals, like other Brutes, had their Females in common; but in this they differed, that the She-*Yahoo* would admit the Male, while she was pregnant, and that the Hees would quarrel and fight with the Females as fiercely as with each other. Both which Practices were such Degrees of infamous Brutality, that no other sensitive Creature ever arrived at.

Another thing he wondered at in the *Yahoos*, was their strange Disposition to Nastiness and Dirt, whereas there appears to be a natural Love of Cleanliness in all other Animals. As to the two former Accusations, I was glad to let them pass without any Reply, because I had not a Word to offer upon them in Defence of my Species, which otherwise I certainly had done from my own Inclinations. But I could have easily vindicated Human Kind from the Imputation of Singularity upon the last Article, if there had been any *Swine* in that Country (as unluckily for me there were not) which although it may be a *sweeter Quadruped* than a *Yahoo*, cannot I humbly conceive in Justice pretend to more Cleanliness; and so his Honour himself must have owned, if he had seen their filthy way of feeding, and their Custom of wallowing and sleeping in the Mud.

My Master likewise mentioned another Quality which his Servants had discovered in several *Yahoos*, and to him was wholly unaccountable. He said, a Fancy would sometimes take a *Yahoo*, to retire into a Corner, to lie down and howl, and groan, and spurn away all that came near him, although he were young and fat, wanted neither Food nor Water; nor did the Servants imagine what could possibly ail him. And the only Remedy they found was to set him to hard Work, after which he would infallibly come to himself. To this I was silent out of Partiality to my own Kind; yet here I could plainly discover the true seeds of *Spleen*,[47] which only seizeth on the *Lazy*, the *Luxurious*, and the *Rich*; who, if they were forced to undergo the *same Regimen* I would undertake for the Cure.

His Honour had further observed, that a Female *Yahoo* would often stand behind a Bank or a Bush, to gaze on the young Males passing by, and then appear, and hide, using many antic Gestures and Grimaces, at which time it was observed, that she had a most *offensive Smell*; and when any of the Males advanced, would slowly retire, looking often back, and with a counterfeit show of Fear, run off into some convenient Place where she knew the Male would follow her.

At other times if a Female Stranger came among them, Three or Four of her own Sex would get about her, and stare and chatter, and grin, and smell her all over, and then turn off with Gestures that seemed to express Contempt and Disdain.

Perhaps my Master might refine a little in these Speculations, which he had drawn from what he observed himself, or had been told him by others: however, I could not reflect without some Amazement, and much Sorrow, that the Rudiments of *Lewdness*, *Coquetry*, *Censure*, and *Scandal*, should have place by Instinct in Womankind.

I expected every Moment that my Master would accuse the *Yahoos* of those unnatural Appetites in both Sexes, so common among us. But Nature it seems hath not been so expert a Schoolmistress; and these politer Pleasures are entirely the Productions of Art and Reason, on our side of the Globe.

CHAP. VIII

The Author relates several Particulars of the Yahoos. *The great Virtues of the* Houyhnhnms. *The Education and Exercise of their Youth. Their general Assembly.*

As I ought to have understood Human Nature much better than I supposed it possible for my Master to do, so it was easy to apply the Character he gave of the *Yahoos* to myself and my Countrymen, and I believed I could yet make farther Discoveries from my own Observation. I therefore often begged his Favour to let me go among the Herds of *Yahoos* in the Neighbourhood, to which he always very graciously consented, being perfectly convinced that the Hatred I bore those Brutes would never suffer me to be corrupted by them; and his Honour ordered one of his Servants, a strong Sorrel Nag, very honest and good-natured, to be my Guard, without whose Protection I durst not undertake such Adventures. For I have already told the Reader how much I was pestered by those odious Animals upon my first Arrival. And I afterwards failed very narrowly three or four times of falling into their Clutches, when I happened to stray at any Distance without my Hanger. And I have reason to believe they had some Imagination that I was of their own Species, which I often assisted myself, by stripping up my Sleeves, and showing my naked Arms and Breast in their sight, when my Protector was with me: At which times they would approach as near as they durst, and imitate my Actions after the manner of Monkeys, but ever with great signs of Hatred, as a tame *Jack-Daw* with Cap and Stockings,[48] is always persecuted by the wild ones, when he happens to be got among them.

They are prodigiously nimble from their Infancy; however, I once caught a young Male of three Years old, and endeavoured by all Marks of Tenderness to make it quiet; but the little Imp fell a squalling, and scratching, and biting with such Violence, that I was forced to let it go, and it was high time, for a whole Troop of old ones came about us at the Noise, but finding the Cub was safe (for away it ran) and my Sorrel Nag being by, they durst not venture near us. I observed the young Animal's Flesh to smell very rank, and the stink was somewhat between a *Weasel* and a *Fox*, but much more disagreeable. I forgot another Circumstance (and perhaps I might have the Reader's Pardon, if it were wholly omitted) that while I held the odious Vermin in my Hands, it voided its filthy Excrements of a Yellow liquid Substance, all over my Clothes; but by good Fortune there was a small Brook hard by, where I washed myself as clean as I could, although I durst not come into my Master's Presence, until I were sufficiently aired.

By what I could discover, the *Yahoos* appear to be the most unteachable of all Animals, their Capacities never reaching higher than to draw or carry Burdens. Yet I am of opinion this Defect ariseth chiefly from a perverse, restive Disposition. For they are cunning, malicious, treacherous and revengeful. They are strong and hardy, but of a cowardly Spirit, and by consequence, insolent, abject, and cruel. It is observed, that the *Red-haired* of both Sexes are more libidinous and mischievous than the rest, whom yet they much exceed in Strength and Activity.

The *Houyhnhnms* keep the *Yahoos* for present use in Huts not far from the House; but the rest are sent abroad to certain Fields, where they dig up Roots, eat several kinds of Herbs, and search about for Carrion, or sometimes catch *Weasels* and *Luhimuhs* (a sort of *wild Rat*) which they greedily devour. Nature hath taught them to dig deep Holes with their Nails on the side of a rising Ground, wherein they lie by themselves; only the Kennels of the Females are larger, sufficient to hold two or three Cubs.

They swim from their Infancy like Frogs, and are able to continue long under Water, where they often take Fish, which the Females carry home to their Young. And upon this Occasion, I hope the Reader will pardon my relating an odd Adventure.

Being one Day abroad with my Protector the Sorrel Nag, and the Weather exceeding hot, I entreated him to let me bathe in a River that was near. He consented, and I immediately stripped myself stark naked, and went down softly into the Stream. It happened that a young Female *Yahoo* standing behind a Bank, saw the whole proceeding, and enflamed by Desire, as the Nag and I conjectured, came running with all speed, and leaped into the Water within five Yards of the Place where I bathed. I was never in my Life so terribly frighted; the Nag was grazing at some distance, not suspecting any Harm. She embraced me after a most fulsome manner; I roared as loud as I could, and the Nag came galloping towards me, whereupon she quitted her Grasp, with the utmost Reluctancy, and leaped upon the opposite Bank, where she stood gazing and howling all the time I was putting on my Clothes.

This was matter of Diversion to my Master and his Family, as well as of Mortification to myself. For now I could no longer deny, that I was a real *Yahoo*, in every Limb and Feature, since the Females had a natural Propensity to me as one of their own Species: Neither was the Hair of this Brute of a Red Colour (which might have been some Excuse for an Appetite a little irregular) but Black as a Sloe,[49] and her Countenance did not make an Appearance altogether so hideous as the rest of the Kind; For, I think, she could not be above eleven Years old.

Having lived three Years in this Country, the Reader I suppose will expect, that I should, like other Travellers, give him some Account of the Manners and Customs of its Inhabitants, which it was indeed my principal Study to learn.

As these Noble *Houyhnhnms* are endowed by Nature with a general Disposition to all Virtues, and have no Conceptions or Ideas of what is

Evil in a Rational Creature, so their grand Maxim is, to cultivate *Reason*, and to be wholly governed by it. Neither is *Reason* among them a Point Problematical as with us, where Men can argue with Plausibility on both sides of a Question; but strikes you with immediate Conviction;[50] as it must needs do where it is not mingled, obscured or discoloured by Passion and Interest. I remember it was with extreme Difficulty that I could bring my Master to understand the meaning of the Word *Opinion*, or how a Point could be disputable; because *Reason* taught us to affirm or deny only where we are certain; and beyond our Knowledge we cannot do either. So that Controversies, Wranglings, Disputes, and Positiveness in false or dubious Propositions are Evils unknown among the *Houyhnhnms*. In the like manner when I used to explain to him our several Systems of *Natural Philosophy*, he would laugh that a Creature pretending to *Reason*, should value itself upon the Knowledge of other People's Conjectures, and in Things, where that Knowledge, if it were certain, could be of no Use. Wherein he agreed entirely with the Sentiments of *Socrates*, as *Plato* delivers them;[51] which I mention as the highest Honour I can do that Prince of Philosophers. I have often since reflected what Destruction such a Doctrine would make in the Libraries of *Europe*, and how many Paths to Fame would be then shut up in the Learned World.

Friendship and *Benevolence* are the two principal Virtues among the *Houyhnhnms*, and these not confined to particular Objects, but universal to the whole Race. For a Stranger from the remotest Part is equally treated with the nearest Neighbour, and wherever he goes, looks upon himself as at home. They preserve *Decency* and *Civility* in the highest Degrees, but are altogether ignorant of *Ceremony*. They have no Fondness for their Colts or Foals, but the Care they take in educating them proceeds entirely from the Dictates of *Reason*. And I observed my Master to show the same Affection to his Neighbour's Issue that he had for his own. They will have it that *Nature* teaches them to love the whole Species, and it is *Reason* only that maketh a Distinction of Persons, where there is a superior Degree of Virtue.

When the Matron *Houyhnhnms* have produced one of each Sex, they no longer accompany with their Consorts, except they lose one of their Issue by some Casualty, which very seldom happens: But in such a Case they meet again, or when the like Accident befalls a Person, whose Wife is past bearing, some other Couple bestows on him one of their own Colts, and then go together again until the Mother is pregnant. This Caution is necessary to prevent the Country from being overburdened with Numbers. But the Race of inferior *Houyhnhnms*, bred up to be Servants is not so strictly limited upon this Article; These are allowed to produce three of each Sex, to be Domestics in the Noble Families.

In their Marriages they are exactly careful to choose such Colours as will not make any disagreeable Mixture in the Breed. *Strength* is chiefly valued in the Male, and *Comeliness* in the Female, not upon the account of *Love*, but to preserve the Race from degenerating; for where a Female happens to excel in *Strength*, a Consort is chosen with regard to *Comeliness*. Courtship, Love, Presents, Jointures,[52] Settlements,[53] have no place in their Thoughts; or Terms whereby to express them in their Language. The young Couple meet and are joined, merely because it is the Determination of their Parents and Friends: It is what they see done every Day, and they look upon it as one of the necessary Actions of a Rational Being. But the Violation of Marriage, or any other Unchastity, was never heard of: And the married Pair pass their Lives with the same Friendship, and mutual Benevolence that they bear to all others of the same Species, who come in their way; without Jealousy, Fondness, Quarrelling, or Discontent.

In educating the Youth of both Sexes, their Method is admirable, and highly deserves our Imitation. These are not suffered to taste a Grain of *Oats*,[54] except upon certain Days, till Eighteen Years old; nor *Milk*, but very rarely; and in Summer they graze two Hours in the Morning, and as long in the Evening, which their Parents likewise observe; but the Servants are not allowed above half that time, and a great Part of their Grass is brought home, which they eat at the most convenient Hours, when they can be best spared from Work.

Temperance, *Industry*, *Exercise* and *Cleanliness*, are the Lessons equally enjoined to the young ones of both Sexes: And my Master thought it monstrous in us to give the Females a different kind of Education from the Males, except in some Articles of Domestic Management; whereby as he truly observed, one half of our Natives were good for nothing but bringing Children into the World: And to trust the Care of our Children to such useless Animals, he said was yet a greater Instance of Brutality.

But the *Houyhnhnms* train up their Youth to Strength, Speed, and Hardiness, by exercising them in running Races up and down steep Hills, and over hard stony Grounds, and when they are all in a Sweat, they are ordered to leap over Head and Ears, into a Pond or River. Four times a Year the Youth of a certain District meet to show their Proficiency in Running, and Leaping, and other Feats of Strength and Agility, where the Victor is rewarded, with a Song made in his or her Praise. On this Festival the Servants drive a Herd of *Yahoos* into the Field, laden with Hay, and Oats, and Milk for a Repast to the *Houyhnhnms*; after which, these Brutes are immediately driven back again, for fear of being noisome to the Assembly.

Every fourth Year at the *Vernal Equinox*, there is a Representative Council of the whole Nation, which meets in a Plain about twenty Miles from our House, and continues about five or six Days. Here they inquire into the State and Condition of the several Districts; whether they abound or be deficient in Hay or Oats, or Cows or *Yahoos*? And wherever there is any Want (which is but seldom) it is immediately supplied by unanimous Consent and Contribution. Here likewise the Regulation of Children is settled: As for Instance, if a *Houyhnhnm* hath two Males, he changeth one of them with another that hath two Females: And when a Child hath been lost by any Casualty, where the Mother is past Breeding, it is determined what Family in the District shall breed another to supply the Loss.

CHAP. IX

A grand Debate at the General Assembly of the Houyhnhnms, *and how it was determined. The Learning of the* Houyhnhnms. *Their Buildings. Their manner of Burials. The Defectiveness of their Language.*

One of these Grand Assemblies was held in my time, about three Months before my Departure, whither my Master went as the Representative of our District. In this Council was resumed their old Debate, and indeed, the only Debate which ever happened in that Country; whereof my Master after his Return gave me a very particular Account.

The Question to be debated, was, whether the *Yahoos* should be exterminated from the Face of the Earth. One of the *Members* for the Affirmative offered several Arguments of great Strength and Weight, alleging, That as the *Yahoos* were the most filthy, noisome, and deformed Animal which Nature ever produced, so they were the most restive and indocible,[55] mischievous and malicious: They would privately suck the Teats of the *Houyhnhnms'* Cows, kill and devour their Cats, trample down their Oats and Grass, if they were not continually watched, and commit a thousand other Extravagances. He took notice of a general Tradition, That *Yahoos* had not been always in that Country: but, that many Ages ago, two of these Brutes appeared together upon a Mountain, whether produced by the Heat of the Sun upon corrupted Mud and Slime, or from the Ooze and Froth of the Sea, was never known. That these *Yahoos* engendered, and their Brood in a short time grew so numerous as to overrun and infest the whole Nation. That the *Houyhnhnms* to get rid of this Evil, made a general Hunting, and at last enclosed the whole Herd, and destroying the elder, every *Houyhnhnm* kept two young Ones in a Kennel, and brought them to such a degree of Tameness, as an Animal so savage by Nature can be capable of acquiring; using them for Draught and Carriage. That there seemed to be much Truth in this Tradition, and that those Creatures could not be *Ylnhniamshy* (or *Aborigines* of the Land) because of the violent Hatred the *Houyhnhnms*, as well as all other Animals, bore them; which although their evil Disposition sufficiently deserved, could never have arrived at so high a Degree, if they had been *Aborigines*, or else they would have long since been rooted out. That the Inhabitants taking a Fancy to use the Service of the *Yahoos*, had very imprudently neglected to cultivate the Breed of *Asses*, which were a comely Animal, easily kept, more tame and orderly, without any offensive Smell, strong enough for Labour, although they yield to the other in Agility of Body; and if their Braying be no agreeable Sound, it is far preferable to the horrible Howlings of the *Yahoos*.

Several others declared their Sentiments to the same purpose, when my Master proposed an Expedient to the Assembly, whereof he had indeed borrowed the Hint from me. He approved of the Tradition,

mentioned by the *Honourable Member*,[56] who spoke before, and affirmed
that the Two *Yahoos* said to be first seen among them had been driven
thither over the Sea; that coming to Land, and being forsaken by their
Companions, they retired to the Mountains, and degenerating by degrees,
became in process of time, much more savage than those of their own
Species in the Country from whence these two Originals came. The reason
of his Assertion was, that he had now in his Possession, a certain wonderful
Yahoo (meaning myself) which most of them had heard of, and many of
them had seen. He then related to them, how he first found me; that my
Body was all covered with an artificial Composure of the Skins and Hairs
of other Animals: That I spoke a Language of my own, and had thoroughly
learned theirs: That I had related to him the Accidents which brought me
thither: That when he saw me without my Covering, I was an exact *Yahoo*
in every Part, only of a whiter Colour, less hairy, and with shorter Claws.
He added, how I had endeavoured to persuade him, that in my own and
other Countries the *Yahoos* acted as the governing, Rational Animal, and
held the *Houyhnhnms* in Servitude: That he observed in me all the Qualities
of a *Yahoo*, only a little more civilized by some Tincture of Reason, which
however was in a degree as far inferior to the *Houyhnhnm* Race, as the *Yahoos*
of their Country were to me: That, among other things, I mentioned a
Custom we had of *Castrating Houyhnhnms* when they were young, in order
to render them tame; that the Operation was easy and safe; that it was no
Shame to learn Wisdom from Brutes, as Industry is taught by the Ant, and
Building by the Swallow (For so I translate the Word *Lyhannh*, although it
be a much larger Fowl). That this Invention might be practised upon the
younger *Yahoos* here, which, besides rendering them tractable and fitter for
Use, would in an Age put an end to the whole Species without destroying
Life. That, in the meantime the *Houyhnhnms* should be *exhorted* to cultivate
the Breed of Asses, which, as they are in all respects more valuable
Brutes, so they have this Advantage, to be fit for Service at five Years
old, which the others are not till twelve.

This was all my Master thought fit to tell me at that time, of what
passed in the Grand Council. But he was pleased to conceal one Particular,
which related personally to myself, whereof I soon felt the unhappy
Effect, as the Reader will know in its proper Place, and from whence I
date all the succeeding Misfortunes of my Life.

The *Houyhnhnms* have no Letters, and consequently, their Knowledge is all Traditional. But there happening few Events of any Moment among a People so well united, naturally disposed to every Virtue, wholly governed by Reason, and cut off from all Commerce with other Nations, the Historical Part is easily preserved without burdening their Memories. I have already observed, that they are subject to no Diseases, and therefore can have no need of Physicians. However, they have excellent Medicines composed of Herbs, to cure accidental Bruises and Cuts in the Pastern or Frog of the Foot by sharp Stones, as well as other Maims and Hurts in the several Parts of the Body.

They calculate the Year by the Revolution of the Sun and the Moon, but use no Subdivisions into Weeks. They are well enough acquainted with the Motions of those two Luminaries, and understand the Nature of *Eclipses*; and this is the utmost Progress of their *Astronomy*.

In *Poetry* they must be allowed to excel all other Mortals; wherein the Justness of their Similes, and the Minuteness, as well as Exactness of their Descriptions, are indeed inimitable. Their Verses abound very much in both of these, and usually contain either some exalted Notions of Friendship and Benevolence, or the Praises of those who were Victors in Races, and other bodily Exercises.[57] Their Buildings, although very rude and simple, are not inconvenient,[58] but well contrived to defend them from all Injuries of Cold and Heat. They have a kind of Tree, which at Forty Years old loosens in the Root, and falls with the first Storm; they grow very straight, and being pointed like Stakes with a sharp Stone (for the *Houyhnhnms* know not the Use of Iron), they stick them erect in the Ground about ten Inches asunder, and then weave in Oat-straw, or sometimes Wattles betwixt them. The Roof is made after the same manner, and so are the Doors.

The *Houyhnhnms* use the hollow Part between the Pastern and the Hoof of their Forefeet, as we do our Hands, and this with greater Dexterity, than I could at first imagine. I have seen a White Mare of our Family thread a Needle (which I lent her on purpose) with that Joint. They milk their Cows, reap their Oats, and do all the Work which requires Hands, in the same manner. They have a kind of hard Flints, which by grinding against other Stones, they form into Instruments, that serve instead of Wedges, Axes, and Hammers. With Tools made of these Flints, they likewise cut their Hay, and reap their Oats, which there groweth naturally in several Fields: The *Yahoos* draw home the Sheaves in Carriages, and the Servants tread them in certain covered Huts, to get out the Grain, which is kept in Stores. They make a rude kind of earthen and wooden Vessels, and bake the former in the Sun.

If they can avoid Casualties, they die only of Old Age, and are buried in the obscurest Places that can be found, their Friends and Relations expressing neither Joy nor Grief at their Departure, nor does the dying Person discover the least Regret that he is leaving the World, any more than if he were upon returning home from a Visit to one of his Neighbours; I remember my Master having once made an Appointment with a Friend and his Family to come to his House upon some Affair of Importance, on the Day fixed, the Mistress and her two Children came very late; she made two Excuses, first for her Husband, who, as she said, happened that very Morning to *Lhnuwnh*. The Word is strongly expressive in their Language, but not easily rendered into *English*, it signifies, *to retire to his first Mother.* Her Excuse for not coming sooner, was that her Husband dying late in the Morning, she was a good while consulting her Servants about a convenient Place where his Body should be laid; and I observed she behaved herself at our House, as cheerfully as the rest, and died about three Months after.

They live generally to Seventy or Seventy-five Years, very seldom to Fourscore: Some Weeks before their Death they feel a gradual Decay, but without Pain. During this time they are much visited by their Friends, because they cannot go abroad, with their usual Ease and Satisfaction. However, about ten Days before their Death, which they seldom fail in computing, they return the Visits that have been made them by those who are nearest in the Neighbourhood, being carried in a convenient Sledge drawn by *Yahoos*, which Vehicle they use, not only upon this Occasion, but when they grow old, upon long Journeys, or when they are lamed by any Accident. And therefore when the dying *Houyhnhnms* return those Visits, they take a solemn leave of their Friends, as if they were going to some remote Part of the Country, where they designed to pass the rest of their Lives.

I know not whether it may be worth observing, that the *Houyhnhnms* have no Word in their Language to express anything that is *Evil*, except what they borrow from the Deformities or ill Qualities of the *Yahoos*. Thus they denote the Folly of a Servant, an Omission of a Child, a Stone that cuts their Feet, a continuance of foul or unseasonable Weather, and the like, by adding to each the Epithet of *Yahoo*. For Instance, *Hhnm Yahoo*, *Whnaholm Yahoo*, *Ynlhmndwihlma Yahoo*, and an ill-contrived House, *Ynholmhnmrohlnw Yahoo*.

I could with great Pleasure enlarge farther upon the Manners and Virtues of this excellent People; but intending in a short time to publish a Volume by itself expressly upon that Subject, I refer the Reader thither. And in the mean time, proceed to relate my own sad Catastrophe.

CHAP. X

The Author's Economy and happy Life among the Houyhnhnms.
*His great Improvement in Virtue, by conversing with them. Their
Conversations. The Author has notice given him by his Master that
he must depart from the Country. He falls into a Swoon for Grief,
but submits. He contrives and finishes a Canoe, by the help of a
Fellow Servant, and puts to Sea at a venture.*

I had settled my little Economy[59] to my own Heart's content. My Master had ordered a Room to be made for me after their manner, about six Yards from the House the Sides and Floors of which I plastered with Clay, and covered with Rush mats of my own contriving; I had beaten Hemp, which there grows wild, and made of it a sort of Ticking:[60] This I filled with the Feathers of several Birds I had taken with Springes made of *Yahoos'* Hairs, and were excellent Food. I had worked two Chairs with my Knife, the Sorrel Nag helping me in the grosser and more laborious Part. When my Clothes were worn to Rags, I made myself others with the Skins of Rabbits, and of a certain beautiful Animal about the same size, called *Nnuhnoh*, the Skin of which is covered with a fine Down. Of these I likewise made very tolerable Stockings. I soled my Shoes with Wood which I cut from a Tree, and fitted to the upper Leather, and when this was worn out, I supplied it with the Skins of *Yahoos* dried in the Sun. I often got Honey out of hollow Trees, which I mingled with Water, or eat with my Bread. No Man could more verify the Truth of these two

Maxims, *That Nature is very easily satisfied*; and, *That Necessity is the Mother of Invention.* I enjoyed perfect Health of Body and Tranquillity of Mind;[61] I did not find the Treachery or Inconstancy of a Friend, nor the Injuries of a secret or open Enemy. I had no occasion of bribing, flattering or pimping, to procure the Favour of any great Man or of his Minion. I wanted no Fence against Fraud or Oppression; Here was neither Physician to destroy my Body, nor Lawyer to ruin my Fortune; No Informer to watch my Words, and Actions, or forge Accusations against me for Hire: Here were no Gibers, Censurers, Backbiters, Pick-pockets, Highwaymen, Housebreakers, Attorneys, Bawds, Buffoons, Gamesters, Politicians, Wits, splenetics, tedious Talkers, Controvertists, Ravishers, Murderers, Robbers, Virtuosos; no Leaders or Followers of Party and Faction; no Encouragers to Vice, by Seducement or Examples: No Dungeon, Axes, Gibbets, Whipping-posts, or Pillories: No cheating Shopkeepers or Mechanics: No Pride, Vanity or Affectation: No Fops, Bullies, Drunkards, strolling Whores, or Poxes: No ranting, lewd, expensive Wives: No stupid, proud Pedants: No importunate, overbearing, quarrelsome, noisy, roaring, empty, conceited, swearing Companions: No Scoundrels, raised from the Dust for the sake of their Vices, or Nobility thrown into it on account of their Virtues: No Lords, Fiddlers, Judges or Dancing-Masters.

I had the favour of being admitted to several *Houyhnhnms*, who came to visit or dine with my Master, where his Honour graciously suffered me to wait in the Room, and listen to their Discourse. Both he and his Company would often descend[62] to ask me Questions, and receive my Answers. I had also sometimes the Honour of attending my Master in his Visits to others. I never presumed to speak, except in answer to a Question, and then I did it with inward Regret, because it was a Loss of so much Time for improving myself: But I was infinitely delighted, with the Station of an humble Auditor in such Conversations, where nothing passed but what was useful, expressed in the fewest and most significant Words: Where the greatest *Decency* was observed, without the least Degree of Ceremony; where no Person spoke without being pleased himself, and pleasing his Companions: Where there was no Interruption, Tediousness, Heat, or Difference of Sentiments. They have a Notion, that when People are met together, a short Silence doth much improve Conversation: This I found to be true; for during those little Intermissions of Talk, new Ideas would arise in their Minds, which very much enlivened the Discourse. Their Subjects are generally on Friendship and Benevolence, or Order and Economy, sometimes upon the visible Operations of Nature, or ancient Traditions; upon the Bounds and Limits of Virtue, upon the unerring Rules of Reason, or upon some Determinations, to be taken at the next great Assembly; and often upon the various Excellencies of *Poetry*. I may add without Vanity, that my Presence often gave them sufficient Matter for Discourse, because it afforded my Master an Occasion of letting his Friends into the History of me and my Country, upon which they were all pleased to descant in a manner not very advantageous to Human Kind; and for that Reason I shall not repeat what they said: Only I may be allowed to observe, That his Honour, to my great Admiration, appeared to understand the Nature of *Yahoos* in all Countries, much better than myself. He went through all our Vices and Follies, and discovered many which I had never mentioned to him, by only supposing what Qualities a *Yahoo* of their Country, with a small proportion of Reason, might be capable of exerting; and concluded, with too much Probability, how vile as well as miserable such a Creature must be.

I freely confess, that all the little Knowledge I have of any value, was acquired by the Lectures I received from my Master, and from hearing the Discourses of him and his Friends; to which I should be prouder to listen, than to dictate to the greatest and wisest Assembly in *Europe*. I admired the Strength, Comeliness, and Speed of the Inhabitants; and such a Constellation of Virtues in such Amiable Persons produced in me the highest Veneration. At first, indeed, I did not feel that natural Awe which the *Yahoos* and all other Animals bear towards them, but it grew upon me by Degrees, much sooner than I imagined, and was mingled with a respectful Love and Gratitude, that they would condescend to distinguish me from the rest of my Species.

When I thought of my Family, my Friends, my Countrymen, or Human Race in general, I considered them as they really were, *Yahoos* in Shape and Disposition, only a little more civilized, and qualified with the Gift of Speech, but making no other use of Reason, than to improve and multiply those Vices, whereof their Brethren in this Country had only the share that Nature allotted them. When I happened to behold the Reflection of my own Form in a Lake or a Fountain, I turned away my

Face in Horror and Detestation of myself, and could better endure the sight of a common *Yahoo*, than of my own Person. By conversing with the *Houyhnhnms*, and looking upon them with Delight, I fell to imitate their Gait and Gesture, which is now grown into an Habit, and my Friends often tell me in a blunt way, that *I trot like a Horse*; which, however, I take for a great Compliment: Neither shall I disown, that in Speaking I am apt to fall into the Voice and manner of the *Houyhnhnms*, and hear myself ridiculed on that account without the least Mortification.

In the midst of all this Happiness, and when I looked upon myself to be fully settled for Life, my Master sent for me one Morning a little earlier than his usual Hour. I observed by his Countenance that he was in some Perplexity, and at a Loss how to begin what he had to speak. After a short Silence, he told me, He did not know how I would take what he was going to say: That in the last general Assembly, when the Affair of the *Yahoos* was entered upon, the Representatives had taken Offence at his keeping a *Yahoo* (meaning myself) in his Family more like a *Houyhnhnm*, than a Brute Animal. That he was known frequently to converse with me, as if he could receive some Advantage or Pleasure in my Company: That such a Practice was not agreeable to Reason or Nature, nor a thing ever heard of before among them. The Assembly did therefore *exhort* him, either to employ me like the rest of my Species, or command me to swim back to the Place from whence I came. That the first of these Expedients was utterly rejected by all the *Houyhnhnms*, who had ever seen me at his House or their own: For they alleged, That because I had some Rudiments of Reason, added to the natural Pravity of those Animals, it was to be feared, I might be able to seduce them into the woody and mountainous Parts of the Country, and bring them in Troops by Night to destroy the *Houyhnhnms'* Cattle, as being naturally of the ravenous Kind, and averse from Labour.

My Master added, That he was daily pressed by the *Houyhnhnms* of the Neighbourhood to have the Assembly's *Exhortation* executed, which he could not put off much longer. He doubted[63] it would be impossible for me to swim to another Country, and therefore wished I would contrive some sort of Vehicle resembling those I had described to him, that might carry me on the Sea, in which Work I should have the Assistance of his own Servants, as well as those of his Neighbours. He concluded, That for his own Part he could have been content to keep me in his Service as long as I lived, because he found I had cured myself of some bad Habits and Dispositions, by endeavouring, as far as my inferior Nature was capable, to imitate the *Houyhnhnms*.

I should here observe to the Reader, That a Decree of the general Assembly in this Country, is expressed by the Word *Hnhloayn*, which signifies an *Exhortation*; as near as I can render it: For they have no Conception how a Rational Creature can be *compelled*, but only advised, or *exhorted*, because no Person can disobey Reason, without giving up his Claim to be a Rational Creature.

I was struck with the utmost Grief and Despair at my Master's Discourse, and being unable to support the Agonies I was under, I fell into a Swoon at his Feet; when I came to myself, he told me, that he concluded I had been dead. (For these People are subject to no such Imbecilities of Nature.) I answered, in a faint Voice, That Death would have been too great an Happiness; that although I could not blame the Assembly's *Exhortation*, or the Urgency of his Friends; yet in my weak and corrupt Judgment, I thought it might consist with Reason to have been less rigorous. That I could not swim a League, and probably the nearest Land to theirs might be distant above an hundred: That many Materials, necessary for making a small Vessel to carry me off, were wholly wanting in this Country, which, however, I would attempt in Obedience and Gratitude to his Honour, although I concluded the Thing to be impossible, and therefore looked on myself as already devoted to Destruction. That the certain Prospect of an unnatural Death, was the least of my Evils: For, supposing I should escape with Life by some strange Adventure, how could I think with Temper, of passing my Days among *Yahoos*, and relapsing into my old Corruptions, for want of Examples to lead and keep me within the Paths of Virtue. That I knew too well upon what solid Reasons all the Determinations of the wise *Houyhnhnms* were founded, not to be shaken by Arguments of mine, a miserable *Yahoo*; and therefore after presenting him with my humble Thanks for the Offer of his Servants' Assistance in making a Vessel, and desiring a reasonable Time for so difficult a Work, I told him I would endeavour to preserve a wretched Being; and, if ever I returned to *England*, was not without Hopes of being useful to my own Species, by celebrating the Praises of the renowned *Houyhnhnms*, and proposing their Virtues to the Imitation of Mankind.

My Master in a few Words made me a very gracious Reply, allowed me the space of two *Months* to finish my Boat; and ordered the Sorrel Nag, my Fellow Servant (for so at this distance I may presume to call him) to follow my Instructions, because I told my Master, that his Help would be sufficient, and I knew he had a Tenderness for me.

In his Company my first Business was to go to that Part of the Coast, where my rebellious Crew had ordered me to be set on Shore. I got upon a Height, and looking on every side into the Sea, fancied I saw a small Island, towards the *North-East*: I took out my Pocket-glass, and could then clearly distinguish it about five Leagues off, as I computed; but it appeared to the Sorrel Nag to be only a blue Cloud: For, as he had no Conception of any Country beside his own, so he could not be as expert in distinguishing remote Objects at Sea, as we who so much converse in that Element.

After I had discovered this Island, I considered no farther; but resolved, it should, if possible, be the first Place of my Banishment, leaving the Consequence to Fortune.

I returned home, and consulting with the Sorrel Nag, we went into a Copse at some distance, where I with my Knife, and he with a sharp Flint fastened very artificially, after their manner, to a wooden Handle, cut down several Oak Wattles about the Thickness of a Walking-staff, and some larger Pieces. But I shall not trouble the Reader with a particular Description of my own Mechanics; let it suffice to say, that in six Weeks time, with the Help of the Sorrel Nag, who performed the Parts that required most Labour, I finished a sort of *Indian* Canoe, but much larger, covering it with the Skins of *Yahoos* well stitched together, with hempen Threads of my own making. My Sail was likewise composed of the Skins of the same Animal; but I made use of the youngest I could get, the older being too tough and thick, and I likewise provided myself with four Paddles. I laid in a Stock of boiled Flesh, of Rabbits and Fowls, and took with me two Vessels, one filled with Milk, and the other with Water.

I tried my Canoe in a large Pond near my Master's House, and then corrected in it what was amiss; stopping all the Chinks with *Yahoos'* Tallow, till I found it stanch,[64] and able to bear me, and my Freight. And when it was as complete as I could possibly make it, I had it drawn on a Carriage very gently by *Yahoos*, to the Seaside, under the Conduct of the Sorrel Nag, and another Servant.

When all was ready, and the Day came for my Departure, I took leave of my Master and Lady, and the whole Family, my Eyes flowing with Tears, and my Heart quite sunk with Grief. But his Honour, out of Curiosity, and perhaps (if I may speak it without Vanity) partly out of Kindness, was determined to see me in my Canoe, and got several of his neighbouring Friends to accompany him. I was forced to wait above an Hour for the Tide, and then observing the Wind very fortunately bearing towards the Island, to which I intended to steer my Course, I took a second Leave of my Master: But as I was going to prostrate myself to kiss his Hoof, he did me the Honour to raise it gently to my Mouth. I am not ignorant how much I have been censured for mentioning this last Particular. For my Detractors are pleased to think it improbable, that so Illustrious a Person should descend to give so great a Mark of Distinction to a Creature so inferior as I. Neither have I forgot, how apt some Travellers are to boast of extraordinary Favours they have received. But if these Censurers were better acquainted with the noble and courteous Disposition of the *Houyhnhnms*, they would soon change their Opinion.

I paid my respects to the rest of the *Houyhnhnms* in his Honour's Company; then getting into my Canoe, I pushed off from Shore.

CHAP. XI

*The Author's dangerous Voyage. He arrives at New-Holland,
hoping to settle there. Is wounded with an Arrow by one of the
Natives. Is seized and carried by Force into a* Portuguese
*Ship. The great Civilities of the Captain. The Author arrives
at* England.

I began this desperate Voyage on *February* 15, 1714/5,[65] at 9 o' Clock in the Morning. The Wind was very favourable; however, I made use at first only of my Paddles, but considering I should soon be weary, and that the Wind might chop about, I ventured to set up my little Sail; and thus, with the help of the Tide, I went at the rate of a League and a half an Hour, as near as I could guess. My Master and his Friends continued on the Shore, till I was almost out of sight; and I often heard the Sorrel Nag (who always loved me) crying out, *Hnuy illa nyha majah Yahoo*,[66] Take care of thyself, gentle *Yahoo*.

My Design was, if possible, to discover some small Island uninhabited, yet sufficient by my Labour to furnish me with the Necessaries of Life, which I would have thought a greater Happiness than to be first Minister in the Politest Court of *Europe*; so horrible was the Idea I conceived of returning to live in the Society and under the Government of *Yahoos*. For in such a Solitude as I desired, I could at least enjoy my own Thoughts, and reflect with Delight on the Virtues of those inimitable *Houyhnhnms*, without any Opportunity of degenerating into the Vices and Corruptions of my own Species.

The Reader may remember what I related when my Crew conspired against me, and confined me to my Cabin. How I continued there several Weeks, without knowing what Course we took; and when I was put ashore in the Long-boat, how the Sailors told me with Oaths, whether true or false, that they knew not in what Part of the World we were. However, I did then believe us to be about ten Degrees *Southward* of the *Cape of Good Hope*, or about 45 Degrees *Southern* Latitude, as I gathered from some general Words I overheard among them, being I supposed to the *South-East* in their intended Voyage to *Madagascar*. And although this were but little better than Conjecture, yet I resolved to steer my Course *Eastward*, hoping to reach the *South-West* Coast of *New Holland*, and perhaps some such Island as I desired, lying *Westward* of it. The Wind was full *West*, and by six in the Evening I computed I had gone *Eastward* at least eighteen Leagues, when I spied a very small Island about half a League off, which I soon reached. It was nothing but a Rock with one Creek naturally arched by the force of Tempests. Here I put in my Canoe, and climbing up a part of the Rock, I could plainly discover Land to the *East*, extending from *South* to *North*. I lay all Night in my Canoe; and repeating my Voyage early in the Morning, I arrived in seven Hours to the *South-East* Point of *New Holland*. This confirmed me in the opinion I have long entertained, that the *Maps* and *Charts* place this Country at least three Degrees more to the *East* than it really is; which Thought I communicated many Years ago to my worthy Friend Mr. *Herman Moll*,[67] and gave him my Reasons for it, although he hath rather chosen to follow other Authors.

I saw no Inhabitants in the Place where I landed, and being unarmed, I was afraid of venturing far into the Country. I found some Shellfish on the Shore, and eat them raw, not daring to kindle a Fire, for fear of being discovered by the Natives. I continued three Days feeding on Oysters and Limpets, to save my own Provisions; and I fortunately found a Brook of excellent Water, which gave me great Relief.

On the fourth Day, venturing out early a little too far, I saw twenty or thirty Natives upon a Height, not above five hundred Yards from me. They were stark naked, Men, Women, and Children, round a Fire, as I could discover by the Smoke. One of them spied me, and gave notice to the rest; five of them advanced towards me leaving the Women and Children at the Fire. I made what haste I could to the Shore, and getting into my Canoe, shoved off: The Savages observing me retreat, ran after me; and before I could get far enough into the Sea, discharged an Arrow, which wounded me deeply on the inside of my left Knee (I shall carry the Mark to my Grave). I apprehended the Arrow might be poisoned, and paddling out of the reach of their Darts (being a calm Day) I made a shift to suck the Wound, and dress it as well as I could.

I was at a Loss what to do, for I durst not return to the same Landing-place, but stood to the *North*,[68] and was forced to paddle; for the Wind although very gentle was against me, blowing *North-West*. As I was looking about for a secure Landing-place, I saw a Sail to the *North North-East*, which appearing every Minute more visible, I was in some Doubt, whether I should wait for them or no, but at last my Detestation of the *Yahoo* Race prevailed, and turning my Canoe, I sailed and paddled together to the *South*, and got into the same Creek from whence I set out in the Morning, choosing rather to trust myself among these *Barbarians*, than live with *European Yahoos*. I drew up my Canoe as close as I could to the Shore, and hid myself behind a Stone by the little Brook, which, as I have already said, was excellent Water.

The Ship came within half a League of this Creek, and sent her Long-boat with Vessels to take in fresh Water (for the Place it seems was very well known) but I did not observe it till the Boat was almost on Shore, and it was too late to seek another Hiding-place. The Seamen at

their landing observed my Canoe, and rummaging it all over, easily
conjectured that the Owner could not be far off. Four of them well-armed
searched every Cranny and Lurking-hole, till at last they found me flat
on my Face behind the Stone. They gazed awhile in admiration at my
strange uncouth Dress, my Coat made of Skins, my wooden-soled Shoes,
and my furred Stockings; from whence, however, they concluded I was
not a Native of the Place, who all go naked. One of the Seamen in
Portuguese bid me rise, and asked who I was. I understood that Language
very well, and getting upon my Feet, said, I was a poor *Yahoo*, banished
from the *Houyhnhnms*, and desired they would please to let me depart.
They admired to hear me answer them in their own Tongue, and saw by
my Complexion I must be an *European*; but were at a loss to know what
I meant by *Yahoos* and *Houyhnhnms*, and at the same time fell a laughing
at my strange Tone in speaking, which resembled the Neighing of a
Horse. I trembled all the while betwixt Fear and Hatred: I again desired
leave to depart, and was gently moving to my Canoe; but they laid hold
on me, desiring to know, What Country I was of? whence I came? with
many other Questions. I told them, I was born in *England*, from whence
I came about five Years ago, and then their Country and ours were at
Peace. I therefore hoped they would not treat me as an Enemy, since I
meant them no harm, but was a poor *Yahoo*, seeking some desolate Place
where to pass the Remainder of his unfortunate Life.

When they began to talk, I thought I never heard or saw anything so
unnatural; for it appeared to me as monstrous as if a Dog or a Cow should
speak in *England*, or a *Yahoo* in *Houyhnhnm-land*. The honest *Portuguese*[69]
were equally amazed at my strange Dress, and the odd manner of
delivering my Words, which however they understood very well. They
spoke to me with great Humanity, and said they were sure their Captain
would carry me *gratis* to *Lisbon*, from whence I might return to my own
Country; that two of the Seamen would go back to the Ship, inform the
Captain of what they had seen, and receive his Orders; in the mean time,
unless I would give my solemn Oath not to fly, they would secure me by
Force. I thought it best to comply with their Proposal. They were very
curious to know my Story, but I gave them very little Satisfaction; and
they all conjectured, that my Misfortunes had impaired my Reason. In
two Hours the Boat, which went loaden with Vessels of Water, returned

with the Captain's Commands to fetch me on Board. I fell on my Knees to preserve my Liberty; but all was in vain, and the Men having tied me with Cords, heaved me into the Boat, from whence I was taken into the Ship, and from thence into the Captain's Cabin.

His Name was *Pedro de Mendez*, he was a very courteous and generous Person; he entreated me to give some Account of myself, and desired to know what I would eat or drink; said, I should be used as well as himself, and spoke so many obliging things, that I wondered to find such Civilities from a *Yahoo*. However, I remained silent and sullen; I was ready to faint at the very smell of him and his Men. At last I desired something to eat out of my own Canoe; but he ordered me a Chicken and some excellent Wine, and then directed that I should be put to Bed in a very clean Cabin. I would not undress myself, but lay on the Bedclothes, and in half an Hour stole out, when I thought the Crew was at Dinner, and getting to the side of the Ship was going to leap into the Sea, and swim for my Life, rather than continue among *Yahoos*. But one of the Seamen prevented me, and having informed the Captain, I was chained to my Cabin.

After Dinner *Don Pedro* came to me, and desired to know my Reason for so desperate an Attempt: assured me he only meant to do me all the Service he was able; and spoke so very movingly, that at last I descended to treat him like an Animal which had some little portion of Reason. I gave him a very short Relation of my Voyage, of the Conspiracy against me by my own Men, of the Country where they set me on Shore, and of my three Years Residence there. All which he looked upon as if it were a Dream or a Vision; whereat I took great Offence; for I had quite forgot the Faculty of Lying, so peculiar to *Yahoos* in all Countries where they preside, and consequently the Disposition of suspecting Truth in others of their own Species. I asked him, Whether it were the Custom in his Country to *say the Thing that was not*? I assured him I had almost forgot what he meant by Falsehood, and if I had lived a thousand Years in *Houyhnhnmland*, I should never have heard a Lie from the meanest Servant; that I was altogether indifferent whether he believed me or no; but however, in return for his Favours, I would give so much Allowance to the Corruption of his Nature, as to answer any Objection he would please to make, and then he might easily discover the Truth.

The Captain, a wise Man, after many Endeavours to catch me tripping in some part of my Story, at last began to have a better Opinion of my Veracity.[70] But he added, that since I professed so inviolable an Attachment to Truth, I must give him my Word of Honour to bear him company in this Voyage without attempting anything against my Life, or else he would continue me a Prisoner till we arrived at *Lisbon*. I gave him the Promise he required; but at the same time protested that I would suffer the greatest Hardships rather than return to live among *Yahoos*.

Our Voyage passed without any considerable Accident. In Gratitude to the Captain I sometimes sat with him at his earnest Request, and strove to conceal my Antipathy to human Kind, although it often broke out, which he suffered to pass without Observation. But the greatest part of the Day, I confined myself to my Cabin, to avoid seeing any of the Crew. The Captain had often entreated me to strip myself of my savage Dress, and offered to lend me the best Suit of Clothes he had. This I would not be prevailed on to accept, abhorring to cover myself with anything that had been on the Back of a *Yahoo*. I only desired he would lend me two clean Shirts, which having been washed since he wore them, I believed would not so much defile me. These I changed every second Day, and washed them myself.

We arrived at *Lisbon*, Nov. 5, 1715. At our landing the Captain forced me to cover myself with his Cloak, to prevent the Rabble from crowding about me. I was conveyed to his own House, and at my earnest Request, he led me up to the highest Room backwards. I conjured him to conceal from all Persons what I had told him of the *Houyhnhnms*, because the least hint of such a Story would not only draw Numbers of People to see me, but probably, put me in Danger of being imprisoned, or burnt by the *Inquisition*.[71] The Captain persuaded me to accept a Suit of Clothes newly made, but I would not suffer the Tailor to take my Measure; however, *Don Pedro* being almost of my Size, they fitted me well enough. He accoutred me with other Necessaries all new, which I aired for twenty-four Hours before I would use them.

The Captain had no Wife, nor above three Servants, none of which were suffered to attend at Meals, and his whole Deportment was so obliging, added to very good *human* Understanding, that I really began to tolerate his Company. He gained so far upon me, that I ventured to look out of the back Window. By degrees I was brought into another

Room, from whence I peeped into the Street, but drew my Head back in a Fright. In a Week's time he seduced me down to the Door. I found my Terror gradually lessened, but my Hatred and Contempt seemed to increase. I was at last bold enough to walk the Street in his Company, but kept my Nose well stopped with Rue,[72] or sometimes with Tobacco.

In ten Days *Don Pedro*, to whom I had given some account of my Domestic Affairs, put it upon me as a Matter of Honour and Conscience, that I ought to return to my native Country, and live at home with my Wife and Children. He told me, there was an *English* Ship in the Port just ready to sail, and he would furnish me with all things necessary. It would be tedious to repeat his Arguments, and my Contradictions. He said it was altogether impossible to find such a solitary Island as I had desired to live in; but I might command in my own House, and pass my time in a manner as recluse as I pleased.

I complied at last, finding I could not do better. I left *Lisbon* the 24th Day of *November*, in an *English* Merchant-Man, but who was the Master I never inquired. *Don Pedro* accompanied me to the Ship, and lent me Twenty Pounds. He took kind leave of me, and embraced me at parting, which I bore as well as I could. During the last Voyage I had no Commerce with the Master or any of his Men, but pretending I was sick kept close in my Cabin. On the Fifth of *December*, 1715, we cast Anchor in the *Downs* about Nine in the Morning, and at Three in the Afternoon I got safe to my House at *Redriff*.

My Wife and Family received me with great Surprise and Joy, because they concluded me certainly dead; but I must freely confess the sight of them filled me only with Hatred, Disgust and Contempt, and the more by reflecting on the near Alliance I had to them. For, although since my unfortunate Exile from the *Houyhnhnm* Country, I had compelled myself to tolerate the Sight of *Yahoos*, and to converse with *Don Pedro de Mendez*; yet my Memory and Imaginations were perpetually filled with the Virtues and Ideas of those exalted *Houyhnhnms*. And when I began to consider, that by copulating with one of the *Yahoo* Species I had become a Parent of more, it struck me with the utmost Shame, Confusion and Horror.

As soon as I entered the House, my Wife took me in her Arms, and kissed me, at which having not been used to the Touch of that odious Animal for so many Years, I fell in a Swoon for almost an Hour. At the Time I am writing it is Five Years since my last Return to *England*: During the first Year I could not endure my Wife or Children in my Presence, the very Smell of them was intolerable; much less could I suffer them to eat in the same Room. To this hour they dare not presume to touch my Bread, or drink out of the same Cup, neither was I ever able to let one of them take me by the Hand.[73] The first Money I laid out was to buy two young Stone-Horses,[74] which I keep in a good Stable, and next to them the Groom is my greatest Favourite; for I feel my Spirits revived by the Smell he contracts in the Stable. My Horses understand me tolerably well; I converse with them at least four Hours every Day. They are Strangers to Bridle or Saddle, they live in great Amity with me, and Friendship to each other.

CHAP. XII

The Author's Veracity. His Design in publishing this Work. His Censure of those Travellers who swerve from the Truth. The Author clears himself from any sinister Ends in writing. An Objection answered. The Method of planting Colonies. His Native Country commended. The Right of the Crown to those Countries described by the Author is justified. The Difficulty of conquering them. The Author takes his last leave of the Reader: proposeth his Manner of Living for the future, gives good Advice, and concludes.

Thus, Gentle Reader, I have given thee a faithful History of my Travels for Sixteen Years, and above Seven Months, wherein I have not been so studious of Ornament as Truth. I could perhaps like others have astonished thee with strange improbable Tales; but I rather chose to relate plain Matter of Fact in the simplest Manner and Style; because my principal Design was to inform, and not to amuse thee.

It is easy for us who travel into remote Countries, which are seldom visited by *Englishmen* or other *Europeans*, to form Descriptions of wonderful Animals both at Sea and Land. Whereas a Traveller's chief Aim should be to make Men wiser and better, and to improve their Minds by the bad as well as good Example of what they deliver concerning foreign Places.

I could heartily wish a Law were enacted, that every Traveller before he were permitted to publish his Voyages, should be obliged to make Oath before the *Lord High Chancellor* that all he intended to print was absolutely true to the best of his Knowledge; for then the World would no longer be deceived as it usually is, while some Writers, to make their Works pass the better upon the Public, impose the grossest Falsities on the unwary Reader. I have perused several Books of Travels with great Delight in my younger Days; but having since gone over most Parts of the Globe, and been able to contradict many fabulous Accounts from my own Observation, it hath given me a great Disgust against this Part of Reading, and some Indignation to see the Credulity of Mankind so impudently abused. Therefore, since my Acquaintance were pleased to think my poor Endeavours might not be unacceptable to my Country, I imposed on myself as a Maxim, never to be swerved from, that I would *strictly adhere to Truth*; neither indeed can I be ever under the least temptation to vary from it, while I retain in my Mind the Lectures and Example of my Noble Master, and the other Illustrious *Houyhnhnms*, of whom I had so long the Honour to be an humble Hearer.

> — Nec si miserum Fortuna Sinonem
> Finxit, vanum etiam, mendacemque improba finget.[75]

I know very well how little Reputation is to be got by Writings which require neither Genius nor Learning, nor indeed any other Talent, except a good Memory, or an exact *Journal*. I know likewise, that Writers of Travels, like *Dictionary*-Makers, are sunk into Oblivion by the Weight and Bulk of those who come after, and therefore lie uppermost. And it is highly probable, that such Travellers who shall hereafter visit the Countries described in this Work of mine, may by detecting my Errors (if there be any) and adding many new Discoveries of their own, justle me out of Vogue, and stand in my Place, making the World forget that I was ever an Author. This indeed would be too great a Mortification if I wrote for Fame: But, as my sole Intention was the PUBLIC GOOD, I cannot be altogether disappointed. For who can read of the Virtues I have mentioned in the Glorious *Houyhnhnms*, without being ashamed of his own Vices, when he considers himself as the reasoning, governing Animal of his Country? I shall say nothing of those remote Nations where *Yahoos*

change was happened

preside, amongst which the least corrupted are the *Brobdingnagians*, whose wise Maxims in Morality and Government, it would be our Happiness to observe. But I forbear descanting farther, and rather leave the Judicious Reader to his own Remarks and Applications.

I am not a little pleased that this Work of mine can possibly meet with no Censurers: For what Objections can be made against a Writer who relates only plain Facts that happened in such distant Countries, where we have not the least Interest with respect either to Trade or Negotiations? I have carefully avoided every Fault with which common Writers of Travels are often too justly charged. Besides, I meddle not the least with any *Party*, but write without Passion, Prejudice, or Ill will against any Man or number of Men whatsoever. I write for the noblest End, to inform and instruct Mankind, over whom I may, without Breach of Modesty, pretend to some Superiority from the Advantages I received by conversing so long among the most accomplished *Houyhnhnms*. I write without any view towards Profit or Praise. I never suffer a Word to pass that may look like Reflection, or possibly give the least Offence even to those who are most ready to take it. So that I hope I may with Justice pronounce myself an Author perfectly blameless, against whom the Tribes of Answerers, Considerers, Observers, Reflectors, Detectors, Remarkers, will never be able to find Matter for exercising their Talents.

I confess, it was whispered to me, that I was bound in Duty as a Subject of *England*, to have given in a Memorial[76] to a Secretary of State, at my first coming over; because, whatever Lands are discovered by a Subject belong to the Crown. But I doubt whether our Conquests in the Countries I treat of, would be as easy as those of *Ferdinando Cortez*[77] over the naked *Americans*. The *Lilliputians* I think, are hardly worth the Charge of a Fleet and Army to reduce them, and I question whether it might be prudent or safe to attempt the *Brobdingnagians*. Or whether an *English* Army would be much at their ease with the Flying Island over their Heads. The *Houyhnhnms*, indeed, appear not to be so well prepared for War, a Science to which they are perfect Strangers, and especially against missive[78] Weapons. However, supposing myself to be a Minister of State, I could never give my Advice for invading them. Their Prudence, Unanimity, Unacquaintedness with Fear, and their Love of their Country would amply supply all Defects in the Military Art. Imagine Twenty thousand of them breaking into the midst of an *European* Army, confounding the Ranks, overturning the Carriages, battering the Warriors' Faces into Mummy, by terrible Yerks[79] from their hinder Hoofs. For they would well deserve the Character given to *Augustus; Recalcitrat undique tutus.*[80] But instead of Proposals for conquering that magnanimous Nation, I rather wish they were in a Capacity or Disposition to send a sufficient Number of their Inhabitants for civilizing *Europe*, by teaching us the first Principles of Honour, Justice, Truth, Temperance, Public Spirit, Fortitude, Chastity, Friendship, Benevolence, and Fidelity. The *Names* of all which Virtues are still retained among us in most Languages, and are to be met with in modern as well as ancient Authors; which I am able to assert from my own small Reading.

But I had another Reason which made me less forward to enlarge his Majesty's Dominions by my Discoveries. To say the truth, I had conceived a few Scruples with relation to the Distributive Justice[81] of Princes upon those Occasions. For instance, a Crew of Pirates are driven by a Storm they know not whither; at length a Boy discovers Land from the Topmast; they go on Shore to Rob and Plunder; they see an harmless People, are entertained with Kindness, they give the Country a new Name, they take formal Possession of it for their King, they set up a rotten Plank or a Stone for a Memorial, they murder two or three Dozen of the Natives, bring away a Couple more by Force for a Sample, return home, and get their Pardon. Here commences a new Dominion acquired with a Title by *Divine Right*. Ships are sent with the first Opportunity, the Natives driven out or destroyed, their Princes tortured to discover their Gold; a free Licence given to all Acts of Inhumanity and Lust, the Earth reeking with the Blood of its Inhabitants: And this execrable Crew of Butchers employed in so pious an Expedition, is a *modern Colony* sent to convert and civilize an idolatrous and barbarous People.

But this Description, I confess, doth by no means affect the *British* Nation, who may be an Example to the whole World for their Wisdom, Care, and Justice in Planting Colonies; their liberal Endowments for the Advancement of Religion and Learning; their Choice of devout and able Pastors to propagate *Christianity*, their Caution in stocking their Provinces with People of sober Lives and Conversations from this the Mother Kingdom; their strict regard to the Distribution of Justice, in supplying the Civil Administration through all their Colonies with Officers of the greatest Abilities, utter strangers to Corruption; and to crown all, by sending the most Vigilant and Virtuous Governors, who have no other Views than the Happiness of the People over whom they preside, and the Honour of the King their Master.

But, as those Countries which I have described, do not appear to have any Desire of being conquered, and enslaved, murdered or driven out by Colonies, nor abound either in Gold, Silver, Sugar, or Tobacco; I did humbly conceive they were by no means proper Objects of our Zeal, our Valour, or our Interest. However, if those whom it more concerns, think fit to be of another Opinion, I am ready to depose, when I shall be lawfully called, That no *European* did ever visit these Countries before me. I mean, if the Inhabitants ought to be believed; unless a Dispute may arise about the two *Yahoos*, said to have been seen many Ages ago on a Mountain in *Houyhnhnmland*, from whence the Opinion is, that the Race of those Brutes hath descended; and these, for anything I know, may have been *English*, which indeed I was apt to suspect from the Lineaments of their Posterity's Countenances, although very much defaced. But, how far that will go to make out a Title, I leave to the Learned in Colony-Law.

But as to the Formality of taking Possession in my Sovereign's Name, it never came once into my Thoughts; and if it had, yet as my Affairs then stood, I should perhaps in point of Prudence and Self-preservation, have put it off to a better Opportunity.

Having thus answered the only objection that can ever be raised against me as a Traveller, I here take a final Leave of all my Courteous Readers, and return to enjoy my own Speculations in my little Garden at *Redriff*, to apply those excellent Lessons of Virtue which I learned among the *Houyhnhnms*, to instruct the *Yahoos* of my own Family as far as I shall find them docible Animals, to behold my Figure often in a Glass, and thus if possible habituate myself by time to tolerate the sight of a human Creature: To lament the Brutality of *Houyhnhnms* in my own Country, but always treat their Persons with Respect, for the sake of my noble Master, his Family, his Friends, and the whole *Houyhnhnm* Race, whom these of ours have the Honour to resemble in all their Lineaments, however their Intellectuals came to degenerate.

I began last Week to permit my Wife to sit at Dinner with me, at the farthest End of a long Table, and to answer (but with the utmost brevity) the few Questions I asked her. Yet the smell of a *Yahoo* continuing very offensive, I always keep my Nose well stopped with Rue, Lavender, or Tobacco leaves. And although it be hard for a Man late in life to remove old Habits, I am not altogether out of Hopes in some time to suffer a Neighbour *Yahoo* in my Company without the Apprehensions I am yet under of his Teeth or his Claws.

My Reconcilement to the *Yahoo* kind in general might not be so difficult, if they would be content with those Vices and Follies only, which Nature hath entitled them to. I am not in the least provoked at the Sight of a Lawyer, a Pick-pocket, a Colonel, a Fool, a Lord, a Gamester, a Politician, a Whore-master, a Physician, an Evidence, a Suborner, an Attorney, a Traitor, or the like: This is all according to the due Course of Things: But when I behold a Lump of Deformity, and Diseases both in Body and Mind, smitten with *Pride*, it immediately breaks all the Measures of my Patience; neither shall I be ever able to comprehend how such an Animal and such a Vice could tally together. The wise and virtuous *Houyhnhnms*, who abound in all Excellencies that can adorn a Rational Creature, have no Name for this Vice in their Language, which hath no Terms to express anything that is evil, except those whereby they describe the detestable Qualities of their *Yahoos*, among which they were not able to distinguish this of Pride, for want of thoroughly understanding Human Nature, as it showeth itself in other Countries, where that Animal presides. But I, who had more Experience, could plainly observe some Rudiments of it among the wild *Yahoos*.

But the *Houyhnhnms*, who live under the Government of Reason, are no more proud of the good Qualities they possess, than I should be for not wanting a Leg or an Arm, which no Man in his Wits would boast of, although he must be miserable without them. I dwell the longer upon this Subject from the Desire I have to make the Society of an *English Yahoo* by any means not insupportable, and therefore I here entreat those who have any Tincture of this absurd Vice, that they will not presume to come in my Sight.

FINIS

NOTES

Abbreviations

Johnson: Samuel Johnson's *Dictionary* (1755)

OED: the *Oxford English Dictionary*, several editions including the online version, http://dictionary.oed.com

Bailey: Nathan Bailey's *Dictionarium Britannicum* (1736)

For many other citations I have used the author's name (and sometimes the date) of a work that appears in Further Reading.

NOTE TO PLATES 1 AND 2

The portrait of Gulliver appeared in three different states in the editions of 1726–7. In the second state, a Latin motto was added: *Compositum jus, fasque animi sanctosque recessus / Mentis, et incoctum generoso pectus honesto* (Persius, *Satires* 2. 73–4). Coming at the end of a poem about the folly of human hopes and wishes, these lines suggest what we should pray for, instead of fame and fortune: 'a heart rightly attuned towards God and man; a mind pure in its inner depths, and a soul steeped in nobleness and honour' (G. G. Ramsay, Loeb Library edition). Gulliver's age matches Swift's age when the *Travels* first appeared on 28 October 1726. In 1735 a different portrait of Gulliver appears with a different motto: *Splendide Mendax* 'a liar, in a noble way', Horace, *Odes* III. 11. The phrase refers to a noble-minded woman who refuses to traduce her husband to satisfy the wishes of her tyrannical father. It has been observed that this portrait, the frontispiece of volume III in Faulkner's edition of the *Works*, resembles the portrait of Swift used as the frontispiece to the whole edition (see Rodino).

The title-page of the edition of 1735 added a Latin tag from Lucretius, *Retroq; / Vulgus abhorret ab his* (*De Rerum Natura*, 4.19–20): Common people recoil from these things [hence I present them in sweet song].

NOTES TO THE 'ADVERTISEMENT'

1. *Mr. Sympson's Letter to Captain Gulliver*: Actually, Gulliver's letter to Sympson.

2. *a Person since deceased*: Benjamin Motte, publisher of the first edition, did not die until 1738, but his close associate, Andrew Tooke, who perhaps made the 'Interpolations', died in 1732. For details about these publishers, see Treadwell, 'Benjamin Motte, Andrew Tooke, and *Gulliver's Travels*'.

3. See p. 231 and p. 304n.

4. *a most intimate Friend of the Author's*: Charles Ford (see A Note on the Text, pp. xxvi–xxviii).

5. *Sheets*: Unbound pages; books were very often purchased in this state at the time; for the interleaved copy referred to here, see A Note on the Text, p. xxvii.

NOTES TO THE LETTER

1. *Letter*: This section first appeared in 1735, although the letter is dated 2 April 1727, shortly before the publication of Motte's 'Second Edition' on 4 May of that year. The name Sympson may allude to William Sympson, the pseudonymous author of *A New Voyage to the East Indies* (1715).

2. *Dampier*: William Dampier, author of *A New Voyage round the World* (1697); Swift owned a copy of the third edition (1698).

3. See p. 304n.

4. *Master Houyhnhnm*: The horse-like creature who takes Gulliver into his home in Book IV.

5. *Godolphin . . . Oxford*: Sidney Godolphin and Robert Harley, Earl of Oxford, occupied the post of High Treasurer successively under Queen Anne. Swift, like his spokesman Gulliver, was in England during part of Anne's reign and served in the Tory government from 1710–14.

6. *say the thing that was not*: The Houyhnhnms' phrase for lying, a non-existent term in their language.

7. *Letter*: Swift instructed Charles Ford to send a letter to Benjamin Motte (3 January 1727) in which he complained about 'Errors of the Press' and the interpolation of the 'flattery' of Queen Anne (Swift's *Correspondence* 3: 194–5). The letter also contained numerous particular corrections to be inserted in 'another Edition'. For a discussion of the letter and its place in the post-publication history of the text, see A Note on the Text.

8. *Yahoos*: The humanoid creatures dominated by the Houyhnhnms in Book IV.

9. *hither*: A 'House, near Newark, in Nottinghamshire' (p. 9).

10. *this little Island*: England.

11. *Pleader*: 'One who argues in a court of justice' (Johnson).

12. *Smithfield*: An open area near the City of London where heretics were burned along with their books in the sixteenth century.

13. *Cotton*: Paper, which was predominantly composed of cotton in the eighteenth century (*OED* II.8. 1752).

14. *Libels, and Keys, and Reflections*: Teerink (pp. 244–6) catalogues eighteen separate lampoons ('Libels'), interpretations ('Keys'), and other responses to *Gulliver's Travels* through 1727, including *Lemuel Gulliver's Travels into Several Remote Nations of the World. Compendiously methodised, for public Benefit* (London: Curb, 1726); each of the four sections was called a 'Key' to *Gulliver's Travels*.

15. *reflecting upon*: Censuring.

16. *original Manuscript*: It was indeed destroyed, as almost all eighteenth-century manuscripts were, after the book was set in type; see A Note on the Text, p. xxvi.

17. *new fangled*: 'Formed with vain or foolish love of novelty' (Johnson).

18. *Utopia*: An imaginary place in Sir Thomas More's work of that name (1516); Swift owned a copy published in 1631.

19. *Shuffling*: To shuffle is 'To play mean tricks; to practise fraud; to evade fair questions' (Johnson, sense 2).

20. *visionary*: 'Imaginary; not real; seen in a dream' (Johnson, sense 2).

NOTES TO
'THE PUBLISHER TO THE READER'

1. *Redriff*: Rotherhithe, a neighbourhood in Southwark, a district in south London, near the river, opposite to Wapping.

2. *Monuments of the Gullivers*: Several tombstones of people named Gulliver actually exist in Banbury, a town between Oxford and Stratford, then known for its Puritanism or extreme Protestantism.

3. *Circumstantial*: 'Full of small events; particular; detailed' (Johnson, sense 3).

4. *Variation*: 'Variation of the compass; deviation of the magnetic needle from an exact parallel with the meridian' (Johnson, sense 7).

PART I

A VOYAGE TO LILLIPUT

1. *Emanuel College in Cambridge*: A college known in the seventeenth century for its sympathy to dissenting views.

2. *Fourteen Years old*: Swift's age when he entered Trinity College, Dublin; young for beginning college at that time but not uncommonly so.

3. *Surgeon*: 'One who cures by manual operation; one whose duty is to act in external maladies by the direction of the physician' (Johnson).

4. *Leiden*: A university in Holland, a country with a more liberal Protestant tradition than that favoured by the Church of England.

5. *Levant*: The old name for the eastern Mediterranean.

6. *Old Jury*: Probably an alternate spelling of Old Jewry, a district in the centre of the City of London inhabited at the time by dissenting Protestants; also the name of the Dissenters' chapel.

7. *Mrs. Mary Burton*: Mrs. is here short for *mistress*, a polite title, rather than *missus*, a married woman's title.

8. *Portion*: 'A wife's fortune' (Johnson); Gulliver gets a substantial middle-class fortune with his wife (at least £60,000 or $100,000 dollars in 2001 money).

9. *Fetter-Lane . . . to Wapping*: The first move takes Gulliver several blocks west in the City of London; the second takes him a considerable distance east of the City to a dock district then inhabited by sailors and prostitutes.

10. *Van Diemen's Land*: An old name for Tasmania, a large island south of Australia, 'discovered' by the Dutch and bisected by the 42nd parallel at 146 degrees longitude. See the fictional map, p. 20.

11. *a Cable's length*: 600 feet.

12. *three Leagues*: Nine nautical miles.

13. *Admiration*: 'Wonder' (Johnson).

14. *Hekinah Degul*: Paul Odell Clark credibly argues that Swift's 'foreign' words are often anagrams complicated by substitutions of letters after the fashion of the baby talk or 'little language' he used in his *Journal to Stella*. According to the method, vowels are nearly all interchangeable, as are the consonants *l* and *r*, *b* and *v*, *b* and *w*, *t* and *c*, among others. This phrase he translates as, 'What in the Devil!' (p. 600). As Clark himself acknowledges, however, intuition and a sensitivity to sound are often more appropriate guides to Swift's linguistic fabrications than methodical or pedantic examination.

15. *Buff Jerkin*: A buffalo leather jacket.

16. *Periods*: Oratorical sentences or statements.

17. *eat*: Past tense, pronounced et.

18. *Hogsheads*: 'Any large barrell' (Johnson, sense 2).

19. *small Wine*: Low in alcoholic content.

20. *Imaginations*: thoughts.

21. *Express*: 'A messenger sent on purpose' (Johnson).

22. *Mechanics*: 'The geometry of motion' (Johnson, quoting the mathematician John Wallis).

23. *Engines*: Machines.

24. *ancient Temple . . . polluted some Years before by an unnatural Murder*: An allusion to Westminster Hall, where Charles I was condemned to death in 1649.

25. *Zeal*: 'Passionate ardour for any person or cause' (Johnson); often used to describe religious feeling and often derogatory; cf. 'Seriousness and zeal in religion is natural to the English' (John Tillotson, quoted in Johnson).

26. *Stang*: A quarter of an acre.

27. *Austrian Lip and arched Nose*: Hapsburg features, a caricature of George I.

28. *High and Low Dutch*: German (*Hochdeutsch*) and Dutch.

29. *Lingua Franca*: A mixture of Italian and other Mediterranean languages used among commercial traders.

30. *Inconveniency*: 'Disadvantage; cause of uneasiness; difficulty' (Johnson, sense 2).

31. *Secretaries of State*: Officers in charge of issuing state papers and royal orders, either domestic or foreign; here, as in England, Swift suggests, their services are venal.

32. *apprehended*: Feared.

33. *Assignments*: 'Legal transference of a right or property' (*OED*, sense 2).

34. *Orders . . . to search me*: Thought to represent the Whig investigation of possible sedition in the Tory government that was turned out with the death of Queen Anne in 1714 and in which Swift had served.

35. *IMPRIMIS*: Legal term meaning 'in the first place'.

36. *Quinbus Flestrin*: Perhaps 'Buskin [kin-bus] dressed in' (Clark, 603).

37. *Perspective*: Telescope, as shown on p. 50.

38. *Flimnap*: Thought to represent Robert Walpole, the powerful Whig minister.

39. *Summerset*: Somersault.

40. *Trencher*: 'A piece of wood upon which meat is cut at table' (Johnson).

41. *Reldresal*: Perhaps Lord Carteret, a friend of Swift's, who, as Lord Lieutenant of Ireland, offered a reward for the identification of the author of Swift's anti-government pamphlets called *The Drapier's Letters*.

42. *one of the King's Cushions*: The duchess of Kendal, mistress to the king, helped Walpole back into favour in 1717; she was also instrumental in the scheme known as Wood's Halfpenny, a plan to sell copper-based coinage in Ireland; Swift's *Drapier's Letters* are an extended attack on this plan.

43. *Blue . . . Red . . . Green*: In 1726 the colours are purple, yellow, and white, apparently to avoid or mask the satire of the noble orders of the Garter, Bath, and Thistle, which are associated with blue, red, and green respectively. The annotated copies of *Gulliver's Travels* seem to restore the orginal colours. However, for a view of these 'restorations' as examples of rewriting, see Lock (1980), p. 79.

44. *discovered*: Showed.

45. *close Chair*: Sedan chair, a closed conveyance, carried on poles by servants.

46. *presently*: Immediately.

47. *Intelligence*: Information.

48. *Colossus*: Like the fabled statue that stood astride the harbour of ancient Rhodes.

49. *Skyresh Bolgolam*: The last name suggests the Duke of Marlborough, an important political enemy of Swift's.

50. *Complexion*: Temperament.

51. *Instrument*: 'A writing containing any contract or order' (Johnson, sense 3).

52. *Corn*: Any grain grown for consumption.

53. *Blefuscu*: France to Lilliput's England in the political allegory of *Gulliver's Travels*.

54. *Mildendo*: A near anagram for London in a word order that brings to mind Mile End, then a poorer place east of the City proper (Clark, p. 607).

55. *five hundred thousand Souls*: Approximately the population of London in 1700.

56. *Pile*: Structure, building.

57. *Tramecksan, and Slamecksan*: Meant to suggest the Tory and Whig parties, which were high and low church parties, respectively.

58. *Heir to the Crown*: The Prince of Wales after 1714, later George II (1727–60), who seemed favourable to the Tories before ascending to the throne but once crowned retained Walpole and his Whig administration.

59. *there are other Kingdoms and States in the World*: An allusion to the eighteenth-century theological controversy about the existence of other inhabited worlds.

60. *his present Majesty's Grandfather*: Often interpreted as Henry VIII, who split with the Catholic Church (Big Endians) and established the Church of England (Little Endians); this bi-partite division leaves out the dissenting Protestants, who have a place in Swift's allegory of religious differences in *A Tale of a Tub*.

61. *one Emperor lost his Life, and another his Crown*: Allusions to Charles I, beheaded in 1649, and James II deposed in 1688.

62. *the whole Party rendered incapable by Law of holding Employments*: An allusion to the Test Acts, laws enacted in the reign of Charles II which restricted service under the Crown to Church of England communicants.

63. *Schism in Religion*: Swift defines *schism* as a breach with the state religion; see *Sentiments of a Church of England Man* (1708) and Johnson's *Dictionary* (s.v. *schism*).

64. *Topics*: Commonplaces, wise sayings (cf. the quotation from Swift's *Letter to a Young Clergyman* in Johnson's *Dictionary* [s.v. *topic*]).

65. *Junto*: 'A cabal; a kind of men combined in any secret design' (Johnson).

66. *Peace*: A reference to the controversial Treaty of Utrecht with France (1714) negotiated by the Tory government to put an end to the war but despised as weak by the Whigs.

67. *Visit in Form*: Formal diplomatic approach.

68. *Maid of Honour . . . reading a Romance*: The derision of women as idle readers of romance goes back at least as far as Juvenal, *Satire* 6.

69. *Flunec*: Sounds appropriately like Latin *flumen*, river.

70. *Capital*: Punishable by death.

71. *the Empress conceiving the greatest Abhorrence of what I had done*: This has been interpreted as a reference to Queen Anne's reaction to *A Tale of a Tub* and her refusal to grant him a bishopric, despite his service to the crown. However, Anne's dismissal of Robert Harley, Lord Oxford, for disrespect to the queen is a better allegorical reading because it fits in with other aspects of the political allegory of the book. For more on the political context of *Gulliver's Travels*, see the Introduction, pp. xv–xviii.

72. *pulling a Lark*: Plucking its feathers.

73. *Cascagians*: A made-up name resembling Casontes or Vascontes, related to modern Basque.

74. *Charges he hath been at*: His legal expenses.

75. *largely*: 'Liberally; bounteously' (Johnson, sense 3).

76. *fence*: Defense.

77. *connived at*: Winked at, overlooked.

78. *Disbelief of a Divine Providence renders a Man uncapable of holding any Public Station*: A compendious statement of the Test Act.

79. *Cottager*: 'A cottager, in law, is one that lives on the common, without paying rent, and without any land of his own' (Johnson).

80. *Docility*: 'Aptness to be taught; readiness to learn' (Johnson).

81. *Quality*: 'Comparative or relative rank' (Johnson, sense 8).

82. *Hospitals*: 'A place built for the reception of the sick, or support of the poor' (Johnson).

83. *Domestic*: Domestic arrangements, but the usage is unexampled in Johnson or *OED*.

84. *Lawn*: 'Fine linen, remarkable for being used in the sleeves of bishops' (Johnson, sense 2).

85. *Bits*: bites.

86. *Exchequer Bills would not circulate under nine per Cent. below Par*: I.e. Government bonds were selling for 91 per cent of their value.

87. *Postillion*: 'One who guides the first pair of a set of six horses in a coach' (Johnson).

88. *Articles of Impeachment* . . . : A parody of the charges pressed against important Tory ministers with whom Swift served, particularly Robert Harley, Lord Oxford and Henry Saint-John, Viscount Bolingbroke.

89. *colour*: Pretence.

90. *poisonous Juice on your Shirts . . . die in the utmost Torture*: A reference to the shirt of Nessus by which Hercules died.

91. *Expedient*: A loaded word in Swift's writing; cf. *A Modest Proposal*, where the mad projector will hear of no other solutions to Irish poverty than his plan to consume the infants: 'Let no Man talk to me of these and the like Expedients'; the proposed blinding of Gulliver suggests the fate of Samson in the Bible (*Judges* 16), but it also parodies the Whig proposal that Oxford and Bolingbroke should be stripped of all their titles for high misdemeanours rather than put to death for treason.

92. *Big-Endian in your Heart*: Oxford was accused of being a Catholic and sympathetic to the Stuart cause.

93. *Establishment*: 'Allowance; income; salary' (Johnson, sense 5, citing this passage).

94. *Lenity*: This and several other words in the passage were italicized in 1735 in order, apparently, to help the reader appreciate Swift's irony.

95. *fled from Justice*: Like Gulliver, Bolingbroke fled to France to avoid his impeachment trial.

96. *Ancient*: 'The flag or streamer of a ship' (Johnson).

97. *North and South-Seas*: North and south Pacific.

98. *the Downs*: An anchorage off the Kent coast of England.

99. *the Advantage of the Woollen Manufacture*: Ironic, because Swift campaigned in print against the English monopoly on Irish wool; see his *Proposal for the Universal Use of Irish Manufacture* (1720).

100. *Epping*: A market town on the northeast edge of what is now greater London.

101. *Black-Bull in Fetter-Lane*: A real inn and its real location in the Holborn district of London.

102. *Grammar School*: 'A school in which the learned languages are grammatically taught' (Johnson).

103. *towardly*: Promising.

104. *Surat*: One of the oldest ports in India, located on the Gulf of Cambay in the Arabian Sea.

PART II

A VOYAGE TO BROBDINGNAG

1. [plate 4]: New Albion was the old name for California and some of the other names are Californian; the Straits of Annian correspond perhaps to San Francisco Bay, but the scatological implication of the name is clearer.

2. *Gale*: 'A wind not tempestuous, yet stronger than a breeze' (Johnson).

3. *Molucca Islands*: Indonesian islands lying east of New Guinea, south of the Philippines, much fought over by early modern European nations until the Dutch gained control.

4. *Line*: The Equator.

5. *overblow*, . . . : This paragraph has been identified by Eddy (p. 143) as a parodic but very close imitation of a passage in Samuel Sturmy's *Mariner's Magazine* (1678); the terms are real (except perhaps 'weather-bowling') but to gloss them would be an exercise in pedantry.

6. *great Tartary*: Northeastern Asia.

7. *Hollow*: '(This is written by neglect of etymology for *holla*.) To shout; to hoot' (Johnson).

8. *human Creatures . . . cruel in Proportion to their Bulk*: In his *Dictionary* (s.v. *giant*) Johnson remarks, 'It is observable, that the idea of a giant is always associated with pride, brutality, and wickedness.'

9. *Lappet*: Lapel.

10. *Hinds*: Servants.

11. *Pistoles*: 'A coin of many countries and many degrees of value' (Johnson).

12. *Water-Mill*: cf. the sound of Gulliver's watch to the Lilliputians (p. 36 above).

13. *arch*: 'Waggish; mirthful; triflingly malicious' (Johnson, sense 2).

14. *London-Bridge to Chelsea*: A distance of four or five miles.

15. *Hanger*: 'A short broad sword' (Johnson).

16. *Belt*: 'A girdle; a cincture in which a sword, so some weapon, is commonly hung' (Johnson).

17. *Baby*: Doll.

18. *Grildrig*: 'Girl-thing' according to Clark's method of decoding (p. 610).

19. *Nanunculus*: Like *Homunceletino*, a made-up word based on *homunculus* but with Latin *nanus* (dwarf) substituted for *homo* (man); hence, a little or not fully formed dwarf.

20. *Glumdalclitch*: Clark decodes as 'Clutch-doll-grim(ly)' (p. 610).

21. *little Language*: Swift's name for the kind of anagrammatic baby-talk that he

used in his letters to Esther Johnson, which make up the *Journal to Stella*.

22. *Pillion*: 'A soft saddle set behind a horseman for a woman to sit on' (Johnson).

23. *Gimlet-holes*: Drill-holes.

24. *Pumpion*: Pumpkin.

25. *Lorbrulgrud*: 'London' in the language Swift uses for Brobdingnag, which is always full of *g*s, *b*s and *r*s (Clark, p. 611).

26. *Bills*: Advertisements.

27. *Sanson's Atlas*: *Atlas nouveau* (1689), a book 20·6 x 20·5 inches.

28. *Moydore*: Portuguese gold coin worth about 27 shillings and 6 pence at this time (*OED*, s.v. *moidore*); 800 moidores would then have been about £1400, well over 1,000 guineas (£1050).

29. *Scrutore*: Escritoire, 'A case of drawers for writing' (Johnson, s.v. *scrutoire*).

30. *Philosophy*: 'The course of sciences read in the schools' (Johnson, sense 4).

31. *Artist*: Artisan, craftsman.

32. *the regular Laws of Nature*: An ironic phrase for Swift.

33. *Virtuosi*: Plural of virtuoso, 'A man skilled in antique or natural curiosities' (Johnson).

34. *Lusus Naturae*: A freak of nature.

35. *occult Causes*: '. . . The Aristotelians gave the name of occult qualities not to manifest qualities, but to such qualities only as they supposed to lie hid in bodies, and to be the unknown causes of manifest effects' (Isaac Newton, quoted by Johnson, s.v. *occult*).

36. *craunch*: '(*Schrantsen*, Dutch; whence the vulgar say more properly to *scraunch*.) To crush in the mouth. The word is used by *Swift*' (Johnson).

37. *Apprehension*: 'The mere contemplation of things, without affirming or denying anything concerning them . . .' (Johnson, quoting Isaac Watts).

38. *Birthday Clothes*: Finery worn at celebrations of a royal birthday.

39. *rallied*: 'To Rally . . . To Treat with slight contempt; to treat with satirical merriment' (Johnson, sense 2).

40. *Dunstable*: A city about 30 miles north of London known in the eighteenth century for its larks.

41. *Gresham College*: Home of the Royal Society and its museum of natural 'rarities'.

42. *Progresses*: 'A journey of state; a circuit' (Johnson, sense 5).

43. *Philosophers*: Natural philosophers, scientists.

44. *Glonglungs*: Ablaut formation from *long* (like *sing-song*), plus *g*, which is characteristic of Brobdingnagian words.

45. *out of Order*: Not feeling well.

46. *Field-Bed*: 'A bed contrived to be easily set up in the field' (Johnson).

47. *complaisant*: 'Civil; desirous to please' (Johnson).

48. *Salisbury Steeple*: At 404 feet, when it was finished in 1362, the steeple was the tallest in England but surpassed by some on the continent.

49. *the Cupola at St. Paul's*: the dome of St Paul's cathedral in London is 112 feet in diameter.

50. *Battalia*: 'The order of battle' (Johnson).

51. *Allusion*: 'A dalliance or Playing with Words alike in Sound, but unlike in Sense, by changing, adding or taking away a Letter or two' (Bailey).

52. *be for my Reputation*: Enhance my reputation.

53. *Espalier*: 'Trees planted and cut so as to join' (Johnson).

54. *nice*: 'Fastidious; squeamish' (Johnson, sense 3).

55. *Smocks*: 'The undergarment of a woman; a shift' (Johnson).

56. *Toilet*: Dressing-table.

57. *Tuns*: 'A vessel containing 252 gallons' (Bailey).

58. *Wherry*: 'A small Boat used for carrying Passengers in a River' (Bailey).

59. *Cistern*: 'A vessel of lead to keep a stock of water for household use' (Bailey).

60. *officiously*: Kindly.

61. *Corking-pin*: 'A pin of the largest size' (Johnson).

62. *Leads*: 'Flat roof to walk on' (Johnson).

63. *distracted*: Mad; frantic.

64. *Levee*: 'The concourse of those who crowd round a man of power in a morning' (Johnson, sense 2).

65. *artificially*: Artfully, skilfully.

66. *Cabinet*: 'A set of boxes or drawers for curiosities; a private box' (Johnson).

67. *deciphered*: Written out (see Johnson, s.v. *decipher*, sense 2).

68. *Consorts*: Concerts or 'music consisting of three or more parts' (Bailey).

69. *Closet*: 'A small room of privacy and retirement' (Johnson).

70. *Demosthenes or Cicero*: The two greatest classical orators, famously compared by Longinus (*On the Sublime* 12. 4–5) and Plutarch (*Lives*, trans. Bernadotte Perrin [1919; rpt. 1994], VII. 210–21).

71. *three mighty Kingdoms*: England, Ireland, and Scotland.

72. *Plantations*: Colonies.

73. *Temperature*: Temperateness.

74. *highest Court of Judicature*: The House of Lords was the highest court in England; the twelve judges of the Supreme Court of Judicature now still sit as members of the House of Lords, comprising the Judicial Committee.

75. *Bishops*: As 'lords spiritual' bishops joined the 'lords temporal' in the House of Lords.

76. *Humour*: Whim.

77. *Prime Minister*: Not an official title until the nineteenth century, it was used derisively of Robert Walpole in the eighteenth.

78. *Chaplain*: ' "He that performs divine service in a chapel, and attends the king or other person, for the instruction of him and his family, to read prayers, and preach." [John] Cowell . . . "A chief governour can never fail of some worthless illiterate *chaplain*, fond of a title and precedence." Swift' (Johnson).

79. *doubt*: Think; suspect.

80. *sifted*: Examined; questioned.

81. *Head*: Point; subject.

82. *Chancery*: The court responsible for trying property and other civil suits.

83. *Corporation*: 'A body politic, authorized by the king's charter to have a common seal . . .' (Johnson, quoting John Cowell).

84. *Issues*: Expenditures.

85. *double*: In *Examiner* 13 (2 November 1710) Swift inveighed against the national debt, which he saw as a consequence of the Glorious Revolution (see Lock [1980], p. 51).

86. *chargeable*: Expensive.

87. *a mercenary standing Army*: A paid military, against which Swift inveighed in *Examiner* 20 (21 December 1710) and elsewhere (see Lock [1980], p. 139), favouring instead the ancient custom of raising a militia for home defence.

88. *Gaming*: Gambling.

89. *Institution*: 'Positive Law . . . "The law and institution founded by Moses was to establish religion, and to make mercy and peace known to the whole earth." Forbes' (Johnson, sense 3).

90. *ennobled*: Raised from commonalty to nobilty (see Johnson).

91. *discover*: 'To make known' (Johnson, sense 2).

92. *Dionysius Halicarnassensis*: A Greek historian who lived at Rome after 30 BCE, author of *Roman Antiquities*, an enthusiastic history; Swift owned an expensive royal paper edition in two volumes folio.

93. *evil Genius . . . the first Contriver*: Milton similarly imagines Satan as the inventor of gunpowder (*Paradise Lost*, 6: 557–627).

94. *the more acute Wits of Europe*: Swift alludes to Machiavellian political thinking, beginning with *The Prince* (1513); Swift owned a folio edition (1695) of the works of Niccolò Machiavelli.

95. *Topics*: Commonplaces.

96. *Ideas, Entities, Abstractions and Transcendentals*: Technical terms important to platonic and scholastic systems of thought.

97. *their Alphabet . . . two and twenty*: The number of letters in the Latin alphabet, according to the common grammars of Swift's time (see, e.g. *Brevissima Institutio Seu Ratio Grammatices* [1596], signature Aii recto).

98. *various*: 'Changeable; uncertain; unfixed; unlike itself' (Johnson, sense 2).

99. *there must have been Giants in former Ages*: A paraphrase of *Genesis* 6: 4; works of

'natural philosophy' that tried to prove Mosaic history, such as Matthew Hale's *Primitive Origination of Mankind* (1677), were common in Swift's time, but none are recorded in his catalogue of his library.

100. *Conduct of Life*: Works of 'practical divinity', such as William Sherlock's *A Practical Discourse concerning Death* (1689), were common and popular, but they do not appear in Swift's library catalogue.

101. *an Army . . . made up of Tradesmen*: Resembling the trained bands or militia favoured by those opposed to a standing army.

102. *Composition*: 'Compact; agreement; terms on which differences are settled' (Johnson, sense 8).

103. *Tumbril*: 'A sort of Dirt or Dung-Cart' (Bailey).

104. *Conveniency of Carriage*: Ease of being carried.

105. *Sagacity*: 'Quickness of scent' (Johnson).

106. *Cataract of Niagara*: Niagara Falls on the border between western New York State and Ontario, Canada; there is no indication that Gulliver has travelled to this place, but the deafening effect of cataracts is a topic at least as far back as the works of Cicero (see Samuel Johnson, *A Voyage to Abyssinia*, ed. Joel Gold [1985], p. 3 and n. 3).

107. *to rights*: 'In a direct line; straight' (Johnson).

108. *sensibly*: From *sensible*, 'Having quick intellectual feeling; being easily or strongly affected' (Johnson, sense 6).

109. *to make*: Reach.

110. *Kentish Pippin*: a small, sharp kind of apple.

111. *winked at*: Overlooked.

112. *Phaeton*: Son of Helios (the Sun); promised a wish by his father, he chose to drive the chariot of the Sun, but, unequal to the task, he nearly scorched the earth and was struck from the skies by Zeus' thunderbolt; cf. Shakespeare, *Richard II*, 3.3.178–9.

113. *Tonquin*: French name for northern Vietnam, given by Jesuit missionaries.

114. *44 Degrees, and of Longitude 143*: If accurate, this would put him in northern Japan.

115. *New-Holland*: Australia, a principal stop on William Dampier's itinerary (see Introduction, p. xi).

PART III

A VOYAGE TO LAPUTA, BALNIBARBI, LUGGNAGG, GLUBBDUBDRIB AND JAPAN

1. *proposed*: Imagined; conceived.

2. *Fort St. George*: Built by the English East India Company in Madras and its headquarters in South India from 1641.

3. *Alliance*: The Dutch Republic and England were joined in an alliance against the French during the War of the Spanish Succession (1701–14), but this broke down in treaty negotiations at the end of the war.

4. *46 N. and of Longitude 183*: Contemporary maps calculated 360 degrees of longitude east of Greenwich; these coordinates (46 north, 177 west) would place him in the northern Pacific, south of the Aleutian Islands.

5. *Burning-glass*: Magnifying glass.

6. *Humours*: 'General turn or temper of mind' (Johnson, sense 3).

7. *Taction*: Touch; a latinism of the kind associated with 'philosophical' (scientific) writing in the eighteenth century.

8. *Kennel*: Gutter.

9. *Vulgar*: Common folk.

10. *Cycloid*: A curve, not a geometrical figure.

11. *Hautboys*: Oboes.

12. *Terms of Art*: Technical terms.

13. *Laputa*: Spanish for 'the whore', though other, additional interpretations are possible, based, for example, on Latin *puto*, to think, or English *put*, a stupid fellow (*OED*, sb. 4; as, perhaps, in *Lilliput*).

14. *Lagado*: Another form of *London* (Clark, p. 613).

15. *Music of the Spheres*: A Pythagorean and Platonic idea of cosmic harmony perpetuated by later mathematicians such as Joannes Kepler (1571–1630)

16. *Joints*: Legs or other cuts of meat for roasting.

17. *Bevil*: 'Any angle that is neither 90 nor 45 degrees' (Bailey).

18. *Mechanic*: 'Mean; servile; of mean profession' (Johnson).

19. *Intellectuals*: Minds; intellectual abilities.

20. *Divider*[s]: 'A pair of fine mathematical compasses' (Bailey).

21. *Judicial Astrology*: 'An Art that teaches or pretends to judge of Influences or Effects of the Stars' (Bailey), opposed to 'natural astrology' which combined aspects of modern astronomy and meteorology.

22. *the Mathematicians I have known in Europe*: In their politics and in their concealed faith in astrology these mathematicians are meant to resemble Isaac Newton,

who backed Walpole in the matter of Wood's Halfpenny (see Introduction, pp. xvii–xviii).

23. *Several Changes they dread in the Celestial Bodies*: All fears expressed by various members of the Royal Academy and recorded in their *Philosophical Transactions*; for details, see Marjorie H. Nicholson and N. M. Mohler, *Annals of Science*, 2 (1937), 405–30.

24. *Philosophical Account*: Scientific report, a parody of articles in the Royal Academy's *Philosophical Transactions*; for details, see Marjorie H. Nicholson and N. M. Mohler, *Annals of Science*, 2 (1937), 110–154.

25. *Flandona Gagnole*: A near anagram for *London, England* (Clark, p. 613).

26. *Glasses*: Telescopes.

27. *two lesser Stars, or Satellites, which revolve about Mars*: This fictional discovery may be based on Kepler's theory that the number of moons should increase geometrically with the planet's distance from the sun – one for Earth, two for Mars, four for Jupiter (the number then accepted), etc. (Turner). Although Kepler's theory was incorrect, Swift's fiction proved true in 1877 when Asaph Hall discovered Phobos and Deimos, the two moons of Mars.

28. *Law of Gravitation*: Swift's satellites obey Kepler's third Law.

29. *keeping the Island hovering over such a Town*: Probably a representation of England's economic tyranny over Ireland and other colonies.

30. *About three years before my Arrival*: . . . *entirely change the Government*. See textual notes. These five paragraphs were written out and tipped into Charles Ford's copy of *Gulliver's Travels* now in the Forster Collection in the Victoria and Albert Museum. The common assumption is that they were part of the original manuscript but omitted by its publishers – Motte in 1726 and 1727 and Faulkner in 1735 – for fear of political reprisals. (They were not published until 1896.) However, F. P. Lock argues that they, like many of the changes in Ford's book, may be revisions rather than restorations of the text (Lock [1980], p. 85). The passage represents Irish resistance to Wood's Halfpenny (see introduction, pp. xvii–xviii above), and Arthur Case has suggested precise allegorical meanings for the various details in the episode (82–4).

31. *Lindalino*: A play on *Dublin* (Clark, p. 613).

32. *Immunities*: Privileges.

33. *a fundamental Law of this Realm* . . . : The Act of Settlement (1701; 12 and 13 William III) states, 'That no person who shall hereafter come to the possession of this crown, shall go out of the dominions of England, Scotland, or Ireland, without consent of parliament.' But, controversially, George I, a native of Hanover, had convinced Parliament to repeal this part of the Act.

34. *Countenance*: 'Patronage; appearance of favour . . .' (Johnson, sense 6).

35. *Lord Munodi* . . . *discharged for Insufficiency*: Various allegorical interpretations

have been advanced including Harley, Bolingbroke, and Temple; the name seems to be short for *mundus odi* (I hate the world), a philosophical tag suitable to any of these important associates of Swift in their retirement from politics.

36. *Plantations*: 'The place planted' (Johnson, sense 2); beds and fields.

37. *Academy of PROJECTORS*: A parody of the Royal Society, which met informally from about 1645, was officially chartered in 1662 and began publishing its *Philosophical Transactions* in 1665; from descriptions of real experiments in this journal Swift drew many of the apparently fantastic schemes he describes in this chapter (see Nicholson and Mohler); *projector* meant, 'One who forms wild impracticable schemes' (Johnson, sense 2).

38. *Commonwealths-men*: A name for partisans of the rebellion in the British Civil War, so here it means 'public-spirited' in an ironic sense.

39. *prevent*: 'To go before; to be before; to anticipate' (Johnson, sense 2).

40. *largely*: 'Copiously; diffusely' (Johnson, sense 2).

41. *growing waste*: Having become unoccupied or empty.

42. *Ingenuity*: 'Wit; invention; genius; subtlety; acuteness' (Johnson, sense 2).

43. *calcine*: 'To burn to a calx or cinder' (Bailey).

44. *Townhouse*: 'The hall where public business is transacted' (Johnson).

45. *foundering*: Getting 'such a soreness and tenderness in a horse's foot that he is unable to set it on the ground' (Johnson).

46. *seminal Virtue*: Scientific jargon meaning the power of procreation.

47. *the Honour entire without a Rival*: Turner cites the rivalry between Newton and Leibnitz for the honour of having invented calculus; the contest about the invention of a method for determining longitude, over which one of Swift's friends committed suicide, may also be on his mind (see *Letters* 3. 240; 27 September 1727).

48. *improving* [the language] *of their own Country*: The Royal Society appointed a committee for this purpose, but it was a subject on which many writers made proposals, including Swift himself in *A Proposal for Correcting, Improving and Ascertaining the English Tongue, in a Letter to the Earl of Oxford* (1712).

49. *Words are only Names for Things*: A commonplace most importantly articulated by John Locke; see *An Essay concerning Human Understanding* (III.II ['*Of the Signification of Words*']).

50. *Artificial*: 'Artful; contrived with skill' (Johnson, sense 3).

51. *Universal Language*: Schemes to this end abounded during Swift's lifetime; for an account of them, see James Knowlson, *Universal Language Schemes in England and France 1600–1800* (University of Toronto Press, 1975).

52. *Cephalic Tincture*: An 'infusion' which is 'medicinal to the head' (Johnson).

53. *Quantum*: '(Latin) The quantity; the amount' (Johnson).

54. *Favourites*: 'One chosen as a companion by his superior; a mean wretch whose whole business is by any means to please' (Johnson, sense 2).

55. *Chimeras*: 'A vain and wild fancy, as remote from reality as the existence of the poetical chimera, a monster feigned to have the head of a lion, the belly of a goat, and the tail of a dragon' (Johnson).

56. *Humours*: 'The different kinds of moisture in man's body, reckoned by the old physicians to be phlegm, blood, choler, and melancholy, which, as they predominated, were supposed to determine the temper of mind' (Johnson, sense 2).

57. *Flatus*: 'Wind gathered in any cavities of the body, caused by indigestion and a gross internal perspiration . . .' (Johnson, quoting John Quincy).

58. *Scrofulous*: Pertaining to scrofula, 'A depravation of the humours of the body, which breaks out in sores; commonly called the king's evil' (Johnson); a form of tuberculosis.

59. *Ructations*: 'A belching arising from wind and indigestion' (Johnson).

60. *Canine Appetites*: '*Canine* hunger, in medicine, is an appetite which cannot be satisfied' (Johnson, sense 2).

61. *Lenitives . . . Acousticks*: Medicines that soothe, open (the bowels), cleanse, wear away, restrain or stanch, ease, relax (the bowels), treat headache, treat jaundice, draw off the humour of phlegm from the blood, and treat hearing disorders, respectively.

62. *Occiput*: '(Latin) The hinder part of the head' (Johnson).

63. *To take a strict View of their Excrements*: A satire on the trial of Bishop Atterbury for Jacobitism in 1722, in which the prosecution used as evidence letters taken from the defendant's chamber pot (Case, p. 91).

64. *I told him . . .* : This paragraph and the next in the Forster copy of *Gulliver's Travels* (but only this in the Morgan copy) are crossed out and others inserted (the second paragraph is revised in the Morgan copy so that it closely resembles the Forster insertion). See Textual Notes. This substitution is very explicit allegorically and, I think, weaker artistically, but editorial consistency requires adoption of it.

65. *Tribnia . . . Langden*: Obvious and therefore uncharacteristic anagrams for Britain and England.

66. *the Opinion of public Credit*: Registered most importantly in the price of treasury bonds.

67. *lame Dog an Invader*: Another allusion to the trial of Francis Atterbury in 1722; a lame French dog of his, named Harlequin, was used to link him, through correspondence with the Earl of Mar, to a treasonous plot to restore the Stuarts to the throne. Swift wrote a satirical poem about the trial in 1722; it was first published by Faulkner in 1735. For details, see *Poems* I: 297–301.

68. *Employment*: 'Office; post of business' (Johnson, sense 3).

69. *sink*: 'A drain; a jakes' or 'Any place where corruption is gathered' (Johnson, senses 1 and 2).

70. *Resist, a Plot is brought Home, The Tour*: To make the anagram work, the letters *i* and *j* must be taken as equivalent, as they usually were at this time; *The Tour* is a reference to a name Bolingbroke used for himself while in France, M. La Tour (Case, p. 91).

71. *Maldonada*: Yet another form of 'London'.

72. *Glubbdubdrib*: A play on 'Dublin' (Clark, p. 615).

73. *Luggnagg*: Another play on 'England' (Clark, p. 615).

74. *29 Degrees North Latitude, and 140 Longitude*: This would be in the middle of the Pacific Ocean; the directions and coordinates here also do not correspond with the fictional map on p. 142.

75. *Bark*: A small ship.

76. *Isle of Wight*: A British island in the English Channel, about 23 miles long and 14 miles wide.

77. *antic*: 'Odd; ridiculously wild; buffoon in gesticulation' (Johnson).

78. *Battle of Arbela*: Now called the battle of Gaugamela (in northern Iraq), where Alexander defeated the Persian emperor Darius III in 331 BCE.

79. *not Poisoned, but died of a Fever by excessive Drinking*: Plutarch asserts that 'most writers . . . think that the story of the poisoning is altogether a fabrication' designed to make a dramatic conclusion to a storied life (77.3); he follows Aristobolus in blaming the death on a fever and the thirst for immoderate drinking of wine it produced (75.4).

80. *Vinegar in his Camp*: A reference to the much ridiculed story retold by Livy that Hannibal cut through mountainous places by building bonfires at the face of impeding rocks and then poured vinegar on them to make them crack and crumble (21.37.2–3).

81. *Caesar and Pompey*: In the decisive battle of the Roman civil war Caesar defeated Pompey at Pharsalus (48 BCE).

82. *Brutus*: Marcus Junius Brutus, a praetor who led the conspiracy to assassinate Caesar and restore the Republic (44 BCE).

83. *Junius*: Lucius Junius Brutus, consul of Rome in 509 BCE, banished the tyrannical family of the Tarquins.

84. *Socrates*: The famous philosopher (469–399 BCE) chose execution over any compromise of his religious or political beliefs.

85. *Epaminondas*: Theban general who broke the Spartan control over many parts of Greece in the fourth century BCE.

86. *Cato the Younger*: Marcus Porcius Cato (95–46 BCE), a hero of the republican cause in Rome who committed suicide rather than see his native Utica brought under Caesar's dominion; before his death he reread Plato's *Phaedo*, which movingly recounts the death of Socrates.

87. *Sir Thomas More*: Author of the political satire *Utopia*, chancellor of England,

beheaded in 1535 for his refusal to accept Henry VIII as head of the Church of England.

88. *his Eyes were the most quick and piercing I ever beheld*: Homer has traditionally been described as blind; Turner shows that Swift here follows Lucian's dialogue with the dead Homer.

89. *Didymus and Eustathius*: Two early (first and twelfth century, respectively), prolific commentators on Homer.

90. *Scotus and Ramus*: Duns Scotus, thirteenth-century scholastic philosopher and commentator on Aristotle; Petrus Ramus, sixteenth-century innovator in logic and rhetoric who opposed many Aristotelian views.

91. *Descartes and Gassendi*: Seventeenth-century French thinkers cited here for their materialist theories of the physical world.

92. *Epicurus*: Fourth-century BCE philosopher, credited with founding atomistic physics.

93. *Attraction*: Gravity, the prime force in Newtonian physics, obviates the need for Descartes's vortices.

94. *Eliogabulus*: Roman Emperor (218–222), infamous for excess and luxury.

95. *Helot of Agesilaus*: A slave of the Spartan king (399–360 BCE) celebrated for his virtue by Xenophon.

96. *Nec Vir fortis, nec Faemina Casta*: Not a man was brave nor a woman pure; Polydore Virgil (d. 1556), a native of Urbino, Italy, who spent most of his life in England, is credited with publishing a collection of proverbs (1498) in addition to his more famous, vast history of England.

97. *Pox*: 'The venereal disease; this is the sense when it has no epithet' (Johnson, sense 2).

98. *practising*: 'To use bad arts or strategems' (Johnson, sense 3).

99. *Anecdotes, or secret History*: Historical works of this kind were prominent in Swift's library; he filled several of them with acrimonious marginalia, including Gilbert Burnet's *History of his own Times* (1724–34), a prime example of a 'secret history'; see *Prose Writings* 5: 241–320.

100. *one Person whose Case appeared a little singular*: Identified as Charles Mordaunt, third Earl of Peterborough, a personal friend of Swift's who fought successfully in the War of the Spanish Succession, lost a son, and failed to receive preferment (Case, pp. 92–4).

101. *Actium*: The battle in which Octavian defeated the fleets of Antony and Cleopatra in 31 BCE; it was popularly believed that the battle was lost when Antony followed a cowardly Cleopatra in flight.

102. *Libertina*: A freed female slave.

103. *Publicola and Agrippa*: Commanders, respectively, of the right and left wings of Octavian's fleet at Actium.

104. *the chief Commander*: Identified by Turner as John Churchill, first Duke of Marlborough, one of Swift's most important political enemies; much decorated commander of British forces from 1702–1711, when he was dismissed by the ministry that Swift served.

105. *Clumegnig*: A play on Latin *flumen* (river), with a diminutive suffix.

106. *Dutch were the only Europeans permitted to enter into that Kingdom*: An uprising of Roman Catholic Japanese (1637–8) was quelled with the help of the Dutch at the battle of Shimbara and led to a policy of *sakoku* or seclusion in which only the Dutch and Chinese were permitted to enter the country after 1638. Attempts to root out Christianity were instituted at this time including *fumi-e*, in which a suspected Christian was forced to stamp on an image of Christ or the Virgin Mary.

107. *lick the Dust before his Footstool*: An Old Testament image: 'They that dwell in the Wilderness shall bow before him [King Solomon]; and his enemies shall lick the dust' (*Psalms* 72: 9; cf. *Isaiah* 49:23 and *Micah* 7: 17).

108. *Shilling*: British coin worth one-twentieth of a pound, phased out of use in 1971.

109. *Establishment*: 'Allowance; income; salary' (Johnson, sense 5).

110. *Longitude . . . Perfection*: A much sought-after and often considered impossible method of determining longitude at sea was finally established by John Harrison in 1773 when he received the Board of Longitude's full prize of £20,000; see Dava Sobel, *Longitude: The True Story of a Lone Genius Who Solved the Greatest Scientific Problem of His Time* (Walker, 1995); perpetual motion and universal medicine were equally popular goals of scientific projectors of the time.

111. *Imbecility*: 'Weakness; feebleness of mind or body' (Johnson).

112. *hard to believe*: Slow to believe (Turner).

113. *unjust*: 'Improper; incorrect' (*OED*, sense 3).

114. *want*: Lack.

115. *of course*: As a matter of course; automatically.

116. *Meers and Bounds*: Boundary lines.

117. *engross*: 'To seize in the gross; to seize the whole of anything' (Johnson, sense 4).

118. *This Account of the Struldbruggs . . . out of the common Way*: Citing Pliny and Lucian, Turner points out that accounts of longevity were commonplace in travellers' tales.

119. *Xamoschi*: Perhaps Choshi, a port town on the trade route to Edo (see below) but situated to the northwest.

120. *Yedo*: Edo, the old name for Tokyo.

121. *Low-Dutch*: Modern Dutch, not German, which was still often called High Dutch at this time.

122. *Nangasac*: Nagasaki, the port for foreign shipping after 1636.

123. *trampling upon the Crucifix*: A practice called *fumi-e*; see note 106 above.

124. *Amboyna*: The name of an island in the East-Indies where in 1623 the Dutch discouraged English traders by an infamous act of torture.

125. *Vangrult*: Perhaps related to German *greuel*, horror, outrage.

126. *Skipper*: Cabin boy.

PART IV

A VOYAGE TO THE COUNTRY OF THE HOUYHNHNMS

1. *Yahoos*: Clark says the word is another form of whinny, minus the nasal sounds (p. 622); since reduplication is so conspicuous in Swift's invented words, *yahoo* might be *you* or part of the word *human*.

2. *Houyhnhnms*: The name incorporates the whinnying sound made by horses, perhaps within the phonemic context of the word *human*.

3. *Purefoy*: Literally, 'pure faith' and, as Turner points out, a play on *Puritan*.

4. *Logwood*: 'Logwood is of a very dense and firm texture . . . It grows both in the East and West Indies, but nowhere so plentifully as on the coast of the bay of Compeche . . . lately introduced in medicine, and is found to be an excellent astringint' (Johnson, quoting John Hill's *Materia Medica*); the Bay of Campeche is an inlet of the Gulf of Mexico bounded on the east by the Yucatán Peninsula of Mexico.

5. *Calentures*: 'A distemper peculiar to sailors, in hot climates; wherin they imagine the sea to be green fields, and will throw themselves into it, if not restrained' (Johnson, quoting John Quincy's *Lexicon Physico-Medicum* [1719]).

6. *Leeward Islands*: The most northerly of the Lesser Antilles, including the Virgin Islands, Saint-Martin, and Montserrat, about 200–300 miles north-north-west of Barbados in the West Indies.

7. *Piece*: 'A hand-gun' (Johnson, sense 6).

8. *Lading*: Cargo.

9. *Toys*: Trinkets.

10. *applying himself*: Approaching for inquiry or solicitation.

11. *expect*: Await.

12. *Philosopher*: Natural philosopher; student of the natural sciences.

13. *Chinese*: The multiplicity of characters in Chinese was seen as an obstacle to its adoption as a universal language, a dream of linguistic projectors in the seventeenth century (James Knowlson, *Universal Language Schemes in England and France 1600–1800* [University of Toronto Press, 1975], pp. 24–7).

14. *Vista*: 'A Prospect or straight Walk through Trees, especially in a Wood, the Trees being cut away' (Bailey).

15. *Withes*: 'A band, properly made of [willow] twigs' (Johnson, sense 2).

16. *complaisant*: 'Civil; desirous to please' (Johnson).

17. *a very insipid Diet, though common enough in many Parts of Europe*: Johnson defines *oats* as 'A grain, which in England is generally given to horses, but in Scotland supports the people'.

18. *Provocative*: 'Anything which revives a decayed or cloyed appetite' (Johnson).

19. *significant*: 'Expressive or representative in an eminent degree; forcible to impress the meaning' (Johnson, sense 3).

20. *Emperor Charles V . . . High-Dutch*: Holy Roman emperor and king of Spain, Charles (1500–1558) is credited with saying he would address his God in Spanish, his mistress in Italian, and his horse in German.

21. *displayed*: 'Spread wide' (Johnson).

22. *Manhood*: Human nature.

23. *their Bodies left to be devoured by Dogs and Birds of Prey*: An echo of *Iliad* 1:4–5 and, generally, of ignoble death, in classical terms.

24. *flying from their Colours*: Running away from the ensign of war set up for their regiment; deserting.

25. *barbarous*: 'Barbarousness' in Johnson means 'Impurity of Language' (sense 2).

26. *Revolution under the Prince of Orange*: The Glorious Revolution, 1688–9, which brought William of Orange to the British throne.

27. *the present queen*: Anne, queen of England, 1702–14.

28. *whether Flesh be Bread . . . dirty or clean, with many more*: An allusion to long-standing disagreements among different denominations of Christians about the meaning of the sacrament of holy communion; the use of music in church services; the veneration of icons and images; and the proper sort of vestments for the clergy, respectively.

29. *reduce*: 'To reform from any disorder' (Johnson).

30. *Culverins*: 'A piece of ordnance of several sizes' (Bailey).

31. *Carabines*: 'A sort of short gun between a musket and a pistol' (Bailey).

32. *Undermines, Countermines*: Military excavations.

33. *Nature and Reason were sufficient Guides for a reasonable Animal*: A concise statement of a long-standing philosophical position, represented by ancient Stoics, such as Zeno of Citium, and by modern Deists, such as William Wollaston, which was a common topic of attack in writers, such as Swift and Samuel Johnson, with more orthodox religious views (for more on this subject, see Turner; also see Gwin Kolb, ed., *Rasselas* [Yale, 1990], p. 83 and n. 1).

34. *I said . . .* : The preceding sentence and the next three paragraphs were written out and tipped into the Forster and Morgan copies of *Gulliver's Travels*, and the original paragraphs were crossed out. In his letter to Motte, Ford wrote that this

passage is 'manifestly most barbarously corrupted, full of Flatnesses, Cant Words, and Softenings unworthy the Dignity, Spirit, Candour & Frankness of the Author. By that admirable Instance of the Cow it is plain the Satire is designed against the Profession in general, & not only against Attorneys or, as they are there smartly styled Pettifoggers. You ought in Justice to restore those twelve Pages to the true Reading.' However, F. P. Lock (1980, p. 83) argues that the original is not less sharp in its satire, though it may be a bit more restricted; he concludes that the new version is a revision, not a correction of the original manuscript. The opening of 1726 seems, in fact, more offensive than the revision or correction, though it then softens. See Textual Notes.

35. *Faculty*: Profession or trade.

36. *Forswearing*: Perjury.

37. *Free-thinking*: Johnson defines 'freethinker' as 'A libertine; a contemner of religion' and quotes Swift's *Argument against Abolishing Christianity*.

38. *Evacuation*: 'The practice of emptying the body by physic [i.e. medicine]. "The usual practice of physic among us, turns in a manner wholly upon evacuation, either by bleeding, vomit, or some purgation." [William] Temple' (Johnson, sense 3).

39. *imaginary* [diseases]: Swift is thinking of such psychological disorders as melancholy, the spleen, and the more temporary vapours; these ill-defined but pervasive ills were roughly the equivalents of ill-defined modern ailments such as depression and chronic fatigue syndrome.

40. See Textual Notes for the passage crossed out in Ford's books and omitted in 1735. In his letter to Motte (see A Note on the Text, p. xxvi), Ford wrote, 'I have an entire Respect for the Memory of the late Queen, and am always pleased when others show the same; but that Paragraph relating to her looks so very much beside the Purpose that I cannot think it to have been written by the same Author. I wish you & your Friends would consider it, and let it be left out in the next Edition. For it is plainly false in Fact, since all the World knows that the Queen during her whole Reign governed by one first Minister or other. Neither do I find the Author to be anywhere given to Flattery, or indeed very favourable to any Prince or Minister whatsoever.'

Motte's desire to avoid offence seems the likeliest reason for his omission of this passage. However, F. P. Lock argues that Motte printed Swift's MS accurately and that this passage represents a severe criticism of George I, by contrast with Anne, which Swift replaced on second thought for stylistic reasons (Lock [1980], pp. 83–5).

41. *Act of Indemnity*: Refers especially to the act passed with the return of the monarchy to England in August 1660 pardoning almost everyone who had fought against the king during the Civil War.

42. *in the last Resort*: A legal term meaning supreme, as in the phrase 'supreme court'.

43. *managing*: 'To deal with or treat carefully' (*OED*, sense 6).

44. *Courts of Equity*: Chancery court, a 'court of equity and conscience, moderating the rigour of other courts, that more streightly tied to the letter of the law . . .' (John Cowell, *The Interpreter*, 1607).

45. *Leader*: 'One at the head of any party or faction: as the detestable [Thomas] Wharton [1648–1716] was the *leader* of the whigs. "The understandings of a senate are enslaved by three or four *leaders*, set to get or to keep employments." Swift' (Johnson, sense 4).

46. *Sagacity*: Means both 'Quickness of scent' and 'Acuteness of discovery' (Johnson, senses 1 and 2).

47. *Spleen*: 'Melancholy; hypochondriacal vapours' (Johnson, sense 4); roughly equivalent to depression.

48. *Jack-Daw*: 'A cock daw [a bird like a crow]; a bird taught to imitate the human voice' (Johnson).

49. *Sloe*: 'The fruit of the blackthorn; a small wild plum' (Johnson).

50. *strikes you with immediate Conviction*: As Turner points out, the phrase recalls John Locke's description of 'intuitive knowledge' (*Essay concerning Human Understanding*, Book 4, chapter 2, section 1); in Locke's system this category is reserved for mathematical truths (such as 'Three are more than Two') and truths by definition (such as 'White is not Black'); the Houyhnhnms apply it much more broadly.

51. *the Sentiments of Socrates, as Plato delivers them*: The closest parallel is in Xenophon's delivery of Socrates' sentiments (*Memorabilia* 1.1.11, as Turner notes), but the position is quintessentially Socratic (e.g., *Apology* 29 D–E) and repeated frequently in antiquity (e.g. *Greek Anthology*, 11.50.5–6: 'On Life, on morals, be thy thoughts employed;/Leave to the schools their atoms and their void' (Johnson, trans., *Rambler* 180).

52. *Jointures*: 'Estate settled on a wife to be enjoyed after her husband's decease' (Johnson).

53. *Settlement*: 'A jointure granted to a wife' (Johnson).

54. *These are not suffered to taste a Grain of Oats*: Because they are a kind of sweet; likewise, Locke restricted children from eating fruit or sweetmeats until late in the day (see *Of Education*, which seems to be a model for many aspects of the Houyhnhnms' regimen).

55. *indocible*: Unteachable.

56. *Honourable Member*: Title of a Member of Parliament or Congress.

57. *Their Verses . . . Victors in Races, and other bodily Exercises*: A kind of classical poetry associated with Sparta and magnificently exemplified in the odes of Pindar (see Turner, pp. 364–5).

58. *inconvenient*: 'Incommodious; disadvantageous' (Johnson).

59. *Economy*: 'The management of a family; the government of a household' (Johnson).

60. *Ticking*: 'A sort of strong Linnen for Bedding' (Bailey).

61. *Health of Body and Tranquillity of Mind*: A Stoic ideal, most famously expressed by Juvenal in his tenth *Satire* (esp. l. 356, '*mens sane in corpore sano*').

62. *descend*: 'To come down ideally, mentally, or morally; to condescend, to stoop . . .' (*OED*, sense 6).

63. *doubted*: Feared.

64. *stanch*: 'Sound' (Johnson).

65. *February 15, 1714/5*: February 15 was 1714 Old Style (according to the Julian Calendar, in which the new year began on 25 March) and 1715 New Style (according to the Gregorian Calendar, which was not adopted in England until 1752).

66. *Hnuy illa nyha majah Yahoo*: Clark translates literally, '(Let) not ill (come) nigh (thee), my Yahoo! (p. 624).

67. *Herman Moll*: Dutch geographer (d. 1732); came to London in 1698; Case shows that Swift consulted Moll with attention (p. 51), particularly his *New and Correct Map of the Whole World* (1719).

68. *stood to the North*: Maintained a northerly course.

69. *honest Portuguese*: The Portuguese were with England in the Grand Alliance in the War of the Spanish Succession (1701–13).

70. *Veracity. But*: Between these two words in 1726 were several lines in which the narrator suggests that the Captain was persuaded of Gulliver's truthfulness because of stories he had recently heard about creatures fitting Gulliver's description of the Yahoos. Assuming that it was removed for stylistic reasons and that Swift was responsible for this, I omit the passage. See Textual Notes.

71. *Inquisition*: 'The court established in some countries subject to the pope for the detection of heresy' (Johnson, sense 4).

72. *Rue*: 'An herb called, herb of grace, because holy water was sprinkled with it . . . "The weasel, to encounter the serpent, arms herself with eating of rue" *More's Antidote against Atheism*' (Johnson).

73. *much less could I suffer them . . . presume to touch my Bread, or drink out of the same Cup . . . take me by the Hand*: There are echoes here of Christ's words in the Gospels and of St Paul's warnings about purity in those who take communion (Turner).

74. *Stone-Horses*: 'A horse not castrated' (Johnson).

75. *–Nec si miserum Fortuna Sinonem / Finxit, vanum etiam, mendacemque improba finget*: The deceitful words of Sinon, whom the Greeks left to convince the Trojans that the invaders had departed leaving behind the gift of the Trojan Horse: 'Nor, if cruel Fortune has made Sinon wretched, should she also make him false and deceitful' (*Aeneid* 2. 79–80).

76. *Memorial*: A record or chronicle.

77. *Ferdinando Cortez*: Hernán Cortes (1485–1547), conqueror of the Aztecs.

78. *missive*: 'Used at a distance' (Johnson, sense 2).

79. *Yerks*: ' "A leaping horse is said to yerk, or strike out his hind legs, when he flings and kicks with his whole hind quarters, stretching out the two hinder legs near together, even to their full extent." *Farrier's Dictionary*' (Johnson, s.v. *to yerk*).

80. *Recalcitrat undique tutus*: He yerks in every direction, making himself safe (Horace, *Satires* 2. 1. 20). This is Horace's description of how Augustus will react to panegyrical verse sent at the wrong time by the wrong person. Horace's friend Trebatius had suggested that he write poems in praise of Augustus, instead of satire, and the poem as a whole is a defence of Horace's calling as a satirical poet.

81. *Distributive Justice*: 'That which allots to each his sentence or claim' (Johnson).

TEXTUAL NOTES

Although they are presented in the traditional form of a critical apparatus, the purpose of these notes is not to provide a complete history of this very vexed text. These notes mainly record significant changes of a word or more made to the copytext (the first edition of 1726) with their sources. Also noted are some significant differences between the first edition of 1726 and Faulkner's edition of 1735, the text often preferred as a basis for modern editions of *Gulliver's Travels*. See A Note on the Text. No effort has been made here to modernize the rejected passages of the first edition. In most cases slight differences among the sources of a preferred reading are not noted: readings from the Forster and Morgan copies, for example, are not distinguished from each other, though there are often variations between them. In recording passages of the accepted text, ellipses are employed to avoid lengthy repetition.

Textual Abbreviations

26: First edition, first issue (Teerink A) of *Travels into Several Remote Nations of the World*, 2 vols. (Motte: London, 1726 [Rothschild copy in the Wren Library, Trinity College, Cambridge]).

26C: Third edition (Teerink B), published by Motte late in 1726. (Williams [1941] is the source for these variants.)

35: Volume III of Swift's *Works* (George Faulkner: Dublin, 1735 [Rothschild copy in the Wren Library, Trinity College, Cambridge]).

FF: Charles Ford's corrections in a large paper copy of 1726 (Teerink A), Forster Collection, National Art Reference Library, Victoria and Albert Museum, London.

FM: Charles Ford's corrections in a large paper copy of 1726 (Teerink A), Pierpont Morgan Library, New York.

Ar: Swift's corrections in a large paper copy of 1726 (Teerink A), Armagh Public
Library, but stolen in December 1999. I relied on a facsimile edition (Delmar,
NY: Scholars' Facsimiles & Reprints, 1976) and Woolley (1978).

PRELIMINARY MATTER

Advertisement: This paragraph first appeared in 1735.
Letter: This section first appeared in 1735.
Plate 1, Mendendo: A mistake for Mildendo, *26, 35*.

PART I

p. 23: my eyes *FF*/mine eyes *26, 35*. This change (or 'mine ears' to 'my ears') is
made 15 times in *FF* but not further recorded in these notes.
p. 24: heard increasing, I knew their Numbers were greater *35*/heard, I knew
their Numbers encreased *26*
p. 25: who held *35*/that held *26*
p. 37: escape *35*/scape *26*
p. 39: Blue, the other Red, and the third Green *FF*, *Ar*, *35*/Purple, the other
Yellow, and the third White *26*
p. 40: Blue . . . Red . . . Green *FF*, *Ar*, *35*/Purple . . . Yellow . . . White *26*
p. 44: 1728 *26C*/1724 *26, 35*; the explanation in the text proves that 1728 was
meant.
p. 44: 1728 *26C*/1724 *26, 35*
p. 44: 1728 *26C*/1724 *26, 35*
p. 55: with observing *35*/observing *26*
p. 55: our Ladies *FM*/Ladies *26, 35*
p. 59: Eleven *26*/Seven *35*
p. 60: their Maxim *35*/the Maxim *26*
p. 60: nine *26*/seven *35*
p. 60: thirteen *26*/eleven *35*
p. 75: *Blefuscu FF, FM, Ar, 35*/Lilliput *26*

PART II

p. 82: However, I *FM*, *FF*, *Ar*, *35*/I *26*
p. 90: towardly *FF 35*/forward *26*

p. 92: Horn and Crown *Ar*/Green *Eagle* 26, 35

p. 96: Majesty perhaps would *FF*, *FM*, *Ar*/Majesty would 26

p. 103: Insects *FF*, *FM*, *Ar*, 35/Creatures 26

p. 105: *European FM*, *FF*, 35/*English* 26

p. 115: Courage *FM*, 35/Honour 26

p. 119: several *FM*, *FF*/all 26/what 35

p. 122: are the proper *FM*, *FF*, 35/may be sometimes the only 26

p. 124: that mighty *FM*, *FF*/that 26

p. 127: the Inclemencies *FF*/Inclemencies 26

p. 128: the Whole Race of Mankind is *FM*, *FF*, 35/so many other Governments are 26

p. 130: just *FM*, *FF*/not directly 26

PART III

p. 144: We stayed 35/stayed 26

p. 144: expect them *emendation*/expect 26, 35

p. 159: For, although their . . . Clearness. This Advantage *FM*, *FF*, 35/For, this Advantage 26

pp. 160–61: fall to the Ground. About three years . . . change the Government. By *FF*/fall to the Ground. By 26, 35

p. 171: Books *FM*, *FF*, *Ar*, 35/both 26

p. 171: emptied 35/employed 26

p. 172: other Project *FF*, 35/other 26

p. 174: thus Ambassadors *FM*, *FF*, 35/the Embassadors 26

pp. 178–9: I told him . . . shall signify *FF*/I told him, that should I happen to live in a Kingdom where Plots and Conspiracies were either in Vogue from the turbulency of the meaner People, or could be turned to the use and service of the higher Rank of them, I first would take care to cherish and encourage the breed of Discoverers, Witnesses, Informers, Accusers, Prosecutors, Evidences, Swearers, together with their several subservient and subaltern Instruments; and when I had got a competent Number of them of all sorts and Capacities, I would put them under the Colour and conduct of some dextrous Persons in sufficient power both to protect and reward them. Men thus qualified and thus empowered might make a most excellent use and advantage of Plots, they might raise their own Characters and pass for most profound Politicians, they might restore new Vigour to a crazy Administration, they might stifle or divert general Discontents; fill their Pockets with Forfeitures, and advance or sink the Opinion of Publick Credit, as either might answer their private

Advantage. This might be done by first agreeing and settling among them-selves what suspected Persons should be accused of a Plot. Then effectual care is taken to secure all their Letters and Papers, and put the Criminal in safe and secure Custody. These Papers might be delivered to a Set of Artists of Dexterity sufficient to find out the mysterious Meanings of Words, Syllables, and Letters. They should be allowed to put what Interpretation they pleased upon them, giving them a Sense not only which has no relation at all to them, but even what is quite contrary to their true Intent and real Meaning; thus for Instance, they may, if they so fancy, interpret a *Sieve* to signify a *Court Lady*, a *lame Dog* an *Invader*, the *Plague* a *standing Army*, a *Buzzard* a *great Statesman*, the *Gout* a *High Priest*, a *Chamber-pot* a *Committee of Grandees*, a *Broom* a *Revolution*, a *Mouse-trap* an *Imployment*, a *Bottomless-pit* a *Treasury*, a *Sink* a *Court*, a *Cap and Bells* a *Favourite*, a *broken Reed* a *Court of Justice*, an *empty Tun* a *General*, a *running Sore* an *Administration*.

BUT should this method fail, recourse might be had to others more effectual, by Learned Men called *Acrosticks* and *Anagrams*. First, might be found Men of Skill and Penetration who can discern that all initial Letters have political Meanings. Thus, *N* shall signify *26*

p. 179: they *26*/who FF, FM, *35*
p. 179: skilful Decipherer FF, FM/Man of Skill in this Art *26*
p. 179: that FF, FM/how *26*
p. 179: Kingdom is FF, Ar, *35*/Kingdom was *26*
p. 182: into the Room *Ar*/in the Room *26*
p. 182: a modern Representative FM, FF, *35*/an Assembly of somewhat a latter Age *26*
p. 188: 1709 FF/1711 *26*/1708 *35*
p. 196: Age, they FM, FF, *35*/Age, *26*
p. 196: Understandings *Ar*/Memories *26, 35*
p. 197: despised *Ar, 35*/deprived *26*

PART IV

p. 205: Second Day of *August, 1710 26*/7th Day of *September 35*
p. 205: I had several Men die *emendation*/I had several Men died *26, 35*
p. 207: and hooked FM, FF/hooked *26*
p. 207: Hair on their Heads, but none on their Faces FF/Hair on their Faces *26*
p. 212: heard *35*/observed *26*
p. 212: those detestable Creatures, which *35*/these detestable Creatures, whom *26*

p. 219: my having *FM*, *FF*, *35*/having *26*

p. 222: weakest *FM*, *FF*/meanest *26*

p. 223: express *35*/represent *26*

p. 223: lifting one of my *FM*, *FF*, *35*/lifting my *26*

p. 224: Trade it *FM*, *FF*/Trade is *26*

p. 224: called a *FM*, *FF*/called *26*

p. 227: these *Ar*, *35*/those *26*

p. 227: is likewise a Kind of beggarly Princes *FM*, *FF*, *35*/are likewise another Kind of Princes *26*

p. 227: Germany and other *Northern FF*/many *Northern 26*

p. 228: Bayonets, Battles, Sieges *FM*, *FF*/Bayonets, Sieges *26*

p. 228: his Hoof *FM*, *FF*, *Ar*, *35*/my Hoof *26*

p. 229–30: what I meant by . . . decreeing accordingly. *FM*, *FF*, *35*/what I meant by *Law* and what sort of Dispensers thereof it could be by whose Practices the Property of any Person could be lost, instead of being preserved. He added, he saw not what great Occasion there could be for this thing called *Law*, since all the Intentions and Purposes of it may be fully answered by following the Dictates of *Nature* and *Reason*, which are sufficient Guides for a Reasonable Animal, as we pretended to be, in shewing us what we ought to do, and what to avoid. I assured his Honour, that Law was a Science wherein I had not much conversed, having little more Knowledge of it than what I had obtained by employing Advocates, in vain, upon some Injustices that had been done me, and by conversing with some others who by the same Method had first lost their Substance and then left their own Country under the mortification of such disappointments, however I would give him all the Satisfaction I was able.

I SAID that those who made profession of this Science were exceedingly multiplied, being almost equal to the Caterpillars in Number; that they were of diverse Degrees, Distinctions and Denominations. The Numerousness of those that dedicated themselves to this Profession were such that the fair and justifiable Advantage and Income of the Profession was not sufficient for the decent and handsome Maintenance of Multitudes of those who followed it. Hence it came to pass that it was found needful to supply that by Artifice and Cunning, which could not be procured by just and honest Methods: The better to bring which about, very many Men among us were bred up from their Youth in the Art of proving by Words multiplied for the Purpose that *White* is *Black*, and *Black* is *White*, according as they are paid. The Greatness of these Mens Assurance and the Boldness of their Pretensions gained upon the Opinion of the Vulgar, whom in a Manner they made Slaves of, and got into their Hands much the largest Share of the Practice of their Profession.

These Practitioners were by Men of Discernment called *Pettifoggers*, (that is, *Confounders*, or rather, *Destroyers of Right*,) as it was my ill Hap as well as the Misfortune of my suffering Acquaintance to be engaged only with this Species of the Profession. I desired his Honour to understand the Description I had to give, and the Ruin I had complained of to relate to these Sectaries only, and how and by what means the Misfortunes we met with were brought upon us by the Management of these Men, might be more easily conceived by explaining to him their Method of Proceeding, which could not be better done than by giving him an Example.

MY Neighbour, said I, I will suppose, has a mind to my *Cow*, he hires one of these Advocates to prove that he ought to have my *Cow* from me. I must then hire another of them to defend my Right, it being against all Rules of *Law* that any Man should be allowed to speak for himself. Now in this case, I who am the Right Owner lie under two great Disadvantages. First, my Advocate, being as I said before practised almost from his Cradle in defending Falshood, is quite out of his Element when he would argue for Right, which as an Office unnatural he attempts with great Awkwardness, if not with an Ill-will. The Second Disadvantage is that my Advocate must proceed with great Caution; for, since the Maintenance of so many depend on the keeping up of Business, should he proceed too summarily, if he does not incur the Displeasure of his Superiors, he is sure to gain the Ill will and Hatred of his Brethren, as being by them esteemed one that would lessen the Practice of the Law. This being the Case, I have but two Methods to preserve my *Cow*. The first is, to gain over my Adversary's Advocate with a double Fee; from the Manner and Design of whose Education before mentioned it is easy to expect he will be induced to drop his Client and let the Ballance fall on my Side. The Second Way is for my Advocate not to insist on the Justice of my Cause, by allowing the *Cow* to belong to my Adversary; and this if it be dexterously and skilfully done will go a great Way towards obtaining a favourable Verdict, it having been found, from a careful Observation of Issues and Events, that the wrong Side, under the Management of such Practitioners, has the fairer Chance for Success, and this more especially if it happens, as it did in mine and my Friend's Case, and may have done since, that the Person appointed to decide all Controversies of Property as well as for the Tryal of Criminals, who should be taken out of the most knowing and wise of his Profession, is by the Recommendation of a great Favourite, or Court-Mistress chosen out of the Sect before mentioned, and so, having been under a strong Biass all his Life against Equity and fair dealing, as it were under a fatal Necessity of favouring, shifting, double dealing and Oppression, and besides through Age, Infirmity, and Distempers grown lazy, unactive, and inattentive, and thereby almost incapacitated from doing any thing becoming the Nature of his Imployment, and the Duty of his Office. In such Cases, the Decisions and Determinations of Men so bred, and so qualified, may with Reason be expected on the wrong side of the Cause, since those who can take Harangue and Noise, (if pursued with Warmth, and drawn out into a Length,) for Reasoning, are not much to be wondered at, if they infer the weight of the Argument from the heaviness of the Pleading.

IT is a Maxim among these Men, That whatever has been done before may legally be done again: And therefore they take special Care to record all the Decisions formerly made, even those which have through Ignorance or Corruption contradicted the Rules of common Justice and the general Reason of Mankind. These, under the Name of *Precedents*, they produce as Authorities, and thereby endeavour to justify the most iniquitous Opinions; and they are so lucky in this Practice, that it rarely fails of Decrees answerable to their Intent and Expectation. *26*

p. 230: have wholly confounded *FM, FF, 35*/have gone near to confound *26*

p. 230: will *FF*/may *26*

p. 230: The Judge first sends . . . preserving all *FF*/For if those in Power, who know well how to choose Instruments fit for their Purpose, take care to recommend and promote out of this Clan a proper Person, his Method of Education and Practice makes it easy to him, when his Patron's Disposition is understood, without Difficulty or Study, either to condemn or acquit the Criminal, and at the same time strictly preserve all *26*

p. 230: Lawyers *FF*/Advocates *26*

p. 231: in all Points . . . and Learning, and *FM, FF, 35*/the Business and Study of their own Calling and Profession so took up all their Thoughts and engrossed all their Time, that they minded nothing else, and that therefore in all points out of their own Trade, many of them were of so great Ignorance and Stupidity that it was hard to pick out of any Profession a Generation of Men more despicable in common Conversation, or who were so much looked upon as avowed Enemies to all Knowledge and Learning, being *26*

p. 231: Profession *FM, FF, 35*/Calling *26*

p. 231: under *Queen* Anne. *The Character of a first Minister in 35/ so well governed by a Queen as to need no first Minister. The Character of such an one in some 26/ The Character of a first Minister in FM, FF*

p. 233: contrary *FF, 35*/the one contrary *26*

p. 233: Bones, Birds, Beasts *FM, FF*/Bones, Beasts *26*

p. 234: inferior posterior *Ar, FM, FF, 35*/ inferior *26*

p. 234: a first or *chief Minister of State*, who was the Person I intended to describe, was a Creature *FM, FF*/our She Governor or Queen having no Ambition to gratify, no Inclination to satisfy of extending her Power to the Injury of her Neighbours, or the Prejudice of her own Subjects, was therefore so far from needing a corrupt Ministry to carry on or cover any sinister Designs, that She not only directs her own Actions to the Good of her People, conducts them by the Direction, and restrains them within the Limitation of the Laws of her own Country; but submits the Behaviour and Acts of those She intrusts with the Administration of Her Affairs to the Examination of Her great Council, and subjects them to the Penalties of the Law; and therefore never puts any such Confidence in any of her Subjects as to entrust them with the whole and entire Administration of her Affairs: But I added, that in some former Reigns here, and in many other Courts of *Europe* now, where Princes grew indolent and careless of their own Affairs through a constant Love and Pursuit of Pleasure, they made use of such an Administrator, as I had mentioned, under the Title of *first* or *chief Minister of State*, the Description of which, as far as it may be collected not only from their Actions, but from the Letters, Memoirs, and Writings published by themselves, the Truth of which has not yet been disputed, may be allowed to be as follows: That he is a Person *26*

p. 235: made *FM, FF*/makes *26*

p. 235: an Expedient called an *Act FM, FF, 35*/an *Act 26*

p. 236: Domestics *FM, 35*/Acquaintance *26*

p. 236: the true Marks of Noble Blood; And a healthy robust Appearance . . . all our Possessions without Appeal. *FM, FF, 35*/no uncommon Marks of a *Great Man;* and a healthy robust Appearance is so far disgraceful in a Man of Quality, that the World is apt to conclude his real Father to have been one of the Inferiors of the Family, especially when it is seen that the Imperfections of his Mind run parallel with those of his Body and are little else than a Composition of Spleen, Dullness, Ignorance, Caprice, Sensuality and Pride. *26*

p. 237: enlarged *FM, FF*/enlightened *26*

p. 240: never *FM, FF*/seldom *26*

p. 241: chatter, and reel and roll, and *35*/chatter, and reel and *FM, FF*/chatter, and *26*

p. 241: known to have been taken with success *FF, 35*/taken myself *26*

p. 241: do here *35*/do *26*

p. 242: the Females *FM, FF, 35*/Females *26*

p. 242: infamous Brutality *35*/Brutality *26*

p. 242: last Article *FM, FF, Ar 35*/Article *26*

p. 244: search about *FM, FF, 35*/scratch about *26*

p. 248: Brutes are *FM, FF, 35*/Brutes were *26*

p. 248: Family in the District shall *FM, FF*/Family shall *26*

p. 249: Ooze and *FM, FF*, 35/Ooze or 26

p. 249: elder *FM, FF*/older 35/old Ones 26

p. 250: spoke a Language 35/had a Language 26

p. 252: certain *FF*, 35/several 26

p. 252: *Lhnuwnh* 35/*Shnuwnh* 26

p. 253: Room to be made for *FM, FF*, 35/Room for 26

p. 253: I likewise *FM, FF*, 35/I 26

p. 255: their Minds 35/their Thoughts *FM, FF*/the Thoughts 26

p. 255: more civilized *FF*, 35/civilized 26

p. 264: Veracity. But 35/ Veracity, and the rather because he confessed, he met with a *Dutch* Skipper, who pretended to have landed with Five others of his Crew upon a certain Island or Continent *South* of *New-Holland*, where they went for fresh Water, and observed a Horse driving before him several Animals exactly resembling those I described under the Name of *Yahoos*, with some other Particulars, which the Captain said he had forgot; because he then concluded them all to be Lies. But 26

p. 265: *Redriff* 35/*Rotherhith* 26

p. 267: were *Ar*/was 26

p. 268: after 26/last 35

p. 269: the least with *FF*, 35/with 26

p. 270: modern *FF*, 35/some modern 26

p. 270: any Desire *FF*/a Desire 26

p. 270: more concerns *FF, FM*/may concern 26

p. 270: believed; unless a Dispute . . . in Colony-Law. 26/believed. 35

p. 270: all my 26/my 35

p. 271: Whore-master 26/*deleted Ar*